SHADOWS FALL

This novel is a work of fiction. Any references to real events, businesses, organizations, and political figures are intended to give the story a sense of reality and authenticity. Any resemblance to actual private persons, living or dead, is entirely coincidental.

Shadows Fall

Copyright © 2018 by JC Brennan
www.jcbrennanbooks.com

All rights reserved.

Published by
TOPSHELF INDIE
www.TopShelfIndie.com

Designed, developed, edited, proofread
by TopShelf Indie Author Services.

ISBN:
978-1-946865-14-4 (Hardcover)
978-1-946865-15-1 (eBook)

Additional books may be purchased through:

Baker & Taylor
INGRAM CONTENT GROUP

SHADOWS FALL

TOPSHELF INDIE

www.TopShelfIndie.com
www.jcbrennanbooks.com

J.C. BRENNAN

For Levi Douglas Holstine.

May you never be afraid to try new things, grow with the will to make your dreams come true, and always be you.

"Some old wounds never truly heal, and bleed again at the slightest word."
~ George R.R. Martin

"Do as the heavens have done, forget your evil; with them forgive yourself."
~ William Shakespeare

"When I discover who I am, I'll be free."
~ Ralph Ellison

The Legend

An ancient legend survives the ages, one of warriors, brothers, and gods. It is a story of love, loss, and betrayal; a legend as old as time and not for the faint of heart. This legend is so archaic in fact, no one is certain of the people from whom it originates. Generation after generation passed this tale down to the next, hoping to keep it alive and educate their youth that there are beings and evils in this world walking among us. The people have preserved the Legend of Two Brothers through the ages, lest we forget.

Lore tells of a majestic, wild tribe; one the people loved and feared in equal measure, for this tribe had power—gifts like no other. Theirs was an impressive and mystical race, one that endured long before our grandparents or the countless generations before. People only dared to whisper when speaking of them for the tribe's pre-eminence struck awe and fear. They saw this magnificent tribe in their dreams and from those dreams bore fairy tales.

Distinguished warriors were the backbone of this majestic tribe, warriors no ordinary man could ever defeat. They were skilled, expert killers, without fear. The killing was not always for food, but they forbid needless slaughter. They were not butchers, nor purveyors of evil. Instead, death was a ritualistic act—the most magnificent sacrifice; one of love and worship to the Goddess herself.

There were, as in any race, a few who were malicious. It was these few who acted out in evil aggression, seething with rage and vengeance, becoming the most savage of these deadly assassins, plaguing mortals in their utmost nightmarish dreams. These tribal members slaughtered innocent men, women, and children. To kill was their morbid insignia.

They violently slaughtered the guiltless. However, were it not for this hellish, rebellious group, this legend would not exist.

In a time before the rebellion and turmoil, two brothers were born to the leader of this great race. The tribe, elated with the birth of their future leaders, celebrated for a fortnight, rejoicing in the two precious gifts the gods bestowed upon them. A great fire burned, its flames reaching the heavens, towering over the tallest trees and seen for miles. Food was abundant; a boar on the fire, fruit from the trees, and vegetables from the earth filled the tribe's bellies. Laughter, dance, and song intoxicated the night, spreading joyful bliss across the sacred lands.

It was the best of times for the tribe, and they would hold these times of jubilance with a rigid grip, preserving the harmonious occasion so long as their memories would allow, for darkness was never far away. It lapped at their feet, preyed on their minds, as their world would change over the years.

Their father, a great leader but also a prolific seer, foretold of this darkness—of the pandemonium to come, just as he prophesied of his own death and that of their mother's. Huddled close to the fire and gathered at his feet, the young boys listened to him with rapt attention. In a soft, trance-like voice and eyes burning with the same intensity as the flames before them, he warned, "My sons, together you are strong and hold the future of our people within your hands. You will lead them to prominence and prosperity, despite the challenges of the ever-changing world ahead. Our race will continue to be celebrated as gods amongst men. But beware, for if you allow jealousy and anger to enter your hearts, evil will permeate your souls and bring forth death and destruction upon us all. Our kind will forever be feared, relegated to the shadows, and spoken of as if in horrific dreams."

For a short time following the death of their parents, the strength of the brothers' bond alleviated the tribe's fear of the vision to come. With a perpetual trust and loyalty in each other, they led their race with the same strength and wisdom as their father before them. None believed anything

could ever separate them. However, it would not last, for something came between them—something that ripped their brotherhood apart forever.

Though one may consider this to be nothing but a tall tale, things aren't always as they seem. Over all other legends that cross the lips of elders, know this, the people of this tribe are much more than fairy tales, fables, or myths. They are real, and some accept them as gods. These people were the first to inhabit the earth and will live long after our bodies are but bone and dust.

Chapter 1

The Bonfire

Detective Levi Ryan Sterling, or just Sterling as his friends and colleagues call him, maneuvers the old Ford through a swarm of people gathering at the scene. Red lights flash and stretch through the night sky like a raven of death as confusion surges. Onlookers cry and mutter speculations, commingling in one loud, incoherent voice, echoing off the buildings and trees. The sound of chaos borders on madness. And why wouldn't the people act as if half-crazed? This is a small town, some would say too small to have a murder. What the people don't realize, but Detective Sterling does, is death happens anywhere and everywhere.

Just another night in the life of a detective, he thinks. A woman in a pale yellow housecoat and pink fluffy slippers staggers aimlessly in front of the car, forcing him to slam on the brakes, which in return, thrusts him forward. "Goddamnit!" he curses, noticing her swollen, red eyes and wet cheeks as she shuffles as if in a trance, not seeing, unaware of what is happening around her.

A man in white pinstripe pajamas is off to Sterling's right. He has thick, brown hair sticking straight up on one side, with his arms around a dark-haired woman, her face buried in his chest. Her shoulders heave with sobs.

Frantic people push their way through the chaotic scene. Their faces smothered in shock as they crowd around the bright, yellow barricade of crime scene tape.

Fear has already solidified. It's oppressive and viscous, making concentration difficult if not impossible for the good folks of Alger, Michigan. Gusts of alarmed cries rip through the once peaceful and serene moonlit night, puncturing Sterling's skull like tiny thorns. The calamity crawls its way under his skin as he puts the car in park and glances into the mirror. "Let's get this done," he says to the no-nonsense, slice through the bullshit eyes reflecting at him, and opens the door.

Sterling emerges from the car—tall, handsome, with stark black hair, hardened features, and mesmerizing emerald-green eyes. He embodies a hard-boiled, mysterious detective from a "40s noir novel. With his head held high—those narrow, all-knowing eyes that never sleep, Sterling strides by the ambulance—solemnity wearing on his brow.

Relentless in their work, the fire department puts out the blaze at the old abandoned house across the road, while police vehicles with their sirens blaring, still rush to the scene. Detective Sterling received a few minor details about some teenagers having a bonfire party. Some sparks from the fire caught brush ablaze, making the old house light up quicker than a New York minute. However, the essential details of the murder were unknown yet.

Men in black pants and light blue shirts, with an arm patch bearing a blue, six-pointed star outlined with a white border and the rod of Asclepius in the center, work helping the few kids hurt when the fire started. As Sterling makes his way to the scene, the musky, sweet scent of burnt flesh, mixed with a sulfurous odor of burnt hair, invades his nose.

A young man whimpers in agony, his raw flesh exposed. The fire left nothing to him but a gaping sore. Scattered patches of hair remain on his bloody, inflamed skull. In some spots, pieces of clothing have melted into the scarce areas of charred skin. With a ragged last gasp, his head falls back, his eyes glass over, and Sterling would swear a smile creases the young man's face. The paramedic shakes his head, pulling the white sheet over the boy's face. This one won't spend time in the hospital—his young life extinguished. As harsh as it may sound, it's a blessing as far as Sterling's concerned. If the boy had lived, what kind of life would he have? How much pain and anguish would he have to suffer? Death is a godsend for him, and that is the gruesome reality.

He looks away, a cough escaping his burning throat, dry and irritated from the intense smoke in the air. A little further up on his right, another young man lies on a gurney, not half as severe as the first—thank God. He's burned, but not as grave as the last. They cut his pant leg on his left side to his thigh, the reddened skin, blistered here and there. He will have one hell of a nasty scar, but this one will make it. His weak, laborious breath wafts through the night as the paramedic places a transparent plastic mask over his nose and mouth, delivering vital oxygen to counter smoke inhalation.

First responders have their hands full striving to keep the growing distress of spectators from rising to manic. A well-dressed woman, her blonde hair pulled up in a stylish, loose fishtail braid, sobs, "Oh God, why?" Men fight the crowd to get to their loved ones. The *lookiloos*, as Sterling calls them, swarm around the scene like a pack of vultures to a fresh carcass, to get a glimpse of the horrors—an unfortunate norm in his line of work.

After all these years, he still grapples with this reaction. He ponders, once more, whether these behaviors are ingrained in the fabric of the human condition, or if people are just fucking sick! Who in their right mind wants to observe death and destruction? It's difficult for him to fathom the human obsession with death.

Sterling's eyes are slits, red and dry from exhaustion and his mind muddles over the bank robbery he's been working on. He awoke at 10pm to a ringing phone telling him a body was found. Ordinarily he would still be awake, but he was up all night the night before working a robbery in West Branch. One robber shot a bank teller in the leg when they made off with five hundred grand. He's sure the burglary is an inside job, after considering the clerk's involvement as a possibility. If he's right, the shooting was a way to sway his attention in another direction. However, he has witnessed that ploy before and isn't falling for it—not until he has proof to tell him otherwise.

Walking over to the marked off area, the yellow police tape seeming too bright, he lifts it over his head for the millionth time in his life. A thousand overlapping voices, ask questions: How'd this happen? Who got hurt? What were they doing out here? Like a swarm of bees piercing his ears and rattling in his head. "Go home, people. This isn't for your eyes," he mutters just above his breath. He recognizes an officer a few feet away, James P. Hamilton.

Hamilton is never hard to miss, his thick mop of dark, red hair a dead giveaway. He's a good-looking guy with steely blue eyes, pleasant enough, and smart as a whip. However, Sterling would wager his season tickets, the kids in school called him Howdy Doody. Children could be so cruel to gingers.

"Hamilton," he calls in his thick, New York accent.

"Hey, Sterling, I'm glad you're here."

"Yeah, it appears you have your hands full with all these lookiloos trying to get a peek at the aftermath."

"Damned people! Isn't there enough devastation in this life? They have to get an eye full, don't they?" Hamilton remarks. Dark bags encircle his eyes making him appear as if he hasn't slept in weeks. "Hey, I'm sorry about calling you. I know you were working on that bank case all night, but we sure have a mess to sort out here."

"I'll survive. Tell me what we have."

"I think it would be best to show you." Hamilton mops his sweat-ridden brow. "But I'm warning you it isn't pretty. I had a few men lose their dinners on this one."

"I'll consider myself warned, my friend."

The two stroll across the primitive, dirt road to a line of stern-faced officers. They're standing shoulder to shoulder creating a human barricade to hide the ugliness behind them from an intrusive crowd that now is buzzing like a hornet's nest.

Why? Why in the hell would anyone want to view the aftermath of murder? It makes little sense; he muses. *What outlandish demented part of the human brain craves to see the execrable sight of human mutilation?* He contemplated these behaviors for years and concluded the human race is a sick breed. There are days he would give his right arm to wash away the sights he had seen in his time as a detective. Yet, every time he arrived on a murder case, a crowd was there waiting to catch a glimpse of something gruesome and repulsive. If he thought about it long enough, it made him nauseous that he was a part of such a mad and twisted breed.

The wall of officers separates as the men approach, revealing the body of a teenage girl sprawled on the ground like a broken down toy, discarded with as much thought as the blink of an eye. "Jesus Christ," Detective Sterling whispers, fighting back the sour sting rising in the back of his throat. However, no one notices Sterling's reaction, for his hardcore expression holds true. He wipes his mouth with the handkerchief from his pocket and the sweat beading up on his brow. It's a warm night for this time of year.

In the darkness, the moon attempts to cut through the dense trees casting imposing shadows, a young girl lay in nature's waste, discarded like garbage and opened like a tuna can. He recognizes her as fifteen-year-old Jody Morrison. It isn't surprising he knows her; small towns are like that. Everyone knows everyone, and it is his job to know the people in this town. What is surprising is this type of murder—a murder period. Sterling has undergone his fill of individuals defiling other people in his years. But for an act this horrific to happen in a peaceful little town is unexpected.

"Who found her?"

"Some kids at the bonfire. Two of the girls got scared when the house went up in flames and ran. One of them tripped over the body—she's rather upset. Randy is taking their statements."

"Not something one so young should see."

Hamilton nods his head in agreement. "Hell, this is something a grown man should never witness."

J.C. Brennan

The instant recognition of the girl, Jody Morrison, may not have come to Sterling if it were not for her clothing—second-hand items. She isn't from a wealthy or middle-class family, for that matter. So, her now shredded, drab brown blouse that looks to be a frock from the "'60s era, her size too big jeans, and K-mart special tennis shoes—though she only has one on now—are a dead giveaway.

Jody is, or was, a quiet girl who lived in the small town of Alger from the time she was two. Her parents were Roger and Sandy Morrison. Sandy died two years prior in a car accident outside Alpena. After that, Roger lost his job due to a drinking habit he acquired after Sandy's death. He isn't a violent drunk, thank God for small favors, but he is a sloppy one. Which means, Jody took care of him, their home, worked, and kept decent grades in school—how? Sterling would never know. The two lived on the wages from Jody's part-time job and what state assistance provided. They didn't have much, but they stayed fed, the house was clean, and Jody never complained. With their financial situation, Jody wore hand-me-downs, so her clothes were not *in fashion*. Most she bought from Goodwill or Saint Mary's. She encountered a significant amount of criticism for the way she dressed, a target for harassment from other kids. Teenagers, they are assholes.

He intruded on their pestering a time or two. Once at the skating rink in West Branch a few years back, a few boys surrounded her, shouting names. Sterling was there with his son on an assigned weekend, which when he turned eighteen, became nonexistent. He could not stand by and let the kids torment her, so he broke it up. Kids, especially teenagers, can be so cruel to someone *different* from the crowd or not part of the *cool kids*.

He still remembered her thanking him, in a timid little voice. Her dark, straight hair, covering most of her face, her faded blue jeans, and puke-green sweater, it was the first time she ever made eye contact with

him. She had a habit of staring at the ground when talking to people, but on that night she looked straight at him.

He noticed she was dry-eyed without the slightest appearance of distress. He found it strange that she wasn't upset about the teasing. At least she disclosed no signs of distraught over the ordeal. Sterling assumed Jody underwent this activity so often that she'd become immune to the constant torment. It was a theory anyway. Yeah, Sterling confirmed she was a strange one but a good girl just the same.

"Anderson," Sterling calls at the site of a dark-haired young man whose face, at the moment, runs deep with worry lines, making him look twenty years older than his age. Kyle Anderson is an edgy kind of fellow, always seeming to be on the brink of a nervous breakdown. He's twenty-one, baby-faced, with pale green eyes, and a square jaw. Sterling doesn't know him well, but there's something all too familiar about the man. Sterling can't put his finger on it, but it makes him vigilant around him. Moments exist where he's confident he met the man somewhere before. He often chalks it up to déjà vu. One thing's for sure, Anderson loves fast, classic muscle cars, fast women, and chewing on those damned toothpicks he's never without.

"Yes, Detective."

It's clear Anderson isn't sure what to do and doesn't want to get in anyone's way. He gnaws on that toothpick—like it'll be the last one he'll ever chew on. His color is pale as he shifts his weight from one foot to the other and rubs his hands together—a nervous twitch, Sterling supposes. His face hangs, as a whiter shade of pale washes over him, and he swallows with effort, appearing as if he may lose his dinner.

Anderson entered the force a year ago, and this is his first murder case. As challenging as a homicide is, this will, with any luck, be his last in this town. At least, Sterling hopes it will be. Murder doesn't happen in a town like Alger. Well, he should say, it doesn't happen with any amount of frequency, which is the sole purpose for his relocation here from New York ten years ago. Besides the occasional shoplifter or reports of a few kids drinking, it's a quiet, uneventful town and that's the kind of town Sterling needed and still does, to unburden his soul of the Belmont case.

"I want you to push the crime tape back fifty feet from where it is right now. Have Matherson help you and get these people the hell out of here."

"Yes, sir."

Sterling heads over, examining the remains of the girl. A phantom breeze twists and teases his hair, the ominous odor of decay drifts with it. He has done this—examining scenes, searching for clues—for a long time, some would say too long. But now the gaze of glassy, lifeless eyes staring back at him brings an all too familiar, unsettling sensation. The eyes of the dead have a way of burning past all a person shows to the world, peering deep into their heart and mind. All the time, the person looking back into the dark, lifeless windows of the dead, becomes riddled with a disturbing awareness, like a bitter wind swiping the nape of their neck. He believes it to be the abrupt understanding that there's nothing left to see; the soul is gone, and all that remains of the person that once was, is a cold, lifeless, empty shell.

Someone or something sliced Jody from the base of her neck to her pelvis. Seeing a lot in his time as a detective, he has to admit he never investigated anything quite like this before. To get a closer look, he squats down and notices the ragged edges of the wound, suggesting the opening wasn't made with a sharp-edged object, but a dull blade. From the looks of her, a few, what could be, claws and bite marks, stray dogs or wild animals made a meal of her corpse.

"Hamilton, has the M.E. been called?"

"Yup, called her myself."

"Good. Is this the way the girl found her?"

"Girls," Hamilton corrects. "Yeah, you see those two girls over there by Johnson?" Hamilton says, pointing behind them to the right.

Randy Johnson is a younger cop, but a good one, nonetheless. On the force for about three years, he works just as hard, sometimes harder, than Hamilton. Johnson isn't seeking glory or promotions, wanting to be the best at what he does. He told Sterling being a cop was a way he could make sure lives got saved. Also, it was a way the grieving family could receive the justice they deserved. *"There's no room for heroes in this game,"* the boy said. Yeah, it's safe to say, Sterling likes Johnson.

"Well, they are the ones who called it in. Besides the little blonde tripping over the body, neither of them touched it. Shoot, they were so distraught when they called, dispatch had a difficult time understanding what they said. Can you imagine being their age and stumbling on this?"

Sterling glances over his shoulder to see two girls about Jody's age, both are shaking. Eyes swollen, damp and red, arms wrapped around themselves as if they needed to hold themselves tight, so they don't fall to pieces. Johnson says something, initiating intense emotion from the little blonde. Sterling watches her drop to her knees and hears her uncontrollable sobs as she shakes her head.

"I can't say I can," he replies. "Do me a favor will ya, Hamilton?"

"Yeah, sure, what do you need?"

"Tell Johnson when he's done getting their statements to take them home."

"Ah, you sure? I mean, shouldn't they go to the station?"

"After what they have been through tonight, they need to be with their family. We have their address if we need anything."

"Ok, will do Sterling... Hey," Hamilton stops in mid-stride, "have you ever investigated anything like this before?"

"I've inspected plenty of the senseless debauchery in my time, don't get me wrong. However, never in my twenty-three years have I seen something like this."

"I hear ya," Hamilton says as he turns, heading over to where the girls and Johnson are.

Chapter 2

The Medical Examiner

The medical examiner, Samantha Montague, enters the crime scene a few minutes later. She's a blonde, with ice-blue eyes, in her mid-thirties, who doesn't look a day over twenty-five and has a body that won't quit. She told Sterling she'd lived in this area most of her life. She married right out of high school to an older well-to-do gentleman, who had put her through college.

Three years ago, her husband died of prostate cancer. Samantha took his death hard and drowned her sorrows in the drink ever since. Her little moonlight rendezvous with the bottle is like a big secret that everyone knows, but no one talks about, so long as it doesn't affect her work. The one thing this town *does* like to talk about is her relationship with her now dead, older husband. Although no one will ever admit it, this town thrives on a juicy situation to arise just to talk behind the back of a supposed friend, neighbor, even a spouse.

Sam is not immune to this attribute of the quiet little town. Some say she married the man solely for his money; other's thought she did it to have a better life than she was born into. However, Sterling knew Sam loved the man—loved him with all her heart. She never saw the age difference between them as a barrier.

Sterling was there to comfort her when her husband died. Though there was no intention, a short, wild fling transpired. And, man, did she live true to the paradigm of passionate. However, they decided, for the sake of their friendship and because of their careers, their relationship needed to be platonic. That was the end of the fling even though there was an emotional tie between them; friends were all they would be after

that. Neither of them let their prior relations affect their work. They were, after all, professionals. Though—professionals or not—Sterling got the sense of tension in her.

Sterling reaches her before she catches sight of the body.

"Hi, Sam, brace yourself, this one is rather unpleasant."

"Aren't they always?" She responds, flashing that pleasant smile of hers.

She comes closer, her perfume—Obsession—dances in the night. Her hair tied in a band reveals her long neck—a neck that's perfect to nuzzle and breathe in her scent. In blue jeans that hug her great ass, a white blouse, and a denim jacket, to onlookers, she appears to be nothing more than another *lookiloo*—one of the crowd and that is the way she likes it. People's responses are different when they're privy to the fact she's a medical examiner—the person who investigates *death*, ooooh. She would rather examine the scene without extreme prejudice.

The night though warm, without a breeze, still sends a chill down his spine as he carries Sam's medical bag. Sterling's hand instinctively goes around her waist as he leads her over to where Jody lies. The chaos vanishes, a sudden flood of memories washes through him. For a moment, it's as if they're strolling in the park. However, the annihilation of this notion evaporates when the body comes into view.

"Holy Mother of God!" Sam whispers. Her eyes are wide with inquisitiveness, not fear. Murder is an oddity, and murder such as this is unprecedented in these parts. Her eyebrows raise, eyes squeeze shut, and her head turns. "Whoa," she says, pushing her hand up to her nose.

"I warned you; this one is a mess."

"That you did."

"Are you going to be alright, Sam?"

"I'm fine," she mutters, squatting down next to Jody. She reaches her hand out, "My kit please." Taking the black bag from him and opening it, she pulls out a small jar of what appears to be Vaseline, applying it under her nose. "Give me a few minutes, and I'll give you an approximate time of death."

It takes Samantha a few moments to get the internal temperature, giving Sterling the time of death. While she does her thing, Sterling inspects the area around the body and surrounding area. It's always tricky finding evidence in the woods at night, although his flashlight helps. Examining Jody's desecrated corpse, which is much smaller resting on the forest floor, he starts from her head and works down her body with the flashlight. Something catches his attention. No ligature marks on her wrist or ankles, indicating she was not bound, nor is there any discoloration around her mouth from a gag, telling him she well might have known her attacker.

"What are these?" Sterling asks as the light hit Jody's legs.

"Let me see."

Dark, purplish-red marks show from under a large rip in her jeans. Lifting the material, Samantha sees what appears to be scratch marks—deep gouges.

"They appear to be marks from animal claws. Some of which are profound and... wait... hold on a minute." Samantha grabs her tweezers.

"What is it?"

"I can't be positive," she says, pulling some foreign object from one wound. "Well, will you look at that?" holding the tweezers for Sterling to see.

"What is that, Sam?"

"I think it's a piece of a fingernail."

"Do you think you can get DNA from it?"

"I won't know until I get back to the lab."

"From examining her, do you think a rape occurred?"

"I'm not showing any signs of that. But I'll conduct a rape kit when I'm able to get her to the lab."

"Good. As soon as you find anything, call me."

"I will," Sam says, turning away from Sterling to continue examining Jody's body.

He lets her get back to her work and heads further into the surrounding woods to inspect the area, hoping to discover something left behind by the assailant. A piece of clothing, a tuft of hair—damn, any little fragment would help. Desiccated dirty yellow-brown leaves and pine needles, obscuring the fertile soil beneath, crunch under his weight as he searches, eager to uncover a speck of blood, a footprint, anything that points toward a killer. However, nothing raises an eyebrow around the body, so he expands his investigation of the ground. The light scans over the dulling autumn colors of oak, ivy, and Persian ironwood leaves, the rot of downed trees, and dead brush, then back again not missing a leaf or a twig that may be out of place. His eyes determined—focused like a hawk. Each movement he makes is with careful precision.

About ten feet from the body, a liquid substance with the consistency of saliva, drips from a withering leaf. Kneeling down, the scent of pine and rich soil sweeps through, and he notices the probable saliva has a red tint to it, offering the briefest bit of vindication. *Jody might have got a decent blow in before he killed her. Good, I hope she knocked the prick so hard his lip split wide open,* he thinks.

"I got something here. I think it's saliva, and it looks as if it might have blood mixed in. I hope she belted the fucker."

"Good for her if that's the case. I wish she would have knocked his damned head off."

"Don't we both," Sterling whispers.

"Get me a sample and I'll test it," Sam replies. "Maybe we can get some DNA and get this psycho."

"I'm on it," he calls back. "Let this give us what we need to catch this guy," he says.

Of course, he's not confident the assailant is of the male persuasion, and the blood could be Jody's. Still, a woman assailant doesn't fit the profile. The thought of a woman carrying out such atrocities on a young girl makes his stomach curl. Nevertheless, it wouldn't be the strangest thing that's ever happened.

Leaves rustling from behind disturb the night. Startled, he stops himself just short of falling on his ass. The flashlight swings around to see what's moving as he curses himself for being caught off guard. A stray black cat hunches its back while pressed against the trunk of a tree growling and spitting. Its eyes glow, two tiny white orbs in the light with its teeth bared. Its ears back touching its head, its body hunkered, eyes fixed and glaring at him. It thumps its tail on the ground as if playing the drums and the vocals—a subtle snarling—rumbles from its depths. The cat's hissing spooks an owl which takes flight, making a loud and clamorous noise. Grousing with a sigh of relief, at ease with the awareness it's just a damned cat; Sterling chuckles and wipes the sweat from his brow.

"Hey little guy, you scared the shit out of me. Now go on, get out of here, I have work to do." He says, flipping his hands at the still hissing creature, as if telling him, *scared you! You bastard, you almost gave me a heart attack.* The cat jumps and takes off in the opposite direction.

"Damned cat!" he repeats, collecting a sample of the unknown substance in a glass container. He places the vial in a bag, seals it, and finishes his search of the areas. The night gets quiet, no crickets, caddis, not even an owl's hoot, it's eerie in the swelter as twigs snap beneath his feet. Nothing else appears as out of place or disturbed so he heads back to Samantha. He scrutinizes the area on his walk back, in case he missed something the first time.

"Do you have an approximate time of death for me, Sam?" Sterling asks, emerging from the shadows to see Sam, bent over the body, swabbing the edge of Jody's open wound.

"Well, this girl died approximately four to six hours ago, the body exhibiting slight signs of postmortem lividity, and her internal temp read 92."

"Are you sure? I would have thought longer with the odor."

"Yeah, me too, but that is not the case."

"Any thoughts as to why?"

"No, I can't explain that yet. But, from what I see, I'd venture to say she died closer to four hours ago. Whoever did this, did not do it here."

"Why's that?"

"From the way she is torn up, there should be blood everywhere. I mean, this area should look like a slaughterhouse, but there's no trace of blood other than on the body."

"I noticed."

"I'll know more when I get her back to my office."

"Don't you mean the morgue?"

"I spend ninety percent of my time there, so if I want to refer to it as my office, I believe I'm entitled."

"Yeah, I can't argue with that." Sterling chuckles. "I'll meet you at the mor... your office, in a little while. I have something to finish up here."

"I can call you when I finish, that way you're not waiting around."

"Thanks, Sam, I appreciate it."

"Can I get her out of here now?"

"Yes, but call me as soon as you're through—take her."

"See you in a while... and, Levi?" Samantha says, with a concerned expression on her face.

"Yeah," Sterling replies, knowing Sam only calls him by his first name when she's worried about him.

"You look like hell," she tells him with a crooked little grin. "You should get sleep."

"I'll consider that. Talk to you soon, Sam."

With a slight throbbing, telling him he has one hell of a headache coming on, he goes over the crime scene one more time. He's nothing if not tenacious and thorough. His dance with an unsolved murder has already transpired, and he does not want another. In fact, after that case, he moved to this town from New York. The big city, with its bright lights, and endless nightlife lost its appeal after the Belmont incident. The luster of New York vanished, and his nightmare began. It wasn't the murder itself that brought the dreams and night terrors; it was the way someone tortured the boy. What kind of fuckin' maniac does something like that to a teenage boy! Yeah, after that case, a quiet, small town suited him fine.

Chapter 3

The Boy

The pain exploding through his body was searing. Nothing in his young life could compare to this agonizing torture. The burns from the cigarettes were a distant memory, though the smell of burning skin, like a steak on the grill at a Sunday barbecue, still tickled his nose. Parts of his flesh were raw as if a steel wire brush, like the one his grandfather used at the body shop, was brushed over his skin repeatedly for a minute or two. However, he was becoming numb to it. After all, one can endure torture for so long before the suffering turned into a long-lost companion in some sick, warped frame of the mind. The cuts made in his flesh by a knife the size of Texas were now a part of a distant brutal dream. All that was left was an intense throbbing still suffered in his posterior, and he prayed to God that pain would end soon.

Fading in and out of consciousness, he is still aware enough to notice the bruises covering his legs—dark purple, shades of blue and yellow—from the men using them like a misshapen kickball. That had gone on for an hour after they entered the tunnels when he could still hear a stereo off in the distance somewhere. Etta James bawled out, *At last, my love has come along*. He recognizes the song because it was one of his mom's favorites.

His face against the cold concrete he wished for death. If he made it out of this, the doctors would never be capable of fixing him. He would never be as he had been before this depraved nightmare. The Devil himself had cursed him, but for what reason? He's unsure.

The fourth man, the short fat one with greasy, black hair that looked as if it had not seen a bar of soap in a week or two, gripped the boy's forehead with one hand and the other went around his waist for leverage. He didn't fight; there was nothing left in him even to try. He was like a rag doll as the fat man's grunts echoed in his ears. The blend of liquor, filth, and cigarettes contributed to the man's stench, making him nauseous.

Another tormented scream cut through the night air, bursting through the tunnels. But nobody came—no one heard—no one saw. Only the walls and rats listened to his cry, and for that at least, he was grateful. He found solitude in knowing other than the men executing these defiling acts; he alone heard his torturous shrieks. Somehow, it made him feel better to know no one would have these harrowing visions waking them up at night in a pool of sweat and glass-shattering screams. Still, he pleaded, in silence so loud it could fracture the earth, *"I wish to die! Please, just let me die now. I will never be right if I survive. I want to die! Please, God, just let me die!"* But no one heard his agonizing words.

His body had received all the punishment it could stand. When the man finished pleasuring himself, he let the youth fall lifeless to the frigid stone floor like a discarded newspaper. His head bounced when it hit the cool, damp floor of the foul-smelling sewer. The boy stared with the vacant eyes of the dying. His lips pulled into a frown though he was no longer sad nor frightened. Emotions were no longer a part of him, as the cold stone beneath him pressed against his warm, wet face.

The toxic aroma of human waste was more potent at this level, making him think he might suffocate, which he wouldn't have a problem with at this point. His body involuntarily responded to the vile odor, wrenching, spewing vomit with what little energy he had left. Under different circumstances, he would have registered crushing pain through his temple, but not tonight. The pain assaulting his body was in his bottom, slight as it was in his state. The agony became further deadened—a stroke of luck.

Though not dead yet, death was tapping at his door, and he welcomed it like a hot cup of cocoa and a warm blanket on a cold winter's night. A slight, bleak smile touched his lips when he realized he would soon welcome the reaper with open arms. He laid on the grime and waste of the concrete surface, staring at the gray-black wall, his mind no longer registering much of anything.

He noticed his face rested on a small, metal grate. Water gurgled, the sound of its sparse, trickling flow below him was the one comforting sound he heard. A faint flash of light. He shifted his tired, red eyes downward toward the brief flicker and noticed the dim light had reflected off the metal edge of a hunting knife. It must have fallen out of the man's pockets.

In the last feeble breaths of stank sewer air he took, the wooden-handled hunting knife imprinted on him maddened mind. He silently cried out, "*Someone—anyone, please! Someone find me! Don't leave my body down here in this vile place—don't leave me in the dark.*"

He was dying, and the knowledge brought an immense, engulfing relief to his broken body and mind. He had wished for death for hours now—perhaps days. All time was lost to him.

The pain, once ripping through his shattered, tortured body, no longer existed—the insensitivity was a godsend. His eyes looked down to his side. He could no longer move his head to see the pool of blood forming on the floor—his life, now floating away into loving, eternal darkness, waiting for him with open arms, telling him, *come, my child, there is no pain here, no anguish, peace awaits.* A blessing descended upon him.

I can see the darkness, she welcomes me with loving, open arms. No more suffering. Thank you. It was the last thought of young Matt Belmont.

It was winter ten years ago, and winters in New York were brutal. This particular winter got worse by the minute. Sterling's department had a record number of deaths that year. Sterling remembered how something—the cold—infected people with crazy. That was the year they found the body of a fifteen-year-old boy, Matt Belmont, off Front Street under the Manhattan Bridge. A woman, on her way to The Bridge Coffee Shop before her shift, was convinced she saw a body and called it in. She told the 911 operator she was sure there was blood but would be damned if she would risk her life to investigate. That was not her responsibility, you see. The police get paid to do the dirty work.

Any officer in the vicinity of Front Street, a one-eighty-seven has been reported. The radio crackled with static as if a bomb was going off, the peacefulness of the morning as Carly Simon's, *You're So Vain* was interrupted on the oldies station. "It's too early for this shit," Sterling groused. It was a long night already, and his state was bordering on the edge of irritation and full-fledged anger. The night had proven to be full of assholes whose cooperation levels were nil, and all he wanted was for his shift to end so he could put another night behind him. But Sterling was close to the area, so he took the call. Now thinking back, he wished he had stayed out of this one.

"Jesus Christ, it's not even 5 a.m. yet!" Grumbling, he turned the car radio off, grabbed the mic, and told dispatch he was on his way.

"Where did she say she saw it?" He asked the faceless voice on the other end of his mic.

"Front Street, Under the Manhattan Bridge." The unseen voice full of static confirmed.

"Ten-four."

Flipping the lights on, he raced to Canal Street. Within fifteen minutes he arrived at the scene. There wasn't a soul in sight as he opened the car door. The negative thirteen-degree wind chill had a hell of a bite, stealing his breath. The cold was unforgiving, just like the city. It's New York, the concrete jungle, a city where dreams are realized and destroyed, all within a day. A place where the streets made you feel brand new and the city's lights inspired you. But if you aren't as durable as bronze, you have no right to be there. Yeah, it's wondrous in the city that never sleeps, but the streets would eat a person alive if they weren't hardened to the core.

Pulling his collar up to fight the bitter cold, he drew a flashlight from his pocket and scanned the area. No more than ten feet to his right, next to one of its massive steel pillars, laid a snow-covered hump. "Shit," he sighed. He'd hope the woman's allegation would amount to a snowdrift, but he couldn't be that lucky. He made his way over to the protrusion, trouncing through the five to seven inches of snow towards the swell, to get a better view. The corner of a tattered piece of old material stuck out of the drift with what could well be blood.

"Shit! Let it be a discarded blanket," he wishes, although experience told him otherwise.

Pulling the material, he sends snow tumbling to reveal a young man's tortured body. The boy is lying on his back, eyes open with a distinctive blue-white haze and pupils dilated. "Shit! Shit! Son, I am so sorry."

Knowing the boy was dead, he squats down still placed his hand on the neck to check for a pulse in the odd chance he was wrong. The skin was cold, solid like touching a block of ice. There was nothing left that would prove he still might be alive. Out of nowhere, something hard struck the back of his head—lights out.

The next thing he remembered was Officer Whitehead, who was frazzled, saying something, but it took a minute to get his bearings.

Officer Alex Whitehead showed up on the scene right after Sterling. He called the incident in, asking for an ambulance and backup. Whitehead was a nice guy with a good head on his shoulders. He was 6' 2", neither muscular nor scrawny, with dark brown hair styled in a way that conjured up images of John Travolta in *Saturday Night Fever*. Always in a black leather jacket, jeans and a permanent five o'clock shadow that maintained the hard-ass from the Bronx front. But truth be told, the male bravado was just a façade, he was all heart underneath. Not to say he wouldn't throw down with a bad guy if the need presented itself. Whitehead was a character, a very intense young man—an old soul if you will. Sterling didn't know the man that well. He had worked with him a few times on other cases, but he was a stand-up guy, the kind of guy that could be trusted.

"Jesus! Levi, Levi!" Whitehead ran over and helped him sit up. His head was bleeding, so Whitehead grabbed his gym towel from the back seat of his squad car to put pressure on the wound. "You alright?"

"Yeah, I'll be fine."

"Did you see who jumped you?".

"Shit, I have no idea who it was, the asshole came from behind."

"Damn it, man. Some hoodlum got you right up proper, my friend. Stay still, the ambulance is on its way."

Whitehead glanced over at the lump under the dirty old blanket. "Is this the body called in?" He asked Sterling, making his way over to the body.

"Yeah, that's the one."

"H-ooo-ly shit!" Whitehead muttered, pulling back just the corner. He spewed his breakfast in the snow.

"That bad, huh? You sure you want to be a detective to deal with this shit day in and day out? It's not all glory and firecrackers." Sterling told him.

"Oh yeah, that's one thing I'm sure of." However, if truth be told, viewing the defilement before him and Sterling's condition, the gash in the man's head, he had to wonder if becoming a detective was the best route for him to take.

"This one is bad—real bad. I've never heard of anything like this."

"Yeah, well get used to it, kid. It's a detective's daily routine, fun, huh?"

A few patrol cars show up and block off the scene to contain those who gathered before they become a swarm.

"Hey, help me up."

"I'm not sure that's the best idea—"

"I'm fine. Give me a hand here, will ya?"

Against his better judgment, Whitehead helped Sterling to his feet as they strode over to the body. What Sterling saw lying under the bridge that day would haunt him for the next ten years of his life. The young teenage boy, he later learned was Matt Belmont, fifteen-years-old, sprawled out under a worn, tattered blanket that covered his brutalized body. It was the nature of the abuse this boy suffered that wormed its way under Sterling's skin. The body showed signs of being tortured, raped, and then beaten to death. Cuts, cigarettes burns, and dark bruises covered Belmont from head to toe. The mercilessness, lack of compassion, complete and utter callousness toward a young boy suggested this was a punishment—towards the boy, doubtful that the perp was someone close to him. He had investigated a few brutal deaths in his time. The lewd acts people commit on one another always astounded. But this boy got to him.

"Damn," Sterling snorted, turning his head for a moment, bile nipping at the back of his throat.

Whoever committed the crime left the boy naked under the bridge. He surmised the blanket belonged to one of the homeless that plagued the city. Not that he had anything against the homeless, it was the fact they were the lost, those that society had forgotten, that bothered him. No one should be forgotten—life's too precious. There was sadness that came with their concealed faces. Invisible, blending into the dark alleys, as thousands of people walked the streets daily, never giving these lost souls a second thought. *The people the world forgot,* are what he called them.

"Christ, we've got one hell of a mess here."

Sterling looks up to see a man with red and gray-peppered hair and a face streaked with age. Officer McNeil was holding his badge out as he crossed the police tape moving toward him.

"Hey Sterling, it's good to see ya. We sure have a predicament here, eh?" McNeil noticed Sterling's head. "Jesus man, someone kicked and booted ya. You alright?"

"Yeah, some bastard jumped me, but I'll be fine. McNeil, you know Officer Whitehead?"

"Ey," he said with a nod, then turned his attention back to Sterling. "You better get that checked out. Ya don't want your noodle all scrambled."

"I will."

McNeil was older, born in Ireland. He came to live with his aunt when his mother died when he was just sixteen. His father passed away before he was born. From what he understood, a dispute in a local Irish pub broke out. His father was an officer of the law over in Ireland, and he took the call that fateful night. A man exceeded his limit of the drink, and although Sterling didn't have all the details, McNeil's father caught a slug in the chest.

"Well, let's take a gander shall we," McNeil said, moving closer to the body.

"I warn you, it is not pleasant."

"Murder never is, my friend."

Sterling wished he prepared McNeil for the sight he was about to see. He's seen so much death in his job but this one, this boy—he was different, more violent, and more sadistic.

He knelt down and lifted the sheet to reveal the mangled face of a boy. A face beaten without mercy stared back at him. Severe swelling, shades of dark purple, green and yellow, mixed with other colors, ravished his skin like some reprehensible rainbow, staring back at him.

"Poor lad. He ain't more than fifteen-sixteen?"

"That isn't the worst of it," Sterling nods, pulling the sheet down, exposing the rest of the body.

"Holy Mother of God," McNeil mutters, making the Sign of the Cross over his torso.

A graying-haired gentleman with a black bag was coming their way. The medical examiner, Lewis was his name, arrived on scene. Behind him, Whitehead led emergency personnel through the ever-growing crowd. "There he is," he said, pointing to Sterling.

"Aw, shit."

"Lad, you should have that looked at," McNeil confirmed.

"Yeah, I guess."

They examined Sterling's head making him sit to clean and wrap the wound. While he sat there, head throbbing, staring at the lump of flesh under a filthy blanket, the M.E. came over, "I'm predicting the boy died between midnight and 3 am."

"Thanks, Lewis. Do me a favor and get the body out of here ASAP."

"No worries, McNeil and Whitehead are clearing a path as we speak. You look like you need to get to the hospital. That's a nasty gash."

"Yeah, thanks."

The female emergency medical technician, EMT, finished wrapping Sterling's head. He wobbled a little rising to his feet as he made his way back to the body being lifted on to a gurney. Lifting the sheet again to see the mangled face, the boy's eyes pop open as an ear-piercing scream comes from him, "*You catch who killed me!*"

The nightmares began.

The EMT's rushed him to the hospital; he passed out after viewing the Belmont kid. With its white sanitary walls, floors buffed to an immaculate shine, the halls filled with the smell of death. They treated his nasty head wound—a slight concussion, with part of his memory stolen from him. The doctor said it was a miracle he didn't suffer worse than a lost past, which became locked away in a cold, dark mental chamber of his mind. Therapy could only help so much. The doctor warned him he might never get it all back.

The hospital released him within a week and back on the job in two. Detective Sims, an older detective who was a couple weeks from retirement, had no problem bringing Sterling up to speed on what he found out or passing the case back to him.

"Listen," Sims said handing Sterling the case file, loosening his tie. The fluorescent office lights put a glare on the large bald spot on his head. "I tried to talk to the mother but half the time she was so damned drunk she didn't have a clue what day it was. So, as you can imagine, I haven't gotten much from her."

"Well, then I will start there," Sterling replied, examining the picture of an attractive woman. "By the way, thanks Sims."

"No need, it helped me pass the time."

"What do you plan on doing with yourself after you retire?"

"I'm taking the Missus to Florida, we have a little cottage on the Keys, and that is where I intend to pass the rest of the years I have left. Alone with my wife and my dog Humphrey."

"Enjoy, you have earned it," Sterling said with a slight chuckle.

Brought up to speed on the case, he began his investigation. Mrs. Belmont—once beautiful, at least from the picture he'd seen on her file—was now an alcoholic. Her face had taken on the traits of anxiety, fatigue, and sadness, along with the telltale signs of alcoholism—broken capillaries on the nose and face, reddening of the nose and cheeks, and yellowing of the eyes. Her skin embellished in a grayish hue, her once vibrant blue eyes were now dull and lifeless, accentuated by dark bags and deep wrinkles. She appeared ten years older than her age. When she invited him in, the stale aroma of liquor lingered in the apartment. The place was immaculate, except for the kitchen table, which he could see through the arched hallway entrance to his right, was loaded with scotch, vodka, and other bottles, all empty, of course.

When he asked her about who could have done this to her son, she blamed the incident on the boy's father. She stated he hated Matt since the day he was born and was always telling her the boy wasn't his. It was a good lead if Matt's father wasn't doing a stint in Adirondack Correctional Facility for a B&E—breaking and entering - which he found out when he ran his name.

Forensics came up empty-handed. No clues were left behind to offer a bearing on who executed the crime. No DNA, fingerprints, or fluids, and no leads. The body was *cleansed*—washed down with bleach.

Sterling had dealt with many—too many as far as he was concerned—child involved homicide cases. They were without a doubt the worst and always took a toll on those who worked them. However, this boy stayed with him in ways he could have never fathomed. He couldn't erase Belmont's mutilated face from his mind no matter how hard he tried.

It was on this case, Sterling lost his faith in humanity—not that he ever had much before. Species that engage in such brutality on the innocent have issues far beyond comprehension. The Belmont case brought him an intimate insight into the real primitive perversion of a man's soul or lack thereof. It makes him sick.

It was the Belmont case that made him view the world as it is—cruel and depraved. To see the world beneath the one where we place polite smiles on our faces, cordially say good morning to our neighbors, and speak our pleasantries at backyard barbecues and parties. The world beneath all the fake personas was a world filled with psychopaths, rapists, child molesters, murderers, and the criminally insane. Who was he trying to kid, humanity was fucking deranged—all of them! Well, not all—there were the innocent. It was protecting them that kept him going—kept him motivated to wade through the vile slime and put the waste of humanity behind bars, or if the situation turned, a bullet in their skull. He never wanted a case to get to the point where killing someone was necessary, but it happened more often than he would like. The thing about killing someone is you were the witness to the light—

the life—as it diminished from their eyes. You could almost see their soul leave their body, and it was never less challenging, for that image stays with a man, it haunts him.

Some are less unbalanced than others, but they are all fucking psychotic, he pondered. *They're out there in the mud and the muck of societal degradation waiting for their next victim. Oh yes, they're the ones who society has turned a blind-eye to, neglected, and pretends to overlook. The people we try not to see, to forget. In the back of our minds, they're there in the decrepit wasteland of humanity. They're the ones we dare not mention or only hear about in the passing breath of a whisper.*

They're hiding in the shadows with the stench of their profane thoughts and broken minds. In the bosom of darkness, they wait. It holds them close and protects them until the next innocent victim is within their grasp. The next man, woman, or child who will become broken, dead, or wish for death long before it comes.

Sterling was vigilant of this shadow world, one he grew to understand thoroughly and had thought he escaped it.

Chapter 4

The Find

Sterling is waking at his antique desk, a 1900 roll top mahogany by Rand Leapold Desk Co., Burlington. It's a beautiful beast, though no one else could see that with the piles of paperwork concealing it. He forces his eyes open to slits; they burn with the scant light peeking from under the window shade. Of course, it breaks through and shines right in his face. Tic. Tic. Tic. The black and mottled tan, 1893 Seth Thomas, Adamantine clock sitting on the desk, thunders in the momentary silence of the house. His head lay atop the desk's cool polished wood. His computer keyboard pushes against the top of his head. Drool forms a small puddle, wetting the side of his face. Songs of birds socializing outside the window mingle with the tic of the clock.

Sitting upright, wiping the spit from his cheek, his head throbs with a sharp twinge like a damned screwdriver rammed through his skull. "Oh, fuck," he says, his voice a hushed slur, while holding his head. "That's the price you pay, asshole. You're not as young as you used to be," he preaches to the empty room and the half-full bottle of bourbon sitting on the desktop.

His neck is knotted something awful, he stretches it and stands with caution, yet very bone in his body protests with snaps and cracks. Pushing on the lower part of his back as he arches as far back as he can, his spine says good morning with multiple pops.

He usually makes it to the comfort of his bed, but considering the bourbon, that the desk served as a pillow last night doesn't surprise him. With a yawn, he peers at his watch and grumbles, *Shit, I got home a couple of hours ago. Maybe Samantha has the results back.* Stretching his arms out to the side and stretching them out before him, he feels the stiffness loosen. Rubbing the long, thick scar on the side of his head—it aches every now and again—he scratches his balls and then his ass, heading into the bathroom.

There was a time in his life, before the Belmont case, when his mornings started much different. A time when he woke up to his wife's beautiful, white smile, her soft skin touching his face, the smell and sound of sizzling bacon, waffles, and warm maple syrup—real maple syrup, not the imitation high fructose corn syrup kind from the store. His son, Josh, getting a running start from the hallway, jumped up in their bed, all smiles and giggles. Ah, but that was a lifetime ago, a time before Matt Belmont; a time he wished he had back.

The bathroom contained a standup shower, a sink, a toilet, and a small linen closet. He had the small room built in the office right after he bought this old place. It's the one place he spent most of his time, so the addition was a matter of convenience more than necessity.

This property sits at the end of a private dirt road. Sterling owns twenty acres, mostly wooded with large old oaks and towering pines. It stretches a thousand feet to the right and three acres to the left. The additional acreage spans back from his two-bedroom home built in the "50s by Jacob Manson, the previous owner until his death eleven years ago. In the mornings, not every morning, but many, he watches deer out the back window of the kitchen or out on the back porch which is a concrete slab he's meant to add a roof and screen wall too. As he drinks his coffee, he sighs, *it doesn't get much better than this.*

Three other homes share Baker Drive. The one at the beginning of the road, about a quarter-mile down, has laid empty since he moved in. The other two are summer getaway homes, occupied a couple of months of the year. He fell in love with the seclusion this place offers, it's his own little piece of heaven and privacy. It's the exact opposite of New York, and it's what he needs to keep what little sanity he has left.

Standing in front of the sink, splashing cold water on his face, sticking his tongue out and rubbing the stubble on his chin, he farts.

"Wow, Levi, what the hell did you eat?" he says as the silence is fractured with the ringing of the phone. *Maybe it's Sam.* In the living room, he picks up the phone.

"Detective Sterling," he answers.

"Sterling you won't believe this," is how the call begins. It isn't Sam as he hoped. Instead, it's Hamilton.

"Hamilton, slow down. What is it?"

"We need you down here, Sterling," he urges, his voice erratic. "W-we have found another body."

"Aw shit, what the hell is going on in this town?"

"I'm not sure, but this one is just like the other girl—Jody."

"Another girl! You're shitting me, right?"

"I wish I were."

"Where?"

"We're down here off of Alger Road about a mile, to a mile and a half past Greenwood. You know, where that old two-track veers off on the right. The one with the thick chain and the faded, yellow private property sign hanging from it."

"Yeah, I know right where you are."

"Well, the property owners came up early this morning. They found her laying in the two-track. The man almost ran her over and, as you can imagine, he's shaken up. I hate to do this, but if you could get here as soon as you can, it will be appreciated."

"It's not far. Give me fifteen. I'll grab a cup of coffee and be on my way. Hey did you call Samantha?"

"Yes, right before I called you. Sam's on her way."

"Good, good. Hold on, I'm on my way."

He grabs his jacket as he hangs up the phone on his way to the kitchen for coffee. The coffeepot's on the end of the wooden countertop, already set up, and starts with a click. Putting a new filter with two scoops of coffee grounds and filling the water reservoir is something he always does when he gets home. It became a habit when he transferred, since he's always on call, never knowing what time the next call will come.

The last couple days he's missed calls on minor incidents. Bank robberies, hunting accidents, home invasions, runaways, all he will take are calls related to these murders. There has only been two so far, but his gut tells him after seeing Jody there will be more, and dammit he hates being right. Homicides just are not something that occurs in Alger, not in the last ten years, anyway. Now, suddenly, they are popping up like flies on shit, and he doesn't like it one bit. He *was* recovering his faith in humanity again in this small town, and someone had to have himself a morbid hay-day on his dime and at the expense of innocent lives.

The sputtering, percolating rhythm of the coffee pot interrupts the morning, bringing an instant smile as he returns to the bathroom. A brush through his hair, a quick toothbrush over his teeth, some deodorant, and a splash of aftershave, he's ready.

The enticing aroma of coffee spills through the house. Three beeps signals completion of the brewing process. The mugs filled, he fumbles through the top drawer to find their lids, and then out the door he hustles.

It's still dark as the crisp morning air hits him. Fresh air with the bitter-sweet fragrance of pine, fills his nose as he gets in the car, shuts the door, and turns the ignition. The road is dark at this hour, making it easy to notice the lights on at the house which has sat abandoned for the last ten years. He notes that it is strange, but a hundred different things could have happened. The owner could have gotten sick, died, hell, life in general, could stop someone from visiting the place. However, he has two corpses dropped in his lap then the house no one has been to in years is suddenly occupied? Strange and it's something he files away for further investigation.

"Well, I'll make it a priority to meet my one and only neighbor real soon," he says aloud. Although with the sudden insanity rearing its ugly

J.C. BRENNAN

head in this town, he's confident he won't have time to socialize.

The sun is just peeking over the horizon as he turns the old black Ford on to Greenwood Road, heading for the location Hamilton directed him to.

It doesn't take him long to arrive at the location. The flashing red and blue lights from the police cars light up the early morning sky like the fourth of July. He sees them half a mile before reaching the two-track turnoff. A lofty, slim officer, yawns with a steaming cup in his hand while standing guard at the entrance. Sterling slows down, holding his badge out the car window.

"Detective Sterling, they're waiting for you."

"How far down?"

"Only about a half mile, you can't miss it," he says, pointing down what looks more like a walking trail than a road.

"Ok, thanks."

Down the two-track, his car bouncing around like a lumber wagon, he curses, "Son—of—a—bitch, I hope she isn't too much further."

The bottom of the car hits a rut, making the wheel jerk to the left. "Fuck!" bellows from his lips with a grip on the steering wheel so firm his hands ache.

Finally, he sees Hamilton waiting for him with Officer Johnson. Hamilton is frazzled. His dark, rust-colored hair a tangled mop, elevated on one side from running his hand through it most likely. The dark circles bordering his recessed bloodshot eyes, stand out like a sore thumb against his pastier than usual skin.

"God, he looks exhausted," Sterling mutters to himself as he parks the Ford sedan off to the side, turns the key, kills the motor, and opens the door. *Today will be a long day*, he surmises.

"Sterling, I'm glad you're here," Hamilton greets him with a distinctly stressed tone.

"Here you go, this should help." Sterling hands him one of the travel mugs. "It looks like you could use it. It's hot and black; I hope that's all right."

"The nectar of the gods. Thanks, man."

"Sorry Johnson, I only brought two coffees."

"I won't hold it against you," Johnson states, raising a large Styrofoam cup.

"So, where's the body?"

"Stay and wait for the medical examiner for me, will ya, Johnson?"

A nod from Johnson is all he needs. Silent, Hamilton leads Sterling down the two-track. Murder is not part of his daily routine though he's dealt with a few deaths during his time as an officer. Mostly accidents, domestic arguments, kids messing where they shouldn't be, but murder? Now, two occur in a twenty-four-hour period, and he is a mess.

Sterling notices Hamilton's hand shakes each time he takes a sip of coffee. He doesn't judge the man, for if he hadn't been through this more times than he could count, he'd be in the same condition. Sterling counts himself lucky, for the past ten years, these violent acts have been absent from his life. Scenes such as that of Matt Belmont had vanished, except in his dreams. The whole purpose for him leaving the sleepless, bright lights of New York, was to be away from horrors such as these. But the powers that be have seen fit to bring them back into his life—the purpose? Unknown yet.

The shadows of the woods lighten with the rising of the sun as they make their way down "road" to the body. "Dammit," Sterling curses, a root protrudes from the ground enough to trip him.

He watches Hamilton reach into his pocket, pulling out a pack of Marlboro and lighting up. He quit smoking a year ago, but tonight, with all this ugliness, the old habit takes him over.

"Can I get one of those?" he asks.

"Sure, here you go. I didn't realize you smoked. You work out all the time; isn't that defeating the purpose?"

"I do every now and again. I used to smoke a pack or two a day back in New York; the stress is what I blamed it on. But, you're right. It's defying my obsession to keep healthy. However, I will need this." Putting the cigarette in his mouth, Hamilton is ready with a light.

A long, profound drag from the cigarette fills his lungs, working its magic. He instantly relaxes. Hamilton also relaxes a little.

"I take it this one is not something I *want* to see."

"Shit, I didn't want to see her. That image is now forever burnt into my head, fuck! No one wants to view something like this." His voice shudders. His knees tremble. Fighting to keep his legs from betraying him; he braces himself against the closest tree and wipes the sweat from his brow.

"Hey, don't lose it on me now?"

"I won't; it's just—"

"I get it—I do. Do you want me to go on without you?"

"No," taking a deep breath he straightens up. "I'm good, really."

He doesn't look good, but Sterling keeps his thoughts to himself. They move in silence for the rest of the half-mile. The body in sight, Sterling's happy he broke a year of being smoke-free.

Sprawled out in the middle of the two-track is a young girl, about the same age as Jody. Her body is filthy, naked, and something ripped open her chest. Four gaping trenches run down the middle of her face from her hairline past her chin. Whatever made the gashes tore out her eyes leaving raw, hollow sockets, making it even more difficult to view her. Additionally gruesome, one of the ruptured remains of an eye mixed with the blood and meat of her lacerated cheek, and the other eye lay caught in her hair.

The flesh of her nose and cheeks lay open, exposing still wet blood and raw meat, hanging by threads of skin. Her lips split down the middle, red-black blood sluggishly trickling down her chin and neck, with blood-stained teeth catching bits of the early morning light. Most of her long, blonde hair is spread over her head, fanning out like millions of thin crimson streaked fingers, sporadically entangled with leaves and sticks.

The severe damage to her face makes identifying her from appearance impossible; identification will probably have to be verified by fingerprints or dental records.

What a fucked-up mess; her mutilated body is horrific and would cause most people years of nightmares. What wriggles its way underneath Sterling's skin is her expression—one of pure unbridled fear, frozen in a preserved state of sheer terror. It's this guise that will cause him more sleepless nights from here on out.

"Holy hell," Sterling breathes, one hand on his hip, the other up to his face massaging the bridge of his nose with his thumb and pointer finger. A strangely sweet odor presents itself, one that should not be here. He can't place it. Glancing over at Hamilton, who has turned away from the body, seeing enough desecration for one day—maybe for the rest of his life—he asks, "Hamilton, do you smell that?"

"Yeah, I smelled it as soon as I got here. It has faded some, but that sweet smell—kind of like honey or something—is still lingering."

"Where is it coming from?"

"Not sure. We've found nothing that should smell like that. But, I have to tell ya, it's better than the smell coming from the body."

"I can't argue with you there." Pinching the bridge of his nose again with the telltale signs of a headache coming on, he asks, "Were you the first person on the scene?"

"Yeah, this is the way I found her." Hamilton's eyes are all but slits now, fatigue has a firm grip on him. He has aged ten years since he first saw him.

"Hey, listen, I've got this under control. Why don't you get some rest and have Johnson wait for Sam?"

"You sure, Sterling?'

"Yeah. You look like hell. Now, get some rest, would ya."

Sterling strode over to the body, noticing the property owner off to the right telling an officer what happened—most likely for the second time. The man's hair is frazzled. His eyes are large and red, his color drained, and he looks as if he might be sick.

The body itself is an appalling sight. The girl's mutilation worse than Jody's, but like Jody, she's found unbound and without a gag. Sterling believes the girls might know their attacker although that idea can change depending on what Sam unveils.

Deep in thought, he doesn't notice Sam walking with Johnson.

"Hey, Sterling, we have another one I see." His body jerks with surprise. "I didn't mean to sneak up on you."

"It's all right, Sam, with as little sleep as I've had and all that's happened in the last twenty-four hours, my nerves are wound tighter than a piano string."

"I can't imagine." Sam is as fresh as the morning dew—not the slightest sign of fatigue or stress. Sterling envies her at the moment.

"So, what did the other girl reveal?"

"Well, she was dead before the creep opened her up—a small blessing. He hit her hard on the back of the head with something about two inches in diameter but with no discernible pattern—a metal bar."

"A crowbar?"

"Could be."

"How hard?"

"Hard enough to fracture her skull; she died on impact. As sad as it is, it was a blessing, for I found much worse."

"I will not want to hear this, will I?" Sterling asks, already knowing the answer. He can sense the corrupt, foul nature of the killer in his bones. Worse, his intuition tells him this case will produce more victims—keeping him awake nights until he catches the sick bastard.

"No, I'm afraid you won't like this at all."

"Well, shit, Sam, don't keep me in suspense, spill it."

"Jody's heart and reproductive organs are missing."

"Hell, I knew it! Shit! Another *freak* case—another fuckin' psychopath on the loose!" Sterling says, louder than intended. The cases he works with unusually morbid circumstances, such as a killer taking body parts, he calls his *freak cases*.

He labeled them early on, for 90% of the time the crimes committed are executed by someone who isn't all there—at least by the standards of what is considered *normal*. Some killers are highly intelligent. However, as in anything, contrary to popular belief due to the fantastical fiction of TV, media, films, and famous authors like Thomas Harris—known for his novels: Silence of the Lambs and Red Dragon—the cultural stereotype that serial killers are to some extent geniuses, is false. Not all serial killers are cunning, criminal geniuses turned mad.

Most of the serial killers Sterling dealt with—which were only a few—knew of the illegality of murder while killing their victims. They knew the difference between right and wrong though this never impeded their crimes. He met quite a few claiming to have an overwhelming desire and impulse, if you will, to kill. They ignored the criminal consequences with total irreverence. Not one of the serial killers he caught over the years was examined and determined to be mentally incompetent to stand trial. However, their lawyers loved to use an insanity defense on their behalf. Sterling cared little for lawyers, but they have a job to do too, just as he does, so despising them was a waste of time.

"What about the sample?" he asks, hands curtly on his hips and eyes staring at the ground.

"Sterling, I wish I had better news but that sample... well, somehow it's corrupted. The sample you gave me had feline DNA in it."

"Fuck! That damned cat."

"What cat?"

"There was a cat that startled the shit out of me by the body, not far from where I found that substance in the woods. It must have gotten into it."

"A black cat?" Samantha asks.

"Yeah, why?"

"I found short, black hairs on Jody's body and in her wounds, but there were also white hairs, both feline."

"Son of a bitch," cursing, he snuffs out his cigarette on the ground. "White feline hairs, hey? I only saw a black cat."

"Whether or not you saw it, one was there at some point."

That old, dark, weighted sensation stretches its long, vexing tentacles, coiling them around the dark edges of his soul, makes his guts tighten. The immense sensations of desperation, frustration, and helplessness producing depraved thoughts, making one contemplate his sanity as they slither into the brain and spread like wildfire. It paralyzes one's thoughts and movements, while silently screaming, *you will lose!*

The thick, dark haze of doubt, he knows so well, grips his core, ripping and tearing, as it loops and weaves through every cell on some deranged conquest, targeting Sterling alone. He will not have another unsolved case. *No, no, no, damn it! Not this time. I'll catch this killer if it's the last thing I do,* the words echo deafeningly through his skull with unwavering conviction.

"Levi, are you alright?" Sam's soft touch, the heat of her hand on his arm brings him out of his self-wallowing. Concern riddles her face, her eyes narrow with anxiety. She, above all others, has every right to worry; there's a maniacal killer on the loose, though Sterling is the focus of her unease.

He's troubled too, not about himself, but the discovery of the *next* unfortunate victim. There *will* be another. There's not verifiable data on this but the feeling—the intuition, call it instinct if you like—is potent, weighs on him like a slick wool blanket soaked with oil. The question spiraling through his head: A killer, targeting young girls—why? He'd witnessed Modus Operandi, MO, change, though rarely. Hoping, and perhaps against all odds, the MO of this killer didn't change. MO's alter when the killer needs to gain control. It's something of a rarity, but it always happens in the freak cases, and that is why it crosses his mind now. This case definitely fit the *freak case* category. He desperately needs a break in this case. He needs to locate this sick son of a bitch soon—preferably before the killer strikes down another victim.

"Yeah, it's this case," he finally answers. "This killer is a particular type of psychopath that I hoped I would never run into again." He runs his hand through his jet black hair, he put his hat back on, "Let's get to work."

The body has his full attention; he investigates the area around it for any sign or evidence the perp may have left. The ground shaded with the sun barely above the horizon. Shrub and smaller trees lay in the shadows of lower light conditions. Grasses, ferns, and wildflowers scatter the landscape with moss peeking out here and there. It's beautiful, peaceful—an atmosphere that should calm but not today, not after the carnage just viewed. The woods are eerily still. *Not a bird's morning song, a chipmunk, or squirrel scurries about—strange*, he concludes.

A scan of the woods, nothing jumps out—no footprints, no scraps, not even the liquid substance he believed was saliva found at the last scene. If the evidence at the scene isn't enough to lead him in a direction, the bodies will pile up. He's confident the killer won't stop on his own.

"Johnson," Sterling yells, after a thorough search around the body.

"Yeah, what do you need?"

"I want you to get two teams together, make sure they have flashlights. Have them scour the woods on either side of this two-track for anything and everything. If it looks out of place, I want pictures, bagged, and tagged. You got me?"

"I'll take care of it, no worries." Johnson wastes no time getting the men organized. Hamilton is his usual go-to person, the one man he can trust to get the job done, but since he's not here, he has no choice but to put his faith in Johnson for the time being.

"Hey, Johnson?"

"Yeah."

"Tell them to be careful. We're uncertain what's out there—at least until the sun rises."

Within a half-hour, two teams of ten men combed the woods on both sides of the two-track. Johnson didn't play around. The sun was over the horizon but still not high enough to brighten the full of the woods. Sterling saw flashlights, now small dots, on both sides of him. The men spread approximately twenty feet apart, and as instructed, they walk straight back a half-mile each direction. Then they turn back the way they came, returning to the two-track, backtracking, taking their time making sure they miss nothing.

There's a fear in most of the men's eyes. Many of them have never worked on a murder case before. The horrific nature of the crimes has them rattled though not enough to detour their determination. In the shadows of tall trees, each man's eyes are resolutely hunting.

They search the fertile soil, low-lying leaves, and branches that can catch on a person's clothing. They inspect the moss, the flowers for anything that could belong to the killer.

Scanning up and down the two-track for any morsel of evidence left behind—Sterling wonders what kind of hell he's mixed up in, as the faces of the girls enter his mind. *I have to stop this guy. This whole town is being turned upside down with these murders. Dammit! The Devil sure is doing his bidding in this sleepy little town.*

The media has not been a problem so far, but that won't last long, it never does. The media are like vultures. They can sniff out a corpse faster than hound dogs on a coon hunt. Just as the thought passes through his mind, a news van appears ahead. Hamilton must've sensed the scavengers would be out before he left, as officers are already on standby to stop the news crew before they can get within sight of the crime scene. However, they're too late. Samantha left with the body out twenty minutes ago. *Ha-ha! You sons a' bitches. Better luck next time.*

The internal laughter is short-lived, hearing a man from the woods yelling he found something. Carefully, but as quickly as he can, Sterling makes his way through the woods towards the voice. Branches snap underfoot and tear across his skin, the stinging sensation of the scratches ignored. He reaches the balding, slightly overweight officer in mere seconds. Furrows pucker the man's round face in perplexity as he hedges over something.

"Did you take pictures?" Sterling asks with heavy breaths before viewing the find.

"Yes, sir. I've taken a couple from different angles."

"Get a few more and get close-ups."

Carefully removing a few leaves, exposing the first real evidence in these two cases, his throat tightens viewing what shouldn't be here—a footprint! Not just any footprint, a print of a cat—a sizable cat—large enough to make an impression as big as his hand. Such an animal is not indigenous to the area, this is Michigan for Christ sakes. The biggest cat one might get a glimpse of is a cougar, and that's if you're lucky. Cougars averaged around 141 pounds—the print left was from a cat weighing a minimal of 220.

"Are you seeing this?" Sterling asks, but not to anyone in particular.

"I see it. I'm not sure I believe it, but I see it." The officer's voice has changed, alarm lines his words. "Is it possible it escaped from a zoo or a nearby circus?"

"Anything is possible." He's surprised to see a cat print, let alone one this size. "What's this," he asks, pointing at a few leaves about a foot away.

"It appears to be blood."

"Take a few pictures."

The officer snaps five to six shots of the area. Then Sterling picks up a leaf, smelling the substance. "It's blood alright. I have to say blood on leaves next to the print of a large cat, is not what I expected."

"You're not the only one."

"*They're known scavengers, Sterling. Why are you so shocked? The damned thing must have smelled the body and stopped for a bite.* Sitting on his hunches a while longer, trying to convince himself of this theory. "Do you have an evidence bag on you?"

"Sure do." The man, Officer Grandson, pulls a couple of bags from his pocket.

"Do me a favor, take more pictures and then collect each leaf with blood on it."

With latex gloves on, Grandson carefully places each specimen into a bag, sealing them, and then hands them off to Sterling.

"I'll get a cast of this print."

"Good, thank you." Deciding to deliver the specimens himself and wait for the results, he calls out to Johnson. "I'm taking these samples to Samantha. Can you finish up here for me?"

"Sure. I'll have the men move down and keep searching for anything else. Do you honestly think a rogue cat committed these murders?"

"No, of course not. However, there's one out there. We need to catch the damned thing before it kills someone. Do me a favor. Inform all the men of the cat and make sure they are armed. I'll call animal control and tell them what we found."

"Alright, I'll take care of things here and call you if we uncover anything else."

"Good enough."

On the way back to his car, Sterling ponders how a large cat could get loose from the zoo, let alone make it this far north. The closest zoo is in Battle Creek, almost three hours from Alger. Not impossible, but unlikely. Some investigation is needed to figure out if any circuses are in, or around, the area and if they are missing a large cat. The animal came from somewhere, and it's a distraction he doesn't need.

Assuming the cat is hungry, scavenging for something to fill its belly, the smell of blood would attract it to the body. Scary when it came right down to it, with men searching these woods and a wild and hungry animal on the loose; it isn't the ideal situation. The last thing anyone needs is for any of them to be attacked or killed by the animal. Enough death is taking place without adding a rather large, hungry cat to it.

Wanting the death toll over and it being over, are two separate things entirely. Sterling's isn't naive, it isn't in his makeup, nor is being lucky, but how he wished for both.

The killer is intelligent and knows what he's doing. The guy understands the forensic procedures for Christ sakes! This killer, as far as Sterling's concerned, is an intelligent psychotic—one hell of a dangerous combination. *The number of deaths will rise*, Sterling deduces with confidence. Suspicion tears at his gut, informing him the murderer is nothing like any he has experienced before. In lieu of what has happened thus far, something unpleasant is coming—something he may not be ready for or equipped to handle.

A long time ago, he learned to listen to his instincts, as if they're engineered to warn him when situations get hairy.

Frustration rages through his veins as he reaches the car. He kicks the front tire and punches the hood which only accomplishes bruising his knuckles. "Fuck! Fuck!" he hisses, throwing open the car door. This situation is bordering on madness, but it will get worse—much worse if he can't stop it from doing so.

Chapter 5

The County Mortuary

"Don't be what I think you are, please, please!" Sam begs, sitting in front of a screen. Her foot anxiously moves in a rhythmic up and down motion, like a tap dancer getting ready for a big show as she waits for the results. San ran numerous tests on biological fluids and tissues taken at the latest crime scene. She has her suspicions with the first girl found, but now with this new girl, she's ready to lose it.

What if the tests are positive? What then? What the hell are we going to do? She surmises, aggravating her nerves into thousands of taunt balls. "Stop this! All you're doing right now is making the waiting worse. Inhale deeply and exhale slowly," she tells herself to calm down. "Wait for the results. If the results come back positive, you know what to do. FUCK! I hate this." She spouts, slamming her hand on the table. "Shit! That hurt. What is wrong with you?"

Thankfully, Sam's the only one in the lab. If she weren't, she would not have the luxury of being herself. She gave her small crew a much-needed day off yesterday evening.

"You've been working around the clock since they found the first body and mistakes happen when people are tired," she said. Though their much-needed rest and the fear of mistakes wasn't the only reason she told them, she would take care of whatever work came in today.

"Are you sure, Sam?" they asked.

"Yes, but make sure all of you get a well-deserved rest and be back first thing Wednesday morning."

She's worried about the test results. If the results come back as she suspects they will, having her crew gone will provide her with the privacy she needs to do what is required. The light flashes and the test results fill the screen.

"Oh, God."

Driving into West Branch, Sterling envisions the bloody, hollows where the girl's beautiful green eyes used to be. The pitiful remnants of life taken before her time and discarded with a little more thought than unwanted trash. Another young life ended in unspeakable violence. Leaving a lifeless, soulless shell of whom and what she once was. A helpless sensation weasels its way into his mind, but he pushes it back. It will be a cold day in hell before he lets another case remain unsolved. Matt—the little boy from New York—would never happen to him again. Matt never received closure, never got justice because Sterling did not solve the case.

"*It will not fucking happen again. I won't let it!*" Fevered with a combination of stress, failure, and being plain pissed off, he pushed down on the gas pedal.

The possibility of not solving the girls' cases has his gut binding into knots. Flipping the dark, gray visor down, an emergency pack of cigarettes falls into his hand. He put the pack there for occasions such as this. Taking one, lighting it, and sucking the sweet, tobacco smoke deep into his lungs, all while hating himself for needing it so bad. But as the smoke fills his lungs, the tension in his neck and back relaxes. "This is the last one," he lies to himself, turning into the morgue's driveway.

With one last, lengthy drag, holding the smoke in while he snuffs out the cigarette, he gives a quick glance in the mirror, then exhales. "Well ol' man, let us see what Sam has discovered," he says to his reflection, then pulls the door handle, shoves the keys in his pocket and exits the car.

The city mortuary is on the lower floor, two floors down from the main lobby of the only hospital within forty miles. The bright white lights practically blind him walking in from outside. The sun is up, but the lights inside the building seem more intense. The elevators are to the left after the second set of electric doors. He pushes the down arrow and waits.

The outside doors burst open. Two EMT's rush a gurney through with a male drenched in blood from his head to his chest. An older woman, yet still attractive and in good shape with salt and pepper hair, appears from around the gleaming, white tiled corner, "What do we have here?" she asks, her stethoscope already at the man's chest. One of the EMT's tells her something about a domestic dispute gone wrong, way wrong from the looks of things, and a stabbing.

Ding, the down arrow of the elevator changes from dark to an illuminated green light. The stainless-steel doors effortlessly slide-open, divulging a 10 X 13 box with a split paneled wall. Flecked black plastic laminate covers the upper portions of the interior walls while stainless-steel conceals the lower. Entering, he retrieves a black leather wallet from his inside pocket, pulls out a blue plastic access card given to him when he started.

Pushing the plastic card into an indistinguishable slot under the button panel—that he would not have known was there if Sam hadn't shown him—he pushes 42568 into a keypad on the right side of the fire button, and then the red lettered LL button underneath. A slight hum and the elevator jolts, traveling down.

In a matter of seconds, the telltale ding sounds once more and the doors glide apart. This part of the hospital isn't as bright as the main floor. As a matter of fact, the lighting down here is depressing. It reminds Sterling of a classic movie; the name escapes him, but the detective is in a dark alley waiting for his perp to come out of a pub with nothing but the weak light from a single lamppost.

He makes a left, then a quick right, the morgue lights illuminate the hallway halfway down. His feet sound heavy on the polished, gray ceramic tile, and with each step, an echo bounces off the concrete walls.

From outside the door, bordered by large, six-foot windows on either side, Sam's engaged in an intense conversation with herself, pacing back and forth. He can hear her grumble, "This makes little sense," as she takes another sip of coffee with a touch of Irish whiskey in it, to calm her nerves. Had she not been working in a small town, her little alcohol infatuation would have gotten her fired by now. However, if the gossip hounds in this small town found out, everyone in a fifty-mile radius would know, and Sam would no longer have a job. She plops down on the oak and brown leather swivel chair with a heavy sigh.

Sam is in black slacks, white lab coat, legs apart, elbow on her knee, and head in hand, cursing under her breath, *what in the hell are you trying to do to me?* Her face twists into a scowl while holding the manila file folder in her right hand. There's no need for her to tell him the results are not in their favor, he already knows.

"Let me guess," Sterling boasts, startling Sam enough to make her jump. "Something has corrupted the test results—feline DNA? Also, you found white—or black—feline hairs in the victim's wounds."

"Jesus Christ, Sterling!" she yells, grabbing at her chest as if she might have a heart attack. He catches the scent of whiskey in the air.

Dammit, Sam, these tests are too important to conduct under the influence, he fumes to himself.

"A little jumpy, aren't we?"

"You shouldn't sneak up on people, Levi. You scared the shit out of me."

"You've been drinking?" he questions, knowing she has.

"I put a drop or two in my coffee to calm my nerves. What are you, the ethics police?" she bites.

Not wanting this to turn into a fight, he switches gears. "I wasn't trying to sneak." Sam's behavior is quite unorthodox tonight, and it's more than he's willing to delve into at the moment. So, he remains focused on the results rather than pry. She's wound up tighter than an eight-day clock and drinking to boot, he knows when to steer clear of a battle. "Are they corrupt?" he asks.

"Yes, they are corrupt. I found feline DNA and white feline hairs. How in the hell did you know?"

"You will not believe this one."

"Oh yeah, try me. The way my day is going, nothing can surprise me. At this point, I would consider just about anything as fact."

"There is a cat loose, an enormous cat."

"Come on Sterling, stop fuckin' with me. I have had a rough day." Sam says smirking though not humored by his revelation in the slightest.

"I'm not. We found a print out there in the woods near to where the body laid."

"Great, just what we need; a monster of a cat running around the woods. Where did it come from?"

"I can't say, possibly a zoo or a local circus."

"Do you think it was at the other site as well?"

"It might well have been, or that could have been the house cat I saw. The two bodies' locations were relatively close, so it's a plausible deduction. Plus, cats aren't above scavenging, big or small, so it would not surprise me if both were at the site. Either way, the damned cats have fucked us." His hand runs through his hair and rhythmically scratches his head in frustration. His frustration is palpable, but at least, they are aware of a large cat wandering around the woods somewhere. This information doesn't help his case at all, it only adds to the current problems. On the plus side, it sheds light on how the evidence became tainted. "Did you discover anything?"

"Nothing new," she says, clearing her throat as she responds. Then her attention turns to the file in hand, she saunters to the examining table where the newest victim rests. Sam is acting strange. He can't explain it, but her mannerisms are abnormal somehow. But, then again, these murders have everyone on edge and Sam is no exception to the rule.

"This girl had her heart and her reproductive organs removed just as in the first one. The torn skin is the same way with no trace left behind. One thing I can tell you, it doesn't appear *le* cat did the damage I see here," she points to the opening in the girl's chest. "It's not possible for an animal to do this. At first glance, it looks as if a scalpel ripped through this girl. However, the cuts in the skin weren't made with a sharp edge—notice the ragged edges?" she glances at Sterling for confirmation and he nods. "Good, you see here," she says, using long tweezers to pick up the edge of the skin. "The tear is clean and straight, but the skin was torn, not cut. Also, the killer removed each organ with surgical precision; no animal could be this precise. The removal of the heart from under the ribs without breaking them is not something a large cat would, or even could do."

"So what are you saying?"

"An animal could only have done part of the damage, such as the deep gouges in her face. A cat, however, couldn't achieve this level of precision when removing the reproductive organs or heart. I doubt a cat did any of the damage done, even a large one. But I cannot verify either way. I will have more when I run further tests." Sterling roughly sweeps his hand over his face in a scrubbing motion sighing heavily. "Sorry Sterling, our killer is careful, dare I say meticulous and well, maybe getting some unexpected help from our animal friends."

"It is what it is, Sam." Frustration and weariness wash over him like a tidal wave. Sam watches as his face falls, seemingly aging right in front of her. "The one thing I'm sure of is, if these murders keep happening, the murderer will toss a monkey wrench in his work, screwing up somehow. The psychotic ones always do. We'll get him and nail his ass to the wall. Let's hope he does something reckless before he can kill another girl."

"If he leaves any trace, I will find it." She's trying to ease some of his exasperation, but her words do not affect his current state. "I promise, I will call the moment I uncover anything, no matter how small."

"Thanks, Sam."

Leaving the way he came, he rubs his eyes, turns, offers Sam a weary smile, then vanishes behind the pale, green concrete wall. It has been a long day though it's only five. With little sleep, his body screams at him that it needs rest.

He turns the air on high when he gets into his car to help him stay awake. Exhaustion plays havoc on him, hitting him with a wallop. Only thirty-minutes until he's home, but he is not taking any chances.

His mind overrun with details, he drives down the long, dark, country road, going over everything from the first to the newest girl found. Why young teen girls? What does he want? What is he trying to prove? With a thousand questions he can't answer, he repeatedly plays each scenario trying to reach a logical conclusion—to detect if something connects.

This repetitive thinking, bordering on madness some would say, is nothing new for him; he goes through this same routine with every case. Although, when it comes to freak cases, his mind lights up like a pinball machine that has done one too many lines of cocaine. Tonight he's on overdrive.

Ever since the Belmont case in New York, freak cases fling his brain in a spiral, working itself into an evaluating, re-evaluating nightmare. Each scene transforms into a repetitive manic soirée of gruesome details until he catches, or kills, or he, himself, ends up in a strait jacket—which so far at least, he has managed to avoid.

La Porte Road's white letters printed on a green street sign brightens in the car's headlights and he turns right.

Chapter 6

The IGA

The old Ford rumbles on Baker Drive, sounding more like a lumber wagon than a car. In the headlights, a white moving truck sits at the old abandoned house. A blue work truck, the kind with access compartments on the side, is parked in the driveway. It has *Dickson's Painting Plus* printed on the driver-side door and tailgate in bold black lettering.

One may perceive it to be high noon the way the yard is lit up. He hadn't noticed the tall, four-lantern post lights on either side of the drive before. They must have installed them today. The house also has a fresh new skin, another little surprise. This morning the home was a dingy brown, the paint weathered and cracked. Now, a clean, bright white color, illuminates the old walls, with new country blue shutters accenting the windows—it's like a completely different house.

The overgrowth, which resembled one of the *Children of the Corn* movies, was cut and removed, leaving behind a decent lawn. It needs work to reclaim its former self, but it's much better than it was. The place looked like it was never left, let alone abandoned for the better part of ten years.

His astonishment doesn't end there, seeing a woman with a killer body standing on the vividly lit front porch. She's an attractive brunette with her hair pulled into a large bun, a few strands sporadically cascade down her elegant neck.

"Wow," Sterling gushes. His mouth dry as a desert and his pulse quickens. Time slows to a crawl taking in the sight of her. High-heels, a form-fitting, black, pencil skirt—the kind with the slit in the back—and seamed, black stockings, is enough to send him into a frenzy. The skirt clings to the toned hips she's sporting while enticing one to wonder how far up those legs go. A wide, black, leather belt accentuates her waistline going up to the slightly see-through, white, silk top—one of those European silk, chiffon blouses with long, balloon sleeves. With her right hand sensually placed on her hip, she speaks with a workman. She's tall with a figure that would stop traffic in a New York minute. He's no expert, but he guesses she's rocking measurements close to 38-26-38, and her curves do hold his attention.

Damn, what a dame, he practically gushes. He hasn't been privy to a figure like hers since the first time he saw Sophia Loren in the 1959 classic *That Kind of Woman*. He, of course, didn't see the movie until 1985 when he and his father watched it together. However, seeing Sophia left one hell of a mark on his impressionable thirteen-year-old mind.

Holy shit, where did you come from? Right as the thought rears through his mind; she turns and stares at him, though, it's as if she gazes right through him. She greets him with a sultry, dark-red, lipstick smile and a thickly lashed wink and then turns her attention back to the man in the dirty, tan Carhartt coveralls.

The way she winks sends a wild sensation right through him, shooting directly to his groin. "Shit, Levi," he grumbles, adjusting himself as indistinct as possible. "You would think you've never seen an attractive woman before." Although it's been two years since he was with a woman—sexually, anyway— he's still surprised by his reaction and grateful to be in a car. *She's certainly not shy now is she? There is no reason for her to be, just look at her.* Sterling muses, giving her a wave.

The car jolts forward when he thrust the gear shift into park. *Christ, what in the hell is wrong with you*, he bitches, opening the car door. A subtle breeze ruffles his hair and sends a little chill through his heated body when he gets out of the car. He heads directly to the weight room.

He hadn't intended on a workout, but he needs to release some sexual frustration he had not known he was harboring until a few minutes ago. His workout room is actually the second bedroom of the home. It's the larger of the two rooms painted in eggshell color, has a full bathroom, wood floors, and a huge picture window facing the serenity of the woods, making it a perfect exercise area. The room has a weight bench with five hundred pounds of free weights, a power tower, an elliptical, and a bar he installed to hang upside down and do stomach crunches.

Pushing his body until every fiber is on fire, he hits the weights hard to clear his head of all the bullshit infecting him and the town lately. The image of the brunette's face replaces it all. *What is it about this woman? Sure she's a looker, but I've met my share of beautiful women, and none of them affected me like this,* he thinks as he pushes 210 pounds from his chest again to finish a set. Something about the woman down the road has woken something within him, something almost primal and most definitely sexual. Why? He doesn't have a clue.

An hour and a half later, hot water from the shower fills the bathroom with dense steam, washing away the sweat. Fifteen minutes later his head hits the down pillow. He doesn't even remember closing his eyes. Tonight his dreams don't fill with dead girls or Matt Belmont—no, not tonight. The smoking hot brunette now occupying the house down the road, whom he has not had the pleasure of meeting in person yet, fills his dreams. They are pleasant, perhaps too pleasing.

His *Jimmy* is hard enough to cut diamonds when he wakes up in his nice warm bed and his bladder screams. However, pissing with an erection isn't wise, not unless he wants to piss on the damn ceiling. The phone rings.

"Sterling here," he says into the receiver.

"Hey, it's Hamilton." his voice is strange and excited, but excited good or excited bad, he's not sure.

"Hey, Hamilton, did you get some rest?"

"Yeah, thanks for letting me go yesterday." The line falls eerily silent for a moment.

"Tell me there hasn't been another murder."

"I wish I could, man," he almost sounds relieved he doesn't have to say the words. "This one is bad—real bad." The silence on the line becomes heavier than it was a second ago but this time it's Sterling's unease that creates the abundant heaviness. "You still there?"

"Yeah, I'm here." Crudely his hand runs down his face. Instantly the room seemingly shrinks, and the temperature shoots up. He abruptly breaks into a sweat as he asks, "What do we have?"

"A kid working the closing shift found a set of twins behind the IGA in Skidway Lake."

"Shit," he hisses.

"You're not going to like this, but press already got wind of this one, and they're all over the place down here—" Hamilton's shaking voice is rambling on so fast he can barely understand him.

"Whoa, slow down. Breathe. Now, what was that?"

"The fucking press is swarming the area like flies on shit."

"Goddamned it! Wait, did you say closing? Christ, what time is it?"

"It's just after midnight. And that's not the worst of it. The kid, he s-saw..."

"What? What did he see?"

"Shit, I'm not sure if he was in shock or what, but what he said he saw, it can't be real."

"Well, what the hell did he say?"

"I'll explain everything when you get here. Get here fast! It's turning into a circus down here."

The line dies. Jumping up from the bed, he runs into the bathroom. The good thing is his erection is gone, but that's the only good thing he has going for him at the moment. Not bothering with a shower, he splashes cold water on his face, grabbing a towel, and looks in the oval mirror hanging above the sink. He feels rested, but the bags under his bloodshot eyes tell a different story.

Not bothering with coffee either, he rushes out the front door, jumping in the Ford, throwing it in reverse as his foot hits the floor. Dirt and rocks soar, dust flies up filling the air around the vehicle. He slams the gear shift into drive and hauls ass to Skidway.

Within fifteen minutes, he's pulling up to what Hamilton called *a circus*—he couldn't have been more accurate in that statement. People are blocking Greenwood Road from Emyer's Hill to approximately a half-mile down to the IGA and past. It's a flippin' madhouse.

Laying on the horn scarcely arouses the *lookiloo's* attention. Irritation instantly runs through his nerves. Like the string on a bow pulled too tight, his nerves feel as if every last one will spontaneously snap within seconds.

"Don't these damn people have better things to do?" he grouses, flipping on his emergency light trying to get people out of the way so he can get himself to the scene. "Son of a bitch, every fucking person in this town is here. Damn it people, go the fuck home," he bitches, pulling the car off to the side of the road.

Getting out, he pushes his way through the crowd, not giving a damn if he's polite or not. It's the only fucking way he's going to the scene. Otherwise, it would take him twenty minutes to get through with the car.

At the barricade, ten officers are doing their best to keep back the press. As soon as the blood-sucking, vultures see him; they're on him like a swarm of locust. Automatically shoving their microphones in his face, screaming questions, he brusquely pushes his way through without a word. Once past the horde, Johnson appears.

"Hey, Johnson."

"I'm glad to see you. Hell of a mess, we sure have our hands full."

"I can see that. Do me a favor; get some men and push this barricade back across the road. These vultures can view whatever there is to see from back there."

"On it," he says with a sigh of relief and a wicked little smile, like a child who was just permitted to have chocolate cake for breakfast.

"Oh, and Johnson?"

"Yeah?"

"Tell the officer if anyone gives them any trouble to arrest them on the spot—that includes the press. You got it?"

"Absolutely." The wicked smile of his widens.

Hell, he can't blame him for being happy. The press is a giant pain in the ass. Yeah, they're just doing what they're paid to do, but their *job* always manages to interfere with his and that pisses him off. The pushier they get, the more pissed off he gets, and he doesn't need anything else on his plate. He will do everything he can to make sure the sons-of-bitches stay as far away as possible from this case.

"Like we need this added bullshit," he fumes.

Sterling searches for Hamilton, but doesn't see him right off, Matherson comes running up, his complexion as pale as the dead.

"You don't look so good, Matherson."

A slight, humorless grin cracks his face. He says nothing leading Sterling back behind the IGA, where Hamilton, a handful of police officers and EMT's are talking.

"Thank God," Hamilton hisses, waving Sterling over to a large, green dumpster. Sterling's face is stern, full of determination and as steady as always as he makes his way over to him. Hamilton wonders how the man can stay so focused, disclosing no sign he's as sick and tired of this vile shit as the rest. "Thanks for getting here so soon."

"Hell of a night, eh?" he notes Hamilton doesn't look well which meant one thing; the bodies they found are as severe as the others were, or worse. From viewing him, he would venture to say they're worse— much worse.

"You can say that again. These murders are getting weirder and more grisly. I can't understand how anyone gets their jollies doing this shit. Fucking sick bastard."

"Yeah, I know."

"Sorry to bring you out here in the middle of the night."

"It's the nature of the game, my friend," Sterling replies, waving Hamilton off. "Listen, what did that boy see? Where is he?"

"They took the boy—Joshua Mitchell, to the hospital. Man, that kid's pretty messed up. I'm not sure if he'll make it."

"Damn it. Well, let's hope he does. What happened, did he surprise the attacker or something?"

"He uttered something... something that makes little sense." Hamilton takes off his hat, running his hand through his thick red hair, and lights a smoke.

"C'mon, Hamilton, what in the hell is that supposed to mean."

"Follow me," Hamilton says brusquely, taking Sterling by the arm, walking him away from the others. "They don't need to hear this. For fuck's sake, I didn't need to hear it."

James' reaction catches Sterling off guard. The man hardly ever used a crossed word and tonight he's cussing like a drunken sailor. It's not that the man is religious or anything, it simply isn't in his nature to curse as most of the officers do, including himself. Whatever the boy, Joshua, said has him unnerved; he's wound up something awful. He can't remember one time in the last ten years he's seen Hamilton in such rough shape. However, in those ten years, the man wasn't dealing with multiple murders, let alone the brutal killings of four young teenage girls either.

Sterling takes a cigarette out, joining Hamilton. If this conversation has him on edge, he figures a cigarette will calm his nerves before all the gruesome details come to light. The two men reach the tan, concrete block back wall of the IGA lined with the small weeds, and rocks beneath their feet. The night air is nippy but not uncomfortable. Hell, if it weren't for the current situation, it was the ideal night for a long walk.

"Jesus, James, I've never seen you like this. What the hell did Joshua tell you?" he asks finally, infringing upon their shared weighty silence.

Hamilton leans his back against the cold concrete, taking a long drag of his smoke. The sound of crickets fills the quiet as a black cat scurries from the side of the building into the tall weeds. He doesn't look at Sterling as he tilts his head slightly back, gazing into the star-filled night sky.

"That kid looked as if the devil himself appeared before him tonight. His eyes were as wide as pool balls, skin as pale as the dead, and he was shaking uncontrollably the whole time I spoke with him. What he said—what he told me, I can't say I believe. I mean, I trust he saw something, but it's... well, shit, let me just tell you." His hand crudely runs across his face, taking another drag from his smoke, he finally tells Sterling what the boy said. "The boy said when he came out to put the nightly garbage in the dumpster, he saw a cat. He thought nothing of it at first because all he saw were a pair of eyes. He thought the damn thing was scavenging for scraps. But then it jumped out from behind the dumpster, and he saw it was a huge devil cat with fur slick as oil on a sun-blazed Arizona highway, green eyes burned through him, and claws with a razor-edge honed more than his daddy's hunting knife after a good sharpening—his words not mine. It scared him so bad he froze, he said he couldn't breathe. A large pure white—"

"Albino, are you telling me that boy saw an Albino Panther?" Sterling cuts Hamilton off abruptly.

"Hell, I don't flippin' know. I'm just telling you what the boy said. Can I finish here?"

"Ok, I'm sorry," Sterling hesitates for a moment. The thought of a panther being on the loose was strange enough, but now the damned thing is some kind of damned oddity.

"As I was saying, the boy told me a large, pure, white cat stared him down, a substance, he was sure was blood, dripped from its mouth. The thing growled at him, showing its teeth and attacked him, but something startled it and it ran off in that direction." Hamilton takes a couple more drags off his smoke. He's having a difficult time trying to process what this boy told him. "He was on the ground, holding his side where claws got him and said he saw a girl lying behind the dumpster. It was then he knew the cat wasn't scavenging scraps, it was eating the girl—at least, that's what he thought. He reached his cell in his back pocket and called 911. He still didn't know there were two girls, not just one." Crushing his smoke out, Hamilton lights another. "Man, that boy..." his voice trails off, he stares vacantly at the sky.

"What is it?"

"What—uh," he stumbles like he forgot they are having a conversation. "Oh yeah, that's not the worst part of the boy's story."

"Dammit, Hamilton, just tell me everything the boy said, would ya?"

"He said when he looked in the direction the thing took off... and I swear; on the grave of my mother, he told me that all he saw was a naked, bloody person running in the woods. He said he thought it was a woman."

"What?! Awe come on now, Hamilton, that boy must have hit his head or was in so much shock, his mind played tricks on him."

"Honestly, I considered that, but you didn't see the confidence in the boy's eyes. He certainly believes that is what he saw, and it about scared the life out of him. I hope he makes it so we can talk to him again."

"Me too. Me too."

Hamilton's silence was deafening as he muddled over the story the boy told him. Can something so bizarre be real or is this boy so traumatized his mind made up the so-called person to make sense of what he saw? At the moment, he's not sure what to think about what the boy told him, but his story is feasible—up to the point of the bloody naked woman, that is. He's positive Joshua told him the truth.

"Is there even such a thing as an Albino Panther?" Sterling asks, pulling him back from his thoughts."

"Yes, I've seen pictures in National Geographic. I guess they're scarce, but they are out there."

"Wow, so we know the cat part of his story is true." Hamilton nods his head but doesn't respond. "Why don't we inspect the bodies and worry about the boy's statement later, what do you say?"

"Yeah, Sterling, sure."

Chapter 7

The Miller Girls

On this beautiful night with its blue-black sky and millions of stars penetrating the void, twinkling like diamonds, the bodies of young twin girls lay amongst the weeds and dirt, discarded like the bags full of trash in the smelly, old, green dumpster in front of them. The condition of the girls is revolting. Of all the murders, the killer did a number on these two little ones.

Whether it's because these two girls are the youngest of the bunch or because of the lack of humanity shown in their desecration, viewing them tightens Sterling's stomach into a tightly twisted coil.

The girls' once angelic faces are left shredded—a mangled mass of grated flesh. Their chests are torn open, not unlike the others. However, this time the killer split the sternum apart. *This is new*, he notes, desperately working to keep his stomach at bay. Neither of them appear to have any organs left from what is visible looking closely into their chest cavity.

"What the fuck is this lunatic doing with their organs?" Hamilton boldly questions, confounded by the site as he chokes back the urge to retch.

"I'm not sure I want the answer to that question."

"To be truthful, neither do I," he responds, his eyes not leaving the mangled corpses.

There is no way to identify the bodies properly with a viewing; they are too disfigured. However, two purple backpacks sit neatly on the ground beside each girl as if carefully placed. The packs have names printed on them in decorative, white-lined, hot pink letters, Christy and

Misty Miller.

Someone gouged the eyes of the girl on the right, next to the Christy backpack out. Most of the left side of her face is gone, leaving a softball size pool of blood, flesh, and brain matter, much smaller than expected. The whole of her neck is also missing, leaving just a few strands of skin and tendons to keep it attached to the body.

The second girl's body is more intact, for which he silently thanks God. Though her chest and sternum are open, they aren't wretched wide enough to reveal what's left inside. Her face is a scarlet inflamed sore, the skin removed, but she still has her eyes. He takes note that her left arm is missing from the body.

"Have we found her arm?"

"What?" Hamilton asks, his eyebrows raised in question as he dryly clears his throat.

"The girl on the left here has an arm missing, have we found it?"

"N-no. We searched the area, but there were no signs. A few men are still scouring the premises though."

"Fine," he examines Hamilton, his complexion is pallid, his mouth pulled tight, so his normally thick lips are but thin strips of flesh. "You going to make it, Hamilton?"

"Yeah. I didn't expect—"

"We never do my friend," Sterling interrupts.

It's an unimaginable feat trying to comprehend the amount of anguish inflicted on these girls and Hamilton? He doesn't even try. He can barely keep his eyes within the vicinity of the bodies, let alone look at them.

"Has anyone contacted the Miller girls' family yet?"

"Yes. We were going to wait, but with the media showing up and a crowd forming, I had Johnson take care of it."

"Good, I don't want them down here. Make sure Johnson gets them to the station. I want these two cleaned up before their parents see them."

"Got it." Walking out of earshot, he relays the message on his walkie.

"Hey, tell them to inform us the minute Samantha gets here," he hollers to Hamilton as he kneels next to the girls. "God, what kind of monster is this?" he asks himself, scanning their bodies. The first thing he notices is their matching purple tops and, what once were, white skirts are torn open, exposing their fragile little bodies. The other two victims were fully dressed. There were rips in their clothes, but it seems like the clothes got snagged—small tears—nothing like this. He thanks God, seeing their panties are still intact. To him, and most any detective, there's nothing worse than uncovering a young, dead, naked body—young and dead is depraved enough.

Exposed flesh typically means a sexual assault. And though he can't definitively say the girls weren't sexually assaulted, it doesn't seem to be the case. *A small blessing, Levi,* he concludes. At least, none of the murdered girls up to this point suffered that fate, so he hopes the test will be negative. From the looks of them, they're no more than thirteen years old. Babies! Damn, Babies! He puts his head down allowing himself a moment to lasso his emotions.

Sterling notices their long, black hair is matted with, what is unquestionably, blood as he views their corpses. There is no lack of blood at this crime scene as in the other two. Which means one of two things, either the girls were murdered by a different individual or this psychotic fucker has changed his MO, not much, but enough to infuriate him. He gets a little closer, careful not to touch anything, the sweet aroma he recalls inhaling at the last crime scene hangs in the surrounding air.

"What in the hell is that?" He asks aloud, not expecting an answer.

"What is what?" Hamilton responds, ambling back to the bodies.

"Take a deep breath and tell me what you smell."

A breath fills his lungs and the phantom aroma evokes his memory. "That's the same aroma we smelled at the last site."

"Yeah, that's more than a coincidence, I'd say."

"But from what? Where's it coming from? I'm going to... Ho-oo-ly shit!" Hamilton's face turns as pallid as death in half a wink—

frozen in place.

"My God, man, what's wrong?"

Hamilton's eyes widened as big as dinner plates. His arm stretches, pointing to the body next to Sterling.

Every fiber in his body simultaneously draws taunt in response to Hamilton's reaction. He rotates ever so slowly to see what has Hamilton so worked up, his eyes fall on the girl with the missing arm. He stumbles backward, falling flat on his ass. "Son of a bitch! What the..." Stammering, he observes the girl's chest move. The chest rises as a low growl emanates from inside her. Shock riddles his expression as his feet involuntarily come off the ground. Carefully, he steps inquisitively towards the body.

Hamilton doesn't move a muscle. Hell, he doesn't seem to breathe. Both jerk back when a grayish-black cat darts out like a bullet from the girl's rib cage. The damned thing hisses and snarls at them before taking off like its ass is on fire.

"Mother fucker!" Sterling bellows. "How in the hell did that damn thing get in there? Shit, when did it get in there?" Whirling around gawking at Hamilton when he doesn't get a response, he sees his face bled of color, standing with a hand on one knee, the other over his heart. "Hamilton, you alright?"

Taking a moment, catching his breath, he stands straight. "Yeah, yeah, I'm ok. Just scared the livin' shit out of me that's—"

"What are the two of you doing? It's a madhouse out front," Samantha's voice bellows from behind them, surprising them once again.

"Goddamnit!" Hamilton shrieks.

"What? What did I do?" She asks, confused.

"Nothing, Sam. We had a good scare is all," Sterling explains.

"A scare? From what?"

"A damned cat got into the dead girl's chest somehow, and it gave us a real jolt when it exited."

"I bet. You both look like you've seen a ghost. Did you catch the cat?"

"No. Shit," he spurts. "Everything happened so unexpectedly I didn't even—"

"No worries. Which one?"

"What?" Sterling asks, still irked by his little scare.

"Which one of the girls had the cat inside them? I might be able to get evidence from her, but I don't believe I'll be able to get clean samples."

"Yes, yes, of course. Misty, there on the left."

"Misty?" Sam questions with a raised eyebrow, wondering how he could know her name.

"Well, we think that's her name. You see the backpack next to her."

"Ah, I see." Samantha strolls over, kneeling down. "It says Misty all right." Her eyes grow intense as she breathes deep. "What is that odor? It smells a little like sweet, musky flowers." The smell compels her to inhale deeper. "Yup, that's what it is. A sweet, musky, floral scent, but from where or what? I do not see flowers around here."

"That's what we were asking ourselves. I smelled that same sweet odor at the last crime scene—it has to be something the killer is wearing or has on his person."

"Well, I can't see a man wearing anything smelling like that. Maybe we're not dealing with a man?"

"It's possible, but I've never witnessed murders of this nature and have the predator turn out to be a woman. Damn freak case! Hell, we could be dealing with the next female serial killer. And, to be frank, I don't give a damn. The only thing I am certain of is we have to stop this psychopath—man or woman—and do it quickly, or we will have another innocent girl ripped apart like some demented fucking jigsaw puzzle." He doesn't mean to be cross, but his aggravation just hit the extreme level.

"Ah, hell Sam, I'm sorry," he says, seeing her blinking expression, instantly he feels like an asshole. "I didn't mean…"

"It's fine, this is a tough time for everyone." Leaning over the bodies, she opens her medical kit. Sterling watches her take out a pair of latex gloves, put them on, and run her hand over one of the girl's head. Reverently she whispers, "I'm so sorry little one." Her eyes focus on the chest wound for a closer examination in the field. "Well, I can tell you it sure seems like the same killer. The prick used the same manner of opening the victims." She evaluates the body a little further. She grabs a thermometer as she examines the wounds and pushes the instrument into the body. After a moment, she says, "I would put the time of death at about seven this evening."

"That matches the time the boy said he brought the trash out," Hamilton explains, his eyes everywhere and on anything other than the bodies.

"I have this. Why don't the two of you do... whatever it is you have left to tackle?" she says, noticing Hamilton's distinctive discomfort. "I'll call you as soon as I'm through."

In no mood to argue, Sterling claps Hamilton on the shoulder, "Let's get out of here, shall we."

Without hesitation, Hamilton keeps pace next to Sterling, heading toward the front of the building. Sterling muses over the mess of shit piled a mile high to work through, and it's on his shoulders to get it done.

They are about to round the corner when Samantha calls, "Hey, I almost forgot, Captain Dixon, is out front and wants to speak with you when you have finished."

"Shit! Here it comes," Sterling grunts.

"Well, you're welcome," Samantha remarks sarcastically, trying to lighten Sterling's mood.

"Sorry, Sam. Thanks. How is he?"

"About as good as you are. To be honest, Cap appears to be tired and pissed off."

"Yeah, he's not the only one. Well, I best take the ass chewing I'm sure I will get. Goddamn, Freak Case!" Lighting another cigarette, he and

Hamilton proceeds towards the front of the store.

"Hey," Sam yells. "As soon as I am done with the preliminary documentation, I'd like to get these bodies out of here. Do you want me to wait for you?"

"No, I'm not sure what kind of lashing I'll be getting from Dixon and I don't want to hold you up."

"You do realize underneath all that *hardass, I'm the boss, do as I say* bullshit, Dixon's a teddy bear."

"More like a grizzly," Sterling snickers.

Sterling sees Dixon as soon as he turns the corner. His salt and pepper hair, more salt than pepper these days, large stature—in good shape for a guy in his fifties—dark gray suit, and "boss" stance, makes him prominent. Dixon always stands with his hands to his sides and straight as a board as if he's in the military standing at attention when he's not happy. Sterling labeled this unique stance of his, the "boss" stance, right after he began working with the man. He wants to avoid this conversation but knows it will transpire whether he wants it to or not. There's no use in prolonging the inevitable. He makes his way over to Dixon.

"You wanted to see me?"

"Yeah, Sterling, how are you holding up?"

"I'm good, sir. This case has got me going in circles, but we'll get him."

"Ah, yeah, the case, I want to talk to you about that." *Here it comes,* Sterling tells himself, but the Captain reads him like an open book. "You're a great detective, but it's this case, it's a little too close to home for you."

"What are you trying to say, Cap?"

"This case is bizarre, just like the one in New York, and you need to back away from it. We don't want the same thing happening here that happened before—"

"Now just a goddamn minute, Cap. I've been working my ass off on this case and there is nothing wrong with me. This isn't New York, and this isn't the New York case."

"Listen dammit! The shit is rolling downhill on this one. I will not be the one that gets his ass reamed if this thing isn't solved toot-sweet, you got me! Now, I will not take you off the case. But if I see the slightest sign—"

"You won't!"

"Good. Then I want this case solved, and I want it solved yesterday."

"I gotcha, Cap."

"I don't have to tell you; this thing is a catastrophe. It has the whole damned county in an uproar. So, you locate this son of a bitch!"

"I will, Cap, you can bet your retirement on that."

"When you unearth this maniac, put him *down* or behind bars, and don't fall apart while doing so—got me? And, Sterling?"

"Yeah, Cap."

"If you need a break from this, you come to me. Don't wait until... No judgments, no repercussions, understand?"

"I understand. Thanks, Cap."

"I'm worried about this one."

"I realize this, but I'm good." He studies Dixon's face and sees that ol' fatherly expression he gets. "I'm fine, really and when I'm not, I'll come to you." Sterling knows Dixon is worried this case might cause him another stint with the bottle.

He fell apart on the Matt Belmont case which included but not limited to, nightly appointments with a bottle of Jack, but only after a few drinks at a local hole-in-the-wall pub. He would stumble home in the wee hours of the morning or not go to bed at all before heading to work the next day. He passed Captain Mansell's office—his Captain in New York—on quite a few occasions traveling to the locker room. Though the hall was a good ten feet from his desk, the man could smell the Jack drifting from him.

After a few weeks of this activity, Captain Mansell called him in his office for a "talk," which was more of a get your shit together conversation. A few weeks after that, he was so inebriated he and his ex-wife had an ugly fight—he didn't hit her, but he'll never forget the fear in her eyes. Sterling put a transfer in the very next day to get away from her, from New York, and from Matt Belmont. Few are knowledgeable about his rendezvous with the bottle or how low he became and Sterling likes it that way. However, whether or not Sterling liked it, that didn't stop Mansell from reporting it all to Dixon before they approved the transfer.

"You do that. I want the report on my desk in the morning. But for now, you look like you could use a good night's sleep." Dixon hates himself for thinking Sterling might fall into the bottle again. But this town and this case can't afford a detective on edge. Against his better judgment, he lets Sterling stay on this case, mainly because the man is the best they have. But one sign he's drinking again, no matter how good he is, and Dixon will pull him.

"I was just heading out."

"Fair enough."

Sterling can't blame the Cap. After all, he still wakes from nightmares of Matt Belmont. That one case won't let him go. However, he's determined not to have a case get to him like that again. *They have to be fucking freak cases!* he broods, walking to his car.

A reporter with dirty-brown hair, a five o'clock shadow, and a screaming, bright red shirt, shoves a damned mic in his face. His fist forms a hard, tight ball and he glances back to see Dixon watching him. What he does at this moment seals his fate on this case, and he knows it. He doesn't hit the man though he wants to with all that's in him. Instead, he pushes his way past the reporter.

"No comment, I cannot comment on an open investigation," he tells the vulture, grinding his teeth and shoving forward, leaving the reporter behind. Giving Dixon a wave and a nod, he lights another smoke off the one burned to the filter before dropping it underfoot. "What a fuckin' day," he mutters, finally reaching his car.

Sterling slams the door shut and shoving the key in the ignition, the car roars to life. He lies on the horn, easing the Ford onto the pavement. The damned crowd has turned into a mob. Alger may be a small town, but Sterling's willing to bet a week's pay every damned person in this town and the next surrounds the IGA.

Trying to move the car through the crowd is an ordeal, it takes time before he finally breaks through the horde and is on his way to the hospital to see the boy. He needs for Joshua to make it, not just to prevent adding another name to the death count, which is becoming quite a list. But he has to know what the boy remembers—to hear what he has to say. It's imperative for the kid to tell him exactly what happened tonight behind the IGA.

Driving toward West Branch, his thoughts turn to the conversation with Captain Dixon—or Roy, off duty. It was brief but to the point, *'unearth this maniac, put him behind bars or put down and don't fall apart while doing so.'* Either one would be perfect for the Captain. But for some strange reason, Sterling has a sneaky suspicion Dixon would rather have him put a bullet in the guy's brain, rather than arresting him. These little towns in Michigan aren't used to this shit, and if he's honest, neither is he anymore.

The Captain didn't yell, didn't show emotion. He told him point blank, *this killer needs to be stopped*—calm, cool, and collective. A typical reaction for the man, he has that way about him when things become serious. Staging himself way too calm, which also means Cap's getting his ass reamed by the authorities. The authorities are the people you never see but hear from endlessly. And he isn't fond of them—hell, truth be told, he hates them.

The 'shit rolls downhill' phrase, is one he'd often heard from Dixon when things got hairy. However, 'I will not go down alone,' meant exactly that! His ass is getting chewed over these murders and if the department—if Sterling—doesn't find this psycho, he'll make damned sure he doesn't go through the grinder alone.

The good thing is things don't get this way with Dixon often. In fact, this is the first time Sterling's seen Dixon so hell-bent and hard wired. Four murders within a week are enough to get everyone in an uproar, and they are. The problem is, he's the person they are looking to solve this.

"Fuck!" Sterling yells, hitting the steering wheel. "I'll get this bastard! I'll get him and nail his ass to the wall." His anger stews, watching the lights from other cars pass. "You have to get into this guy's head. What does he want? Is he trying to make a statement of some kind or is he a sick bastard that has a thing for ripping apart young girls?!" The latter is what his money is on. This guy's morbid. There's no rhyme or reason for his acts. He gets his fucking jollies off killing and mutilating these girls.

However, Sterling came up with a rough profile: a white male in his late twenties, early thirties. From a well-to-do family. The work this unsub puts into the girls makes it highly unlike he has a full-time job. He's highly intelligent with some education, possibly a bachelor's degree, or work history in the medical field. He may not be correct on all bases, but he trusts he's pretty damned close.

Sam's at the inside door waiting when Sterling pulls into the parking lot. Hamilton called and let her know he was on his way. "Shit!" she breathes, watching him walk up. She has some bad news and the way Sterling's looking; she doesn't want to deliver it.

"Hey. Jesus, you look like hell."

"Yeah, did you expect any less?"

"No, not really."

"Listen, Sam, I would love to chat with you about what you found, but I have more pressing issues at the moment. I have to talk to that boy."

"Sterling wait—" Sam grabs his arm.

"What!" he yells, pulling his arm away. Now more pissed for losing his temper with Sam, he rams his hand through his hair, grinds his teeth until they hurt, turns away from her and then back. "What Samantha?" he asks more calmly, but his voice has that all too familiar edge to it.

Alright, full name, he's really pissed, she concludes.

"What is it?"

"It's just... the boy... um, he died about twenty minutes ago."

"Fuck! Shit!" Sterling grabs Sam by her shoulders, a little too hard. "Did he say anything? Anything at all that might help catch this son of a bitch."

"You're hurting me—let go."

Surprised at his action, he drops his grip, puts his head down. His eyes flash as remorse sweeps over him. Disgusted with himself for losing control, he can't look her in the eye. This case has his nerves shot, but that's no excuse.

"No," she huffs. "The boy said what he told Hamilton before to a tee. Not once did he waver in what he saw. He stated a huge cat came into view and the next thing he knew there was a bloody, naked figure, possibly a woman, walking away from him in the woods. That's all he said."

"I'm sorry, Sam..."

Rubbing her arm, a little unnerved herself, she tells him, "It's all right, Sterling, no need to apologize. This case has everyone on edge."

"No, I'm sorry. I shouldn't have grabbed you like that." His stance full of tension, he put his hands roughly on his hips, biting his bottom lip. "A woman? He said he saw a woman?"

"Not exactly, he said it *could* have been a woman, he wasn't sure, just like he admitted before." She wraps her arms around her waist, composes herself, reining in her emotions before she continues. "You don't think a woman is committing these awful murders, do you?"

"No, no, I don't. But I'm not ruling out anything at this point—not on this one. Did your examination of the twins reveal anything?"

"Not initially." Instantly she falls right into medical examiner mode. "There is no DNA, other than that belonging to the girls—nothing."

"What about that saliva or whatever it was? It looked to have blood in it."

"It was saliva and there was blood. However, it was feline on both counts."

"So that damned cat?"

She understood Sterling's frustration but what could she do. "All I can say is, someone opened them with the same method, using the same instrument as the others. I haven't completed my examination yet; we may get lucky. There's still no trace of anything that can lead us to a suspect."

At this moment, for some reason, he notices she has on the blue blouse he bought for her birthday a few years back. He always liked how that shirt looks on her. How it accentuates her breasts and her slim, toned waist.

"Sterling, did you hear me?"

"Yeah, I'm sorry, Sam. I can't seem to concentrate tonight."

"I understand." She doesn't though. It's the first time she's seen him so-so, agitated. *He's not himself at all,* she muses.

"Do me a favor and contact me the moment you have something," He says, heading for the entrance and then he stops. "And Sam, thank you."

"Anytime. Now go home and get a little sleep. I promise if I discover anything new, I'll call."

Offering a smile, the door slides open, and he leaves.

The drive home feels too long. His head filled with the details of the crime. The faces of the girls run in a vicious loop, tormenting him until his head throbs. "I'll figure this out, and when I catch this bastard, I'll cut off his balls and make him choke on them." He tells himself, applying a bit more pressure on the gas pedal.

He can't say what time he came through his front door—he doesn't even make it to his bed. The sofa will have to do. He's exhausted, and he dreams.

Chapter 8

The Dream

The wind blows through the screen of the open window fluttering the sheer curtains as the scent of evergreen fills the room. Sterling snaps out of dead sleep, confusion runs sluggish through the misty shadows of his clouded mind. Cold sweat runs down his back and face.

"Oh God," he says, jumping off the sofa still groggy, though the bewilderment is wearing off, he runs for the bathroom. The old nightmares are becoming more frequent, and he can't say he's all too happy about this. "Oh God," he repeats, turning on the faucet, splashing cold water on his skin. Looking into the mirror at his face, he hardly recognizes the reflection full of terror.

"It's just a dream, Sterling, just a dream." Leaning on the vanity allowing the grogginess to wear off, he grabs a towel, drying his face before leaving the room. The watch on his wrist reads 5:30 in the morning.

"Aw hell," he protests, going to his room. His time for sleep is over; there's no way he'd be able to go back to sleep, even if he tries. Since he's awake, a morning run is in order. If nothing else, maybe he can jog the lingering remnants of the nightmare off.

The solid-wood door to his bedroom creaks as he opens it. He has meant to oil the damned thing for a while now, but can never get a moment to do it—for that's all it will take, a moment.

His answering machine flashes; its green light blinking off and on, silently shouting at him, *you have messages*! Sterling pushes the play button and Captain's voice stems from the box, 'Hey, I know you're knee deep in this case, but I want you to take tomorrow off. It's Saturday, you know, go have fun. Go somewhere and do something other than work on this case. Don't argue with me about this. My mind's made up. But you best have your ass back here first thing Monday morning.' His voice squawks in no uncertain terms. There's a moment of silence before Cap's voice says, 'Oh, and Sterling, that's an order! I don't want to see your face around here tomorrow; you got me.' The machine beeps again. Dixon's is the only message. Sterling is perturbed and yet relieved. His finger hovers over the erase button, but he doesn't push it. It's not often that the Cap is in a giving mood, and more so, he wants to cover his ass, in case Cap forgets.

"Well, I have a day to myself. A nice run then a day of relaxation sounds like just what the doctor ordered," he mumbles to himself with a crooked smile.

He turns to the dresser to pull out a pair of shorts and a gray sweatshirt he cut the arms off of last year. He ripped a sleeve that got caught on a thorn when he cleared out the rose bed on the side of the house. He wasn't going to throw it out just because the sleeve got torn wide open; the rest of the shirt was acceptable.

It only takes a moment for him to change his clothes and lace up a pair of running shoes. Walking through the living room heading for the kitchen, he peers out the picture window that takes up most of the outer wall as rays of sunshine peeking over the trees, brightly beams through the only vase he owns, empty, of course, creating a rainbow on the furthest wall. *A gorgeous day, not a cloud in the sky,* he thinks.

In the kitchen, he pushes the brew button on the coffee pot sitting at the end of the polished marble counter. The kitchen is a large country style with a lot of woodwork. The man who built the home also made the cabinet of *real* oak, not pressboard or whatever crap they're making furniture from these days. No, these cabinets are made of the genuine article and he admired the workmanship.

Beautifully crafted, they remind him of the 1940s Hoosier cabinets, naturally finished, and sturdy—they'll last longer than he will. Sitting at the table waiting for the beep signaling the coffee was ready, his thoughts keep going back to his dream, "It was a fucking dream, you idiot. It was a damned nightmare!" he yells at the beige walls. The sweet, robust scent of coffee fills the room. The faces of the dead present themselves stiffly in his mind's eye. He realizes the dreams are a part of him now. They have been since his first case. It's as if the dead won't let him go. "Leave me the *fuck* alone," he gripes. The piercing sound of the phone's ring starts his head throbbing. He shuts it off without looking at who called, presses his hands to his head and stares at the oak plank floor.

Beep... Beep... Beep.

The coffee pot sounds startling Sterling out of a moment of self-pity. He rises, pours a cup of hot coffee, and takes a sip. The warm, rich fluid runs smoothly down his throat, easing the throb in his skull. He turns on the radio to hear the newsman say:

In today's news, tragedy struck the small town of Skidway Lake last night when the mutilated bodies of two young teen girls were found at the IGA. Also at the scene, a young boy was attacked and received fatal injuries from an unknown assailant. The local Police have declined to comment on the situation.

Sterling quickly turns it off. His frustration is at an all-time high, his thoughts cry out; *Christ, I want just one day not to think of this case.* He slams the rest of his coffee, burning his tongue. "Fuckin' freak cases," he mutters, making his way to the front door. He sits the coffee mug on the cherry console table by the door he leans against to take a few breaths.

More composed, he opens the door and listens to the birds sing, a squirrel perches itself on the free-standing bird feeder that is graying with age. He assumes the man who built this house, built the feeder. Suddenly an acute gnawing sound comes into play. He takes a few minutes to figure out that the sound is from a squirrel scraping at whatever it's eating. Exiting the front door, he leaves for a morning run.

He completes this running routine three—sometimes four—times a week. It's nice in the woods this time of day—quiet and peaceful. The wind whistles through the trees, birds chirp, and small animals scurry through the bush. He sees two chipmunks playing tag. One chasing the other and then switch it around so the second one does the chasing. They bring a smile to his face.

Two doe come into sight. They stand but twenty yards from his running path. One is yearling. They stop feeding long enough to raise their heads. Big, brown eyes view him with vigilance, watching him jog by then go back to their breakfast. They're so beautiful. No cars, no people, no civilization, just him and nature alone, leaving the world behind for a while. *I wish it could be like this all the time*, he thinks. Though he knows for this to happen, he will need another profession.

The course he cuts through the woods is a mile and a half out and the same distance back. It runs through the woods and around to exit at the beginning of Baker Drive—the road he lives on. The dirt drive is private, which means the city does not take care of it—he does. This is fine with him. The less he's bothered back here, the better he feels. Some might see this as anti-social, but he couldn't care less. "Opinions are like assholes, everybody has one," he recites, with a smirk.

He bought a small road grader, nothing fancy, the year after he moved here. It's a long blade which helps to give the road a semi-flat surface, keeping the ruts and dips within the usable parameter. He also has an old plow to clear away the snow. His home is the last on the two-mile road, getting snowed in is something he can't afford, so the plow was a must. He's the only one who lives there full-time. He has his privacy. It's him and nature when the day is through. *As it should be*, he muses.

Breaking from the woods onto Baker Drive, sweat drips from his brow. His sweatshirt is soaked with perspiration.

The newly occupied home is the first house on the road and what surprises him is the mystery woman and Sam are standing on the front porch talking. Sam's face is in a rare scowl and it doesn't appear they're having a pleasant conversation. The mystery woman notices Sterling, giving him a wave. Sam snaps her head around, forces a smile and waves too. Sterling may have been born, but it wasn't yesterday. He isn't blind either. The smile Sam offers is as fake as a three-dollar bill.

"Hi, Sterling," Sam says, with strained cheerfulness. As soon as their eyes meet, she knows she isn't pulling the wool over Sterling.

"Hey Sam, a little early for you, isn't it? I didn't realize you two ladies knew each other." He grins, holding out his hand to the mystery woman. "My name is Levi, Levi Sterling, but everyone around these parts calls me Sterling. It's nice to meet you. I live down the road."

The mystery woman takes his hand as Sam makes the introductions. "Sterling, this is my—well my friend, Nefertiti, but I've called her Neffi ever since I can remember. W-we went to college together." She says in an unsteady tone.

"You've never mentioned her before. Did you know she was coming to our little town?" Sterling questions, immediately realizing that Sam is hiding something—the tone of her voice gives her away. He knows her well, but the reason behind her deceit escapes him. He didn't hear their conversation, but he would bet dollars to donuts they were arguing over something.

"No, it was a surprise," Nefertiti responds with a thick accent that Sterling can't quite place, inserting herself into the conversation.

"Yes. Yes. Entirely a surprise," Sam stammers, unconvincingly. Her stance rigid, lips in a grimace of distaste, and her expression sullen.

"Yes, and Samantha, I should have called," Nefertiti replies with a natural sultry voice. Unlike Sam, her relaxed, uninhibited composure doesn't waiver. "You see, Levi—you don't mind if I call you by your first name, do you?"

"No, of course not."

"Good. You see, Levi, my Uncle David Chalthoum owned this property. He left it to me in his will when he passed last year. It took me some time to get things together to come to see the property," she explains. Her eyes never abandon his.

"I see. I'm sorry to hear about your uncle's passing. I never had the pleasure of meeting him. This place has been empty for years."

"No need for apologies," she responds, her voice is hypnotic. "It was quite a shock when a lawyer explained an uncle I hardly knew left twenty acres of land with a house on it to me."

"I can't imagine. Are you going to be staying with us long?"

"I'll be staying for some time—this is my home for now."

"Well then, let me be the first to welcome you to our little neighborhood. I hope you enjoy peace and quiet, for it stays that way until summer comes. I'm the only other person who lives on this road full-time."

"It's a pleasure to meet you. I'm a little confused, though, isn't it summer right now?"

"It feels like. However, everyone who owns property back here left the last week of June. It's an unusually warm August."

"Ah, well then, it's nice to meet my sole neighbor until summer comes again."

Nefertiti is extraordinary. She is smart, beautiful, and mysterious. The sense of déjà vu' creeps over him, though if he met her before he wouldn't forget, he's confident of this. Staring at Nefertiti a little too long, Sam interrupts his gaze.

"I'm going to get going. Nefertiti, it's nice to have you here," she states. The tension in her voice is harsh; her strained smirk borders on a sneer. Sterling catches her eyes for a moment and a moment is all he needs to see the anger swirling in them like a massive, red wave rising from a tsunami. Her hands curl into fists at her sides as she turns toward the direction of her car.

Confused by her actions, he is unsure why she is acting so hostile. He's never understood women. Jamie used to tell him he was blind to the cues women gave. "Well, if you have something to say, just say it," he remembers telling her. "Why do you women expect us to guess what the hell you're thinking? We're not mind-readers." To this day, he never understood why a woman couldn't come out and say what's eating at them instead of the ho-hum bullshit that men have to try to figure out.

"Hey, Sam?" he asks with care, not knowing how she will react.

"Yeah." She stops but doesn't turn to face him and her voice still has that cutting edge to it.

"Is there anything new on those girls?"

"No Sterling," she bites. "Nothing to provide any clues—didn't Dixon order you to take the day off from this case?"

"How did…" he thinks a minute. "Damn it, Cap," he mutters under his breath. With a shake of his head, he tells her, "I am. I want you to keep me in the loop, though."

"I see. Well, I'll call if a new development occurs. Enjoy your day off, Sterling," she grouses, sarcastically, dropping all effort to hide her mood. She glances at her friend with daggers, "Goodbye, Nefertiti."

What is wrong with Sam, he wonders, turning to Nefertiti for clues. Then watches her march away as if on a mission. *Man, she's pissed.*

"Goodbye," Nefertiti replies as if she doesn't notice Sam's unpleasant state. They watch her get into her car, back out of the drive and speed off leaving a trail of dust behind.

"Would you like a cup of coffee?" Nefertiti asks, returning her attention to Sterling.

"I don't want to impose. Plus, I need a shower."

"Are you sure? There's some already brewed, and we can sit out here on the porch if you like. Come, I'll get you a cup."

"How can I refuse," Sterling says, following her in the house.

Chapter 9

The Tale

The interior of Nefertiti's home isn't at all what he expected. Not that he's sure what he expected, but this indeed isn't it. Walking in the front door is like walking into the jungle. Large exotic plants with striking broad-leafs swallow him up. Two miniature waterfalls run adjacent to him. The sound of the water flowing down, running along the outer edge of this little jungle is welcoming and relaxing. Jesus, someone could get lost just by walking in the door.

Beyond the plants, the walls are a deep, vibrant, dark green. The floors as dark and vivid as the green on the walls—*mahogany* he thinks, as they move further into the home.

On the left is a library; a massive desk sits in the middle of the room. The desk looks to be from the 19th century; hand-carved mahogany. Brass handles grace the carved drawer fronts and doors. Three of the four walls have built-in bookshelves holding old books.

"I'll be right back," Nefertiti announces, shaking Sterling loose from his awe. "Make yourself at home." He watches as she disappears around the corner.

Sterling's senses become overloaded entering the library through double French doors. A trace of old book smell wafts through the room combining with the aromatic aroma of jasmine. At first, he can't place where the jasmine fragrance is coming from. Then to his right, on a beautiful 19th century, Chinese carved table sits a gilt-bronze incense burner. He believes it's Korean, from about the 5th or 6th century, though he could be way off. One thing's for sure, the artifacts in this room have his attention and he's very intrigued.

Inspecting this room is like taking a journey back in time. Antique books line the shelves, some he never thought he'd have the pleasure to see. *The Greek New Testament* produced by Robert Stephanus from 1550; an *American Cruisers* book from 1874, it's cover carved with the name 'Capt. J C Pease, Oswego; 1460 *Invectives Against the Sect of Waldensians*, and numerous others he heard of but never seen before.

With J C Pease's book in hand, he turns to see the wall not endowed with books. Instead of full bookshelves lining the wall, various masks decorate its surface. A Zambian, Lovale, Wooden Deity Dance, African Tribal, and a Kuba helmet along with many others. The masks adorn the wall from ceiling to floor, and if Sterling isn't wrong, the oldest are at the top.

A large portrait steals his interest. The frame is an intriguing antique gold with a very ornate, intricate design that includes large cats. Though impressive, the aged picture of a woman, identical to Nefertiti, has him hypnotized. It's a painted portrait of a dark-haired woman in what he assumes is 1800s era dress with immense black panthers at her side, posing in front of a circus wagon. But it isn't the cart or the huge, beautiful, black cats that have Sterling's attention; it's the woman. Her eyes—deep, dark, mysterious—just like Nefertiti's, captivate him. His mind sweeps away, lost in their gaze. Whispers of ages long passed infiltrate his ears. Although he can't make out what the voices say, he's entranced nonetheless.

"Isn't she beautiful," Nefertiti says, startling Sterling out of his trance. So much so, he jumps. "Oh, Levi, I'm sorry. I didn't mean to startle you."

"That's all right," he replies, as Nefertiti hands him a steaming hot cup of coffee. "I guess I've been a little on edge lately. Who is this?" He asks, looking back at the cryptic woman in the painting.

"That is my great, great, great-grandmother. She was born in Egypt. Her name—well, her stage name—was Madam Dalaminia. Yes, I do. I guess we have strong genes in my family."

"Yes, I suppose you do. She's exotic and so is her name. You look so much like her that if I didn't know better, I would swear it was you. You have her eyes."

"Well, thank you, that's a charming compliment. As for her stage name, oh yes, exotic indeed; it was meant to be. Of course, her given name was Camila—I assume that name did not provide the air of intrigue and mystery that Madam Dalaminia offered her." Nefertiti's eyes widen. She swipes her hand through the air as she says this with a breathy, deepened voice for effect. "Camila was beautiful. She had a gift for telling the future and a magic touch with felines, notably panthers. She had already taken up with the circus by the time my great, great, great, grandfather, Jonathan Chalthoum, laid eyes on her. In his journal, he states Camila had magic in her and a mystical touch with large cats. His exact words were, 'It's as if she knows what they are thinking and they know her mind as well—they and she are one. I have never witnessed such a talent and connection between human and beast—it's extraordinary.' He also states that Camila enveloped his senses the moment he saw her—that she must have cast a spell, for he was in love at a glance."

"Wow, it almost sounds like a fairy tale. I can't believe your family still has his journal."

"Oh, yes, my family keeps everything. They thought future generations must learn of their past—where they originated. As for Camila and Jonathan, their love was very much like a fairy tale. They married in 1802, traveled all over the world with the circus, and had five children, two boys, and three girls. They had a long life together until..." Nefertiti's face falls. Her words fade off. She's stolen—taken somewhere else for a moment.

"Are you ok, Nefertiti?"

"Oh, yes. I'm sorry, sometimes I dream about what it must have been like for them, being in the circus and all. From the journal entries, you would never meet two people so in love. They were happy. Oh, but listen to me prattling on like an old hen..."

"No. No, please continue, Egypt is intriguing."

"Yes, it is. It's a mysterious place and so beautiful." Nefertiti smiles.

"So, you've lived there?"

"Yes, I was raised there."

"And your grandmother was born there, correct?"

"She was. She was born in a little village off the banks of the Nile. She left Egypt after meeting my grandfather. It was her home, and she loved Egypt but something happened, something terrible and they fled the country."

"What happened?"

"Grandfather's brother betrayed him, and many died." Her eyes study him carefully as if she's expecting some response he doesn't comprehend.

"That's awful," he thinks. The betrayal of a family member, he can't imagine anything more scarring.

"It is," she replies, sorrow entrenched in her eyes.

"How did his brother betray him?"

"He became obsessed with power and nothing grandmother or grandfather did could change his direction. In fact, their words ignited a fury within him. He and some followers he'd gained, killed the innocent."

"That's harsh, even if he wanted power."

"Yes, but from the history written in my grandmother's diary, the man was quite mad. I have read it many times."

"It sounds it. You've had her diary all these years."

"I have, it was passed down to me by my mother. In its pages, she speaks of many things, but more than any other is her love for my grandfather. He was her life, and her love for him was powerful."

"Your family has a remarkable history."

"They do, one that goes back centuries."

"What is it you do, Nefertiti?"

"Oh, I'm a zoologist. Some will tell you I'm one of the best, but honestly, I love animals."

"That is amazing. Are you around the animals a lot?"

"Not as much as I'd like to be. I am more of a consultant for zoos and wildlife preserves these days."

"What brought you here? I mean, besides your uncle's generous inheritance. Do you work around here?"

"I've been consulting with some different wildlife preserves here in Michigan, mainly Grand Rapids. But, enough about me, let's drink the rest of this coffee on the porch, shall we?"

Sitting on the porch with Nefertiti is a treat. Sterling hasn't been able to relax and not worry about the murders for some time. However, the tension hasn't left him and Nefertiti picks up on his anxiety.

"So, Levi Sterling, it would seem your job has plenty of stress attached to it. You must be working on something important. You seem so tense."

"What? Oh, yes, that obvious, huh?"

"Well, a little. I hate to be so bold but what happened?"

"It's these cases. They have me running in circles."

"Want to talk about it? I'm all ears." She beams with her too-white smile along with a wink of a long, dark-lashed eye. Her mere presence sends chills through his body.

Though aware talking about this case with anyone is frowned upon, he can't resist her charm. "Yeah, sure," he says. "If you won't be too bored listening."

"I doubt that."

"There has been a rash of murders here. The clues make little to no sense whatsoever."

"Murders? Here?"

"Yes. I have to tell you; you couldn't have picked a worse time to move to our little town."

"Can you tell me about them? If you can't, I understand. Police business and all."

"You don't want to hear about the gory details I live with every day."

"Oh, but I do—at least, what you can tell me. It is frightening but mystifying."

"I can tell you there has been a rash of deaths here lately—very strange for this small town. The part that bothers me most is they're all teen girls—well, at least, so far."

"Someone is killing young girls!" Her forehead furrows with concern. "No wonder there's so much anxiety encircling you. Do you think there will be more? Are there any clues to who may be involved in such atrocities?"

"There could be more, though I hope not. As for clues, well, there's a few." He knew he shouldn't talk about the case with Nefertiti, but there was something so comforting about her—so trusting, it compelled him. If he didn't know better, he'd swear he'd met her somewhere before; the feeling was intense. *Either that or you're just a lonely ol' coot that has had no one other than co-workers to talk to in a long time. That may be the case, but it is nice to speak with someone new*, he thought as he continued. "But at the one scene, there was a peculiar piece of evidence."

"Like what? Can you tell me?"

"I shouldn't be telling you any of this, but you might be able to help—I mean with your experience in animal behavior and all."

"Oh, I'd love to help if I can. What did you find?"

"There was evidence of a large cat, a white panther to be exact, and a boy saw it."

"A white panther, my God!"

"What, what is it?" he asks. Her face displays more than just surprise. There's something else in her expression—something off.

"White Panthers are very rare. I've only seen one myself. It must be a magnificent animal. So, this boy..." she questions, exhibiting reluctance in doing so.

"He didn't make it. He died a few hours before I could speak with him."

"I'm sorry, Levi," she says, placing her hand on his knee. The look on her face is sincere; it may be the most candid look he's witnessed in some time.

"Thank you. Though I didn't know the boy, I never feel right when young lives end well before their time. But, you know, the strange thing is I don't believe he was the target. I believe he merely got in a lunatic's way."

Nefertiti doesn't reply. Observing her, he notices she's either hiding or uncomfortable about something. So, he asks, "What is it about white panthers? You're not telling me something."

"You are a good detective, aren't you?" She says, blushing. "Well, there are native tribes that believed seeing or hearing a white panther's screams is an omen—meaning, something evil is coming. Also, tribes have for centuries, associated the white panther with witchcraft."

"I'm not worried about witchcraft. I have concerns that a dangerous animal is out there. How do you know all of this stuff, anyway?"

"I read a lot of books, that's all." She said dismissively—too dismissively for Sterling's liking. He realizes there is much more to this beauty than meets the eye. She is hiding something—but what? Then, more enthusiastic, she asks, "So, tell me more about these gruesome murders."

"Are you into strange deaths or something?" he chuckles, nervously.

Nefertiti reddens a couple of shades, "No, I'm sorry. What you do is interesting, that's all and if I can help, I'd like to."

He's pleased with her curiosity. Not to say she might be the one who can help or at least, give him some insight into the behavior of panthers. "Well," he begins, "the deaths don't fit animal attacks. They're too precise and skilled for an animal to have done the deed, so to speak. However, all clues are pointing to the large white cat."

"Now, that is strange," Nefertiti confirms.

"What do you mean?"

"Well, from what I know from working with large cats, they won't attack a person for no reason, let alone, singularly select young, teen girls. You see, they are scavengers. The blood could have attracted the one you say got loose. But for a panther to attack with such prejudice—well it's highly implausible."

"That was my conclusion. I may not know much about the everyday behaviors of a large cat, but these deeds don't seem to fit the actions of an animal. This case just isn't adding up."

"What you're describing reminds me of an old folklore—a legend, if you will—from Egypt."

"More witchcraft," Sterling chuckles. Nefertiti's face turns down a little, making Sterling feel like an ass. "I'm sorry, tell me, please. I would love to hear the legend."

"I'm sure you have more important things to do than listen to me prattle on."

"Actually, I don't. I would love nothing more than to hear the story. I'm sorry. I'm an ass at times, but I am intrigued. I want to hear it."

Nefertiti studies Levi for a moment to see if he's mocking her. When she is satisfied that he's not, she begins her story.

"Well, as I said, it's just a legend. However, as the legend goes, the Egyptians held the cat in godliness. The felines have been the most revered and worshiped animal throughout the history of our culture as I'm sure you know. However, the cats are—or were, held in such high regard, to the point that the people revered them as gods.

"There is a legend of the first feline goddess, named Mafdet. Mafdet was a feline deity whose existence is said to date back to the First Dynasty of Egypt 3,000 BC to 300 BC. She takes the form of a woman—one with mesmerizing beauty. She could shape-shift into a cat, her head being the first part of her to transform. Many throughout the centuries have witnessed the body of a woman with the head of a cheetah. However, her transformation into the impressive cheetah was only one of the feline forms she could assume. Eyewitnesses wrote accounts of the goddess turning into a leopard, a lynx or even a mongoose. But the ancient people described her most predominant form as that of a mythical and powerful panther.

"It's alleged the goddess was gifted with the power to protect against venomous bites, such as those of snakes and scorpions. The tribes celebrated her as the goddess of judgment, justice, execution—the warrior goddess of sunset, destruction, death, rebirth, and wisdom. Those who were judged and found at fault were sure to feel her claws, twice as deadly as the serpent or scorpion, sending them to the underworld."

As she spoke these words Sterling saw the excitement flow through her; lighting up her eyes like rays of light on diamonds. The enthusiasm wafting from her is contagious and he finds himself being carried to a past that is not his own.

"The legend tells that our ancient ancestors loved and adored Mafdet with such powerful reverence they would sacrifice their children to her. It was their way of showing their undying loyalty to the goddess for her protection.

"Mafdet fell in love with an ailuranthrope..."

"I am sorry," Sterling interrupts. "An ailuranthrope?"

"Yes, more commonly known as a skinwalker or werecat."

"I see," he says although thinking, *what rubbish*. "Please continue," he says. Even though he does not buy into imaginary entities like skinwalkers, the story is entertaining.

She eyes him for a moment to see if he has anything else to say before she continues. "Now, where was I?"

"Mafdet falls in love."

"Ah yes, his name was Le-Banyo, and he became a great king. Their passion generated three daughters, each born human. However, like their father, they were skinwalkers and held power to alter to the panther.

"Two of her daughters were blessed, said to transform into the great white cats. The problem that arose was, unlike the goddess, the daughters needed the fresh blood of a virgin female child to change back to their human form. Therefore, for centuries, the Egyptians who worshiped the goddess would choose virgin girls to sacrifice to the deity.

"After centuries of virgin sacrifices, the daughters' transformation came easily—they needed no more blood to transform from cat to human. After that time, however, the legend says, the daughters killed virtuous young girls to preserve their youth. It's told that one girl, blessed with the power of the white panther, became jealous of her black cat sister. She became so enraged with envy she tried to kill her own blood. If it were not for their other sister, the girl would have died. The night she attempted to murder her sister, she disappeared. Whether she ever came back, the legend doesn't say."

"She tried to take her sister's life, not very loyal was she?"

"Oh, but she was loyal!" she says this like she knew the girl from the story or something. "She just had a hard time controlling her emotions. Jealousy, as you know, is a powerful emotion that can make people do strange things."

"I suppose," he replies. "So, what is supposed to have happened to these daughters of Mafdet?"

"Well, the legend pretty much ends there, however, the elders say the daughters of the goddess walk among us to this day. They believe the daughters walk among us, taking innocent blood to keep their youth—death shall never befall them. Whether this legend is true is yet to be seen."

"Wow, that's one hell of a legend," he says and means it. "In fact, if it weren't legend, it would explain the unfortunate murders of these girls." It would too. Shit, it fits this case to a tee. But a human, cat, god mix? Impossible! Although the combination would explain the situation if it weren't so damned ridiculous, he thought. "That is amazing—dark, but amazing. This legend of your people is incredible."

"Yes, it is quite the story, isn't it," she admits. "It is, of course, immersed in a formidable amount of drama."

"Oh, but it's fascinating. Thank you for sharing it with me."

"You're welcome. That particular legend has always intrigued me; I'm quite fond of it." Nefertiti laughs, nervously.

"So, are there any other compelling legends of your ancestors?"

"Too many. More than I could ever remember. However, I can tell you about a strange incident that happened to me when I was a child."

"Now, I am intrigued. Please, go on, tell me."

"Well, when a child, my aunt took me to the circus. While we were there, I saw an old woman—you know one of those fortune tellers. She was mesmerizing, with her dark clothes, deep lined face, and eyes as black as opals. I went to her and—well, I'll never forget what she told me."

Apprehension swathes Nefertiti. She appears nervous to tell Sterling what the old woman said. The very thought of it strikes a tremendous fear in her.

"What did she say?" he urges.

"I know it's just the ramblings of an old woman, but it scared me—it still does."

"God, that is awful. Tell me what she said to you."

"It was like a poem. I'm not sure what it meant, but the words the old woman told haunt me to this day.

> *When shadows fall, she walks in taciturnity—a creature of the night, Strong and powerful, with jaws of might. Prowling for a female youth of virtuous accord, To cure her incessant appetite Whose formative years she must absorb.*

Nefertiti shutters at the thought of the old woman's words.

"Come on, Nefertiti; don't let the words of a crazy old lady get to you. I'm sure she was trying to scare you, and from the looks of it, she accomplished that."

"Maybe," Nefertiti replies, studying Sterling's face. It's obvious something else is bothering him. "I don't mean to pry, but there's something else—something old—that torments you."

"Wow, after that legend and the words of a senile old woman terrifying you half to death, you're worried about me... are you a mind reader too?"

"I've told fortunes in my time," Nefertiti laughs. "Now what dark secrets are you hiding?"

"Me? I'm not hiding anything."

"Ah, but you are; I can see it. Deep within you, something is eating at you piece by piece."

Sterling isn't sure why he tells Nefertiti of the boy. Maybe, it's because this woman relaxes him, which lately, isn't a condition he often has. Or, perhaps it was because it's as if he's known her for a lifetime. She has that air about her, one that makes people feel content. He feels he can tell her anything—everything! Or maybe, it's the fact he's never had anyone to talk to about it and getting it off his chest may prove to be the best medicine.

"I was in New York," he begins. Nefertiti pulls her chair closer, listening intently. "I had a rough case. A boy—Matt Belmont, was his name—was found under the Manhattan Bridge. He'd been defiled, tortured, and the body was left naked and lifeless in the snow."

"Oh, my," she gushes, traces of terror in her eyes. "That's awful! Who would commit such terrible acts against a boy?"

"That's the thing, no clues were left behind, and we never found out who executed such vile acts on the boy. So his killer or killers were never brought to justice." He looks into her eyes, and with more honesty than he believes he has ever had, he tells her, "I spent long hours working on the case, searching the case file, studying the crime photos, beating the streets and nothing ever came to the surface. I questioned the boy's mother, but she was so distraught it was obvious she didn't know who could do such a thing."

"And his father?"

"He was doing time for breaking and entering at the time of the murder, so he was ruled out. I dove into the case giving it all I had and more; it affected me in a profound way."

"I can't imagine the horror you went through back then. It must have taken a toll on you."

"It did. I fell into a destructive cycle that cost me my family and almost cost me my job."

"You were married?"

"Yes, and I have a son as well." He doesn't want to get into this conversation with Nefertiti—dredging up Matt Belmont is one thing, his divorce is another. So, to change the subject, he says, "All those old feelings from back then have been brought to the surface with these new murders. And to be perfectly frank, Matt Belmont still haunts me."

"And this? she asks, touching his scar.

"That is from the same case. Just over ten years ago, I received this little gift." He rubs his scar. "A perp got the jump on me and well, I ended up with a nice memento."

"It is a deep scar from a harsh wound, but you wear it well."

"Thank you. The doctor believed someone hit me with a metal pipe and it took most of my long-term memory with it." As he runs a hand through his hair, grazing over his scar, Matt's body lying in the snow flashes through his mind.

"I see, how dreadful for you. You still have nightmares about that boy don't you?"

"You *can* read minds," Sterling replies, with a nervous chuckle.

"I am sorry, Levi. I shouldn't pry."

"Nefertiti, it's all right. The incident with the boy happened a long time ago. I can't seem to get him out of my head. Yes, I dream about him. It's as if he's trying to tell me something." He can't believe he said this aloud to a complete stranger. *What is it with this woman that compels me to share this darkness?* he struggles with this idea. Though it's a bizarre compulsion, it's not altogether uncomfortable either. There's something almost proverbial about her. "This all must sound much too melodramatic, but—well, there it is."

"No, Levi, it doesn't. What does the boy say? I mean in your dreams, what does he say to you?"

"Why, what does it matter? They're just dreams," he lets out a nervous snicker slip.

"Oh, but they're not just dreams," Nefertiti replies. "We trust dreams are a way for the dead to communicate with us."

"That's an unsettling thought, dead people invading our dreams."

"As unusual as it may be to you, can you humor me this one time?"

What she asks of him is weird and bizarre indeed, but thinks, *Oh hell, what's it going to hurt?*

"Well, he says nothing until the end of the dream." An icy shiver shoots down his spine. "He says, "˜You never found who killed me.'"

"So, he is trying to tell you something."

"Or he's plain pissed off I didn't catch the bastard," Sterling utters.

"Levi, I accept there's a spirit world," she says, ignoring his outburst. "A world beyond our reality. Those who've died a violent death are in a state of confusion and turmoil. They had not prepared to continue and travel to the netherworld. They're angry, confused; their souls and spirits cannot rest until they've acquired what they want. Restless spirits, such as the boy you've spoken of, can assist or harm the living. They have the power to reveal details of what they need to rest—all we need do is listen."

"Nefertiti, I don't mean to offend." He clears his throat, stifling a snicker. "But you realize this all sounds like a bunch of mystic bullshit."

"That may be, but I can open your mind. I mean, I can open it to the spirit world so you can receive this boy's message."

"Really," he laughs. "Well that sounds interesting, but I don't believe in this hoodoo, voodoo, mystic stuff."

"You don't have to and if you don't believe in it, what can it hurt? It will be a new experience for you."

"Naw, Nefertiti, I'm not sure I want someone messing around with my head."

"C'mon, it's not as if I can get into your mind and make you a different person. I'll open it up to the spirit of the boy, so you know what he wants." Sterling observes her with apprehension, so she tries again, "Think of it as an adventure... please. If you don't believe in it, what can it hurt?"

"Ok, ok," he says, more bitter than intended. He doesn't give credence to any of this, but Nefertiti has conviction in what she believes. So, to appease her, he agrees to be a guinea pig. "What do I have to do?" he says with subduing respire.

"Close your eyes," Nefertiti tells him, smiling and perhaps with a little more excitement than he's comfortable with, as she scoots her chair in closer and puts her hands on either side of his head. Reluctantly, he closes his eyes. "Now, try to relax and clear your mind."

"I feel like a complete fool," he grouses, half opening his left eye.

"No peeking. It will not work if you don't trust me. You trust me, don't you, Levi?"

"Ok, I trust you," he grunts and shuts his eye again.

"Listen to my voice; there's no one else around you, let yourself relax, clear everything from your mind. Picture yourself in a large, dark, empty room. You are alone in the vast, dark room. You're relaxed, warm, and sitting in your favorite chair. You're very comfortable, all your muscles are loose, and your mind is clear. You are opening your mind. There is nothing that can harm you here.

"In front of you is the soft glow of a candle, illuminating a single word on a black chalkboard. The word is out of focus, obstructed by the darkness. You float closer—relaxed and comfortable. As you move closer, the word becomes clearer—more defined. The letters are enhancing—larger, bolder. You can now read the word, SLEEP..."

Chapter 10

The Spirits

He observes a beautiful, young, long-haired girl standing before a small assembly. She's in a light linen tunic, wearing a crown of flowers, and intricate symbols shroud her bronze skin—whether painted on or tattooed, he can't tell. Fear prevails in her large, dark, almond-shaped eyes as she stands stagnant in a deep trance.

An old woman dressed in black, her face covered except for her milky white eyes, makes her way through the flock of chanters. She takes the young girl by the hand and leads her to the fire. Sterling steadily moves in closer to see a cave hidden partially beneath the sands. The old woman guides the girl to an opening in the cave. She stands her in front of it and rejoins the incanting cluster. The whole time the insufferable humming endures in repeated harmony.

He sees *it. Oh god, no! NO!* he screams. Stunned. Confused. Before he can move, the young girl is yanked backward into the darkness by a massive claw. Blood sprays from the darkness, coating the opening with a crimson splatter. The chanting becomes louder causing his head to ache. *"NO!"* emanates from him with the force of the Thunder God. The ominous crowd turns and faces him, still chanting their bustling message of death.

"Awwrgh!" Sterling bellows, tumbling out of the chair. "NO!" he wails, tears streaming down his face mixing with the sweat from his brow. He's scared, unhinged, it takes him a moment to realize where he is.

"My God, Sterling, are you ok?" Nefertiti asks, her eyes as big as saucers. "Here, let me help you." She takes him by the arm as he gets to his feet. "Sterling? Speak to me!" Nefertiti's voice quivers.

"I'm fine—I think."

"What happened? I mean one second you were calm and the next... well, you screamed, crying like someone was torturing you."

"That's what they did! They sacrificed her! Oh, God!"

"Sterling, what are talking about? Sacrificed who? Did you see Matt? What did he say?"

"No, Nefertiti, it wasn't Matt I saw. I saw a young girl in a faraway place she was young and beautiful and her people sacrificed her to a...to a..." Frantic, Sterling fights to keep his knees from buckling. "I don't understand. It makes little sense."

"It's alright. I'm sorry this didn't bring you the answers you were looking for, Sterling. I was trying to help."

"Nefertiti, I'm sorry I have to go—I'm sorry."

"But—"

Nefertiti doesn't have time to say anymore. Sterling jumps up clumsily. He runs as if his life depends on it until he reaches his front door. When he gets inside, he slams and locks the door. *Holy shit, what the hell just happened?* He asks himself. Stumbling to the sofa, he plops down. His mind replays the vision—dream, or whatever the hell that was he saw. That girl! The blood! He recognizes none of it, so how could it be a memory of his as Nefertiti told him if he has no recollection of such sights. The vision shown to him was old—ancient—there's no way in heaven or hell it can be his. Something is not right.

Someone help me! Echoes in the darkness are fading from Sterling's mind. His eyes pop open; inexplicable anxiety clutches every nerve as he wipes frantically at the fogged glass of the shower to discover he *is* alone. "Come on Sterling! Pull your head out of your ass, ol' boy. You fell to sleep that's all." Slapping his face, he turns off the shower, reaches out the glass door, and grabs a towel to wrap around his midsection.

He steps from the shower into the room now filled with steam reminding him of a heavy fog over a lake. He leans on the sink, wiping the mist from the mirror, leaving behind moisture beads that run down the glass. Staring at a clear view of his reflection, his green eyes seem unfamiliar as if they're the eyes of a stranger—yet not quite a stranger, an old acquaintance—looking back at him. "Ah, hell, it's nothing, just some kind of voodoo trick or something." He turns and heads out of the room and toward the kitchen.

The phone rings, startling him. "Son of a Bitch!" Sterling shouts. "Shit! Fuck, that hurt," he grumbles, as he struggles to stand on one foot after stubbing his toe. Holding a foot in one hand and the phone in the other, he answers, "Hello!"

"Sterling? It's Samantha, you ok?"

"Yeah, my clumsy ass just smacked my damn toe on the table. What's up?"

"Ouch," she responds, cringing at the thought. Toes aren't something people think about often until they smack them on one thing or another, then they can't help but be aware of them. "I'm sorry to bother you on your little vacation, but I found something you should know about."

"Great! What?"

"I went through the girls' clothing and found a spot on one of the dresses. I figured, what the hell, and ran it. Sterling, I found female DNA on that dress that didn't match the victim. I ran it through the National DNA Index, but there wasn't a match."

"I wish you had. So, either this is this perp's first time, which I have a difficult time believing. Or the son of a bitch has never been caught before. Damn!"

"That's the way it looks. However, you get me a suspect, and I'll be able to match it up."

Momentarily deep in contemplation, he can't trust this psycho hasn't done something of this nature before. The crimes are too clean. But more than that, he's having one hell of a time wrapping his head around the idea he's looking for a woman.

"Female, are you sure?" He asks.

"I'm positive—it's just about the only thing I *am* confident of lately. I couldn't believe it either. I double-checked the sample to make sure. I mean, with the nature of the crimes, I'd have bet my house the perp was a male. I'm still in shock that a female is committing such..."

"I know. Thanks. Oh?"

"Yes, Sterling."

"Keep this information between us for now."

"You got it. See you on Monday."

Sterling starts a pot of coffee and looks at the clock; it's only 2 p.m. As he stands there staring at the second hand going around in its stutter motion, he considers the female DNA. *How can a woman commit such atrocitie*s? He contemplates. He isn't an idiot. He has seen women do some terrible acts, but this is unusual for a woman serial killer.

"Shit, for that matter, women serial killers aren't in abundance, especially ones that target young girls. What in the hell is this world coming to!" The coffee pot beeps finally as his phone rings again. "Christ, it's becoming Grand Central Station around here," Sterling bitches.

"Hello."

"Sterling, it's Nefertiti, I called to check on you, you left in such a hurry."

"I'm fine. I'm sorry I left like that, I was—well, just a little off-kilter. What exactly did you do to me?"

"There's no need to apologize, I understand. All I did was open your mind to the spirit realm. I have to say, I wasn't sure it would work. I mean, no one's ever reacted quite the way you did. Are you better?"

"Yes, I am." He genuinely is too. The shower did him a world of good. "Hey, are you doing anything right now?"

"No, not at all."

"Would you like to have a late lunch, early dinner with me? I don't have much, but I have some T-Bone, and it's a beautiful day to grill."

"That sounds terrific. I'll be down in a few."

"Great, see you then." Sterling hangs up the phone. As he seasons the steaks a voice resonates through his mind, *you need to find this killer.* "I'll catch the bastard!" Sterling washes his hands, slips out the sliding-glass door to the backyard, and starts the grill.

Nefertiti knocks at the front door a few moments later wearing a dark pink sweatshirt that exposes her midriff and jeans, she looks amazing. Sterling notices she has a tribal-like tattoo around her bellybutton, which is strange—she doesn't seem the type, though it's alluringly sexy. "Come on in. I have the grill warming and the steaks seasoned."

"I brought red wine—I hope you like wine."

"Yes, I do. Thank you."

"Is there anything I can do to help?"

"Well, I was about to get a salad ready—would you like to help cut vegetables?"

"Absolutely, lead the way."

The day is perfect. So is Nefertiti. Laughter fills the air between the two. Sterling can't remember a time he's enjoyed the company of a woman so much—not even Sam made him feel as if he were invincible. He's able to forget about the girl's murders and the killing of the boy so long ago—at least, for a short period.

As the day becomes night, Sterling dreads ending the time he has with Nefertiti as he walks her home. Standing on her front porch, she looks like an angel in the soft light radiating the outside light. The luminescence wraps around her, holding her tenderly casting a thin shadow and softening her frame, sharp borders of her body soften in the light creating a glow that makes her look like an angel gazing deeply into Sterling's eyes.

"Thank you, Levi. I had a great time tonight, and you're a fantastic cook."

"I'm not sure grilling is quite the same as actual cooking, but I'll take it. It was a nice evening. Thank you."

Nefertiti waits for a few more minutes, her dark eyes seemingly looking deep into his soul. "Good night, Levi," Nefertiti says, kissing Sterling on the cheek.

"Good night, Nefertiti."

Without warning, Nefertiti's lips passionately lock on his. Sterling feels the warmth of her kiss move from his lips to his neck, his chest, and expanding throughout his body like warm, sweet, cocoa on a cold night. He is a little stunned by her actions, but he'd be lying if he said it isn't a pleasant surprise. As quickly as she began, it ends.

"Good night," She says once again, as she disappears into the darkness of her now open front door. The door shuts and Sterling stands there for a moment relishing in the aftermath of her kiss and slowly turns to go home. When he hits the road, he feels like a teenager with a crush. His insides become electrified, he jumps up clicking his heels together, and if he didn't know any better, he would swear he skipped back to his house.

Chapter 11

The Boy Scout Camp

Vrrrr, vrrrr, the phone vibrates against the wood of the nightstand loud enough to wake Captain Dixon. Glaring at it for a moment, he falls back on his pillow. "I need a new profession," he moans. He figures most people in any public service job—police, firefighters, doctors, you name it—wish the same thing from time to time. "Shit!" he gripes under his breath, sitting upright, scratching his head with aggravation.

With a twist of his wrist, he sees what time it is and appreciates the watch for a moment as he always does. The wristwatch is a Rolex made during World War I. It was left to him by his grandfather, who was given the watch by a man whose life he saved during that war. He had been one of the few who served in a combat unit, back when most African Americans were limited to labor battalions—his grandfather was one of the lucky ones. The man he saved was a white man, Sargent Jason Singer. He pushed the man out of the way during an ambush and took a bullet in the leg for his trouble. Because of his actions, Sargent Singer gave him the watch and his lifelong friendship. Grandad always said his friendship meant more than the watch. The watch has a dark leather band the color of rich walnut and a large circular case onto which wire lugs were soldered so a strap could be attached. The hands of the watch tell him it's barely 4 a.m.

"Son of a bitch! You've got to be kidding me," he mutters in a gruff whisper as he gets quietly out of bed, so as not to wake Maggie, his wife. She looks so peaceful with the moonlight radiating on her caramel skin. *God how I love you*, he admits inwardly, while lightly kissing her forehead. He tiptoes to the door and once outside the bedroom, he answers the still vibrating phone.

"This had better be good."

"Captain Dixon, sir, I'm sorry to wake you, but we have another one." The all too familiar voice of Hamilton states. He'd recognize Hamilton's voice in a crowd. It's raspy and rough—reminding him of Max Martini.

"Dammit," he swears, passing his hand crudely over his face. With a long sigh, he asks, "have you been out to the scene yet?"

"Anderson and I are on our way now."

"Where was this victim found?"

"This one is out at the Boy Scout camp there on Rifle River. Dispatch said some kids found her on the river bank. As you can imagine, Cap, the boys who found the body are not in the best mental condition."

"Shit!" he spouts, making his way down the dark hallway illuminated by only a night light Maggie bought. It isn't very bright but helps him make it down the hall without destroying a toe on the table or knocking things to the floor. "If this victim has the same MO," he continues, "Yeah, I can imagine the state of those boys. The only positive I see is that you're good with kids. So get out there, check things out, and get those boys' statements."

"Will do, Cap."

"Call me as soon as you get confirmation if there are signs of the same MO." He pauses, thinking longer than he should have whether he wants to involve Sterling yet. Finally, he says, "Listen, Hamilton; don't call Sterling until you're sure this case relates to the others but call me first."

"But, Cap."

"Don't argue, just discover if the MO's are the same first."

"Will do," Hamilton replies, not liking keeping this from Sterling one bit.

Dixon slams his cell down a little harder than he intends and *fuck* comes spilling from his mouth much louder than he anticipates.

"Roy, honey, is everything all right?" Maggie appears in her white robe, hair ruffled with pillow head, wiping the sleep from her weary eyes.

"Oh, baby, I'm sorry. I didn't mean to wake you."

In her house slippers with a drowsy smile on her face, she shuffles over to him and wraps her arms around his waist. "You're a cop, Roy, a captain. If I had a problem with being woken up all hours of the night, I wouldn't have married you."

"You're an understanding woman, my dear," he chuckles as he kisses her on the check. "I love you."

"I know," she says playfully. "I'll make some coffee." She stops in the doorway, "Is it another girl?"

"Yeah, honey, it is."

Maggie's head drops, shaking from side to side. "Those poor babies," she mumbles as she disappears behind the wall.

Hamilton and Anderson pull into the dirt circle drop-off of the Boy Scout base. The camp's Scout manager, Paul Spencer, is pacing back and forth in the entrance impatiently. He's a short man, decently built, in his early forties. He's wearing khaki pants, a short-sleeve tan shirt with numerous patches on each side; an olive green baseball hat with the Boy Scouts of America logo embroidered on its front, and an olive green tie hangs from his neck. Hamilton notices that the boys, the ones he presumes found their victim are inside the main office building sitting with parents, faces riddled with stress.

"Officer Hamilton, I'm glad they sent you. Not that anyone needs to see... I mean," Paul takes off his cap, grabbing the hanky out of his pocket to wipe his brow and bald head that are both noticeably speckled with sweat. "What I mean is, you work well with the boys. They all know you."

"Paul, it's all right. Man, are you ok?"

Paul bends over slightly, hands on his knees. He takes a few long breaths then straightens and looks Hamilton right in the eye. "Yeah, I'll be alright. It's just a shock. I mean nothing like this has ever happened here; the boys are in a state as you can imagine. A couple of them have been in the restroom since they found her."

"So, our vic is a female."

"Yeah, at least, that's what the boys say. They hauled ass out of those woods, screaming to high heaven, white as ghosts. Scared the living bejesus out of me, I don't mind tellin' ya."

"I bet."

Paul's color is off. His face has a red hue to it. After what he has been through, who wouldn't be a little off kilter? "Are you sure you're good?"

"Yeah, just give me a minute to get my thoughts together. Damn shock is all."

"Sure, sure, take your time."

Paul stands in the same spot for a few minutes, trying to wrap his head around what's transpired. It isn't easy for a cop to see or hear about these things; Hamilton can imagine what poor Paul is bearing. "Ok, I'm sorry about that. All of this just got my blood pressure up."

"No need to apologize, I understand."

"Yeah, you would, wouldn't ya. I don't know how you boys do this every day. I'd be in the crazy house—surprised I'm not there now."

"It's not something you ever get used to, that's for sure." Hamilton senses Paul's anxiety hang in the air like a thick, wet wool blanket. He's unsettled and who could blame him.

"Paul, can you answer a few questions for me?"

"Yeah, I can do that."

"How long ago did the boys come out of the woods?"

"Just before I called you, about twenty minutes ago."

"What were the boys doing out in those woods at this hour?"

"We have Troop 193. The troop's leader is Mitch Parkinson. You know him, the dark-haired man, used to be a Marine."

"Yeah, I remember him," Hamilton replies.

"Well, he's the father of one of the boys, and a camp counselor. His troop is camping down-river at a campsite on the south end. Some of the boys got up early hoping to see a deer or other animals. They're trying to meet all the qualifications to receive the Nature Merit Badge."

"Yeah, I remember those days. I took forever earning that badge," Hamilton guffaws, remembering his childhood days spent at this very base.

"Then you realize how determined these boys can get."

"That I do."

"The boys weren't doing any harm, they were just trying to identify three wild mammals in the field. You remember, don't cha?"

"Yeah, I do. It's a shame what those boys discovered wasn't more pleasant. I want to talk to the kids before you take me down to the body."

"Sure, come with me. Try to remember these boys have had a fright. They're rather shaken up."

"Don't worry, Paul, we'll use a gentle hand." Hamilton calls over to Anderson, "Hey, come on. Let's talk with these boys."

For five boys to discover a body of a young girl on the bank of the river was more than they bargained for. Inside the main office cabin, an old desk sits near the east wall. In the corner, a Smokey the Bear statue, larger and taller than Hamilton, with his telltale yellow hat holding a shovel, and a sign that reads, "Only you can prevent forest fires," sits with an eternal blank stare. Two dark-haired boys sit next to each other, their wide eyes staring blankly, obviously in shock.

He sees it's useless to talk to them. He has Anderson call an ambulance. The two are in such rough shape, a doctor should examine them. The other three, though shaken up, can tell him exactly what took place down to the last detail.

The talkative twelve-year-old with golden blonde hair and fair skin, Robbie Freeman, has a black eye.

"How did you get the shiner, Robbie?"

"Ah, it's nothin'; Pete and I were screwin' off and not payin' attention on the trail. There was a branch hangin' in the way, and he grabbed it to go through, but let it go before I passed and it snapped back and caught me in the eye."

"It looks pretty bad."

"Naw, it'll be ok. My ma's none too happy about it though."

Hamilton snickers while the boy's mom gives him a disapproving look and Hamilton squashes his humor.

"Robbie's a good boy," she snaps. "But he gets into trouble more often than not."

She doesn't need to tell him that Robbie's good; he can see that for himself. Robbie's always been helpful, a ball of energy this one is. Trouble has a way of sniffing out the good ones, at least from Hamilton's experience. It's too bad too; the boy has a heart of gold, he just makes the wrong choices. He hopes the boy grows out of it and will learn to stay away from the bad elements in this small town.

"Robbie, can you tell me everything that happened this morning?"

"We set my watch alarm—the watch my dad got me for Christmas, see?" He puts out his arm to show Hamilton a Jacques Farel quartz wristwatch with a black leather band, a cartoon shark on the face with dark blue numbers.

"Very nice."

"Yeah, it's waterproof and everything. Anyway, I set it so we could get up early enough and hopefully see some wildlife. We are all trying to get our Nature badges. I have thirty-two, and the Nature badge will make thirty-three."

"Thirty-two! That's amazing, Robbie. I only earned thirty in my whole time with the Scouts." Hamilton knew putting the boy at ease will make the conversation easier. He was in the Scouts as a boy so he can relate to Robbie's determination to get the nature badge, it's not an easy one to earn.

"You were a Scout too, Officer Hamilton?"

"Sure was, came to this same camp when I was your age."

"Wow, so we're Scout brothers."

"We sure are," he smiled, putting three fingers up with his pinky and thumb touching. "So, Robbie, it's important that you tell me to the best of your memory everything that happened after you boys got up and went looking for the animals."

"Well, we went down the trail to the river. We thought we might get a glimpse of a deer or two or maybe a black bear. John, he was out front, turned to tell me something and tripped. He fell hard and sprained his ankle. When we went to help him up, we all saw wh-what he'd tripped on..." The boy is doing his best, but tears spew from his big, green eyes and trickle down his cheek. He wipes them away forcefully, angry at himself for allowing it to happen.

"It's alright, Robbie. No one will judge you. Please tell me the rest. You're doing great."

"Ok," he sniffs and continues, "Th—there's a girl, a dead girl, laying right on the riverbank!" His voice reduces to a whisper as he leans in closer to Hamilton, "and she didn't have any clothes on." His face turns beet red with the words, and he can't look directly at Hamilton when saying them. "I ain't ever seen nothing' like that before. S-someone cut her full open."

That's it. Robbie has been strong enough for one night. He breaks down into full-blown tears. He buries his head in Hamilton's shoulder, sobbing, "It was awful, Officer Hamilton, just awful. I never want to see it again."

Wrapping his arm around Robbie, he pats his back, "I know it was. You have been such a big help, thank you, Robbie."

Hamilton eyes Paul as he comes over. "Hey, Robbie, why don't you and your mom go with Mitch here; he will take your information down in case we need to speak with you again."

"Ok."

Paul leads them into his office off the main entranceway where Officer Mitch Brady is waiting. He had shown up not long after Anderson made the call for backup.

"Thanks for getting here so quick," Hamilton says.

"No problem. I'll take care of them," he replies nodding his head toward Robbie and his mom.

"I know." Hamilton walks out behind them to see the two other boys sitting with their parents.

"Do either of you have anything to add to your statements?" he asks, squatting down, sitting on his hunches, so he's eye to eye with the boys.

"I do," Pete says.

Its Pete Ostrander's first year in the Boy Scouts. He and his mom moved to this area a little over two years ago. He's a taciturn boy with few friends; most are boys from his troop. "Ok, Pete, what do you have to tell me."

"After John fell, and we saw that girl, we ran. We had flashlights because of it still being dark. I pointed my flashlight at the ground, so I didn't trip—my dad taught me that when he was still here." He turned his head glancing at his mom. Her eyes are watery as she touches his shoulder, showing her support. "Andy was running in front of me, but he stopped cuz he got sick—that's when I saw it."

"Saw what, Pete?"

"I saw a track. It was a cat print, a big cat too."

"A cat print, are you sure?"

"You better believe him," Paul interjects walking back into the main room. "This kid knows his tracks. He earned his Tracking Merit Badge within two weeks of joining. He can tell you what animal left what footprint in the aftermath of a stampede. The boy is good," Paul explains. "He's even better at tracking than I am."

114

"No kidding, huh? That's amazing, Pete. Can show me where that track was?"

"Sure I ca—"

"No! You can't mean to take him back out to that—that place!" Pete's mom protests.

"Mrs.—"

"It's Miss. Pete's dad died five years ago. And my name is Jenny."

"Jenny, I'm not taking Pete out to the place where they found the girl, only to where he saw the track. Paul will be with us and so will Officer Anderson. Paul, here, will bring him back to you as soon as he takes us to the paw print."

After a few moments of prodding and Paul promising he will bring Pete right back, Jenny gives her permission, allowing Pete to go. Hamilton can't criticize her for being so cautious; her son has just witnessed a girl found torn apart.

The men follow Pete, stopping at the paved road; he looks both ways before crossing. He takes them down the densely wooded trail. Tree branches grab at their uniforms and roots seemingly spawn from the ground out of nowhere, trying to catch their feet. It is tricky getting through the bush, for the men anyway. Pete, on the other hand, has no problem. He guides them straight to where he saw the print without missing a step. He is good—excellent, actually—at tracking and it impresses Hamilton.

When they reach the area, Pete's face lights up like the 4th of July and yells, "Here it is." He's careful not to get too close to the print, which surprises Hamilton again. *This boy is something. Is there a class of prodigy for tracking?* he contemplates, staring down at a perfectly preserved track, a big one at that.

"Thank you, Pete," he tells the boy who beams with a smile bright enough to light up Texas. "Now, you better go back with Paul, so your mother doesn't worry."

"Aw, do I have ta?"

"Yes, your mother will have me and Paul skinned alive if we don't get you back straight away."

"Ok," Pete says, kicking at the ground. However, the boy turns around and takes Paul's hand with no more fuss.

"Yeah," he stops and turns to Hamilton.

"If I am not mistaken, I believe you and Robbie have earned the Nature Merit Badge." Looking up at Paul, he winks.

"Really!" his excitement now through the roof.

"Yes, I believe Officer Hamilton's correct," Paul tells him. "I will talk to your troop leader when we get back, and Officer Hamilton can sign off on them when he's finished."

"Sure will."

"Wow, this is awesome!" Pete shouts, gleefully. "I can't wait to tell Robbie," He says, pulling on Paul's hand to race back to the office.

"Good kid," Hamilton comments to Anderson, who's examining the track.

With a splinter of a pick in his mouth, he murmurs, "Huh?"

"Pete, the boy, he's a good kid."

"Oh, yeah, he's an incredible tracker, too," he says, putting the fragment of wood in his pocket and pulling out another toothpick to replace it. "Hey, come here and look at this." His eyes bright with contemplation, his brow forming ruts as he shines the light towards the track.

Hamilton walks over, looking carefully at the print. He sees a few white hairs stuck in the dirt next to the track. "So the cat left us a print and some hair I see."

"It's the track of a panther."

"How do you know that?"

"Zoology is a hobby of mine."

"Impressive."

"No big deal." Anderson shrugs. "But the print isn't what I wanted you to see." he says, moving the light a little to the right and Hamilton following it with his eyes, "That is."

"I'll be damned, is that blood?" Hamilton says, leaning close to the substance.

"It looks like it."

"Let's mark it and get this area taped off. I'll go down, look at the body and inspect the area. Do you have this?"

"Yeah, I'll call the M.E. and get some backup out here. I'll wait here until they arrive."

"Thanks. Alert me when some help gets here."

Hamilton makes his way further down the trail. During this time of the year, the foliage is thick, but the damned mosquitoes are the most prominent obstacle at the moment, it like trying to break through a spider web made of the flying bastards. He doesn't have far to go; the print is only about 500 feet from the riverbank. It's an easy little jaunt if he wasn't being eaten alive by the damned bugs before he makes it back to the base.

He smells her before he sees her. "Goddamn," he grunts, putting his hand to his nose. "I'll never get used to that smell." Hamilton kneels down beside a redheaded, waterlogged body. He reaches over and moves her hair to view her face. "Jesus Christ!" He yelps.

A fleshless face stars back with dead obscured eyes. A milky white film conceals what he's sure was once brilliant green. From her look, clothes, and size, she can't be over twelve or fourteen. "I am so sorry, little one. Violent acts like this should never happen to any of you." Something tore her chest opened, and her innards are missing, just like the other girls. "Damn it! We have to stop this sick son of a bitch."

He has no doubt a human is committing these murders as he carefully inspects the body. *This isn't the work of an animal; it can't be*, he surmises. Why the skin on her face is missing isn't something he wants to know. The cuts made on the body are precise. *There's no way a cat, or any other animal for that matter, could do this.* Yanking the cell from his pocket, he dials Cap's number. The phone only rings once before he hears Dixon saying, *Hello.*

"Hey, Cap, it's unquestionably connected to the others. The difference

I can see off the top is this girl has been here a few days; there's no way this is recent." Hamilton gets a closer look as he talks. "From the looks of her, she's been in the water for a while. She most likely just washed up here. There's no evidence around the body I can see, but there's a large cat print about 500 feet up the path with some hair and what looks like blood."

"Shit! Ok, call the M.E. and get Sterling out there. I sure hope we catch this lunatic soon."

"Already had Anderson call Sam, she should be on the way. I'll give Sterling a call as soon as we hang up. This guy is seriously sick, Cap."

"Yeah, he is. So until we catch up with him, let's be thorough. Scan that area and make sure we don't miss a crumb."

"I'm on it, Cap," he confirms, hitting the end call button. It only takes him a second to search Sterling's number, when Anderson appears.

"Hey, Hamilton," Anderson hollers, covering his nose and mouth with the sleeve of his blue uniform jacket. "Christ, I don't think I'll ever get used to that smell."

"Let's hope not. What did you need?"

His eyes fall on the body. "For the love of—" he bawls jumping back.

"Yeah, it's a bad one," Hamilton states.

"Bad my ass, what the hell happened to her face?"

"The perp skinned her."

"What the hell for?! Jesus Christ, that's some sick shit!"

"Don't I know it," Hamilton agrees. Anderson stands stiff as a board, wide-eyed with a mixture of revulsion and amazement encumbering his face. Hamilton asks, "Was there something you wanted to tell me?"

"Yeah," he says, his eyes unwavering, viewing the body as if it were something from outer space. "I called Sam. She said she'd be out ASAP. Backup is on the way. I'm going back to finish setting up the perimeter. Do you need anything else?"

"Just to nail this son of a bitch."

"I hear ya," Anderson utters, shaking his head in disgust.

Chapter 12

The Missing

At 2 a.m. Sterling crawled out of bed, he hasn't had a good night's sleep in years—not since Matt Belmont. Sitting at the kitchen table, he's reading Christopher Pike's *The Last Vampire,* a book he has meant to read for quite some time. He's on chapter six where Alisa Perne, a blonde-haired, blue-eyed vampire, has six guns on her, and she is finally meeting the mysterious Mr. Slim.

Sterling reads, setting the hand holding the book against the table, rubbing his eyes with the other. The fatigue from lack of decent sleep is getting to him; it leads to the lack of control he has over his life. Reading on, Alisa puts on the handcuffs and goes with Mr. Slim. He must admit he is enjoying reading again, getting lost in a dramatic compilation of words fashioned together in such a way to take him out of the abundant troubles of reality for a while. He admires those with any creative talent, for he has none.

The rhythmic hum of his cell vibrating against the table forcibly pulls his nose out of the book.

"Sterling here," he says, more exhausted than he's been in ages. *Man, this case is getting to me,* he thinks, picking up the bookmark, placing it between pages 96 and 97, and sitting the book face up on the oak tabletop. A man with an unnerved expression riddling his face, and an attractive blonde standing behind him in what looks to be a cave of some sort, gleams back at him.

"Sterling, hey listen, I didn't want to call..."

"You've found another one."

"Shit, Sterling, I'm sorry, but yes, we did."

"Where?" he automatically responds, too tired to get all riled up about this shit today.

"Boy Scout Camp off Greenwood."

"Give me fifteen." Glancing at his watch, the fluorescent green 5:15 glows back at him. "Well, let's see what this bitch has left me this time," he mutters as he grabs the cover to his coffee mug, slapping it on as he crosses the kitchen to the living room and opens the front door. Startling a possum and her cubs, he watches them scurry across the yard.

"I apologize, ma'am," he chuckles. The morning air is cool and crisp, giving him some much-needed revival with each breath. "At least the weather will be nice today if nothing else," he says, walking out to the car. Something rustling in the bushes seizes his attention. It's too big to be the possum he saw. Whatever's out there is also much larger than a coon, cat, or some other little critter. The bushes rustle again. Whatever is in there is large—too big for Sterling's liking.

"Who's there?" He questions as a sudden chill ravishes his body. "Son of a Bit—"

"Hamilton," Anderson bellows, trekking down the trail to the river.

"Yeah."

"I have everything taped off. Did ya call Cap?"

"I called."

"So, is Sterling on his way?" Anderson asks.

"He is. I called him about ten minutes ago. He should pull up anytime. Hey, come here and look at this."

"Ya got something?" Anderson strolls over and squats down next to him. "What is that?"

"We may have our first piece of real evidence. This," Hamilton says, holding up a soggy fragment of material. "This, my friend, is a piece of silk. The branches ripped it off whoever was wearing it. Hopefully, it came from our killer."

"Silk? Shit, so you're telling me we have a well-dressed murderer?" Anderson spouts in disbelief.

"Maybe."

"Interesting."

"Do you have an evidence bag?"

"Sure do. Here," Anderson says, pulling out a wad of clear plastic bags rolled up neatly in his pocket.

"You have enough of those?"

"You can never be too prepared," Anderson tells him, handing over an evidence bag. Placing the fragment of material in the bag and sealing it, Hamilton inspects the item a few minutes longer with a questioning expression on his face. "What are you thinking?" Anderson finally asks.

"Kyle, how many men do you know around here who wear silk shirts?"

For a second he scratches his head considering the point Hamilton makes. "None, now that you mention it. Why?"

"I don't think we're looking for a man."

"Come on, Hamilton; you don't believe a woman could do what someone did to these girls, do you?"

"I wouldn't have an hour ago but come with me; I want to show you something else." He leads Anderson off the path in the woods a little way. A large oak with some of its leaves turning color occupies the small clearing as if nature has given it a space to call its own. "Look at this." Hamilton points down at the ground. There, lying in the dry leaves is a woman's shoe—one of those slip-on canvas kinds you can buy anywhere.

"I'll be damned. But you know as well as I do that could be from one of the Girl Scout bases; they camp up here too."

"Maybe, but I'm not taking anything on chance. A piece of silk and now a woman's shoe? If they're not connected, it's a hell of a coincidence, don't ya think?"

Anderson can't argue his conclusion. Yes, this all could be a coincidence, but cases don't get solved if every angle isn't exhausted. He shrugs his shoulder, "You have a point."

"Get a few pictures and let's bag it."

He takes a couple pictures. Hamilton bags the shoe, marks the spot they found it with a yellow marker and the two walk back to the trail.

Anderson is overly quiet and twitchy, so Hamilton asks, "What's up?"

"Huh, oh, I'm just trying to wrap my head around this killer being a female. I know there have been female serial killers throughout the ages, but I don't recall any conducting such depraved acts, do you?"

"Delphine La Laurie did despicable things to her slaves in the 1800s. It's said, she sewed her victim's lips shut, forced men to have a sex change, bodies of women were found without skin, and officers discovered in her home's attic, body parts strewn over the floor. Belle Gunness killed and dismembered her victims, Delfina and Maria De Jesus Gonzales dismembered and buried their victims, and one of the people who come to mind with this case is, Enriqueta Marti. From what I've read, she was a real psycho. They called her Enriqueta 'The Vampire of Barcelona' Marti."

"How do you and, more importantly, why would you ever *want* to know all this shit? Do you harbor a weird fascination for female killers or something?"

"Not quite a fascination, let's call it a hobby."

"That's creepy, don't ya think?" Anderson scoffs but has to admit he's curious about this Vampire thing. "Why did they call Enriqueta *The Vampire of Barcelona*? What did she do?"

"Enriqueta had a special kind of sickness. She butchered children to make potions, which she then sold to people. Two young girls escaped and when the police searched Marti's place, they found children's body parts, blood, and fat she kept in a jar. They also found her *recipe* book."

"Damn, that's some sick shit, Hamilton. Seriously, they actually found that stuff?"

"Oh, yeah, it's the truth, and sick doesn't even touch what she did to those kids. But, if you think about it, it's not any more demented than what we're dealing with now."

"No, I guess not," Anderson says, turning just in time to run smack dab into Samantha, knocking her off her feet. "Oh, Sam. I'm so sorry," he apologizes, offering his hand to help her up from the ground.

"I think my ass will mend." She takes his hand, pulling herself up. "So," she says, brushing herself off, "where's the body?"

"Follow me," Hamilton tells her. They walk back down the path to the riverbank. "Hey, you didn't see Sterling, did you?"

"Sterling? I thought he was *ordered* to stay away from the case until tomorrow."

"Well, he was, until we found our newest vic which has the same MO." Hamilton points to where the body lays. His face flushes with concern glancing at his watch.

"Is everything alright?"

"I'm not sure. I called Sterling twenty-five minutes ago, and he told me he'd be here in fifteen."

"Maybe he got held up."

"Yeah, perhaps. But Sterling usually calls if he's delayed." He digs in his pocket retrieving his cell.

"Are you calling him?"

"I am. I have a bad feeling that something isn't right."

"You're right; it doesn't sound like Sterling at all." She replies, observing the scene. "So, tell me what you've found here so far." He hands Sam the evidence they'd collected as he hits redial. Inspecting the bag, she asks, "Where was this found? It looks like silk. Silk from a woman's shirt, maybe."

"Yeah, that's what we conclude, it's a little bizarre, don't cha think?"

"It is."

"It was in the mud next to the body, and the shoe wasn't far off the trail—a woman's shoe. We marked where we found it and took... just a minute, Sam." Hamilton speaks to the receiving end of his cell. "Hey,

Sterling, it's Hamilton. We're getting a little worried out here. Where are you? Call me when you get this, ok." Hamilton's face falls, pained with worry.

"No answer?"

"No. I don't mind telling you I am bothered by this."

"Don't worry," she says, trying not to get herself in a twist. "This is Sterling we're talking about here. He's probably pulling up right now."

"Yeah, you're right," he replies unconvinced.

"So what were you saying about the shoe?"

"Yeah, right, we took pictures of everything we found. I can take you back to where we found it if you'd like?"

"Maybe in a few," she replies, preoccupied with the body sprawled out on the ground in front of her. "Wow, this asshole did a number on this girl, didn't he?"

"Yeah, it's not pretty that's for sure."

"She's been out here for a few days judging by the amount of decomp and bloating."

Hamilton's cell rings, "It's Cap. Just a minute, Sam, ok?"

"Of course."

"Hi, Cap." He answers, pacing back and forth.

"Is Sterling there yet?"

"No. I called, and he said he'd be here in fifteen, but it's been well over twenty-five. I called him again but only got his voicemail. Sam's here, though."

"His voice mail, that doesn't sound like Sterling."

"I know. I have no idea where he is, Cap."

The line's silent for a minute. While Dixon doesn't want to cause a panic, he knows he needs to be straightforward with Hamilton and replies, "Listen, we both know it's not like Sterling to ignore a phone call. Give him another five to ten minutes, at the most. If he doesn't show up by then, I want you to drive to his house and see if he's still there. Keep it quiet; don't make a big exhibition of it. When you find out what's going on with him, you call me immediately."

"Ok, Cap... uh, Cap, what if something..."

"Not now, Hamilton, we can't afford that line of thinking. Let's see if he's home? If he's not there, then we will figure out what to do next."

"I understand," Hamilton utters, hearing the line disconnect. "Shit!"

"Everything alright, Hamilton?" Sam asks.

Hiding the fact he is unnerved and surprised, he responds, "Yeah, no worries," he replies with a feeble grin on his face. He places his hands on his hip and stands there for a second or two. Then abruptly he asks, "Hey, do you need me for anything else?"

"No, I need to get this body processed," Sam answers and begins to applying menthol paste under her nose and pulling on latex gloves. She holds out the small container with the menthol paste, "You want some?"

"No, thank you. I'm good. Listen, I have something I have to do. Can you tell Anderson to stay here with you? I'll be back in a few."

"Yeah, sure. What's up?"

"Just a few things I need to check on. Be back in a bit." He disappears down the path, leaving Sam to her work.

In the parking lot, Hamilton notices a few more squad cars. Backup has arrived. Officer Raymond Martinez is standing, talking with Paul. Martinez has been on the force for two years. In high school, he was the football quarterback that all the girls swooned over. However, he's down to earth and though he was one hell of a quarterback, he always wanted to be a cop.

His father was a police officer in Flint for twenty years but was killed in the line of duty when Martinez was five years old. After his father's death, he and his mother moved to Skidway Lake. He was a good kid and a better adult. It's safe to say, Hamilton likes the man.

"Martinez," He calls over to him.

Martinez gets closer so no one else can hear and replies, "Hey, this is getting ridiculous, isn't it?"

"Without a doubt. Listen, I have to check on something. Anderson is down with the M.E.. Can you look after things up here until I get back?"

"Sure. What do you need the guys to do?"

"Containment is the most important thing right now. I don't want anyone going down that path across the road." Hamilton points to the opening of the path. "Station men there and make sure no one gets by them—especially the damned media—"

Martinez's eyes widen, "Well, speak of the Devil."

Hamilton twists around to see what Martinez is talking about and sees a white news van headed in their direction. Martinez slaps him on the back, "I have this."

"Thanks, Martinez," Hamilton yells after him, collecting a couple of men closest to the mouth of the path.

With things under control at the crime scene, Hamilton gets into his squad car, pulls to the main road, making a right and heads for Sterling's. *God, just let him be all right,* Hamilton thinks, traveling down Greenwood Road. He doesn't flip on his emergency lights until he's clear of the Boy Scout camp, then flicks the switch and pushes the gas pedal to the floor, hauling ass.

He hit Sterling's road in nine minutes flat, "Not bad, not bad at all," he praises himself, applying the brakes. One doesn't want to enter Sterling's road at a speed over forty miles an hour—it isn't a good idea. Baker Drive is not much wider than a two-track; a private road, which means those living on the road take care of it, not the city.

Sterling has done a decent job of keeping the road up, but there are still some sizable pits in it. You hit one of those damned things too hard, you and your car will be halfway up a tree. Hamilton just got a new squad car and plans to keep it in the condition it is in for as long as he can.

"You better be home," Hamilton tensely drones as Sterling's house comes into view. The lights are on which causes suspicion. *If the light is on, he's home, so why wouldn't he answer his phone?* His internal dialog is cut short pulling into the driveway as anxiety ripples through his nerves. The front door is wide open. Hamilton throws the car into park and turns off the ignition. The atmosphere is foreboding as he exits the vehicle. An unsettling silence screams its warning. He undoes the snap on his holster and draws his gun. There is no sign of Sterling.

"Sterling," he calls, but there's no response. Reaching the door, he calls again, "Hey, Sterling." No answer. "Son of a bitch," he curses to himself, his anxiety edging its way to fear.

Leaning against the door frame, gripping the gun tight, he takes a deep breath and quickly glances inside. Seeing nothing, he takes another moment to steady his nerves, and then enters the home. Following his gun, held firmly in front of him, he slowly clears each room—there's not a soul. Inspecting the rooms, no signs of a struggle are apparent, which isn't helping his current predicament. "Shit, Sterling, where the hell are you?!"

With no sign of Sterling inside the house, he deliberately makes his way outside. *He has to be here somewhere*; he thinks. *Just let him be alive.* The sun is peeking through the trees making the lower portion of the woods seem much darker than they should be. Taking out his flashlight, he places it next to the gun in his grip in such a way they are one.

One foot in front of the other, cautiously, he scans the ground in front of him with the light looking for any trace of Sterling. A glint of light bounces off an object to his right; it's Sterling's phone lying on the ground. "H-o-o-o-ly fuc—!" He steps over to the phone, picking it up. "Sterling?!" he hollers, scanning the woods the flashlight but sees nothing. "Dammit, Sterling where the fuck are you?!" Cautiously, fully alert, he proceeds toward the backyard.

"Sterling, you back here?" he calls. Panic surges through him, tightening his chest. "Le—" he calls once more. "Shit!" He sees Sterling lying on the ground, towards the woods that line the backyard. Running over, praying he isn't dead, a thousand scenarios race through his thoughts in a single minute. Maybe he fell or tripped and knocked himself out.

He realizes that's not the case reaching Sterling. Blood drenches his shirt, four gouges stretch across his chest. "Sterling! Jesus Christ." Scanning the woods and the surrounding area wildly—making sure nothing comes raging at him like a rabid wolf—he kneels down, dialing 911 on Sterling's phone as he does.

He takes Sterling's wrist, checking for a pulse. At first, he can't feel one. *Breathe and take your time, Hamilton,* he tells himself and puts two fingers to his neck, checking again. "There!" He yells aloud. "There it is. Come on, Levi, don't you fuckin' die on me." Taking off his shirt, he folds it up, using it as a pad and applies pressure. "Sterling," he says, shaking him some. "Sterling, you hang in there, buddy. Damn it, talk to me!"

"911 operator. What's your emergency?" comes blasting through over the line.

"This is Officer James Hamilton. I have a man down at 4385 Baker Drive. I need medical personnel ASAP!"

A moment of silence is like a lifetime. His grip tightens on the cell to the point his knuckles turn white. The feminine voice breaks on the line, "They're on their way, Officer Hamilton. Can you—"

Hamilton drops the phone on the ground, feeling for Sterling's pulse once more. It's weak but steady, at least he has one. Letting out a sigh of momentary relief, he whispers, "Sterling, listen, I'm here, so you fight. You stay with me, you hear me!"

Still applying pressure, he scrutinizes the area to see if there's any clue to explain what the hell happened here. The light of the morning sun rising over the dense trees creates shadows that sway in the breeze, rustling the leaves and making them chase one another in a playful dance.

The birds sing, chirping in the trees next to them, two squirrels chase one another, and a small, gray rabbit sits at the edge of the wood grazing voraciously on the leafy vegetation. It's as if the world came to life, and he wasn't paying attention, but nothing jumps out at him saying, *hey, look what Sterling's attacker left behind!*

"We'll get you, you bastard. I know you did this," he mumbles, still inspecting the ground. His friend's blood on his hands, he's convinced this is the work of their killer or has something to do with the case. He has that sixth sense, he believes most cops who have spent time on the force do, making his bones ache.

With his nerves wound up tighter than Mary Jane's jeans on a Saturday night, time drags, minutes seem like hours, and though he knows it hasn't been as long as it feels like, his patience wears thin. "Come on, where in the hell is that ambulance!"

"You just called them," a weak, barely audible voice says. "For the love of God, man, give them some time."

Shock, relief, and joy all rolled up in one massive tidal wave of emotion, flushes over Hamilton. "You son of a bitch, Levi! You scared the shit out of me. I thought you would die right here in my arms."

"Not today. I'm too damned stubborn for that," Sterling tells him through a choked cough. "Help me sit up, would ya."

"Maybe that's not such a—"

"Ah hell, come on, Hamilton, give me a hand," he grumbles in a low, hoarse voice.

"Yeah, ok." He carefully lifts Sterling to a sitting position. "What in the hell happened here?"

The sirens of the ambulance blare in the distance

"It won't be long now," Hamilton announces.

"Good, I hope they get here soon. I have one hell of a headache," Sterling says, feeling the back of his head where it's warm and wet. Pulling a blood coated hand back, disbelief manifest in his eyes. "I must have smacked my head on a rock or something."

"Let me have a look." Hamilton pulls a penlight from his pocket. Although the sun has risen some, it's still not high enough to cut through the darkness engulfing the woods. Long, black shadows fall across the property, helping the darkness to flourish instead of fade. "These damned woods are dark," he states the obvious, examining the back of Sterling's head. An inch to an inch and a half long gash streaks his hair with dark crimson fluid. "Son of a bitch!" he hisses. "This is a doozy of a laceration you've got back here."

"It'll be alright. You are always telling me how hard-headed I am." Sterling jokes, but Hamilton isn't laughing.

"You realize I will get my ass chewed by Dixon for moving you with a head injury."

"Don't worry so much. I got your back."

"That won't matter, and you know it."

"Yeah, well, I am fine. So, no harm, no foul." Looking at his bloodied hand, he asks, "How bad is it?"

"I'm no doctor but, I'd say you'll need stitches back here."

"Fuckin' fantastic."

"Hey, from what I can see, you're damn lucky to be alive."

"I don't feel lucky. Every inch of me aches."

Hamilton's phone booms; *I shot the Sheriff* blares from it. "Looks like Cap was listening to his radio. I better get this."

"*I shot the Sheriff*, really?" Sterling says, his words dripping with sarcasm. Hamilton doesn't dignify his shrewd comment with a verbal response. He flips up his middle finger with a devilish smirk, which makes Sterling laugh out loud, thereby sending a piercing pain through his head, "Fuck."

"That will teach ya," he guffaws, watching Sterling cradle his head in his hands, though he doesn't mean a word. He's worried about Sterling and more than that, he's worried about who in the hell did this to him. Nothing in this world would give him more pleasure than tracking down this asshole and nailing his balls to the wall. *I shot the Sheriff*, shrieks vigorously over the sounds of nature and Sterling's face twists in pain once again. "Alright," he mutters, answering the phone. "Hey, Cap, I'm here with him. He's talking, but he needs to go to the hospital."

Sterling listens to the one-sided conversation with a reasonably good idea of the dialog on the other end.

"Judging by the siren, the ambulance is just turning onto his road. No, I haven't been here that long, Cap." Watching Hamilton's facial expressions, his eyes close, his finger pressed against his temple, and his eyebrows raise almost comically, confirms that Dixon isn't in a pleasant mood. "Of course. Yeah, sure will. As soon as I know, you'll know." He pushes "end call" and gripes, *'Shit,'* pushing his phone back in his pants pocket just as the ambulance enters the driveway.

"We're back here," He calls out.

Men in dark blue uniforms with a white stripe around their short-sleeved shirts and one running down the outside of their pants, come rushing to where Sterling and Hamilton are, carrying a stretcher. One is a tall, thin, blonde hair, blue-eyed fella in his early twenties. The other, a well-built man with short, dark hair and brown-eyed, in his late twenties to early thirties, Hamilton guesses. They don't hesitate, getting right to work on Sterling. The older of the two sets his bag next to him, opens it and takes out one of those blood pressure bands and stethoscope. Wrapping the cuff around Sterling's upper arm and securing, he squeezes the pump bulb as he places the end of the stethoscope on his chest, listening to his heart. When done, he lifts the makeshift shirt Hamilton formed into a pad to help stop the bleeding, since the blonde guy has already checked his head wound and has it almost wrapped.

"Are you the one who found him?" the older EMT asks.

"Yeah. He was laying here unconscious when I got here. He came to a little while after."

"Did you see what did this to him?" He asks. By this time he had removed the shirt Hamilton used to stop the bleeding and replaced it with a clean white pad, blood already appears on its surface. The blonde guy supports him while the other wraps the pad with gauze.

"No. Whatever did this was long gone by the time I got here."

Done with dressing his wounds, Hamilton steps back further out of their way as the men position themselves at Sterling's head and feet. The dark-haired man counts, "One, two, three," and on three, they lift him up and place him on the stretcher. "His wounds are deep," he tells Hamilton. "But he'll live. We'll get him to the hospital and let the doctor's work their magic."

Relief washes over him with the knowledge Sterling will make it through his ordeal. He's about to thank them when a very attractive woman comes running in from the front yard. "My God, what happened?"

"Who are you?" Hamilton asks, stopping her before she can reach Sterling.

"James, this is my new neighbor, Nefertiti," Sterling says, as the EMT's pull a sheet up to his chest and fastens straps around him.

"You must lay still, Detective Sterling," the man scolds.

"Ok, boss. Do as you will."

"He will be fine," Hamilton snorts. "Hi, I'm James. It's nice to meet you." Hamilton smiles, holding out his hand to Nefertiti. "As far as what happened, I still haven't gotten that out of him."

Nefertiti glances over at Sterling, a strange expression creases her face, which Hamilton chalks up to concern. She relaxes some seeing Sterling is in good hands and turns back to Hamilton.

"Hi, it's nice to meet you as well. Will you be going to the hospital with him?"

"Yes, ma'am."

"Can you take my number," Nefertiti has a card in her hand. "Call me when... well, after the doctor looks at him. I know it's a lot to ask but..."

"No. No, not at all. I will call you." He takes her card smiling, then stops her when she starts walking away. "Hey, lock your doors and stay inside tonight."

"Oh, thank you, I will." She walks over to Sterling, "Levi, you listen to these men. I'll be down to see you as soon as I can, ok."

"You don't need—"

"Hush now." Kissing his forehead, she smiles then turns and walks back the way she came. Hamilton watches her walk, her hips swaying from side to side, as she vanishes around the front of the house. Sterling notices the sly smirk on his face when he turns back around.

"What?"

"Wow, what an ass," Hamilton exclaims with the same shit-eating grin. "I might have to look into purchasing land here. I am enjoying the scenery."

"You don't have a chance. Not on your best day," he teases hoarsely, but the EMT hushes him as they lift him onto the stretcher and lock it in place. The men, with some effort, push the cot, its wheels sink into the black soil.

"I'll meet you at the hospital," Hamilton laughs. "You better do what these guys say, they work with needles."

Sterling only smirks, his eyes close, and he looks peaceful roughly rolling away. In record time, he's loaded into the back of the ambulance and on his way to the hospital.

Chapter 13

The Results

Hamilton, Captain Dixon, and Nefertiti, who James calls not long after they arrive at the hospital, sit in the waiting room with a couple other people. An old woman with thin, short, white hair sits quietly looking through a Reader's Digest magazine. Across the way, a man with his eyes closed and his head back against the pale, green wall supporting two painted scenery prints, holds his sleeping daughter. A rerun of *In the Heat of the Night* plays on the television hanging in the corner. An older man with thick, gray hair, a light blue shirt, dark blue tie, and a long, white coat enters the room.

"The Sterling party?" he says.

"Here." Dixon stands and then asks, "How is he, Doc?"

"He has deep lacerations on his chest and a concussion. It took twenty-one stitches to close the gash on his head. Whatever made the injuries to his chest, nicked two of his rib bones but did not break them." He informs them. "He'll have one hell of a headache, but he's lucky; things could have been much worse. More importantly, he will recover nicely."

"Can we see him?" Nefertiti asks.

"Not yet. We're taking x-rays to make sure we haven't overlooked anything. Also, a foreign object lodged in one of the lacerations. I have to go in and get it before we can finish stitching him up. He's being prepared for that as we speak."

"Foreign object?" Dixon asks.

"I can't be entirely sure what it is until I get in there. The one thing I know, it's not from Sterling."

"Will you send whatever you pull out to the department's lab for identification? It may help us catch who did this."

"Absolutely," he responds, then disappears out the door.

Everyone waits to hear how the surgery has gone. From what the doctor said, it's a minor thing, but any operation has its risk. For three hours they watch people come and go. The little old lady who sat reading had been waiting for news on her husband. He fell taking out the garbage. A doctor came in a little while after the update on Sterling and asked her to follow him. He told her on the way out not to worry; her husband would recover nicely. The man with the sleeping daughter has been waiting for news of his second child. "It's a boy," a female doctor lets him know. His daughter squeals with delight and asks, "Can I see my new baby brother?" The doctor laughs, "Of course you can," and takes them both down the hall.

A man and woman come in after the little girl practically runs the doctor over getting out the door. The woman's eyes are red, swollen, and full of tears. They overhear that the couple's son was in a car accident and is in critical condition. Although the doctor is whispering, they hear him say, "it will be touch and go, but know we're doing all we can."

Finally, the doctor who came in earlier appears. Hamilton, who'd been pacing back and forth for the last hour, sprints over to the physician.

"Doc," he says, shaking the man's hand. "How is he?"

"He will be just fine. He's a very fortunate man. The lacerations he received were deep, but he escaped with no damage to his lungs, bones, or any arteries—someone was watching over him. He does, however, have numerous stitches in his head and chest, and a slight concussion, as I mentioned before. He's resting peacefully now—at least, as peaceful as a man like Sterling can rest."

"Thank you, Doc. Did you identify the object lodged inside him?" Dixon asks flatly.

"It appears to be a piece of a nail or bone. We had it taken to the lab as you requested."

"That's odd," Dixon mutters, more to himself than to the doctor.

"It could be from the person who did this to him."

"We'll know soon enough," Dixon replies, his head already trying to work out how a fragment of bone got into his detective. "How long will he need to stay?"

"I'm recommending he stays at least a week—possibly two depending on how he heals up."

"Thanks again, Doc. I'm not sure what the department would do without him. He's a damn good man." He hesitates for a moment then adds, "I wish you luck trying to keep him here over 24 hours."

"Yeah, he's already asked me twice when he can get out of here," Doc chuckles. "I'm just happy it wasn't any worse. You can see Mr. Sterling tomorrow, but no more than two at a time, ok?"

"Deal," Cap agrees, peering intensely at Hamilton. He's well aware Hamilton will be here first thing in the morning, and if he could sneak into Sterling's room without detection, he'd try. However, Hamilton doesn't notice Cap's, *don't do anything stupid*, glare, he's distracted by his thoughts.

"Ah, Doc?" Hamilton stops the doctor before he leaves. "Can you make sure Sterling has this?" Hamilton hands the doctor Sterling's phone. "He dropped it during the attack, and I know he'd want to have it."

"I'll have the nurse put it in his room."

"Thank you."

The doctor disappears into the hallway. A weight lifts from the room knowing Sterling will recover. Now it's back to business. Capturing who in the hell did this to him has become a top priority, and though no one says it, all are thinking Sterling's attack ties in with the rash of murders somehow.

"Hamilton," Dixon says. "Go back to the station to get whatever updates there are on the case."

"Cap, I'd like to go back to Sterling's house and check things out. See if there's anything to tell us what happened."

"Ok, but I don't want you to go alone, so pickup Anderson and then head out there."

"Thanks, Cap."

"And Hamilton?"

"Yeah?"

"You discover anything; I want to know about it."

"You got it." With the Captain's approval, he wastes no time leaving. Something or someone nearly killed a detective, and not just any detective, his friend. He's hell-bent on uncovering what took place out at Sterling's house if it's the last thing he does.

After Hamilton leaves, Dixon notices Nefertiti looking as if she's a misplaced puzzle piece. "Do you need a ride home?" He asks Nefertiti. Nefertiti's sudden appearance in the middle of these murders has not escaped him. He wants to keep an eye on her.

"No, I have my car, and I am all right to drive. Thank you for the offer."

"Can you do me a favor?"

"What do you need?" She questions, with a hesitant expression.

"When you get back home, stay close to the house and lock your doors tonight. We're not sure what's out there or who's doing this. I would feel better knowing you're safe," he says, not hinting to his suspicions.

"I believe I can do that. Thank you again, Captain Dixon."

"Drive safe, ma'am."

"I will."

J.C. Brennan

Anderson maneuvers his black, mint condition, 1967 Pontiac GTO—which he affectionately named Lucille—into the station's parking lot. He's obsessed with the classics, but who can blame him, Lucille is a beauty. The sun bears down on the asphalt which comes across as weird, for in his mind it should be dusk. "God, it has been a long day," he gripes, opening the door. Getting out of the comfortable black leather seat, he closes Lucille's door gently and makes his way back to the rear of the car. Opening the trunk, he pulls out a cardboard box that has red tape running over its top marked *evidence,* as Hamilton roars into the parking lot in his squad car next to Lucille.

Hamilton doesn't bother leaving his car; he rolls down the window. "Anderson, come on, we need to check out Sterling's place."

"Yeah, I heard the call over the wire. Why didn't you call me?"

"C'mon, man. I was a little distracted."

"Yeah, I'll forgive you this once. How is Sterling?"

"The doctor said he'll be ok. But we need to know what happened over there. This bastard has gone too far."

"I agree with you. Didn't Sterling tell you anything?"

"No, he was out cold when I got there. When he came to, the ambulance was almost there, and when we got to the hospital, they took him right into X-ray—we didn't have much time to talk." Hamilton barks, frustrated. "None of that matters right now, let's get over there and see what's there if anything." He doesn't tell Anderson he asked Sterling a couple of times what happened and his questions were diverted and never answered. He can't be sure why Sterling didn't tell him, maybe he didn't remember. After all, he took a good blow to the head.

"Don't go getting your panties in a twist. I have to get this inside. I'll be right there."

"Well, hurry. I want to check the grounds thoroughly."

"I'm movin'. Damn, you're impatient today."

"Yeah, I know," Hamilton says, under his breath watching Anderson scurry into the station. *Oh hell, whom am I kidding? This case has just gotten under my skin*, he thinks, hitting the steering wheel. *I hope we nail this psycho before he takes someone else out.* The pressure of the murders and now Sterling's little run-in is weighing down on him.

"You good?" Anderson asks, getting back to the parking lot in record time.

"Yeah, I'm ok," Hamilton replies. *Yeah sure, you're fine. Shit, none of this is alright and won't be until we get this crazy fuck off the streets*, he broods.

It's plain to see Hamilton is on edge, which is unusual for him or at least it was before this mess started. So, Anderson surmises, smart-ass comments are best left unsaid. *No reason to throw gas on the fire*, he thinks. "Well, let's get out there and see if we can't figure out what happened this morning."

They are loading into the squad car when they hear, "Hey, hold up!" It's Martinez exiting the station. "Hey guys, you headed over to Sterling's?"

"Yeah, we need to go over the scene."

"You need an extra hand?"

"Sure, jump in, kid."

Martinez wastes no time climbing in the back of Hamilton's squad car. He's a good kid, and reliable, which can be rare for newbies, especially those barely in their twenties. He's half Latin from his father's side and half French from his mother's. The combination of ancestries produced a handsome, light caramel-skinned, dark-haired, dark-eyed, prominent-nosed man with a neat mustache and well-kept, extended goatee. He only has a high school education, but he has common sense, and that is more than some college graduates have.

They're hauling ass down M-33. Sterling's house is 25 to 30 minutes from the precinct, but Hamilton's in a troublesome mood, his speeding a clear indication. "Hey Hamilton, I'm not trying to tell you how to drive but—" Martinez begins

"Good, then don't!"

He decides not to push it, so he sits back and shuts his mouth. This case is making everyone crazy, and he isn't as immune to it as he'd like to be. The trees are a massive blur looking out the side window of the cruiser as he wonders what they may uncover at Sterling's. The distorted haze outside the car window puts him is a relaxed, almost hypnotic state, that's soon fractured by Anderson's screams, "Hamilton, look out!"

Hamilton jerks the steering wheel more out of shock than anything else. The tires screech as they leave rubber on the pavement. The car drifts uncontrolled, whirling into a 360 spin.

"Ah, shit, hold on," Anderson bellows.

Before any of them truly knows what the hell just happened, the car lurches sideways. The humming of tires on the pavement turned to an ear-piercing screech, filling the air with the smell of burning rubber. The vehicle flips end over end as the men slam violently inside the car, their bodies slam into the dash and the doors.

Martinez's head smacks hard against the window with a cracking thud. Panic rushes in as the earth and sky seem to become one and the same. Their ears thunder with the sound of crunching metal. Glass shatters, spewing shards in all directions. Then, abruptly, the tumbling stops. The car rocks slightly back and forth on its roof, steam hissing from the radiator, its metal groans from the punishment it has taken.

For what feels like a long time, all is still. Martinez's ears fill with an annoying ring. Anderson and Hamilton hear nothing but their breathing. It's incredible how in certain situations, silence is so loud. None of them move, time slows to a crawl, and nothing seems real. Then a squeak, sounding like a scratched record skipping, coming from one tire spinning slow on its axle is the catalyst for time rushing to the present. It makes Martinez queasy, or maybe his sudden nausea is from the crack he received to his skull.

"Is everyone all right?" Hamilton's voice rips through the

unbearable hush.

"I'm fine, I think. My head, on the other hand, may not be, but it's not bleeding."

Anderson doesn't answer, hanging upside down, staring straight ahead, eyes wide. "Anderson," Hamilton nudges him, "Are you ok?"

Anderson lets out a heavy breath like he's been holding it in the whole time. "Did you see that thing? It was fucking huge."

"Of course, I saw the damned thing. Are you alright?"

"Yeah, I think so."

"Good, let's get out of here."

"You gonna call it in, or you want me too?"

"I'll take care of it. Do you need a hand?"

"No, I think I can manage."

"Martinez?"

"I'm good," he responds with a groan.

Supporting his weight on the one hand, he unclips the seat belt and falls to his hands and knees. He notices the minor cuts on his arms as he crawls out of the overturned car. *Damn, we were lucky* he thinks, grabbing hold of the radio mic. "Dispatch this is car four-eight-seven."

"Go ahead four-eight-seven."

"We have a ten-forty-nine out on M-76 about a mile from LaPorte Road, ambulance needed."

"Ten-four." A moment of silence then, "four-eight-seven, the ambulance is in route," blares from the mic.

"Fuck!" he spouts, after dispatch states help's on the way, throwing the mic as hard as he can at the car. Pieces of black plastic go flying on impact when it hits the ground and breaks in two, exposing its inner workings.

Dixon shows up right behind the ambulance. Concern mixed with irritation entrenches his expression as he strolls with purpose over to what's left of the police cruiser. Martinez sits on the pavement, his arms on his knees and head down.

"Martinez! Hey, you alright?"

"I'll be fine, Cap, just knocked my head around."

The paramedics examine him, poking and prodding to see if he broke anything. One of them says, "He may have a concussion, minor scrapes, and bruises, but no serious injuries."

"What happened?" Dixon kneels down and asks.

"Honestly, Cap, it all happened so fast I can't say."

"Ok, you hang in there, son," he says, patting Martinez's shoulder. He stands up and walks over to where Hamilton and Anderson are. Anderson's skin is ashen, and he looks to be in shock. Hamilton is steady with a few minor cuts on his left arm and appears to be pissed off.

"Hamilton, Jesus Christ, what the hell happened here?"

"Something—something large—sprung in front of the car. It was so fast," he replies in disbelief, more to himself than to Dixon.

"What was it?"

"It came out of nowhere, Cap," he states as if he didn't hear the question Dixon asked. "And, well, it startled me. I wasn't expecting it. I jerked the wheel, and that's all she wrote."

"What *was* it?" Dixon asks again, trying his best to have patience. He usually doesn't, but these men are shaken up. He's never seen Hamilton so unnerved, so it is best to keep a level tone on this one.

"I'm not sure. It was big, white, and so fast, I didn't get a good look at it."

"I did." Anderson finally snaps out of his daze and speaks up.

"Well?"

"It was a cat. A *white* panther."

"What? How hard did you hit your head?"

"Hell, Cap, I don't blame you for not believing me. I wouldn't believe it either if I didn't see it myself. But this thing was huge. A panther averages in size anywhere from 65 to 200 pounds, this thing had to be pushing 300-320. I've seen nothing like it."

"You're not kidding," Dixon says, baffled.

"No, I am not. I saw it. It was real."

"How do you know so much about panthers?"

"Large cats have always fascinated me. I even took a few courses in college on Zoology, Animal Behavior, and such."

"And you're a hundred percent sure what you saw was a white panther?"

"As sure as I am standing here in front of you right now, Cap."

"That would make this cat rare, I'd think."

"Oh yes, very."

Dixon has a hard time swallowing the idea that some big cat, a rare one at that, is running around in Alger, but Anderson's eyewitness account seems forthright. "Well," he finally replies. "let these people look you over to make sure you're not hurt." His mind is racing with the information he received and looking over the car, these men are damned lucky they weren't hurt any worse. Then the question, *Where in the hell did a panther come from?* Overrides his thoughts. *"I'm too old for this shit,"* he says under his breath and walks over to Hamilton.

"How are you feeling?"

"I'm good, Cap. I'm more wound up than anything."

"You're damned lucky none of you got hurt any worse." Dixon stands there for a moment rubbing his chin and mutters, "A Cat, a panther." Then glancing at Hamilton, he informs, "I'm going to check out Sterling's place—"

"I'll go with you."

"The hell if you will. You get your ass in that ambulance and go to the hospital."

"But, Cap, I'm fine."

"But, nothing! Hamilton, you go to the damn hospital and don't leave until the doctor clears you, do you understand me? It's an order, not a request, son."

143

"Cap, you can't go out there alone. Shit, you don't know what's waiting out in those woods."

"I'm not. I'll have Summerton with me. Now go, get to the hospital and get checked out."

"Summerton, but I thought he was on vacation."

"He was, but when he heard about all this crazy shit going on, he cut it short."

"All right, but as soon as the doc—"

"As soon as they release you, you best get your ass home. You have the rest of the night off."

"Come on, Cap—" Hamilton protests, but Dixon isn't having it.

"Dammit, Hamilton. Do you want a write-up for insubordination to go along with your bumps and bruises? I'm not fucking around here. I need every good man I have. So, you *will* go home and rest tonight. But your ass *best* be back in the office first thing in the morning."

Hamilton punches the side of the turned over squad car with a grunt. He doesn't like this at all, but what choice does he have? Dixon has a look on his face Hamilton knows all too well. It's a look that says, *I'm not fucking around*. Hamilton storms away, climbing into the back of the ambulance.

"First thing in the morning, Hamilton," Dixon yells, as the paramedic's load Martinez into the ambulance and Anderson climbs in behind them. "Goddamn hard-headed son of a bitch," he grumbles, heading back to his vehicle. Opening the car door, he gets in.

"Everything ok?" Summerton asks.

"No, it's not," he replies, without further explanation. "Let's check out Sterling's place." Throwing the car into drive, Dixon hit the gas a little harder than planned. The tires squawk, a puff of black smoke billows behind the car as it roars down the road.

Pulling up to Sterling's home, Dixon and Summerton get more than they bargain for—there's blood everywhere. It's a scene from a slasher flick. Sterling's yard looks as if a massacre has taken place, but there's not a body in sight—at least, this is Dixon's first impression.

"Shit," Summerton mutters. "This is a—"

"Yeah, well, don't jump to conclusions," he utters. "Let's get a closer look, shall we?" Dixon says, exiting the car. Summerton follows his lead but stays quiet.

They stand in front of the car staring at the blood-soaked yard. A breeze carries a sweet, metallic pungency as it grabs withered, blood-splattered leaves in a morbid game of chase. Summerton's green eyes are wide as saucers, his mouth gasps in disbelief, trying to make sense of the sight before him. However, his brain isn't allowing it to register. It's like having a nightmare when you're awake.

Dixon moves toward the yard to get a better look and assess the morbid scene. It's at moments such as these, he wishes he would have done something else with his life. Starting out as a cop, he saw his share of devastation and brutality, but this? It's a horrid spectacle from a movie—something people hear about but never see. It's like a phantom rumor told to frighten people that circulates throughout the years, spreading fear in the imagination but one never realized—that is, until today.

"Are you coming or what?"

"Oh, yeah. Sorry, Cap," Summerton apologizes. He walks forward with caution and proceeds to where Dixon is standing with his hands on his hips at the edge of carnage.

This isn't a thing a man should ever have to see, he surmises, assessing that all this blood is only a part of this gruesome display. He sees pieces of bodies mixed with the bloody chaos. "Who in the name of God, would do something like this?" he questions and then thinks, *it's not God we're dealing with.*

Walking forward, he steps on something that slopes his foot to the side. Looking down, he sees he is stepping on the remains of a human hand. "Christ!" he exclaims, stumbling backward, barely keeping his balance.

"What or who could have done this?" Summerton asks, looking a little gray around the edges.

"I have no idea, but we need to stop this lunatic's rampage."

Dixon hustles back to the squad car. Wiping away the cold sweat, which has formed on his brow, he reaches through the open car window and grabs the radio mic.

"Dispatch, this is Captain Dixon, do you copy?"

"Go ahead, Captain."

"I need all available units out to 4385 Baker Drive, ASAP! Get the coroner and an ambulance here, pronto!"

"Ten-four."

Heading back over to Summerton, being extra careful of where he walks, Dixon has a deep-seated fear settle in his bones unlike anything he's ever felt before. *This guy is a certifiable psychopath! Where in the hell did he come from? More importantly, where is he now?* Wondering if this lunatic was right under his nose the whole time, waiting for the day when he thoroughly lost control over his demented urges or was this someone who came to their quiet little town from somewhere else? These questions now plague him and terrify him in equal measure.

"We will get this guy."

"I sure hope so, Cap."

"Oh my, what happened here?" comes from behind them. Dixon spins around to see Nefertiti standing with her hands up to her mouth like she's praying. He doesn't trust her, but he also cannot fathom a woman doing this kind of damage. It's not that women don't kill. God knows, they're not immune to the sickness. But women kill differently than men. From his experience, they aren't prone to do the damage this scene is showing him.

"Nefertiti, you shouldn't be here."

"I'm sorry, but I saw your car and... for the love of... who could have done this?"

"We don't know, Nefertiti. Did you see or hear anything?" he asks, still not excluding her as a suspect. In his mind, she isn't from this town, and she showed up not long after the murders began. So, even if she didn't do this, she might be in on it somehow.

"No, I didn't. I was in my office working on some paperwork when I heard you come down the road."

The sight mortified Nefertiti, so much so, she's visibly shaking. Dixon notices and from the horrid expression on her pretty little mug; he realizes she isn't lying about this at least.

"Come on, let's get you back home." He wraps his arm around her back, guiding her back to the road.

"Captain Dixon, I'm good, honest. You don't have to walk me home. You have more important things to attend to right now."

"Are you sure? I don't mind getting you home."

"Yes, I'm sure, but thank you," Nefertiti tells him walking toward the road.

"Nefertiti," Dixon calls after her.

"Yes, Captain?"

"You're a zoologist, right?" He shouldn't be asking someone he doesn't completely rule out as being a suspect, a question such as this. But she is a zoologist, so maybe she can shed light on this panther that's on the loose.

"That's correct."

"Could a panther do something like this?"

"A panther?"

"Yes. I had officers on their way over here earlier, but they were in an accident avoiding a rather large cat."

"Well, of course, any large cat can kill a person, but this? No. What you're seeing isn't a large cat attack."

"Can you tell me why you believe a panther couldn't have done this?"

"First, large cats such as panthers are scavengers and are, mostly, afraid of people. Second, these body parts are scattered all over the place. It looks more like a person stumbled onto a landmine. If a large feline had been involved, there'd be a carcass left, not little pieces spread over the length of the yard. A cat attack would not result in this, this mess if that's what you're asking."

"Yeah, that's what I am asking."

"For panther involvement in the act of this nature, that animal would need extensive training by a highly skilled trainer. To teach a panther to do something like this would take hundreds of long hours. Then you would still need human interference to scatter bits of a person around as you're witnessing here. I'm not saying if it were hungry, it wouldn't smell the blood and come to eat. Still, a panther wouldn't leave a scene like this. There has to be human intervention here. Honestly, Captain, this looks more like the work of a human monster than an animal one."

"Thank you, Nefertiti... ah, you sure I can't walk you home?"

"I'm sure, Captain Dixon. I'll be fine," Nefertiti tells him as she makes her way down the road to her house. Dixon watches her walk until she disappears behind the trees.

"Dammit! It'll be a long day," Dixon groans, strolling back to the mess left for them.

In his thirty years as a detective, eleven as Captain of this small town, he's never dealt with such debauchery, and he hopes he never will again. A starting point slightly overwhelms him, though, at this point, it doesn't matter. They need to get pictures taken, samples collected, evidence bagged—they will need help. Summerton has already immortalized the scene, taking photos.

"Please let us catch this sick son of a bitch soon," he prays.

Backup shows up in record time, for once. Dixon wastes no time, he breaks the men up into three groups of four. Two of the groups comb the area around the house and woods surrounding it for any further evidence. The other group, loaded with evidence bags and cameras, gather the remains distributed around the yard. He's about to go with one of the wood-searching teams when his phone plays Beethoven, which means a call from the station.

"Captain Dixon," he answers.

"Captain Dixon, I don't mean to disturb you," a female voice says on the other end. "But I have a Detective Whitehead on the other line. He says it's urgent."

Dixon thinks for a moment, *Whitehead, Whitehead, where do I know that name?* "Go ahead, transfer the call, Jenny."

There's a moment of silence and then a deep, male voice comes on the line.

"Captain Dixon, my name is Detective Whitehead. You don't know me, but I worked with Detective Levi Sterling on a few cases here in New York."

Where he'd recognize the name instantly pops into his head with the mention of New York. *Ah, yes, the Belmont case!* "Yes, Detective Whitehead, I've heard of you. What can I do for you?"

"Well, sir, I've been trying to reach Levi, and I keep getting his voice mail. Now, I know you all have been busy, but it's unlike Levi not to respond. You see, he's been waiting for my call."

"Detective Whitehead, I hate to be the bearer of bad news, but Sterling is in the hospital—"

"What! God, what happened? Is he alright?"

"Yes, he's going to recover. He just had a little mishap working on this case."

"Aw, man, I can't believe it. I'm happy to hear he'll recover though."

"What was it you needed to speak with him about?"

"I wanted to give him an update on an old case we worked together."

"It doesn't concern the Matt Belmont case, does it?"

The voice on the other line chuckles, humorlessly. "Yeah, I figured you'd know about that case," Detective Whitehead says. "I know—well, I'm sure you also know how that case affected Levi."

"Yes, I do."

"Then you know how bad it got for him."

"I do... ah, what's this about, Detective Whitehead?"

"Please, call me Alex. Listen, Captain Dixon, I mean no disrespect, but I'd rather speak with Levi first. He can tell you about our conversation afterward if he likes."

"I don't *like* it, but I understand. When Sterling wakes up, I'll make sure he gets any message you have for him."

"That won't be necessary. I'm on the next plane going to Michigan."

Before Dixon can respond, the line goes silent; Whitehead hung up. "Shit!" he curses, shoving his phone back into his pocket.

"Hey, Cap!" Summerton calls from the backyard. "You have *got* to see this."

Forgetting about the call, for now, he has more important things to worry about than Sterling's old cases and acquaintances.

As Dixon runs to the back of the house, Summerton is kneeling down examining something on the ground. A few other officers near him are standing about twenty feet from the back tree line.

"What did you find?" He calls, trotting over.

"Well, have a look," Summerton replies when Dixon closes the gap. "Can you believe this?"

Squatting next to Summerton, uncompromised prints of a large cat comes into view. He notices the position of the track. There's turned up dirt and spray-back that indicates the cat readied itself here and jumped into the wood.

"We may have an escaped panther on our hand's boys. It most likely smelled the blood and came in for a snack." Dixon announces.

"Ah, Cap, you need to see this, before you jump to any conclusions." Dixon gazes upon Summerton's puzzled expression. He stands up and treads just beyond the tree line. "Look, Cap," Summerton says, pointing to a spot not a half a foot in front of him.

Kneeling once again in the soft, rich dirt of the forest floor, he sees a partial print of human toes along with the outer edge of a foot. "You have *got* to be fucking kidding me," Dixon exclaims.

"God knows, I wish I were," Summerton answers, a bit alarmed. "What do you make of it, Cap?"

Dixon sits there, one knee on the ground, the other supporting his elbow, gazing at the print, not knowing what in the hell to think about any of this. "I'm not sure. Are there any other footprints—human footprints—further up?"

"No, Cap, not a one. It's like whoever made this one disappeared."

Dixon exhales, exasperated by it all. "Ok, I want pictures of these two tracks, a cast made, and mark this area off," he orders Summerton. "Hey, you men," he waves to the officers still standing where he'd left them. "I want the three of you to form a line about 20 feet apart and walk through these woods about a half mile back. Anything—and I mean anything—that's not supposed to be there, consider it evidence. You bag it and tag it, do you understand?" The men nod and go to work without a word. "Christ, this is turning into a fuckin' nightmare," Dixon mumbles, wiping sweat from his brow.

Summerton wants to tell Dixon this situation is giving him the creeps but decides he's stressed enough. He resolves to keep his mouth shut.

The search in the woods continues.

Chapter 14

The Hospital

Sterling hears his name called from outside the kitchen window. He just hung up the phone with Hamilton who let him know there's been another murder. Levi, a voice calls. He opens the back patio door.
"Who's there?" he asks, but no one answers. Levi, it's a woman's voice he hears coming from the woods, and although morning, the woods are too dark to see anything. A silhouette races thought the shadowy depths of the wood.
"Who's out there?" he inquires louder, but no response is given. Deciding to investigate, he cautiously heads out the door toward the tree. The silhouette flashes before him, this time closer. "This is private—" Glowing eyes. Glistening fangs. Razor-sharp claws. Blood. A scream—

Sterling shoots straight up in his hospital bed, fighting to unravel the covers tangling him. Wet with perspiration, shaking, and madly gawking around the room; he almost forgets where he is. The beating of his heart is erratic and vigorously threatening to burst from his chest at any moment. "It was just a dream," he gasps. "Oh, sweet Jesus, just a dream." He flops back on the somewhat uncomfortable hospital bed with his head throbbing.

The television blares from the corner. A weatherman informs his viewers of what the five-day forecast will bring—clear skies and sunshine. Then another male with a blue suit, white shirt, and light, blue tie comes on:

"Thank you, Jim. In other news; today in New York, four men were found brutally murdered. The police haven't commented on the case and no leads have established who committed this heinous crime. However, our sources say the men were members of a notorious New York gang, the Latin Boys"

A sharp pain rips through Sterling's skull. He shuts his eyes, opens them again slowly, and does his best to focus on the white wall in front of him. "It's about fucking time someone got those pieces of shit."

"Hey, man, how are you feeling?" a male voice speaks off to his left and startles him. He whips his head around causing a momentary sense of disorientation.

"Fuck!" he curses himself, focusing hard on bringing into view the man before him.

"Holy shit, Alex? Is that you?"

"In the flesh," Alex says. He is sitting in the puke green chair in the corner. After ten years, his black hair is showing signs of aging with sparse graying around the edges and his eyes have a few more laugh lines. Other than that, the blue jeans and leather jacket are the same as he remembers.

"God man, it's good to see you. When did you get here?"

"I flew in yesterday." He says, flashing a genuine smile. It surprises Sterling to see Alex. As shocked as Sterling is seeing a fellow officer from New York, Alex is more so but for a different reason. Sterling looks unerringly the same since New York. No graying hair, no extra creases in his face due to age—it's remarkable. *He has some good genes*, he thinks, still grinning.

"Hell man, I've seen ya lookin' betta."

"Aw hell, it's just a few bumps and bruises. What day is it?"

"It's Wednesday."

Sterling sits up too fast making his head spin. For a second he fears he will lose consciousness, the disorientation making his stomach flip-flop.

"Ah Levi, you ok?"

He gives himself a minute or two to get his head to halt the disoriented spinning. "I'll be ok, just give me a second," he says, finally able to swing his legs over the side of the bed without tumbling to the floor.

"I don't mind saying, you look like hell."

"I'm fine, just a bad dream that's all."

"Still havin' the nightmares, huh?"

"Yeah, not the same ones but still creepy as shit."

"How are you—I mean as far as what happened in New York?"

"I'm better," Sterling replies and quickly alters the subject. "What day did you say it was?"

"Wednesday," Alex responds, deciding not to press the issue.

"Wednesday! Holy shit, I've been here for three days?" Sterling exclaims, surprised by the number of days that have passed. *Jesus man, I must have taken quite a wallop.*

"Here," handing Sterling a bottle of water. "It looks like you could use this."

"Thanks," he replies, taking the bottle and finishing it in one gulp. "I can't believe It's been that long already."

"Yeah, from what I understand, you went through a hell of an ordeal..." Alex's eyes flash, shining with pride as he continues. "We got them, Sterling. We got those no-good, sick bastards. Well, *we* didn't get them, but I guarantee they'll never hurt a kid again."

"Whoa, Alex, slow down. We got who?"

"Those sick sons-of-a-bitches that killed that kid, Matt Belmont."

"No shit."

"Yeah. And you'll never guess who it was." Alex was dragging out his little surprise on purpose. He liked to present an air of the dramatic at times like this. His smug grin told Sterling it was someone notable.

"Well, are you going to tell me or make me guess?"

"It was the Latin Boys. We got 'em, man."

"The Latin Boys! Huh, I never would've guessed their crew would do something like what was done to Matt."

"Yeah, they've done some despicable shit in their day, but this? I was as shocked as you are."

"How? How did you figure it out?"

"That was easy enough once I found a knife down in the old sewer. You know the one that the city never finished."

"Yeah, I know the place. But how did you know to look in the sewer? I know we suspected the place during our investigation, but nothing ever came of it."

"Call it a hunch. One morning I woke up early and went for a walk. I swear I had no prior notion to head down to that place but, for some reason, I gave it a second look, and that is when I found the knife there under a grate. Tiny must have dropped it when they were defiling the kid. It was the knife he always carried on him."

"I know the one. That overweight piece of shit with that nasty scar on the right side of his face and a gold tooth may not have been good for anything, but the bastard could, sure enough, wield a knife."

"You ain't lyin'. It was the knife and the symbol LB with intertwined snakes in the carved handle that led me to Tiny and his band of demons."

"Yup, I remember the one. No one had a knife like that, and the damn idiot left it down in the sewer—imagine that." Sterling says, shaking his head. "You said you didn't get them, but they won't hurt anyone again. So, who got to them?"

"The Latin boys."

"They went after their own, hey?"

"That they did, with a little push. The Latin boys were none too thrilled when they found out. They, of course, didn't believe a word I said at first—"

"You went to them alone! Christ man, did you have a death wish."

"No, and at first, I thought I might end up a statistic. But when I presented the evidence and showed them the crime photos of what Tiny and his friends did to that boy, they took care of them. I'll tell ya; I don't recall ever seeing Radman so infuriated in my life."

"I can imagine."

"Get this, his crazy ass brother, Vadim, gets right in my face and says, 'We handle our own' as he cracked his knuckles. 'You don't need to know anything else, Copper.' You know, in that Latin, broken-English accent of his. Hell, I didn't want to know anymore."

He stands there musing as if in disbelief. If the truth be told, he'd been scared to death to confront them with evidence against one of their own. With a snort, Alex continues, "The one thing I can tell ya is whatever Matt suffered ten years ago—well, let's just say those four men suffered tenfold. Man, what a fucking mess they were when we found them."

"I can't say I'm sorry. So you found the knife in that old sewer system, huh? I knew there was something about that place. I knew it back then."

"It was your persistence about that place that made me head back down there. You kept going back there, remember?"

"Yeah, I remember."

"You said there was something we were missing and after that old bag woman... what was her name?"

"Mildred. No, that wasn't it. Milly! Yeah, that was it, Milly Buckles."

"After she said she heard screams coming from the place and no one believed her—she was three sheets to the wind half the time, but you believed her."

"And she was right."

"Yeah, she was, wasn't she," Alex confirms with a slight edge of disquiet.

Milly was a drunk, and half the time her mind wasn't all there, but there was something about her story the day after they found Matt under the bridge that gnawed at Sterling. He wasn't precisely positive of what particular piece of information it was or if it was the way she said the words, but he could not let it go. And now, over ten years later old Milly proved to have had a lucid moment.

"I'm just relieved the Matt Belmont case finally got put to bed."

"Yeah, me too."

Sterling lays thinking about the nightmare he has lived for over ten years is finally over. He glances over at Alex, "So you came all this way to tell me about this—you could've just called."

"Well, after the Latin boys finished with those men. and we found them, I did call. Your Captain told me you were in the hospital—didn't give me the whole story—but I was on the next plane out here. What happened to you out there?"

"Alex, I don't think you'd believe me if I told you."

"Try me. After the Matt Belmont case, I can believe just about anything."

"I think a panther attacked me."

Alex's eyes squint to slits, questioning. "A panther—here?"

"Yeah, there's some strange shit going on around here. We found five murdered girls that I know of—young girls mind you. Young girls who went through some gruesome acts of brutality."

"You're fucking with me, right?"

"I wish I were." Sterling shakes his head and goes silent.

Alex has not seen him in ten years, but he knows him well enough to realize this case is eating at him. Hell, it's a part of this fucking job. Being detectives, they see some of the most grisly acts humanity has to offer and deal with the worst rot and depravity of man. It's bound to get under a man's skin at some point. However, fate has it out for Sterling. The Belmont case put him over the edge, ran him out of New York into this sleepy little nowhere town, and now the cold-blooded murders of young girls—Alex worries about his friend.

"Hey, listen, Sterling, I can stick around for a few extra days."

Sterling's face breaks into a smile. It's kind of Alex to offer, even after all this time. "Ah hell, New York has its share—more than its share—of fucked up crimes and freak cases, you need to get back to it."

"Freak cases," Alex smirks. "I haven't heard that phrase since you left.

Hey, listen, Sterling, are you sure? I can take a few more days. Hell, I don't mind being out of the hustle and bustle of the big city. But damn, did ya have to move into a switchback, no-name, country-fuck, redneck town like this? Does this place even have a bar?" Alex ribs.

Sterling laughs and then replies, "Yeah, it's a small town, but I like it here." He glances at Alex sideways and says in his best redneck voice, "And our waterin' hole just be a stone's throw down the road."

Alex bursts out. His laughter resonates off the cold, unappealing concrete walls, filling the dismal room with a refreshing perk. He laughs so hard that Sterling can't stop from joining in. It takes a minute for them to each catch their breath when the laughter dies down.

"It's good to see you again, Levi—real good to see ya."

His persona becomes serious. He's concerned this case may push Sterling back down the ugly road he traveled before. He was there during the Belmont case; he witnessed what it did to Sterling. Three packs of cigs a day, a couple of bottles of bourbon a night, his divorce, and little to no sleep. He doesn't want to see a good detective wander into no-man's-land again, fearing this time he wouldn't make his way back.

Sterling takes his cases to a level most detectives steer clear. He views each victim as if they're his family—his blood. Matt Belmont could have been his son the way he went after that case. But it's this trait that makes him so damn good at his job. It's also this trait that takes a psychological and physical toll on him. Alex, by no means, wants to see Sterling at the point where he becomes lost again—he's fearful he'll end up in a grave this time.

"Sterling, listen, I know you don't want me to stay—I get it, but do me a favor. If you need to talk, pick up the damned phone, day or night, I'll be here."

"Well, I see our patient has woken up," a nurse says, entering the room before Sterling can respond. She sets a tray down on the bedside table, taking him by the wrist to check his pulse and shoving a thermometer in his mouth.

He observes the tray sitting on the table. Tape, gauze, sterilized pads, and a few other items arranged neatly on the shiny, silver tray with a sterile, blue liner. A clipboard sits next to it holding a paper with his name printed neatly at the top and other writings, which he assumes are notes from the nurse's prior visits.

"Well, now." The nurse says, smiling. "Your pulse is much better." She pulls the thermometer from his mouth, "98, that's good. Your fever has broken. It's still a little elevated but much better. The doctor will be happy to hear that." She takes the clipboard off the table, jots a few notes, and then turns to Alex. "Sir, would you mind? I have to change his bandages."

"Oh, of course. Hey, Sterling, I'll be out in the hall." Sterling watches Alex leave the room.

"Thank you," she calls after him, adjusting Sterling's bed. "Well, let's see how those wounds are healing up," She says, pulling down the white blanket that covers him and carefully removes the tape away from his skin. When she draws back the dressing, her eyes become large, mixed with disbelief and fear. Her jaw drops simultaneously with a small gasp. She hurriedly places the dressing back and utters, "Um, I'll be back in just a moment." She's doing her best to stay professional but failing miserably.

"Is something wrong?" Sterling asks.

"No. Nothing's wrong. I'll be right back." She replies, scurrying out of the room. She doesn't look back, and he hears her say, *excuse me*. Sterling presumes she ran into Alex in her hastened state.

"What in the hell was that all about?" Alex asks, popping his head through the door.

"I don't have a clue. She removed my bandage and then said she'd be right back. Shit, she practically ran out of here—strange."

"I know. The woman about ran me over."

Sterling glares curiously and somewhat disturbingly at Alex, then down at his bandage. "Damn it; don't tell me this thing is infected—or worse gangrene has taken root."

"Aw c'mon, you're being overly dramatic, don't you think?"

"Maybe," he replies, glancing back down at the gauze, then back at Alex. After some hesitation he lifts the bandage, keeping his eyes on Alex and peels the bandage off to reveal what lies beneath.

"Holy shit!" Alex exclaims. "How is that possible?"

Sterling looks down at his practically healed chest. "Your guess is as good as mine. No wonder the nurse rushed out of here."

"No shit! I'm sure it surprised her. Damn, Levi. You're not even going to end up with much of a scar by the looks of things. What, did someone place a healing spell on you or something?" Alex says jokingly, but there's a notable undertone of unease in his voice.

"C'mon, Alex. I heal quickly, it's no big deal. I work out, take my vitamins, and eat right. Besides the occasional shot of bourbon and smoke, I'm a healthy guy. Don't make this into something it isn't, and for god's sake, stop looking at me like that!"

The door opens saving Alex from having to respond. A tall, lanky, gray-haired man in a long, white jacket with a stethoscope around his neck, walks in with the shaken nurse behind him.

"Mr. Sterling, I'm Doctor Bushman. It's good to see you awake. Nurse Pearson tells me you have some amazing healing going on; shall we look?" The man bends down, examining Sterling's wounds. Straightening without changing his expression, he chuckles and says, "Well, it looks as if you have a unique quality I wish more of my patients had."

"So, is there something wrong with me, doc?"

"No. Is your rapid healing strange? Yes. Is it rare? Very. But I don't think it's anything to be alarmed over. We'll take a few blood tests to make sure there's nothing that raises concern. I believe you'll heal nicely and be out of here in the next couple days."

"Doc, what would account for such hasty healing to occur? I mean, this isn't normal, is it?"

"Well, it could be as simple as elevated testosterone levels."

"I'm not sure what you mean."

"Testosterone plays a critical role in the recovery and regeneration processes of males. When elevated, it can contribute to accelerated healing. However, don't worry; the blood test should reveal more. Nurse Pearson will take some, and we should have the results by tomorrow."

"Thanks, Doc."

The man smiles, leaving the room while Nurse Pearson—still looking staggered by the whole ordeal—ties a tourniquet, pushes on his vein a moment, and jabs the needle in his arm, and gentle she's not. Sterling watches his blood fill up three tubes. Nurse Pearson puts a folded piece of gauze over the needle mark on his arm, tapes it, picks up the tray with the newly retrieved blood, and hurriedly leaves the room.

"I don't think she likes you very much," Alex jokes.

"Me neither," Sterling snickers, rubbing his arm.

Chapter 15

The Curiosity

Dixon calls off the search of the woods surrounding Sterling's place after six hours. The men search for every possible piece of evidence, but they didn't recover much. *If we haven't discovered something substantial by now we're not going to,* are his thoughts.

"Ok, men, let's pack it in and get back to the station. Give whatever you've bagged and tagged to Summerton," He shouts to those still in the woods, his voice carrying, bouncing off the trees and disturbing some nearby birds who take flight.

The men come in from the woods. They look haggard from the long day's search. Words escape the Captain seeing the trivial amount of potential evidence. The case has them rattled. He secretly wishes for Sterling to return soon. *God, please be with me on this one and let that man heal fast,* he says a silent prayer as the last of the men come into view. Only one has an evidence bag.

Thursday morning Captain Dixon sits at his oak desk, staring out the only window in his office, at a Northern Cardinal who decides to keep him company while he waits for the results from the evidence collected. The sun is bright, and the sky is clear, excluding a single, sparse cloud. He watches the cardinal with his bright, red color, the distinctive head crest and the black mask on its face, as he stares back at Dixon for a good fifteen minutes before losing interest and flying away.

A slight tap comes at his open door. Mildred, his long-time secretary, is standing there with a cup of coffee in her hand in a white blouse and black slacks, her brown hair touched by gray, neatly pulled back.

"I thought you could use this," she says, entering and sitting the steaming cup down on his desk. "Black and sweet," she tells him.

"Thank you, Mildred."

"If you need anything else, just buzz. Also, Sam said she'd bring you the results of their test the moment they finish." Smiling at him, she retreats, leaving Dixon alone once again. The one thing he always liked about Mildred is the fact she keeps things simple and to the point. She never asks questions and does what's asked of her.

Samantha has been there 36 hours straight, going through the evidence and running tests on related crime scenes. She isn't alone, but she only has two others on her team—Amy and Brendan. They have one hell of a testing regime to go through in this case.

No matter what Sam and her crew come across, Dixon thinks, *if anyone can exhume the underlying cause of this case, it's Sterling*. He's confident, of all the men he has under him, Sterling is the only one who can put an end to these murders. Not that Sterling is any better than the rest; it's an engulfing feeling Dixon has. Call it a premonition or a gut feeling, whatever you call it, it's powerful. It gnaws at his guts although he isn't sure why. The one thing he is sure of is if they solve the murders of these girls his troubles will be over, for the moment, anyway.

Freak Cases crosses his mind—for what reason and though it doesn't matter, he thinks of where in the hell he's heard the phrase before. *Oh, yeah, that's right, Sterling calls specific cases by that name occasionally*, but why this is coming to him at the moment is a mystery. "These damn cases fall under Sterling's definition of a Freak Case, no doubt about that," he says aloud to his empty office.

Staring at the old oak bookcase full of books across the room that wraps around one wall to the other, he contemplates the number of times in the interrogation room with a suspect who was without a doubt guilty of the crime. A few would go on spouting some crazed shit about the devil made him do it, acting as if he's a dead actor or president, or going on babbling about the sick acts he suffered by his mother—all trying to get off with the plea of insanity. The bitch of it was, most of the time—too many times—it worked. This aggravates Dixon more than anything else in his work. However, in this case, he's sure the assailant won't be one of those. He won't consider himself a freak, someone who is medicating themselves with the newest drug, or spout the standard bullshit that his mother doesn't love him or abused him when he was a baby. Nope, not this guy—this one is special.

Dixon's mindset is that this guy isn't your average low-life. This guy will be the intellectual type—crazy, yes—insane, possibly, but still intelligent. It takes intelligence—a certain amount of knowledge—to accomplish the mutilations this man performed. *Shit, he removed the girls' organs with surgical precision; we're not dealing with an ordinary psychopath,* Dixon muses. He sits back in his comfortable brown leather chair with his fingers laced tight behind his head, lost in thoughts of this maddening case when another knock comes at the door.

He looks up to see Mildred with a striking middle-aged man who he recognized as Detective Whitehead. The reason Dixon is familiar with the man is the pictures he reviewed in Sterling's cases files when he transferred. It isn't standard procedure, but because of the Belmont case and what it did to Sterling, his captain in New York had copied the files and faxed them to Dixon. The faceless man on the phone said, "Sterling's a good man and a great detective, but this case put him over the edge for a while. I figured since he's transferring out there, I should bring you up to speed." Dixon remembers how grateful he was for the New York Captain, Miers was his name, for being so forthright.

"Captain, this is—"

"Detective Whitehead," Dixon interrupts, with Mildred taking this as her cue and leaving them to whatever business they have.

"Hi, Captain Dixon, I don't mean to bother—"

"Yeah, I know. But you need to speak to me, right? Come on in and sit down. Is this about Levi Sterling, perhaps?"

"Yeah, it is," Whitehead smirks, shaking his head. "Can we talk?"

"Well, come on in, sit down… and do me a favor, shut the door." The tall, dark-haired man in a black, distressed-tooled leather bomber jacket with an asymmetrical zipper reminds Dixon of Corey Allen in Rebel without a Cause as he shuts the door, strolls into the office and sits in the chair in front of his desk.

"This place has too many ears if you know what I mean," Dixon cautions.

"Don't all precincts?" Whitehead responds in his thick Bronx accent.

"Yeah, I guess you're right," Dixon laughs. "What can I do for you?"

"Listen, Captain, I know you're aware of the Belmont case and that Sterling left New York because of it."

"Yeah, from what I heard and read, that case was enough to drive any detective out of a job for good. But this force got lucky when he stayed… uh, what's your point?" Dixon wasn't sure where this was leading but to be frank, he didn't like it much.

"Well, what you may not know is what that case did to Levi—I'm talking mentally. I was there; I saw what he went through. The pain. The obsession."

"The obsession?"

"Sterling wouldn't let it go. He spent long hours—I mean days without sleep—following up with any lead he could find, going over the file, going back to the crime scene. The man was relentless."

"That is what detectives do. You of all people should know that."

"Yes, but not as he went after that case; he was like a bulldog put on a short chain with a stake placed just out of his reach. He lost weight—at least twenty pounds—his complexion was ashen, and he had dark, puffy bags under his eyes. I didn't even recognize him after a while. The misery and secret demons tore at him, with bourbon becoming his reprieve. I guess what I'm trying to… well, shit, I'm worried—real worried. I don't want to see Levi go down that hole again. He's a good detective—one of the best. But a case like the one your department is dealing with, it's the kind of case that gets under his skin so deep he lives and breathes it. Just watch him, please don't let him go down that road again. Can you do that for me?"

Dixon doesn't drop his eyes from the man before him. He recognized the man's conviction, though he wondered why he would believe his finest detective might go off the rails now.

"Detective—"

"Alex. Please, call me, Alex."

"Alex, did Sterling say something or did you see something in him that makes you think he's on edge?"

It would be a cold day in hell before Alex betrayed Sterling's confidence, but then again, the man sat there and told him he believed a giant goddamned cat attacked him. Still, he couldn't tell Dixon this.

"No, but this case has similar factors. It's another case involving murdered kids. I would feel better if I knew you were keeping a close eye on him, is all."

"I knew about the drinking and the obsession; his captain in New York filled me in when he came here. Ah, hell, I don't want to lose a good detective as much as you don't want your friend to go down a dangerous road. I promise I'll watch him—we all will."

Whitehead gets up, offering his hand to Dixon. "Thank you, Captain, thank you," he says. The concern Alex has from Levi isn't hard to see, but there's something else in him Dixon has little difficulty distinguishing, and that's fear. He's pallid with a noticeable tremble running through him.

"Listen," he says. "I have to leave in the morning. My flight is at 6am. Can you do me a favor, tell Levi I said goodbye?"

"Goodbye? Aren't you going to see him before you leave?"

"No, I'd go over there, but I'm afraid I won't leave if I do. Levi made it clear he doesn't want me to stay to help." With a snort he tells Dixon, "He said New York has more than its fill of Freak Cases. Tell him to call me, would ya?"

"I will, and don't worry about Levi, he's in good hands. Ah, Detective?"

"Yeah?"

Dixon pauses, something's nagging at the man before him. Generally, he'd leave it alone, but one of his best men has caused Alex's distress. He wants to know if he needs to be looking for anything in particular.

"What's bothering you?"

"What do you mean?"

"C'mon, I'm not some rookie you're talking to here. I've been working with men for far too long not to see something is eating at you."

Running his hand through his dark brown hair, Alex sits back down. He says nothing for a moment as he leans in the chair. Then with a frustrated sigh, he says, "Have you ever noticed how young Levi seems? I bet he looks the same as he did when he got here. Shit, he hasn't aged a day since I've known him."

"Good genes," the Captain snuffs. "We should all be that lucky."

"Yeah, maybe." Dixon notices Alex is struggling. He doesn't say a word, letting him work through it and hoping he will devalue what's eating at him. "I went to the hospital yesterday," Alex says. "And well, Levi's wounds are almost healed."

"What?"

"Yeah, and I'm talking to the point they'll discharge him soon. Isn't that abnormal? I mean, no one heals that fast."

Sterling's rapid healing is unusual, but Dixon will not get all worked up over it, there are too many other situations to worry about. "The man has good genes, nothing strange about that. What did the doctor say?"

"The doc said he'll run a few tests. But, Cap, his lack of aging, his ability to heal... Ah hell, maybe I need sleep." Alex realizes he sounds crazy, but dammit, the man hasn't aged in ten years. Now with this accelerated healing, something is not right.

"Maybe," Dixon responds. He keeps his poker face although his mind is racing. "I know these things with Levi are out of the ordinary, but what are you getting at?"

"I don't know," Alex says, running his hand over his face. "It all is *too* coincidental. I'm just tired I guess. Captain, I've taken up enough of your time. Tell Levi what I said, ok."

"I will, Alex. It's good to meet you in person—and don't worry, I'll look after Detective Sterling and look more into what else is happening."

With that, Whitehead gives Dixon a wiry smile and leaves his office.

Dixon thinks about the conversation. He didn't let Alex see how much of what he was telling him bothered him. Of course, it's strange how little Sterling aged, if at all and how quickly he's healing. But shit, lately more unusual things have happened. *Maybe Sterling has been taking damn good vitamins*, he wittily thought, trying to make light of Whitehead's allegation.

The accusation Whitehead posed of something being out of sorts with Sterling, lingers in his mind. *Curiosity killed the cat*, he jests with little humor. *That is all I need, to have something wrong with Sterling,* is the more prevailing thought going through his head. *Hasn't the man been put through enough?! Please, God, I need this detective. He deserves a break. Not now. Please, not now,* he silently pleads.

However, with as much as the department requires Sterling's expertise on this case, Dixon decides to do some digging into Sterling's past. He has to.

Chapter 16

The Inquisition

Sterling wears a trench in the floor pacing while waiting for his release papers. He has memorized every inch of this room with its sterile, white walls and spotless tile floor. He's never been one for being cooped up, and this damned place is driving him nuts. He is about ready to go and look for a nurse to see how much longer his release will take when the doctor walks in.

"Good afternoon, Mr. Sterling. I see you're more than ready to get out of here."

"Yes, I am. I've never been big on hospitals." Trying to relax and calm his nerves, Sterling asks, "So, did the results come back?"

"Yes, I have them right here."

"And?" Sterling's becoming more impatient with the doctor's aloofness.

"Mr. Sterling, sit please," the doctor tells him, extending his hand to the chair nearest Sterling.

"I think I'll stand if it's all the same to you, Doc. Tell me what the results show."

"Well, you're completely normal—better than normal, actually. Your antibodies are enhanced, which provide you with the healing effects you're experiencing."

"Enhanced?"

"Yes, think of it as antibodies that were giving a booster shot. Now, this could be from your intake of proteins and vitamins, or you were born with an excellent immune system. However, nothing in the test results shows anything to worry about—curious, yes. Worry, no."

Breathe, Sterling, just breathe. He let out a sigh of relief. "So, can I get out of here?"

"Of course. I have the papers ready for your signature. I want you to make a follow-up appointment for a week from Monday, but you're free to go." A nurse—the same nurse who freaked out when she saw his healing—enters the room to collect Sterling's discharge papers as the doctor departs. The doctor stops and turns back to Sterling, holding a piece of paper in his hand.

"You may need this," he says.

"What is it?" Sterling asks, taking the paper from him.

"It's your clearance for work."

"Yeah, Dixon won't let me near the station without this." Sterling takes the paper, shoving it in his pocket as he watches the doctor continue out the door. He completes the paperwork needing his John Hancock without question. The nurse insists he has to be taken out in the wheelchair, not something Sterling's looking forward to, but arguing isn't doing him any good.

"Do you have a ride home, Mister Sterling?" She asks, pushing him down the corridor.

"I'm calling a cab—"

"No need for that, Levi," he hears from somewhere behind them. "I'll be taking you home."

Sterling cocks his head to see Captain Dixon. "Hey Cap, I didn't know you'd be coming today." Taking the paper doc gave him from his pocket, "I got my work release," he says, waving the paper with a cocky grin.

"Good, it'll be nice to have you back on this case, but we can talk about that later."

They are out in the discharge area within ten minutes. The nurse was relentless with the hospital regulation about the wheelchair, wheeling him out to Dixon's car a few moments later.

"Thank you," he tells her once they're at the car and gets up from the wheelchair. She offers him a wry grin, heading back to the door they exited.

"Damn, for a minute there I thought she might wheel me all the way home," he tells Dixon, climbing in and shutting the door. Dixon doesn't say a word until the hospital is out of sight and the scenery changes to the green of spruce and fir pines, along with large bur and red oaks.

"Everything alright, Cap?"

Dixon keeps his eyes on the road; he doesn't want to engage in this interrogation, but there's no other choice. "Levi, I have to ask you some questions, but I don't want you to get yourself all twisted about it."

"Ok, what's going on?"

"Alex stopped by my office before he left—"

"Alex left!" Sterling exclaims with surprise. In a subdued voice, he says, "He didn't even say goodbye."

"No, he asked me to tell you for him. He had to go back to New York. I'm sure his precinct needs him."

"Yeah, I was hoping to see him before he left." If Levi is honest with himself, he's a little hurt Alex didn't say goodbye. After all, they hadn't seen one another in ten years.

"Why did Alex stop in to see you and what does it have to do with me?" Dixon doesn't answer the question. He rubs his hand under his lip, contemplating how to go about asking Sterling the sensitive questions. Sterling sees him struggling with whatever it is he wants to question him about. *What did Alex stir up?* He thinks, his mind reeling over what has Cap in a twist. "Listen, Cap, if you have something you're curious about, ask. I have nothing to hide."

"Are you sure, Sterling?"

"Now, just what in the hell is that supposed to mean!" Sterling snorts. He's becoming uncomfortable and frustrated by the way Dixon's acting. *Christ, Alex, what did you say to get me into this?* He wonders.

"Back on the Belmont case, someone hit in the head with a pipe, damned hard as I understand, and you lost most of your memory from that head injury, right?"

"Yeah, that's no big secret. You've known about this before I transferred."

"I know, just stick with me on this, Sterling, and tell me how far back in your life can you remember?"

"Come on, Ca—"

"No! Now, dammit, Sterling, I want to know. How far back can you remember? Do you remember your wedding to Jamie or the birth of your son? How about your college years?"

"Christ, Cap, what is this, an interrogation! I haven't seen Alex in ten years. He comes out and says something that gets you all twisted—what in the hell did he say?!" Sterling's pissed, but he is also struggling to remember as far back as his broken mind will allow.

"Alex is concerned about you. After what happened during the Belmont case he has the right, don't you think?"

"Maybe, but why are *you* so concerned? Shit, that case was a long time ago."

"C'mon, Levi, humor me, would ya? Think and tell me how far back you remember."

Sterling hadn't thought about his past since before the knock he took on the noggin. Now, thinking about it makes his head throb. Dixon is right about his memory, but Cap already knew the blow he took back then wiped most of it. However, Cap must have a good reason for asking—at least, he damn well better.

Thinking back, pushing his memory as far as his misfiring synapses will allow, Sterling is quiet for a long time. His head throbs with a piercing pain he has not felt in a while. The scar on his head has a pulse as the day he found Matt Belmont enters his memory with a sheer force. Back further, dinner with Jamie and his son. The aroma of corn, sweet potatoes, and brown sugar swirl in the air. The table is set as Jamie enters the room carrying a serving platter with a ham. Josh, about five years old, says, 'it smells good, mom.'

And further, his head is throbbing, a thick haze hangs in the darkened corners of his mind. He pushes through his memory banks, which causes him pain, to penetrate the snapped connection.

Its summer, the sun is shining, birds sing in the big oak above his house. He takes his hanky from his back pocket to swab his sweat-soaked face. The day is sweltering hot.

He's at a baseball game; people are all around him cheering and heckling. He recognized Mr. Baker and his wife, Linda, who were the parents of Josh's best friend—what was his name? Brian! Yes, that was it. Brian.

A man in a blue baseball cap, white shirt, and denim shorts from below them bellows, "C'mon Eddie, fire it in there! Let's strike this one out!"

He looks to the player on the plate; it's Josh in his gray uniform, the bat held back waiting for the pitch.

Jamie jumps up beside him, "Josh you can do it! Hit it to the bleachers."

The pitcher, Eddie, spits, takes the ball in his hand, glances at the runner on the plates, and then fires a pitch at Josh. He swings, it connects, and the ball flies over the fence—

"HOMERUN!" Jamie squeals.

With all his concentration he pushes further but to no avail, all he sees in the deep hollows of his memory after this game is unfathomable darkness—emptiness and silence. It's as if his life was put on hold at that point.

Dixon watches him intently. Tiny beads of sweat form across his brow and run warily down the sides of his face. Just when Dixon is confident Sterling isn't going to answer, Sterling quietly says, "I remember Josh's little league game."

"Josh's little league game?"

"Yeah, he was seven, and the day was hot as hell—a real scorcher. He'd practice every night; at lunch, on weekends, to get better at his swing. That game he hit the winning home run. It was the best day I

173

think I ever had with him—took him and the team out for pizza and ice cream. I was so proud of him." Sterling relishes in the memory. He may not remember all his past but that memory he's grateful to keep. "Now, what is all of this about, Cap?"

"Listen to what I have to say before you blow a gasket. Listen carefully to everything I'm about to tell you, can you do that?"

Sterling's already annoyed, but the look on Dixon's face is unnerving. He wants to know what has him so upset. Apparently, it's something about him—about his past—something he can't remember.

Rubbing his temples and then his scar, he answers, "Yeah. Sure. Whatever."

What Dixon reveals is more than unnerving. Sterling feels he's the butt of some sick joke. However, Dixon's voice, his expression—Sterling knows the man isn't trying to pull a fast one on him.

"Levi, I've looked, prodded, called anyone that may have been able to verify they knew you or Jamie Peterson—your wife's maiden name right?" Sterling nods his head. "I'm not sure what's going on Sterling, but Jamie Peterson never existed until 1984 and you... well, there's nothing much to lead to a past of any sort. The hospital you were supposedly born in closed down the same yea—"

"Supposedly! Fuckin' supposedly!"

"Now, Sterling, you promised."

Deep breaths my man, deep breaths. It takes time, telling and willing himself into calm—a forced calm, but calm all the same.

"What are you suggesting, Cap?" he finally asks.

"Dammit, Sterling, give me the time to tell you what I know!"

Sterling falls silent, pissed, but silent. Alex must have told Dixon a doozy to get him curious enough to dig into his past. *Shit, Alex! What in the fuck did you do this time?!* His head feels like it will split in two. Still, he tries to stay pacified while pushing his memory past the point of the baseball game but nothing but darkness answers.

"Can I finish?" Dixon barks.

Sterling just nods.

"Good, now let me tell you everything before you go off." He waits a moment to determine Sterling's state, but the man sits next to him with an expressionless face. "Ok," he sighs. "There's nothing, no birth records, no driver's license, no social security card—not one piece of ID before that date for your wife. As for you, your parents died in a fire when you were fifteen—I'm sure you already knew that..." Dixon doesn't get a twinge from him, but the words get through.

My parents? He thinks. He can't picture them, their faces, the color of their hair, the smell of their skin. *My parents? Who were they?* He tries hard to remember, forcefully pushing past the darkness in his brain—nothing. His head fervently throbs now.

"I found out about the hospital closing, and in the relocation of files they lost your birth records."

"That's impossible!" Sterling's stress is mounting. *Breathe ol' boy, he thinks, there has to be an explanation for all this. Jesus, Jamie! What in the hell is up with that!* He coaxes himself to stay calm, feeling anything but. "Ok, well, if you need a copy of my birth certificate I have one. I am who I am. I'm not trying to hide anything from you, Cap, if that's what you're thinking." Sharp pains shoot through his temples. His ears sing as if someone's beating on his brain like a bass drum. Unsure of what was going on or why Cap has dug into Jamie's background.

"That's unnecessary, Sterling. I have found some strange things about you and your family's history and I'd like—"

Blood drips from Sterling's nose as a piercing pain rips through his skull.

"God, Sterling," Dixon huffs, wide-eyed. "Here." He hands him a handkerchief. Sterling's color is off and his discomfort is clear. "Are you—"

"I am fine. My head is fucking killing me!" His temperament is stretched to its limits at this point. He wipes away the blood and squeezes his nose until the blood subsides. Anger rushes through him. He's mad at

Dixon for digging into his past without his consent and furious with Alex for whatever it is he said to start this. He's also pissed off at himself for not being able to remember shit about his history.

"First of all, why are you investigating my ex-wife and me?" he spits out, failing horribly at keeping his tone even.

"After my talk with Alex, I was worried. I looked into your past because I give a shit about what happens to you! Also, I am the fucking Captain around here and if I feel it necessary to gather information on one of my detectives, I'll damned well do so!"

"What? Can't you just ask me? Fuck! I'd tell you whatever you wanted to know."

"But you don't remember everything, now do you?" Dixon questions.

"So, that gives you the right to go snooping around—looking into my past!"

The last thing he wanted was an argument, but Sterling's pissing him off. "Dammit, Levi! There's more—much more."

Having difficulty finding his calm, thinking this whole ordeal is insane. He forcefully thrusts his escalating anger and anxiety deep inside and swallows hard to steady himself. He feels a breakdown lingering on the edge of his sanity.

"This isn't something I will want to hear, is it?"

"Maybe not, but you need to. I tried to call Jamie, but the number listed for her isn't in service. She isn't working where you told me she was. They've never even heard of a Jamie Peterson, let alone Jamie Sterling. When was the last time you spoke with her?"

"I don't know. I mean, after the divorce, we didn't talk much unless I had Josh for the weekend. At eighteen... well, I haven't spoken to him or her for any length of time. It's been a few years, why?"

"We don't know where she is. The place she was living has been empty for the last couple of years. I talked to the property owner. He told me she paid a full year of rent, but she up and left in the middle of the night a few years back. She said nothing, didn't leave a forwarding address, just up and vanished."

"What?!" The pounding in his head came back with a vengeance. "That can't be," he says aloud, but to himself, not Dixon. "Have you called Josh? He will know where his mother is."

Dixon's nerves are tighter than piano strings. He has to tell Sterling, but damn it all to hell, he doesn't want to be the one to do it. "That's something else—we can't locate him either."

"To hell you say! Have you called the university?"

"We did and Levi..."

Sterling knows it's serious with the use of his first name, Cap hardly ever uses it.

"I know it sounds bizarre, something out of the twilight zone, even. But, New York State has no records of Josh ever enrolled there."

"No fuckin' way!" Sterling jumps as if someone shot him in the ass. His head pays the price. "Fuck!" he bitches, punching the dashboard. His vision blurs from the immense pain, so he squeezes his eyes shut and lays his head back on the headrest. "So, what?" He asks with sarcastic composure. "He mysteriously vanished?! I have pictures of him on campus. I-I have pictures! It-It can't be."

Dixon doesn't say anything else. He hates to be the one to tell Sterling all of this, particularly since he's the one who dug into Sterling's past without his knowledge. However, it's better Sterling hears it from someone he trusts—well, maybe not after this, but he did before this conversation.

"Levi, I have something else—"

"No! I can't take any more surprises, especially when it concerns my bogus wife, whoever she is, or my son, who is now missing. I just can't..."

Fully aware of Detective Sterling's agitated state, Dixon believes it best, for now, not to tell him anything else he found. He gives Sterling some time to absorb the current information about his family. God only knows what kind of basket case he'll create if he tells him everything.

He contacted the school, but he also reached out to the hospital Josh was born in—according to the records the department has on file. However, the hospital has no records of the mother or child. Someone is messing with his detective, and he can't be entirely sure if Sterling is in on it. He lost his memory, so it's possible before the memory loss he knew about all this. However, knowing Sterling the way he does, he can't believe the man has anything to do with it, and he fears Sterling is a target in someone's sick game. A game that may be attached to these murders in some way, and he intends to figure out what's going on if it kills him.

For the moment, he lets Sterling digest all he's told him. For one, the man appears as if he might have a complete breakdown, and for two, it will give him more time to investigate deeper and figure this out. He's getting close; he can feel it.

"Ok, Levi. We can talk later. However, we *need* to talk."

"I gotcha, Cap. I'm just trying to imagine why Jamie would do something like this. Where is she? Where is my son? Shit, my family are damned ghosts." Wiping off the sweat that formed on his brow, his head turns into a full-blown hurricane. He struggles to recall memories, images, conversations—fuck this is insane!

Grabbing his cell out of his pants pocket, he pushes number one. The speed dial number assigned to his son. He doesn't use it much. Josh made it abundantly clear a year ago he wanted nothing to do with him.

"Shit! Shit!" Sterling curses at the electronic recording as it plays, *the number you have reached is no longer in service.* "I don't know what the hell is going on, but I damn well intend to find out."

"Sterling, why don't you leave that to me for the time being? I'll work on this while you get back to work on the case."

"Cap..." He stops, knowing damned well the argument he's about to present is over before it starts. "Ok, Cap, but promise me you'll track down my son."

"I'll do what I can. With all the resources available to the department, there has to be a logical explanation." Dixon says the words but doesn't believe them. He doesn't want to think Sterling is hiding something he does not know about, but until he can get to the guts of this, he has to consider Sterling may not be who he thinks he is.

He hasn't ruled out the idea someone is fucking with Sterling. He's heard of this kind of thing before, people wanting something—money, silence, etc.—from an individual, so they hoodwink that person until they get what they want. What this person may want from Sterling, he doesn't know yet. Sterling isn't wealthy, doesn't have any particular influence in high society—so this is highly unusual. Also, having him remain on the case keeps him under the radar so Dixon can watch him.

"What I need from you is to stay focused. We have too many heartbroken parents that expect justice here. I'll take care of figuring out what's going on with your family, but you get the son of a bitch who killed these girls. Deal?"

"Yeah, Cap, I'll get to the bottom of it."

No reassurance comes to Dixon from the lack of conviction in Sterling's voice, but it will have to do for now. There's too much on the line, and he has to get Sterling's head back in the game.

"Sam is waiting at the office. I went through the partial results of the cases you missed..." Dixon stumbles. In his absorption of this mess in Sterling's personal life, he forgot Sterling doesn't know what has happened to Hamilton, Anderson, and Martinez or what they found at his house. So much for trying not to stress him out any further.

"Well, you going to tell me about the cases or are you going to make me guess?" Sterling spouts, a slight edge to his voice.

"I haven't told you about what happened out at your house yet—"

"What in the hell happened—no, no, let me guess; the Devil has a vendetta against me and has unleashed hell to get his revenge."

Now Sterling is being contemptuous, but considering the circumstances, Dixon disregards his abrasive statement. "Someone decided to the leave remains of one or more body slung over your yard."

"What?!"

"It looks as if they're sending you a message, Sterling. We have an officer on your property until this is cleared up."

"Perfect! Bad enough we have a psychotic broad killing innocent you—"

"A woman?" Dixon questions. "What are you talking about?"

Dammit, Levi. You've done it this time. Kicking himself in the ass for letting his mouth overrun his head, Sterling tells Dixon about what Samantha found. "Listen, Cap, I know I should have said something earlier, but it looks like we may have a female serial killer on our hands."

"You're damned right you should have told me. What in the hell is wrong with you?"

"Cap, I wanted to keep it under wraps for a little while. I'm trying to figure this thing out. I wasn't expecting to get attacked in my front yard by some crazed, runaway circus cat either."

"I don't give a good shit if a creature from Mars attacked you, you best damn well keep me in the loop on this thing! Are you getting me, Sterling?!"

There's silence until Dixon pulls into the precinct. Neither of them is in the right state of mind. Driving his car into his parking space and shut off the ignition, he stares at Sterling for a moment, though Sterling looks straight ahead with a head full of jumbled thoughts and an ache that could hit a nine on the Richter scale if the pain was an earthquake.

"Listen to me," Dixon begins. "Hamilton and the other men could have been killed out there. That damned cat ran right in front of their car, causing an accident. They all went to the hospital and were damned lucky to have only minor injuries. I'm down men on this Sterling, so I need to know you're up for this. If not, you need to let me know now."

"I am, Cap. I *will* solve this case."

Dixon studies Sterling's face for a good long time and this time Sterling's eye do not waiver from the Captain's. Satisfied he can keep his head in the game, he says, "You need to be careful out there. Someone might be gunning for you and until we know who that is..."

"Cap, I'll be fine. Besides, you'll have a car at my house, so I'll have backup if needed."

"Yeah, then why don't I feel any better?"

"That's your nature. You worry too much." Sterling's face breaks into a grin.

"That's my job."

They get out of the car, walking toward the entrance. "So, what exactly happened at my place?" Sterling asks.

"Let's get inside. I think showing you the crime photos will explain it better than I can."

The two enter the building, a building that has stood in the center of town for over a hundred years. Sterling never thought about it before, but this place holds plenty of secrets and histories. He wishes it held the secrets to unlock his past. He also wishes he didn't see the doubt in Dixon's eyes which he tries so hard to hide.

As they enter the hall leading down to Dixon's office, both men hope for a stroke of luck to come their way. However, both know luck is in short order lately. *Damned freak cases* is the shared thought. Dixon also thinks about his detective cloaked up in a personal freak case. Not his fault by any means—or at least, Dixon prays it's not. Even so, it's vital for him to discover what happened in Sterling's past and do it fast. He isn't fond of how Sterling's lack of knowledge of his previous years is shaping up.

Chapter 17

The Stranger Things

Sterling heads straight to his desk feeling as if the old office is drearier than he remembered it a few days ago. It could be the fact the sun has stayed hidden behind clouds all day. However, he believes it has more to do with the way this case is affecting everyone or maybe just him. Still, he tries to smile as his colleagues pat him on the back and give the ol', *it's good to have you back* lingo as he passes. When he reaches his desk, manila folders grace its top. His work desk is always neat; files put away, no clutter, a computer, a phone, a black, plastic organizer holding a few pens and a couple of pencils, with a stapler, and a box of staples—quite the opposite of his desk at home. Before he looks at the file, he boots up his computer. He decided after his talk with Dixon to do some searching of his own. Pulling up a browser he types in his name. *There has to be a mistake*, he says looking at the screen that only shows old newspaper articles from the Belmont case. One displays a picture of him with his hands on his hips over the body.

No, this can't be right, he thinks, running Jamie's name than his son's name. Dixon was right there is nothing before 1984 on Jamie and nothing at all when he types in Josh's name. "What the fuck is going on," he mutters. He tries the DMV, CODIS, and NDIS—nothing. "Impossible," he says, bringing his fist down on his desk startling those around him. "Sorry," he apologizes and stares at the screen for a few moments. *Ah hell, you have other things to worry about right now*, he surmises though his brain racks up reasons like cue balls of why his family has no goddamned past!

He picks up the file from Sam and sees she attached a sticky note:

I had to leave early. Wanted to make sure you got these results.
—Sam
P.S. Welcome back

That's strange; Samantha never takes off early, must have been significant, he muses. Sitting down, he grabs the rest of the folders and sees the one labeled with the date of his attack on it. *This is the victim from the Boy Scout camp*; he mulls, thumbing through the crime scene photos. Even on an empty stomach, he isn't sure he'll stop himself from being sick. *The sick bitch did a number on this kid.*

The photos show the skinned face of a girl. *Why in the hell would she remove the face?* He flips back to the first page of the report.

Name: Jacqueline Myers
Hair: Auburn
Eyes: Green
Birth Date: 5, February 2002
Height: 5' 3"
Weight: 101 lbs.

There is also a picture attached. It's a picture of Jacqueline before the attack, most likely given to them by her parents. It's a school picture of a lovely young lady with a slightly crooked smile—a slight imperfection that adds to her charm. Long, auburn hair like silk, eyes shining, pale skin dusted with a smidgen of freckles, without a care in the world. A cold chill lodges in his spine. "She *was* a pretty girl. At least, until some sick, twisted bitch roaming around the woods removed her face," he grumbles, scanning through the rest of the photos in the file.

The results from the blood on a shoe found in the woods a hundred yards from the body isn't the girl's blood, it isn't female, and no CODIS hit.

"Son of a Bitch!" This time, Sterling didn't mumble as he slams the folders down on his desk.

"Hey, Sterling," he hears a voice say off to his right. "You good?"

Turning, he sees Hamilton standing there, face streaked with concern. He notices the bandage on his arm.

"Shouldn't I be the one asking you that?" he replies, nodding toward the wrapped arm.

"It's just flesh wounds. I take it you talked to Dixon?"

"Yeah, I heard you came close to meeting your maker out there."

"Hell, it could have been worse."

"Oh yeah, how?"

"We could've ended up like you," Hamilton smirks.

"Hilarious, asshole," Sterling chuckles. It's good to see Hamilton, but he looks as if he hasn't slept in days. His color is off and his eyes are sporting bags packed for a year-long trip. "So, how are Anderson and Martinez?"

"Anderson will be out for a few more days. His neck took a good jolt when the accident happened. As for Martinez, he's chewing at the collar the doc put around him. But he suffered a concussion and is on sick leave for a month."

"Damn, sounds like you guys are lucky to be alive."

"You know us; we're tough sons of bitches."

Ah, that humor. Sterling missed hearing it from Hamilton. "So, what did you guys find? Anything to lead us to the perp?" he asks.

"Nothing. This guy's pissing me off," he mutters bitterly, instantly frazzled and indignant.

Dammit, Sterling, when will you learn to keep your mouth shut, he thinks. *You're a real piece of work Sterling. You should have told him already.* The last thing he wanted to do was hide information from Hamilton, but he had to make sure that a female was involved.

"It's not only a man we're looking for."

"What?"

With a heavy sigh, Sterling explains, "From prior reports, the DNA suggests our killer is female."

"No fuckin' way," Hamilton spouts, grabbing Sam's reports off Sterling's desk. He roughly browses the pages of results. "It can't be," clamoring once more, bemused. Setting the folders down, an unreserved skepticism manifest in his features, he hisses, "Seriously, a woman! What kind of woman does… Ah hell, I guess women can be as repulsive as men. But damn, I wouldn't suspect—"

"Yeah, I know. We have to pinpoint this she-devil and her mate before they kill again."

"They?" Hamilton questions.

"Yeah, I don't believe she is working along."

"But the evidence…"

"I know. I don't have proof but I have a gut feeling on this one."

"You've never led us wrong," Hamilton says. "I agree, it doesn't seem like *they* will stop on their own accord. What do you need?" Hamilton's eyes are intent, brows furled with determination. "I'm here to help."

Sterling thinks for a moment, wondering where they should start. "You want to take a ride over to the Boy Scout camp? They still have it marked off, right?"

"Yeah, Dixon wants to make sure we scour every inch of that place and yours."

"Well, let's not disappoint him. We'll start with the camp and then head to my house."

"Sounds like a plan."

The police cruiser pulls into the parking area of the Boy Scout camp. The place looks deserted as they exit the car.

"Where is everyone?"

"Paul sent the boys home. He said it was almost time to shut the camp down for winter and after a dead girl washing up on the banks of the river, he decided he would close it up early."

"I can't say I blame him."

"It's over this way," Hamilton says, leading Sterling across the road. They head down the path to the river where a few days earlier they found the body of Jacqueline Myers. The brush is thick, and though the day is cloudy, it's hot for this time of year. The spurs of an autumn olive tree scratch deeply into Sterling, piercing the skin on his arm. He cusses, pushing the branch aside and following close behind Hamilton. The path opens up to the river bank where there's much less vegetation.

"This is it, but it's not the death scene. Her body was laying right there on the river bank. We speculate her body floated downriver." Hamilton points to the faded white online of a body.

"Have you been able to establish where she was killed?"

"No, but from the forensic report—"

"Yeah, I read it. Her body had been in the water for about 24-48 hours."

"It looked like it too, when we found her. God, it was awful—those poor boys that found her, I don't think they'll ever get that image out of their heads."

"No, I don't believe they will. It's the part of this job I hate—exploitation of the innocent."

Shaking his head slightly, Hamilton explains, "We've had three search parties scouring the area upriver. They've covered two miles up and about the same distance east and west—nothing yet."

Sterling strolls over to the white lines that marked where Jaqueline once laid. Kneeling down to get a closer look at the area, though he isn't sure what he's looking for, he hopes he'll uncover something—anything to help guide them in a direction.

"Was anything found around the body?"

"No, but about 500 feet up the trail, there was a footprint—a cat footprint. We found the shoe back in the woods a ways."

Sterling desperately scans the area not seeing anything that can help them. "Well, let's go see the area where the shoe was found." Taking a last look, the clouds break, allowing the sun to shine through. Out of the corner of his eye, the sun's rays glint off something shiny. "Whoa, wait a minute."

"Did you find something?"

"I'm not sure. Do you have gloves on you?"

Hamilton pulls a pair of latex gloves from his pocket. "Always," he says, handing them to Sterling.

Putting on the gloves, Sterling digs in the soft dark soil and removes a round, silver object. He gently wipes away the dirt to reveal a disc about one and a half inches in diameter. In its center is a green crystal cat eye with strange carvings around its edges. Sterling feels strange holding the object. The energy coming off it vibrates up his arm.

"Would you look at that," Hamilton says in admiration of the piece while snapping some pictures. "It looks old—ancient."

Sterling's head spins. He suddenly isn't feeling well.

"Are you alright?" Hamilton asks, his expression turning from one of wonder and amazement to alarm.

"Yeah. I think so. I felt strange for a minute there." Shaking the feeling off, he gets a grip on the whirling sensation in his head.

"You sure?"

"Yes. I'm not sure what happened, but I'm fine now."

"What is it?" Hamilton questions, gawking at the object in Sterling's hand.

"I'm not sure, but I swear I've seen this—well, something like this, somewhere before."

"It looks antique. Maybe you saw it in a shop or something."

"It does, doesn't it? That has to be it. I must have seen something like this in one of those antique shops, a movie, or something." Sterling confirms, though not entirely convinced that is where he'd seen this symbol before. "We better get this back to forensics. Maybe we'll get lucky and useful trace will be on it."

At the precinct, Hamilton takes the coin, amulet, or whatever it is to trace, Sterling following when Dixon stops him. "What did you fin... hey, you look like shit."

"Yeah, I'm not feeling so well. I didn't eat breakfast this morning. Maybe I need some food."

"I think it's more than that, Sterling, you're pale—very pale. Why don't you take the rest of the day? If you're not feeling like yourself in the morning, you need to go back and see the doctor."

"I'm fine, Ca—"

"Don't feed me that load of bullshit. Now, get the hell out of here and get some rest!"

Dixon will not budge, and Sterling is too bilious to fight with him. "Ok, ok. I'll go home and get some rest," He says, turning to make his way back to his desk. "Oh, Cap, we found some sort of coin where they found the Myers girl. It looks old. Hamilton's taking it to forensics."

"Good, maybe we can catch a break. Now, get out of here. Oh, and Sterling?"

"Yeah, Cap."

"That *is* an order." Dixon has his classic "hard ass" expression embedded on his face. It's a trait he has to ensure his men know when he's not fucking around. But a smile still cracks through the *tough guy* routine.

"On my way, Captain, on my way," Sterling says, reaching in his desk. He grabs the files, waves to the guys in the office, and walks to the hallway leading to the exit doors. It has been a long day already. He's glad Cap let him have the rest of the day off. As he walks down the long, dimly lit hall, with its flat beige colored walls and polished tile floor, his footsteps loudly echo, making it seem like he's the last man in the world.

Outside, the clouds briefly break, rays of sunlight bursting through the window. His head spins again as light shocks of electricity pulse through his hand and arms. *What in the hell is wrong with me?* He thinks, reaching his car. Opening the door, he extends and contracts his right-hand's fingers a few times and the pulsing stops. He chalks it up to lack of sleep and being subjected to some strange shit lately. As he turns the key and his old Ford roars to life, he's promptly aware something isn't right with that coin they found. It's an irrational thought, but the way it affects him isn't logical either.

Chapter 18

The Wicked Storm

The foreboding skies held back no longer and a downpour burst from the heavens on his way home. Rain falls in sheets making visibility difficult even with his wipers on full speed. The wind has picked up aggressively, thrusting against the car, causing his arms to ache counteracting the force it takes to keep it on the road. Mother Nature matches his mood with her darkened sky and unforgiving winds, giving the impression it's later than it is.

Sterling doesn't mind so much because he likes the rain, but this he has to admit, is a little much. The storm has caused the temperature to drop, providing some reprieve from the unusually warm August they are having.

The dirt of Baker Road turns into a mud-ridden mess. He manages the car through the push and pulls of thickening sludge and maneuvers proficiently around, or through, the ever-growing puddles. As he enters the driveway, a rush of nausea hits him again, rendering him more tired than he's been in days.

"Shit!" hurriedly, he swings open the driver side door barely in time, so he doesn't dispatch his stomach content over his lap and the seat. "What's wrong with me?" he grumbles, wiping his mouth. He has never been prone to sickness his whole life. and he can't remember one time he's ever had illness befall him. Now that he's thinking about it, he finds the trait strange. Exiting the car, careful not to step in the vomit now spreading across the dirt, he hurriedly makes his way to the front door.

Standing stationary for a moment before going in, he allows the rain to hit his face. It's wet, coolness feels pleasant, even through the intensity of its descent is as if millions of tiny, dull pinpoints are pelting him.

"Ok, ol' man; get your ass in the house before you catch your death out here." Sterling laughs to himself, "Wouldn't it just be the way. I can see the headlines now, 'Well regarded Detective dies of pneumonia after a strange, when an unexpected storm hits the county.' Shaking his head, "I know, I know, I need some sleep. I think I'm losing the bit of sanity I have left."

Opening the front door, he kicks off his shoes and heads straight to the bathroom for a towel. Pulling a clean one from the linen closet, he undresses, dries off, and then pulls on a pair of sweats and a T-shirt. He glances in the mirror at a face with puffy, swollen bags framing his eyes, causing him to look older than he did this morning.

After Dixon's little deluge of inconvenient facts about his life and his own escapade that revealed his family is some kind of fabrication—someone's attempt at a sick fuckin' joke, he's surprised he doesn't look much older. "Josh," he whispers, his heart picking up its pace, speeding, pounding vigorously in his chest, wondering why Jamie would do this to him. *Maybe she was forced. Perhaps someone is out to get me, but who? And where in the hell is my son?*

He picks up the phone and tries Jamie's number. The recorded voice tells him that the number has been disconnected. He dials Josh's number—the same recording.

"Stop this! There's not a damned thing you can do about this now," he advises aloud to four walls void of judgment. Irritated, confused, and more than disturbed, he proceeds to the kitchen to set up the coffeemaker.

Opening the cupboard, he takes out the can of coffee, putting two scoops into the maker systematically, as if his body is completing the task without his command. His eyes are heavy; he has difficulty keeping them open as he puts the coffee back into its place. Returning to the living room, he lies on the sofa. His body refuses to take another step, let alone producing enough energy to accomplish the task of making it to the bedroom. "I need to close my eyes just for a minute... just a minute..."

Lightning assaults the sky, forceful and violent, as if the world has just pissed off the Greek sky and Thunder God, Zeus. Thunder explodes reverberating through the area—raucous, deafening, shaking the whole house.

"Son of a—" Sterling shoots up from the sofa, taking a moment to get his bearings. *I must have crashed hard,* he assesses, sitting on the edge of the sofa rubbing his eyes clear of sleep. Smacking his cheeks with little repetitive slaps, endeavoring to become fully awake, *as if this is helping to wake me up,* he thinks, as lightning rips through the sky once again. Thunder erupts in an angry rage, shaking the house with a force he can feel through the floor.

"Holy hell, someone pissed Mother Nature off," he says, standing and stretching his back and neck.

With the clamorous roaring of rolling thunder, he doesn't hear the rhythmic, hollow knocking of knuckles on his front door right away.

Boom... Boom... Boom...

A pounding sound echoes through the front room as the thunder rumbles, howling its rage through the night. Knocking, the sound of flesh on wood becomes clear, and the thunder dissipates. "Who in the name of God would be out in this shit," he questions, strolling over to the door.

Bewilderment washes over him as he opens the door to expose Nefertiti standing soaking wet on the front porch. More of a shock is that she's wearing a thin, white nightgown, clinging to her naked body underneath.

"Ah... um... Nefertiti, come in. What are you do—"

Nefertiti rushes in, almost knocking him to the floor. "We need to talk, Levi."

Confused by her presence at this hour—though he has no idea what time it is—and her being out in this Godforsaken weather, he closes the door. "I'll get you a towel."

"No! I'm fine. Please, there is something I need to tell you. Something you will not believe, but you must."

She's shaking, sopping wet, with water dripping from the ends of her saturated hair. Her persona feels different, but he can't put a finger on how.

"Alright, let's sit down. You look frozen."

She sits tense and determined on the arm of the sofa; her eyes are dark and penetrating. Her actions are causing an unsettling sensation to rise in his gut. He sits in the chair across from the sofa so he can face her.

"What is it, Nefertiti? What's so important that it could not wait until the morning?"

"Levi, you're not who you think you are. The blow you suffered stole your true identity, and you need to remember."

"What," he laughs, rising from the chair. "Did Hamilton put you up to this?"

"You must listen," she says forcefully. "Jamie. Josh."

"What?! Now wait just a damn minute, how do you know about my family."

"They are not who you believe them to be. You must listen. Please, you have to—"

Sterling doesn't much care for her tone. He always loves a good joke but bringing his family into this is taking it too far. "No! Nefertiti, I don't know what kind of game you're playing, but it stops now!"

Nefertiti's eyes flash—turning bright green—cat-like. Sterling stumbles back, shock and disbelief rush through him. Fangs extend from between her lips as sharp claws tear through the skin of the knuckles on her hands. "You will listen," her voice is deep and menacing as if something or someone has taken over her very being. Her face mutates and twists, morphing into something between human and panther. She rushes him, thrashing him against the far wall, sharp claws embedding themselves deep in his back, ripping through the skin. Blood trickles down the small of his back as she shrieks profoundly in a ravenous voice, "You have to remember, NOW!"

"Holy Fuck!" Sterling screams, falling to the floor from the sofa, crashing against the coffee table, knocking it over to its side. "What in the HELL?!" he bellows, sitting on the floor, hands over the wound on his back, his body shaking.

Lightning flashes, illuminating the sparsely lit house, bouncing shadows across the walls. A loud continuous pounding comes from the front door then the heavens erupt as howling thunder bellows, crashing through the night like a warning siren.

Roughly rubbing his face, he fervently feels his chest and pinches his arm to make sure he's awake and not dreaming this time. It takes a moment for the impending feeling of his dream to wear off. *I must have fallen asleep,* he thinks rising to his feet.

"Ouch!" He shouts, pinching himself hard again for good measure. "Ok... I'm awake," he tells himself, though not wholly convinced.

The pounding on the door surges through the house again. With caution, he makes his way to the front entrance, still unsure if this is reality or a dream. With an air of caution, he opens the door to see Nefertiti standing, drenched from the down pouring rain.

"Levi, Levi! Is everything ok?" she asks, concern riddling her features.

He hesitates before responding. Glancing at the wall mirror—still hanging by the door where it's been since purchasing the place—he sees a frazzled, wild-eyed man staring back at him. *Good God, man, get it together. It was just a dream,* he muses.

Gazing back on Nefertiti who is soaked just as before, but not in a clinging nightgown, he realizes that this is real. She's wearing a raincoat and has an umbrella hovering over her head, though it isn't helping much as he watches droplets of water drip from the ends of her wet hair.

"Levi, you look like hell, are you feeling ok?"

He stands there like a damned fool just staring at her as she asks with a touch of frustration.

"Are you going to let me in?"

"Oh, I'm sorry. Yes, come in," he invites, leading her through the threshold. As he shuts the door, thunder rumbles, the sky brighten with the lightning that tears through the darkness. The room Illuminates like a floodlight was switched on and then off again. "Sorry it's so dark," he says, switching on the lamp as he enters the living room. "Why are you out in this weather?"

"The lights went out. This storm must have knocked the power out. I couldn't find the damned candles in the dark. But I noticed your lights were still on, so I came down to see if you had any extra candles I may borrow. I was going to come down earlier, but I thought you'd be resting, just coming from the hospital and all. From the looks of you, I was right." Nefertiti takes off her soaked raincoat, putting it on the hook by the door, and sets her umbrella in the corner. "Um... how are your lights still on?"

"I have a generator that kicks in when there's a power outage. You may want to invest in one yourself. When the stormy season comes calling, you're guaranteed to lose power."

"I'll have to look into that. Are you sure you're feeling ok?" She questions. "I mean, I know you just got out of the hospital, but forgiving me for saying this, you look terrible. Your color is erratic," she says, placing her surprisingly warm hand to his forehead. "I heard a loud ruckus and..."

Her concern touches Sterling even though there is no need. He feels fine, well besides the unsettling dream he had. "No, I'm good. I fell asleep on the sofa and the thunder startled me out of a dead sleep that's all."

"Are you certain? You're extremely pale and rather muddled."

"Honestly, I had a good jolt is all. Let me get you a towel to dry off with before you end up catching your death." Turning, he walks toward the guest bathroom and takes a clean towel from the rack. No one, including himself, uses this bathroom except on rare occasions, which means he also has a clean guest towel hanging on the rack just in case. Nefertiti's still scrutinizing him as he hands her the towel, a questionable expression swarms her features.

"Thank you," she says, taking the towel.

"I'm fine, really," he repeats to reassure her. "Would you like some coffee? I have hot cocoa if you prefer."

"Coffee sounds lovely," Nefertiti answers, moving further into the house and examining the turned over coffee table. "You really must have had one heck of a fright."

"I'm sorry?" he asks, pausing his exit to the kitchen and turning to face her.

"You must have had quite a fright," she repeats, glancing down at the turned over table.

"Yeah, it was a heck of a dream." He doesn't look directly into her eyes when he says this. "I'll start the coffee. Please make yourself comfortable."

When he turns to walk into the kitchen, Nefertiti gasps, "My God, Levi, what did you do to yourself?!" Blood covers the back, right side of Sterling's T-shirt.

"What do you mean," he asks, perplexed by her outburst.

"Your back, it's bleeding."

"What?!" Sterling cranks his head as far back as he can, knowing damned well he won't be able to see. Reaching his right hand across his chest, he feels nothing. Then he does the same with his left, feeling the thick, clinging dampness of his shirt. "Shit," he snorts, taking off his shirt. "I have no idea what I did."

Nefertiti goes to the bathroom, coming out with a damp washcloth. "Here let me see," she says, motioning for him to turn around. She isn't able to see the wound clearly until she carefully pats away the blood. What she sees radiated a sporadic set of icy chills through her body; three gouges from his right shoulder to almost his spine.

"What do you see?" Sterling asks.

"Ah... um..." she hesitates.

"Well," Sterling urges, impatiently.

"It looks as if you may have ripped open your stitches from your attack."

"I didn't have any wounds on my back from the assault. At least, I don't remember any."

"Well, you have wounds on your back, and you took a good bang on the head, right?"

"I did."

"They look like claw marks. But they could be from your fall. Maybe you caught yourself on some sharp edges. But without any other explanation..." she leaves the sentence unfinished, examining the wound.

He thinks about it for a moment. He's not positive there weren't any marks on his back. He assumed they were only on his chest, but never asked otherwise. Hell, he never felt them and still doesn't.

"That's true. But I didn't think... it doesn't matter."

Still holding the washcloth, blotting the wound to soak up the blood, Nefertiti asks, "Do you have Band-Aids or a first-aid kit somewhere?"

Puzzled but more irritated than anything, Sterling tells her, "The first-aid kit is in the hall closet." As she gets what she needs, he thinks, *how? How could I not have known about the wounds on my back?* His dream of Nefertiti flashes through his mind, the claws gouging his back, her face altering into that of a panther. *That's ridiculous, Levi. Keep it together, old man.*

"Here we are." Nefertiti comes back, the first-aid kit in one hand and peroxide in the other. "I'll have you fixed up in a few minutes. I have to say you have one of the best stocked first-aid kits I've ever witnessed."

"Living out in these woods you never know what you'll need," Sterling replies. "The funny thing is I never had one in New York. But the first week I was here, I bought this kit and added to it as the years went on."

"Good thing you did. I believe I can close the wounds well enough you won't need to get re-stitched. That is, if you can be careful not to open them again."

"Didn't mean to open them up this time—didn't even know they were... sssss," Sterling hisses.

"Sorry, this will sting."

"Yeah, I got that."

"Don't be such a baby," Nefertiti states, taping up the wounds. "There that should do it. Coffee?" She asks, getting up and heading to the kitchen.

"Ah, yeah," Sterling replies.

Heading to his bathroom, he grabs a hand mirror from the cabinet. He found the mirror after he moved in, left behind from the last owners. It's large, carved vintage hand mirror with a filigree antique, bronze finish, was quite the fetching little item. *Someone sure must have had some fascination with mirrors,* he broods, positioning himself in front of the mirror to see his back in the wall mirror. There's a little blood seeping through the gauze but nothing to cause alarm. *Huh, she does good work,* he thinks.

"So have I passed the skill test?"

"Jesus!" Sterling jumps, hissing through clenched teeth and holding his chest.

"I'm sorry, Levi. You are quite jumpy tonight. Coffee?" She holds out a mug of the steaming liquid.

"Yeah, I guess I am," Sterling answers, taking the mug from her. "Thank you."

"We need to talk, Levi," Nefertiti says and her demeanor changes. She's anxious.

"About what?"

"It's important—essential—and you may not believe me, but I swear everything I'm going to tell you is true." She taps her nail on the side of the coffee cup. "This may not be a pleasant conversation for you."

His dream streaks through his mind, but he pushes that absurd fantasy aside. He notices Nefertiti is physically shaking, her eyes fill with agitation and apprehension, making Sterling very curious about what she has to say.

"Hell, it can't be any worse than the *pleasantries* I've been through for the last couple weeks," he conveys with some sarcasm and a humorless guffaw.

She doesn't look at him. She stares blankly at an indiscernible spot before her. Lips at the edge of the steaming mug of coffee, she blows gently to cool it. Her color washed from her skin.

"Now, you're the one whose pale. You look as if you've seen a ghost. It can't be that bad."

"Oh, but it can, Levi."

"Then why don't we sit and you can say your piece."

Nefertiti's anxiety is palpable, filling the room with its thickness. Click, click, click, her nail taps the side of the white enamel mug. Whatever she is planning to tell him, he believes what she's said about it not being welcoming information. However, he doesn't get to hear what she's so eager to tell him. A booming racket comes from outside before Sterling can sit down—and it isn't the thunder.

"What in the hell was that!" Sterling shouts, turning toward the door.

"I don't know," Nefertiti says, shooting up from her seated position as Sterling moves to the front door. "Levi, don't go out there."

"I have to see who is out there, Nefertiti. Its sound like the side of the house is being ripped off."

"Please, Levi," She's shaking, rushing to his side. "I don't have a good feeling about this."

"Jesus, you're frightened. I can feel you trembling." He wraps his arms around her, "I'll be alright. I'm just going to look. You stay here."

He ignores Nefertiti's pleas, seizing the flashlight out of the drawer in the console by the door, grabs his gun sitting on its top, and walks outside. The storm is raging. Rain falls like sheets, making visibility impossible. The treetops lash, swaying back and forth uninhibited in the blustering wind. A clamorous crack fractures the night simultaneously the sky lights up as lightning streaks through its stark blackness. He catches movement in the corner of his eye.

"Who's out here?" He bellows although the thunder conceals his voice. He hears another crash off to his left and swings his flashlight around.

A wicked, abrupt pain races through the back of his skull. Darkness overtakes him—

Chapter 19

The Sands of Time

The sands of time flashed before Sterling's eyes, slamming displays of his life and all life before his, in a whirlwind of organized chaos. Sterling is rocketing backward in time. Wars, the settling of America, voyages across the sea, the building of Machu Picchu, the Colosseum, the Great Wall of China, the Pyramids and Stonehenge.

Backward he flies like a hasten tour of a mass historical timeline. The onslaught stings his face like thousands of pinpricks, whirling him back further through time until he stops abruptly.

Sterling is lying on the hot sand. He lifts himself up bewildered, his head throbbing. "Son of a bitch," erupts from his excessively dry mouth. Disorientation devastates his senses. "Where in the fu—"

A slow, steady, subdued chanting is coming up from behind him, sounding in his ears in a language that's ancient. Yet, he comprehends the dialect, this antediluvian tongue of bizarre voices.

Turning, he sees people cloaked in dark tunics arranged in a semi-circle around a raging fire. He tramps closer, rubbing his eyes. "Levi, you're dreaming." Squeezing his eyes shut tight, he opens them again with a slight shake of his head, but the vision is still before him. The people he's seeing don't seem to notice him.

He moves hesitantly closer toward the persistently chanting flock; their words produce a low constant droning. *"Great Mafdet we summon you."*

An attractive, young, long-haired girl wearing a light linen tunic stands in front of the inhabitants gathered. Unlike the others, a coronet of colorful flowers, intertwined twigs, and vibrant greenery cover her crown. Intricate symbols blanket her bronze skin. Fear pervades her large, dark eyes though she stands perfectly still, seemingly in a deep trance.

A woman dressed in black, her face covered excluding her milky white eyes, moves snake-like through the flock of chanters, taking the girl by the hand and leads her to the fire. Sterling steadily steps in to see a dark cave, hidden beneath the sands. The old woman guides the girl to the mouth of the cave, placing her in front of it like a trophy. The old woman turns to the crowd, raising her hands towards the sky the chanting quiets to nothing more than a murmuring hum as she says, *"Oh, the great Mafdet we summon you. We honor you with this gift of innocence and blood."* The incanting cluster's volume rises to a buzz of the hypnotic harmony like a massive beehive, repeatedly chanting *innocence and blood*.

He sees *it*. Stunned. Confused. Before he can react, the young girl is jerked back into the darkness by a massive claw. Blood sprays from the cave, coating the opening with crimson splatter, blood trickling down like rainwater. The chanting becomes louder, causing his head to whirl, pounding with their obsessive chanting.

"NO!" emanates from him with the force of the Thunder God. The ominous crowd spins to face him, still chanting their bustling message of death.

In a moment of fevered delirium, his eyes flicker. A blurred image of a ceiling is momentarily in his view. He hears harsh voices, abrasively whispering somewhere in the distance.

> *Have you lost your mind! What do you think you're doing?*
> *Don't give me your 'holier than thou' tone! I'm sick of this game.*
> *Damn it! You must handle this with delicate gloves. What are you trying to do, kill him?! I'm warning you—*

Don't you dare! Don't you try to threaten me! We have waited and coddled him long enough. Ten years have passed. You must tell him! If you don't, I swear I will—
You'll what sister? You know all too well...

"We honor you with this gift of innocence and blood," buzzes with a hypnotic rhythm with dark, empty eyes piercing his very soul. From the blood-soaked cave, a dark, long-haired, half-naked woman appears. She's hauntingly paralyzing, her beauty unmatched. Levi observes her as she slowly faces him. In her arms is something he can't quite make out. Slowly, she approaches him; her big, dark, hypnotizing eyes intense, searing through his essence. He shockingly feels no fear and the young girl is a distant, concerning memory.

In an instant, she's inches in front of him. He can feel her strange, mysterious, inviting energy. The heat of her essence pulls him, calling some primal influence within him.

He can't think; she has engulfed his very being. He can't move, frozen in place as if made of stone.

She's familiar, proverbially so. He tries, but his head won't allow him to recollect where he knows her.

She holds the bundle she has in her arms out to him. For a moment, Levi can't pull his eyes from hers to look down at what she carries. A smile creases her face as his eyes fall to see a child wrapped in linen. An emblem lay on the child's chest, just like the coin he found at the scene of Jacqueline Myers' murder. She takes the withered cloth from the child's face, revealing bright green eyes of his own.

"NO! NO! It can't be," he whispers in bitter disbelief. His head slowly rises as his eyes meet hers once again. With blazing speed, the face he beholds is now one of a raging panther.

"Nooo!"

Arrrgh! Dull pain fires through his body as he slams to the floor. Erratically breathing in a fit of confusion, Sterling lies on his back with his hand on his chest feeling his heart pounding. He stares up at the white tiles of his home's ceiling, feeling the rough wood of floor beneath him.

It was a dream.

"Levi, Oh my god, Levi," he hears, seemingly in the distance, a flustered voice of a woman. "Levi! Jesus, let me help you."

He slowly twists his aching head to see the troubled-filled eyes of Nefertiti.

"Levi, speak to me," she begs, kneeling down beside him.

He tries to sit up, but a sharp pain rips through his head, forcing him back to the floor. "Dammit!" he grumbles, carefully clutching the back of his head.

"Please, lay still. You took one heck of a knock." She takes a pillow off the bed and places it beneath his head.

"From what?" he asks, hoarsely.

"The storm. Don't you remember?"

"Not really," he replies, still discombobulated and unsure of what's real.

"Last night—"

"Last night!" Screams from his lips and immediately he wishes he had kept his voice down. A pain streaking through his skull—a pulverizing pounding as if Neil Peart from Rush is playing a drum solo on his brain—he lets out a slight moan.

"Please, Levi, you must rest for a moment." Nefertiti rises, going to the bathroom. She comes back with a glass of water in one hand and two aspirins in the other. "Here take these," she says, supporting his head.

"What are they?"

"Aspirin, it's the only thing you have. Didn't the doctor give you a prescription?"

"Yeah, I flushed them."

"Why?!"

Sterling ignores Nefertiti's question. "So, what happened last night?"

"We heard a loud commotion outside. You went to see what was going on, against my better judgment, mind you." She had to throw that little dig in there. Her scowled expression shows she's none too happy with his decision. "The storm was raging and the wind had kicked up something awful. I tried to stop you, but you went out, nonetheless. A hard smack on the head from a fallen tree branch is all you gained from your stubbornness."

"Christ, no wonder I feel like I have the hangover of the century," he says, raspy. His throat parched.

"Here, let me help get you to bed."

"What time is it?"

"2 a.m.," she tells him with a weary smile.

"And you stayed?"

"I couldn't just leave you. You took quite a knock you know."

"Yeah, I guess so. Thank you, Nefertiti. Thank you for staying with me."

"No worries. Now get some sleep. I'll be on the sofa if you need anyth—"

"No, stay. Please lay with me."

Nefertiti gives him a curious look for a moment but climbs into bed next to him. He wraps his arm around her as she places her head on his chest. Her warmth fills him with a sense of safety; the light scent of her perfume, musk of some kind fills him with tranquility. She listens to his steady heartbeat and wraps her arms around his waist. Sleep comes effortlessly to them both.

Chapter 20

The Grizzly Death

Vrrr, vrrr, vrrr, Sterling's cell vibrates on the nightstand. Slowly he slips from dream to a conscious state, trying to eliminate the haziness of his drowsy eyes. Vrrr, vrrr, vrrr, the phone is screaming at him.

"Jesus Christ," he grumbles, holding his aching head. Picking up his cell and clearing his voice he utters, "Yeah, this is Sterling."

An erratic voice practically shouts on the other line. "Sterling! God, man, where have you been?! Oh God! You're not going to believe this! Shit, this is crazy. It's a damn nightmare—"

"Whoa, slow down. Hamilton?"

"Yeah, it's me... Sterling, there's been another murder at the Dixon's. It's a—"

"Wait, the Dixon's?!"

"Yes!" Some heavy breaths of frustration radiate through the receiver.

"Ok, Hamilton, slow down and tell me what happened."

"We got a distress call early this morning from the Dixon house. Though I don't know all the details, the call shook the 911 operator. I was the first on the scene... Oh God! Sterling, it's a fucking massacre!" Hamilton's voice cracks.

"Hamilton, hold it together. I'll be there shortly."

"Yeah, yeah, I'll try."

"I'll be right there. Just wait for me. I'll be right th—" The line dies. "Shit!" Sterling jumps out of bed, throws on his jeans and the shirt he wore the night before since it was the closest thing to him.

Glancing at his watch, he's surprised it's 9 am already. *What in the hell is wrong with me?* At that moment, he notices Nefertiti isn't there.

On his way out, he sees a note lining the stand by the door. The letters scratched across the paper in black ink say:

We need to talk.
~Nefertiti

"Yeah, well sweetheart, that will have to wait," he declares, hustling out the door and into his car.

Christ, what in the hell is going on in this town, he thinks as he races down the familiar muddy road to the Dixon home.

Sirens blare, lights flash, and a crowd has already configured outside the stone ranch home of the Dixon's.

"Damned, wretched *lookiloos*," he mutters, pulling his car to the curb. Cameras and reporters rush him when he opens the car door. They sure *are* assertive bastards. Nothing would give him more pleasure than to shove these cameras right up their pushy asses.

"Detective Sterling. Detective Sterling," thunders in his ears crudely, while he pushes his way through the masses.

"Hey, come on people, back off. Back the hell off, NOW!" a voice bellows above the swarm. "Sterling," Hamilton says roughly, pushing through the wave of cameras and reporters. He reaches Sterling and wraps his arm around his shoulders. "Parasites," rumbles from his mouth as they make their way to the yellow tape surrounding the Dixon home. Hamilton's tone is harsh, his eyes red and glassy, his body rigid. This one is personal, and Hamilton is showing the telltale signs of mixed emotion raging through him. And from what Sterling can see, he has reached a hard-boiled attitude. People handle the death of those close to them in different ways; some cry, some close off. But Hamilton? He becomes a thick-skinned vigilante wanting nothing less than revenge.

Just then, some insane part of his brain gushes a phrase from a movie he's seen *'a man's heart is stonier.'* Hamilton is a prime example of that phrase at the moment. The problem with seeing Hamilton like this means the scene that awaits him inside won't be pleasant.

"Thanks," he tells Hamilton, although the man doesn't look at him, keeping his rough, hardened expression and eyes on the ground. "Hey, you going to be ok."

Hamilton still doesn't say a word, he keeps pushing rigorously through the horde.

"Hamilton?"

"It's Roy and Maggie for fuck sakes!" he finally replies in a harsh, hushed tone.

His language is a dead giveaway that he's at the threshold of a frenzied calm. Sterling watches a light, misty haze form in his eyes, betraying the hard-boiled expression on his face. He stops Hamilton after they reach the other side of the yellow tape with bold black letters— POLICE LINE DO NOT CROSS. "James, listen, I need to know you will keep it together. I know this is hard on everyone. Shit, I have known them for ten years, and they're like my surrogate father and mother, but I need you. They need you to pull it together," he says, putting his hand on Hamilton's shoulder. "Ok?"

"Yeah."

Studying his face for a moment longer, Sterling observes the struggle within him but concludes he'll make it through this. *Hell, what did you expect, this is the Dixons!* He thinks. After all, he's grasping at every ounce of determination he has to keep a level head when all he truly wants to do is mourn the death of his friends. *Buck up, Levi, ol' boy, the last thing you need is to fall apart. Not now, not yet,* he tells himself taking a cleansing breath before speaking to James. "Good. Now, where in the hell did all these reporters come from so quickly?"

"Hell, I don't know. I think they're enabled with a sixth sense for devastation and others despair I guess." Hamilton replies, critically. "By the way, where have you been?"

"Why are you carrying on like an overprotective woman? I was just at the office yesterday."

"No, Sterling, you were at the office on Friday; it's Monday."

Sterling's face falls. Utter confusion dominates his expression. "That's not possible," he breathes.

"You sure *you're* ok, Levi?" Hamilton asks, with some concern and a touch of sarcasm.

He lets it slide, understanding the situation. "Yeah, I guess the smack in the head knocked me out longer than I had thought."

"What?"

"The storm. There was a ruckus outside that night. When I went to check it out, a tree limb fell and hit me on the head. Nefertiti took care of me. I must have had a slight concussion."

"Concussions are nothing to play around with, Sterling. Maybe you shouldn't be here."

"No, I should be here. I'm good, just a headache."

"If you say so." His firm expression has lifted some, but not much. However, there's an underlying amount of concern now present.

"Shit, you know me."

"Even tough guys need to take care, you know," Hamilton tells him with a grim smirk. Nonetheless, his eyes broadcast his unease.

"I'll manage," Sterling states, harsher than he intends.

"Ok," Hamilton huffs, worry furling his brow. "Ah, Sterling, I think we should talk before you go in there. I want to warn you it's gruesome—the worst I've seen. What happened to the Cap and his wife… it… well, it's—"

"Hamilton, I'll take care… and thanks."

Hamilton doesn't say a thing, only pats him on the back. Sterling walks to the door. He stops, noticing Hamilton isn't following. "You coming?"

"No, I've seen enough," he says, unsteadily and for a moment profound sadness reaches his eyes, though quickly, the rigidity comes back. It had to, this is how James copes with this more than unpleasant situation. "I'll stay out here and keep these vultures back."

Sterling nods in understanding. *God, what in the hell has this lunatic done to the Dixons?* He asks himself, not wanting the answer. It would come soon enough and that fact creates a lump like a stone in his throat. Pausing at the door to catch his breath, quickly wiping his eyes he hadn't realized watered up. He prepares for the atrocity he's sure to see inside. *Prepared, hell! No one can be ready to see their murdered friends. Who are you trying to kid?* He thinks and for a moment, wishes he selected a different profession. A prophesying sensation sweeps over him as he reaches for the door handle. One that cries *'brace yourself, ol' boy. There are horrors behind this door you can never unsee.'*

He's nearly slammed on his ass when the door swings violently open. An officer, one hand clutching his stomach, the other over his mouth, comes barreling out on the porch. The officer leans over the rail and vomits in the bushes. Sterling squeezes his eyes closed, inhales deeply, and ambles inside.

The first thing he notices is the smell. A thick coppery aroma fused with a pungent fragrance of rot, urine, and excrement hangs heavy in the air. The scent assaults his senses, clawing its way into his nostrils fighting to become a part of him. It coats his tongue with its reeking bouquet. The site welcoming him is a partial leg lying in a large pool of blood in the middle of the floor, yellow markers bordering it. The size and the fact it's unshaven, tells Sterling it belongs to Dixon.

Sterling takes shallow breaths as he reaches into his pocket for a hanky. His stomach tightens viewing the limb once attached to a man he loved, looked up to, and respected. He eyes threaten to reveal his pain, but he pushes the emotion down, keeping it at bay, though it is difficult to keep his staunch front from collapsing. Shielding his mouth and nose, he makes his way to the severed leg.

As he kneels down, the coppery odor of blood grows more potent. However, it's not strong enough to mask the foul mixture that accompanies it. These are the rancid fragrance he has regrettably grown, more or less, used to. But this, among other unsavory things, day after day, becomes 'the norm.'

Getting a closer look at the detached extremity, he surmised the appendage was torn from the body. *How is this possible?* He muses. *Ounce for ounce, bone is stronger than steel.* The force it took to do something like this to Roy Dixon is mind-boggling. He straightens, rattling conceivable causes around in his brain while he approaches the hallway.

The rancid odor of death thickens the closer he gets to the hall. His stomach churns and tightens painfully. *Come on Levi. It isn't your first rodeo*; he tells himself. *Damn it! Sterling, keep your head straight. Pull yourself together and do your damn job!* his head screams. At this point, whatever has happened to Dixon and his wife can't be any worse than what he'd already seen in his time as a detective. The fact of the matter is, he knows these people, considered them friends. Whoever's doing this has made it personal.

Nearing the corner of the hallway, he runs into Brendan, one of the people on Sam's forensic team. "Shit!" Sterling spouts, as the two men collide.

"Oh, God," Brendan yelps, visibly startled. "I'm sorry, Detective Sterling. I should watch where I am going."

The young man before him is struggling with his emotions, doing his very best to steady himself so he can do his job. His puffy, bloodshot eyes are a dead giveaway to his current emotional state. There's a slight tremor in his person, Sterling notices. *This kid is really shaken up*, he thinks, placing a steady hand on the young man's shoulder.

"No, I'm as much to blame," Sterling informs him. "This case has everyone on edge."

"I never—well, I *hoped*, I'd never have to work a friend's case."

"I hear ya."

Brendan has on a white lab coat over a blue sweatshirt and jeans. Latex gloves cover his hands, with an empty, plastic vial in one hand and a swab in the other. He's mid-twenties, with dirty-blonde hair that never lies properly, narrow hazel eyes, and is thin, almost comically so. He wears thick, black glasses that add to the mad scientist look he sports, and is very young, but Sam admires the man's skills. Which brings him to question, *where is Sam?*

"So," Sterling asks, "How bad is it back there?"

"I haven't ever seen anything like it, Detective. To be honest, I wish I'd never been back there, and hope I never have to witness anything like it again. I wish Samantha were here."

"Samantha isn't here? Where is she?"

"That's a damned good question," he says, turning around. "Sam left the office early on Friday and hasn't been back. We've called her cell and don't even get the voicemail. Amy and I went to her house, but no one is home. It's just not like her."

"No, it's not like her at all." *Fuck, that's all we need a missing M.E.! Keep it together Sterling; you'll have to worry about this later,* he thinks. Keeping his voice steady Sterling asks, "So, where are they... Roy and Maggie?"

"You mean what's left of them?" Brendan says, swallowing hard and immediately regretting his words observing Sterling's intense expression. "Man, I'm sorry. I—"

"Don't. I understand."

Brendan wipes his misted brow on the sleeve of his lab coat. "C'mon, I'll take you back," he says with a wave of his hand, but his reluctance is palpable. He places the swab inside the plastic vial and snaps it shut. Then deposits the vile in a black kit that reminds Sterling of an extravagant tackle box.

"Oh, and stay on the left," He informs Sterling, moving toward the hall.

Sterling follows Brendan. Entering the hallway he sees blood on the floor and wall. His insides tighten; a burning sensation flourishes in the pit of his stomach. On the corner is a perfectly preserved handprint in blood. He assumes this is where Dixon pulled himself from the floor with a dangling shredded limb, using all his strength to make it down to the bedroom. He can practically see the scene playing out in the depths of his mind. Dixon, his face twisted, fraught with agony and despair, struggling to get to Maggie, yelling her name. Physically shaking the image from his mind's eye, he continues to take in the wretched display before him.

Roy Dixon, after the excruciating removal of his leg, still had the will to do everything he could to advance down the hall to their bedroom. A pronounced blood trail on the ceramic tile, bloody handprints on the beige wall, smears of one bloody footprint. "God," is all Sterling can manage, taking in the brutality, the pain, the struggle. A couple of pictures lay on the floor, shards of glass spread across the hall from where either Roy or the prep knocked them from their hangers.

As they continued down to the last room on the right-hand side, the hard knot that formed in his throat grows. On the door frame, another handprint line oozes down from the print of dried blood. *His hand was soaked with blood, he was losing too much*; the thought is so loud in his skull it sends a cold chill down his back. No matter what the scene in this room is, he knows for a fact he's not ready to witness it.

Brendan points, not attempting to enter the room. Sterling nods with understanding and Brendan leaves back the way they came. Sterling stands outside the room, images of the nightmare that awaits behind the door flash through his head. He takes hold of the doorknob, his heartbeat quickens, his pulse races, as he feels a bead of sweat trickle down his temple.

Any other case would have been just that, another case. But this was *not* another case, this was the Dixon's. The people who took him in like family and showed him strength, love, and compassion when he needed it the most. When he thought he might never pull himself out of the bowels of desperation and the bottom of an Old No. 7 bottle, Roy Dixon was there keeping him focused, keeping him going, so he could move on. *I will damn well catch this bitch and whoever's helping her. I'll bury them or put a fucking bullet in their heads!* he thinks, giving himself his version of a pep talk.

He waits a minute, gathering up all the courage he can before entering to view what horrors await him just beyond this door.

Levi, do this for their sake. It's a case, work it, he reasons. *It is not just another case! This is Roy and Maggie! The people you love! People you've known for ten fucking years for Christ's sake. And some jack-wad took them from you, so buck up and do your fucking job!* His internal dialog courses anger through his veins and the anger sets his head straight, providing him the much-needed fortitude to witness what's behind the next door, at least for the moment.

Entering the room, the scene before him looks like a bad horror flick—a damn Manson family reunion or something. Dixon lay on the floor, his head cocked to the left. Around his thigh, just above the missing part of his leg is a belt tightly fitted—a tourniquet to stop the flow of blood. His left arm stretches out from his side toward the bed.

On the bed is a body—at least pieces of one. The remains on the bed, rationally, are of Maggie. Although to look at them, no one can say whether it's her confidently. DNA will have to confirm it's her. Her body looks more like pulverized meat that a butcher put through a grinder. Blood's everywhere—the floor, the windows, the walls, and is still sluggishly dripping off the bedding making a thick, sickening sound as drops gradually fall into the puddle beneath.

"Son of a bitch," Sterling mutters, pushing the hanky tighter to his face. Stomach rumbling with constricting pressure, he almost doubles over. His head throbs, his heartbeat fills his ears. It hasn't been long since the murders, but a smell assaults his senses. It's a God-awful smell, one that recalls the scent of decomp mixed with burning hair, and a wet dog who bathed in swamp water. The door handle solely supports his weight as his knees grow weak, fighting to defy him. The room is worse than he could ever conjure in his head and as his eyes take in the excessive carnage before him, another emotion breaks through, one he knows well. An emotion more comforting than the heart gripping grief. One he can use to get through this. Molten anger rolls over every nerve with rage flooding his veins, and just when he thinks he will erupt, he sees tufts of blonde hair bobbing from the other side of the bed.

From the end of the bedpost, he realizes the blonde hair belongs to Amy, another person from Sam's team. She is on her knees with a pair of tweezers in one of her gloved hands and a plastic bag in the other.

"Amy," Sterling croaks, his fist clenched so tight his knuckles are white.

"Jesus Christ!" Amy yells, startled, about dropping the bag and tweezers she holds. "Dammit Sterling, don't do that. Shit! I am already on edge!" she scowls.

"I didn't mean too..." the wretched odor is more pungent on this side of the room. "What's that smell? It reeks like Satan's ass in here."

With an expression of wanting to ring his neck still embracing her features, Amy tells him, "I'm not sure about the smell but you're right it's rancid."

As he treads lighter in the storm he has created, a glint of something silver catches his eye. "What is that?" he points to what Amy holds in her hand.

"It looks to be some rather strange coin or something." She says, holding the bag up to her face inspecting the object.

"A coin, like the one found down by the Rifle River?"

"Now that you mention it, yeah, it could be similar to that one."

"Where was it?" He asks, staring at the peculiar artifact, feeling the familiar sensation of slight dizziness and nausea he felt when they found the last one.

"Down here next to the bed covered in blood, so I can't honestly make it out. As soon as I get it back to the lab, I'll clean it up and compare the two."

"Good," Sterling breathes, scrutinizing the mangled body on the bed.

"What in the hell could have done this?"

"Your guess is as good as mine at this point. I have no idea. Whatever or whoever it was, was strong—very strong." She says, sealing the evidence bag and putting it with the others in her kit.

"I gathered that from Roy's leg."

"That's not all," she says, rising and pointing toward the wall above the mutilated body, "You see the blood there?" She asks and Sterling nods. "Those series of spatter patterns are from the last few beats of Mrs. Dixon's heart. These patterns are from severing the carotid artery. Now that isn't particularly unusual, but how it was done is."

"What do you mean?"

She moves to the other side of the bed, maneuvering with expertise around the evidence. "Look here," she gestures to what looks to be nothing but raw meat. "Do you see this?"

Sterling leans to identify what Amy is pointing to. In about the only part of Maggie that isn't minced up like hamburger meat, are three rather large puncture holes in her neck. "What could have done that?"

"I can't confirm that yet, but it appears someone shoved their fingers through the skin, severing her artery."

"Christ," Sterling mutters, his gut the burns like a punch to the groan.

"However," Amy continues, either not noticing his current state, or he's doing one hell of a job hiding it. "She suffered a great deal more torture before whoever did this performed the deed." Amy walks to the window, "Look here."

Sterling progresses closer, there's a print in blood, "A handprint."

"Yeah, it matches Mrs. Dixon perfectly, which tells me she was bleeding out fairly well by this point."

"Could it be from her trying to help Roy?"

"It could, but Sterling, I think she was in bed when the attack started. Have you had a good look down the hall?"

"Yeah. What a mess."

They walk over to the door and peer down the hallway at the trail of blood left by Roy. "I can't verify it yet, but I surmise Mrs. Dixon was in here asleep, the radio was on when we came in. With the door closed, the radio on, and asleep…"

"She may not have heard Roy scream."

"Exactly! He dragged himself down here to get to her before, whatever in the fires of hell, got to her first. However, he doesn't make it."

"No. He doesn't."

"The thing that creeps me out more than anything else is Mr. Dixon's expression."

"What do you mean?"

"After he made it in here," Amy turns to Dixon's body. "Just before his throat got ripped out something stuck an unparalleled terror in him."

"Wait, his throats ripped out?!"

"Come here and have a look."

Sterling's head feels as if a pianist is playing Wolfgang Amadeus Mozart's Piano Sonata No. 16 on his brain, but instead of the delicate piano hammers that hit the strings, the pianist opted to use bongo mallets instead. With a greater effort than he imagines, he makes his way over to Dixon's corpse and kneels down. Dixon's lifeless eyes are wide, a dark-looming glaze, like two pools of lusterless black holes. His facial expression borders on pure, unbridled terror. He can't bear to look at him, but he can't seem to tear his gaze away either. His pulse races, his heart's pumping so rapidly, it feels like a runaway train ready to derail its tracks. Without warning, images flash through his mind. Blood splatter. Dixon's horror-stricken face. Maggie's screams. Flesh ripping from bodies. Fangs. Claws.

"Sterling," Amy urges, witnessing the color drain from his skin. "Sterling, are you with me?"

Startled, he scampers backward, falling on his ass.

"Sterling! Jesus man, are you alright?!"

Abruptly, he snaps out of the death trance and stammers, "Ah, yeah. Yeah, I'm fine."

"Jesus, Sterling, you're sweating and your color—"

"I'm fine!" Sterling snaps.

Amy's face contorts with concern and confusion.

"I'm sor... Amy, this case is just..."

"I know. Trust me, everyone's on edge." She examines him questionably, "Seriously though, you gonna make it? You don't look so good. You look as if you've seen a ghost."

"I'm good. I just wasn't expecting all of this. It caught me off guard, is all." He wasn't about to tell her about the wallop he took on the noggin, knocking him out for a while. He should be resting, not investigating, but he couldn't let anyone else take the lead on this case. Not this one. He wouldn't let Roy and Maggie down like that.

Her expression speaks louder than words, telling him she's not convinced, but she asks, "You sure you want to see this? You don't have to, you know."

"No, I do. I need to see everything," he tells her in a choked voice.

"Look here," she instructs, moving Dixon's shoulder carefully off the floor to expose his neck. A dark, red, raw, gaping hole greets him. Shredded pieces of skin hang to either side as part of the carotid artery dangles from the wound and a portion of the trachea is exposed. She's right; Roy's throat was ripped out, and he didn't need to see it.

"Christ," he sputters and glances back at the body on the bed. "Where's the blood? I mean, shouldn't there be more blood?"

"I haven't had time to figure that one out yet."

Sterling ponders for a second, running the bizarre scenario through his mind. "Come with me he says."

Without question, she follows him down the hall and out to the living room by the door. "Stay with me now," he says, walking methodically through the crime scene. "So, Dixon is attacked as soon as he answers the door," he opens and shuts the door, turning toward the interior of the house. "The perp and Dixon struggle and in the process, somehow, the perp rips Roy's leg from his body before heading down the hall toward the bedroom. Does that sound about right?" he asks Amy.

"So far," Amy confirms, nodding her head

"But how does he know Maggie's in the bedroom?"

In unison, they say, "The music!"

"Right, so Roy gives chase," he continues down the hallway. "He's struggling, but Maggie's screams keep him going. When he finally makes it to the room, he sees this psycho butchering Maggie. He probably tries to pull the fiend off of her, but the perp turns and tears Roy's throat out before he can do much to stop what's happening to Maggie. Does that sound about right?"

"That's what the evidence is showing at this point."

"Now, with Roy taken care of, the perp can torture and mutilate Maggie at his leisure."

"Right," Amy confirms.

"But it makes little sense," Sterling asserts to himself more than to Amy. "Why didn't he finish off Roy before going to Maggie? Was Maggie the target?"

"I don't think so. Maybe he's a psycho that needed an audience or the asshole might have wanted Roy to know Maggie would not survive."

"Maybe," Sterling mutters, unconvinced.

"But who has a grudge against the Dixons? Or could this be related to the death of those girls? I mean they were ripped up—nothing like Maggie, but still."

"I don't know, Amy. I genuinely do not know." Anger and helplessness surge through him in equal measure. Well, not equal; he's sure there's more anger as he once again glances around the room. It's a puzzle he needs to solve quickly. Now that this severely deranged lunatic has killed the Captain, he'll have no qualms anymore. Although he can't verify it's the same killer, his gut tells him it's related, and they *have*, without a doubt, a killing twosome. *The slaughtering duo*, he thinks, turning back to Amy.

"Listen, as soon as you finish up, I want you and Brendan back at the lab to run tests," He informs her. "I'm going over to Samantha's. Something's terribly wrong. Let's hope she hasn't met the same fate."

"You don't think—"

"Amy, right now, I'm not sure of anything." Sterling leaves the room and heads out of the home. He has turned all his emotions inward, using them to propel forward. If he takes a split-second to allow himself to grieve, it's all over; he'll be as useful as a dried up watering hole. Keep your head straight and track down this mother fucker!

Outside, he sees Anderson talking to Hamilton. Both men are distraught. "Kyle, I wasn't expecting to see you back so soon."

"Hey, Sterling. I heard it on the radio and figured that an extra hand couldn't hurt on this one."

"Thanks, Kyle. You don't want to go in there."

"I heard. Not the Dixons. Man, this isn't right." Watching Kyle choke back his emotions, he knows the kid can't go inside. "It is seriously that bad?"

"Let's just put it this way, it's pretty damned close to a Green Inferno nightmare in there."

"Green Inferno?" Kyle replies, confused.

"Never mind; just know it's nothing you want to see. Images like that get into your head and don't leave."

"Ah, shit."

"There's plenty to do out here keeping those vultures at bay," he says, glaring at the reporters on the other side of the police tape.

"Yeah. I had a hell of a time getting through them."

"I can imagine. Damned buzzards here to pick at the carnage of devastation to get their fuckin' story," he spits, shoving his hands in his pockets. "I'm going to go over to Samantha's. She has been MIA for the last few days. I want to check out her house, see if there is something that can tell us where she might be."

"You want company," Hamilton asks.

"No, things are a mess here. The two of you can help keep the reporters and *lookiloos* back. I'll call if anything turns up... you got your cell?"

"Always," Hamilton confirms as Sterling heads for the barricade tape. "Hey, Sterling?"

"Yeah?"

"Be careful. Something vile has infected this town. We don't need to lose you too."

"Keep your phone on," he says, pulling open his jacket revealing the Beretta strapped across his chest. "I'll meet you back at the precinct."

Sterling pushes through the growing crowd and ignores the reporters. He makes it to his car, slamming the door. "Fuck!" He mutters as he puts the key in the ignition and starts the car. Honking his horn to get the assholes out of his way, he's finally able to break clear of the crowd.

Chapter 21

The Barren Home

Pushing eighty the whole way, it doesn't take Sterling long to arrive at Sam's house. When her home comes into view, the windows are dark, the garage door closed, and her vehicle is nowhere in sight. *Where is she?* he thinks, pulling into the driveway. *Come on Sam, we can't lose you too.*

The first thing he notices, other than the obvious, is the open, overstuffed mailbox and the drawn drapes. "What's going on? She's only been missing for a few days," he mutters out loud to himself.

The drawn drapes don't discourage him. After all, the plan isn't to peek through the windows. He still has the key Sam gave him years back. He asked her if she wanted it back when they decided their relationship wasn't what either of them wanted, but she told him to keep it.

"Listen, Levi," she'd said. *"We're still good friends, and I would feel better if someone I trusted had a key just in case."*

He remembered asking, *"in case of what? Come on, Sam. We live in the most uneventful town in the United States."*

"You know as well as I do, routine or not, things happen all the time. Who better to trust than one of New York's finest?"

"Ex-New York's finest. Remember, I moved out here to the middle of nowhere."

"New York's finest just the same." She'd said and kissed him on the cheek.

A smile creases his face with the memory. Putting the car in park, turning off the ignition, Sterling gets out of the car. Searching the ring, he finds the right key and strolls up to the house. The house's darkness isn't all that's off; there's also an unsettling quiet as he slips the key into the lock and enters the house.

"Hey Samantha, you here?" he calls, walking out of the foyer. "Shit," he spouts when he saunters around the corner. Sam isn't just missing. She packed up and left. The house is empty of furniture. Only the drapes and a few empty boxes lay haphazardly on the floor in the living room. Random wires, screws, and clean patches where a picture once hung, adorn barren walls.

In disbelief, Sterling rushes to Sam's bedroom. Empty. He looks in the closet, the adjoining bathroom. Nothing. Running to the kitchen all there is to greet him are empty drawers—some open—and bare cupboards. There's nothing. Not a sign anyone has ever lived here.

"What in the fuck is going on!" he grumbles, yanking his cell from his pocket. He pushes number three; Hamilton's speed-dial number.

It rings once before Hamilton's voice graces the line. "Hey, Sterling, did anything turn up? Were you able to figure out where Sam went off to?"

"Her house is empty, Hamilton."

"What? Don't mess with me, man, I don't think I can take anymore."

"I'm not fucking around, Hamilton! I'm telling you, she's gone! She packed up everything she owned and left. There isn't one damned thing in the house besides a few empty boxes and some nails in the wall. That's it. Sam's gone, Hamilton! Departed, vanished, moved out—capeesh?"

"What the hell! Sam wouldn't just leave without telling someone? Hell, for that matter, where would she go?"

"Well, she did, and I don't have a clue where she is. I don't mind telling you, this isn't adding up and something smells rotten!"

"No shit."

"Listen, how much longer do you have over there?"

"About an hour. The forensic team just finished up. They're getting ready to take the bodies back to the lab. After that, it's just locking the house up tight."

"I'll meet you there. I'll put an APB out on her car and do a run on her credit cards."

"Be there as soon as I can, Sterling."

Cramming his cell back into his pocket, he locks the house. This day is becoming one he wished he'd slept through. The Dixons and now Sam. He hopes she's alive.

He gets in his car and drives straight to the station. Samantha's actions are bizarre. He isn't only going to do what he told Hamilton. Sterling has every intention to go through her desk, files, and locker—whatever it takes to get answers. *Something has to disclose where she disappeared to. A piece of paper, a note, or reservation lying around somewhere*, he thinks, laying his foot a touch too hard on the accelerator. The *'why'* of the reason she left, will have to wait until she shows up, or she's found, and he *will* find her, one way or another.

Forty minutes later he pulls the old Ford into the precinct. Shutting her off, she moans and hisses at him. He's pushed the old girl to her limit the last couple of weeks, and she is protesting. "Hold on ol' girl, we all have a job to do here," he says, running his hand along her warm hood.

Once inside, he heads directly to Sam's office. He doesn't have a key, but he doesn't plan on using one. He kicks the door in, and a few small pieces of wood break away from the frame and flies to the floor. The door smashes against the wall with a loud clatter, and he goes into her office. Sterling shuffles through Sam's desk side drawers but finds nothing of interest.

Trying the middle drawer, he discovers it locked. Removing a jackknife from his back pocket, he uses it to jimmy the drawer open. The drawer's void of anything but a piece of paper with Sam's handwriting on it.

Levi,

If anyone reads this, it will be you. I had to leave. Things are happening that I can't explain. I know it makes little sense, but please don't come looking for me and don't put an APB out for me. You won't locate me but don't worry I'm a big girl, and I'll be alright. Know, I hate myself for putting you through all of this, but I can't change it either.

*Love,
Your friend,
Sam—*

"Now, what in the hell is that supposed to mean, Sam," Sterling curses, crumpling the letter in his hand. "Fuck, Sam! Where are you?" he howls, while kicking the desk before leaving the office. Just as he's exiting the office door, he hears Hamilton.

"Hamilton, I wasn't expecting you back so soon," he addresses James, emerging from the office.

"Yeah, me neither. As soon as you left, the crowd dispersed as if the people lost interest. Amy and Brendan completed collecting evidence and well, all I had to do is delegate a couple of men to make sure everything was sealed up nice and tight." He doesn't like the expression on Sterling's face. "What is it? What's wrong?"

Sterling doesn't say a thing as he hands him the note he found.

Suspicion clutches in Hamilton's features as he takes the letter. "What's this," he asks.

"Just read the damned thing, would ya."

Hamilton opens the crinkled paper and reads the message, "What in the hell is this! Are we supposed to be some kind of psychics now?" He practically shouts. "Shoot, we don't have time for these little riddles."

"You're telling me. Hell, I didn't even know she was going through anything, did you?"

"No, I don't think anyone did." Hamilton's eyes the words again and examines Sterling, "So, what are you going to do? And, what does she mean by she can't change it?"

"I can't say, but I will figure this out." Thinking for a moment, he asks. "Can you do me a favor and run Samantha's credit cards? See when she used them last. "

"On it... ah, what are you doing?"

"I'm going to go home—"

"What! What good is that going to do?"

"Not much, but my head feels like a bass drum is pounding out the Star-Spangled Banner. I won't do much good if I stay."

"Ok, I understand. There isn't much else we can do here but wait for the lab results to come back. Anderson and I already questioned everyone associated with Dixon and his wife. We didn't get much. Most of the people were so unsettled they could barely put words together to form a sentence. The rest were in shock."

"I can imagine. I'll be back in the morning bright and early. We'll get on this first thing."

"You bet," Hamilton replies. "You know, I didn't want to say anything earlier, but you honestly look like shit." A cheeky grin crosses his lips.

"Yeah, well, I feel worse," Sterling chuckles. "I'll see you tomorrow at 6 a.m. sharp," he hollers on his way out.

"6! Hey, wait," but it's too late; Sterling disappears out the door. "Son of a bit... 6 a.m. my rump," he says, with the same brazen grin on his face.

On the way home the words Samantha wrote, roll around in his brain like a scratched record. *What did she mean, 'I can't change it either.' Why? Why can't she change her decision?* None of what happened over the last couple days makes much sense. Now, there's Sam's disappearance and a letter that's as confusing as a riled hive of bees. Sterling's head aches, it pounds more violently with every new thought. He needs a drink.

Within minutes, he turns onto LaPorte Road. Glancing at Nefertiti's house when he drives by, he thinks about stopping but decides against it. It appears no one's home anyway. The lights are off and the door is shut. Looking at the clock on the dashboard, it's already 4:30 in the afternoon. *Man, time flew today,* crosses his mind. It's a little strange that Nefertiti isn't home yet but he isn't her keeper either. *Shit, we aren't even dating. Then again, she could have insight on what the dickens was going on with Sam,* he thinks. "Christ Levi, you're losing it. The *'dickens'* seriously! What is this some PG flick?" He scolds himself, making a mental note to stop by Nefertiti's tomorrow on his way home from work.

Pulling into the driveway, the sun is lowering in the sky. He watches a pair of chipmunks scurry across the yard as he's turning off the engine. Getting out of the car, birds chirp in the trees above and some leaves dance in the light wind chasing one another in nature's game of tag. He inhales the fresh air and is reminded once more how much he loves this place as he strolls towards the house.

He notices the door is open. "What in the *hell* is going on now," he grouses, stepping cautiously closer. Pulling his gun from its holster, he pushes the door open further, "Hello," he calls, but only silence answers. Carefully he steps through the threshold, gun in hand leading his movements as he inspects the living room. Nothing. He makes his way steadily through the living room to the bedroom, the light of the late afternoon casting shadows. No one's here either.

Turning, he heads to the kitchen. "Anyone here?" he asks with no answer. Seeing that the kitchen is empty too, he grabs a beer from the fridge, and sucks down half of it before he bellows, "Hey, is anyone here?" He gulps down the rest of the bottle and grabs another, holstering his gun and placing it on the kitchen table.

"You walked right by me, Levi. I'm in the living room." Nefertiti's voice rings back, startling him to the point he almost drops his beer.

"Shit," he grumbles as some beer splashes on his pants. He heads back to the living room, wipes his pants with his hand, knowing for a fact Nefertiti wasn't there just a moment ago.

"Where in the hell did you come from?" he asks as she comes into sight.

"I've been sitting right here. You just passed me."

"You weren't here a second ago, Nefertiti. I would have seen you." Tilting his beer, he downs a quarter of it. "You really should be more careful, I could have shot you!" He barks, still wondering how the hell he missed her. *Maybe this whole situation with the girls and now the Dixons is getting to me more than I thought*, he muses, gazing at her suspiciously.

"Rough day I take it?" she asks.

"Rough day is an understatement," he says, plopping down on the sofa. "They found Roy, Captain Dixon, and his wife, Maggie, this morning murdered."

Nefertiti touches his shoulder in response.

"I don't know what's going on in this damned town anymore," he mutters, turning his gaze to her deep, dark eyes.

He's a little unnerved by the flat, cold expression on her face. He stares at her for a brief moment and figures he's an emotional mess. After all, it isn't as if Nefertiti knew them for the last ten years. She was barely introduced to Roy and never met Maggie. Still, the distant taciturnity in her isn't right; something is off with her. "So, why are you here?" he curtly snaps.

"I left you a note that we needed to talk."

"Ah hell," he exclaims, getting up and emptying his beer. "I've had a terrible day—most likely, the worst day of my life. The last thing I want to do right now is *talk*."

"Now that is rude," Nefertiti snidely tells him. "I don't think I deserve for you to speak to me in that manner."

"And who in the hell are you?!" Sterling shouts. *Fuck she's acting like we're married or some shit!* He deems. He's had a shitty day, and the last thing he needs is this woman talking to him as if they're a couple. He's already been through that, and he'll be damned if he goes through it again. "I've had a rotten fucking day. I come home the door is wide open, you're here—without permission mind you, and you expect me to be *ok* with this." Now he's pissed. His voice is at a level he hasn't used in years. "How in the hell did you unlock the door? You know what, it doesn't matter. You need to leave."

Nefertiti gets up. It appears she's going to leave as asked, but she shuts the front door. She doesn't turn around as she practically growls at him in a harsh, crude voice, "I said we need to *talk*!"

Shock races through him along with anger. *Who in the hell does she think she is?* He silently questions as he storms over, grabbing her arm and spinning her around to face him. "Listen, I don't know what has gotten into you, but I want you to lea—"

Before he finishes his sentence, Nefertiti's face alters into something that's not human. "Arrrgh," she screeches in a voice more animalistic than human, and he sprawls backward.

The next thing he knows, he's on the floor losing consciousness. He vaguely hears female voices arguing but his vision is blurred, he can't see a damn thing. His head is splitting, something wet trickles down the side of his face, and a familiar fragrance—musk flowers—engulfs him, but he can't seem to remember where he has smelled it before. He lifts his head a bit, his vision hazy, and two female forms are some distance away from him, he's sure of it. They're yelling, but they seem so far away.

"I told you not to hit him in the head anymore. You're going to cause brain damage or something. For fucks sake, what is wrong with you?!"

"What in the hell did you want me to do? He was angry! He grabbed you! Ugh, I should have *never* listened to you. You and your flippin' fantastic plan to gently bring his memory back. We should have done what I sa—"

"Shut up! Do you think I wanted this?"

"How am I supposed to know what the hell you want? All I know for sure, *sister*, is if we had done what I suggested, this would *not* be happening."

"You know why I did things this way, so stop with your sanctimonious bullshit and help me, would you? Jesus, sometimes you piss me off, you know that?"

"What else is new?"

"Let's just get this done. We have little time."

His body moves; he feels as if he's floating. His mind dims—consciousness leaves him.

Chapter 22

The Missing Detective

Hamilton is on his cell, listening to the continuous ringing. *C'mon Sterling, where are you*, he questions, frustration turning into panic. "That's it!" he yells, slamming his phone on the desk. "I'm headed out to Sterling's house. Something is wrong."

"Hey, wait," Anderson calls, grabbing his jacket. "I'm coming with you."

He's relieved Anderson offers to join him. Going anywhere alone has proven to be a bad idea for anyone in the department. For that matter, going without a damned tactical unit is a bad idea, he thinks, pulling his hood over his head before rushing out the door. Having Anderson along for backup doesn't make him feel a whole lot better, for who knows what's waiting for them or what has happened to Sterling, if anything. *Hell, he could be on the shitter for all I know*, he considers, although he knows better. He has a gut feeling, and it's the kind of feeling telling him something is off, and he's not going to like it.

When the men get into the squad car, they're soaked. A storm rolled in fast, and the heavens are dumping water to the earth like the oceans themselves have sprung a leak. Lightning flashes angrily, ripping white-hot streaks against a stormy darkened sky as thunder cracks with the force of a sonic boom. Nature has matched Hamilton's mood tonight. *Let's hope the road doesn't wash out*, he deems, buckling his seat belt.

"You don't think something has happened to him, do you? I mean, like what happened to the Dixons?" Anderson asks. The glare in Hamilton's eyes makes him wish he'd kept his mouth shut.

"Anderson, I'm going to forget you just said that," Hamilton replies, through clenched teeth.

"Sorry James, there's just some crazy shit going on in this town." Anderson recants, understanding Hamilton's frustration with all the jacked-up events as of late.

"Yeah, and we will figure out who is behind it, mark my words," Hamilton replies, slamming the car into reverse and then into drive. They leave tread on the concrete parking lot along with a cloud of black smoke as the car barrels out onto the primary road. Anderson reaches down, flips on the lights and siren. If Hamilton's going to drive like he's about to take the lead in the Indy 500, he wants people to get the hell out of their way. It was a good thing too, by the time they hit old 76, the pedal is to the floor, and the speedometer is reading ninety-eight. He says a silent prayer and double checks his seat belt but says nothing.

The man barely touches the brake when they come to La Porte Road. To his surprise, Hamilton drifts the car flawlessly, making the right-hand turn. The tires throw water and wet gravel high, spraying rocks over the yard to the left. He says another little prayer in thanks that the house on the lot sits back a substantial distance, or a window or two, would have broken—of this he's sure.

Anderson's confident that there are perfect impressions of his fingers on the door handle as the car straightens out, and they continue to haul ass down the muddy road. His heart races and his eyes are as wide as saucers watching Hamilton maneuver the car at warp speed—ok, not warp, but he's going much too fast for these conditions. If they were playing Grand Theft Auto, he'd be excited to see moves like this. But in real life, it's not much fun. In fact, it's damned well frightening.

Closing in on Baker Drive, Hamilton has no choice but to slow down. The road is private; it's kept, but not in any kind of shape to cruise a hundred miles an hour. If they tried to go down it at their current speed, they will end up in, or wrapped around a tree, let alone leaving the car's suspension lying in the mud.

The headlights and emergency lights brighten the obscure wood, where the darkness in the densest part is so profound, it gives Anderson the creeps. The blackness shrouds everything, like a living entity that swallows anything in its path. The light scarcely breaks through the heavy rain, his gut tells him something's not right and the dark shadows of night add an extra sense of doom.

They make it down the rough, sloppy road being tossed around like ping-pong balls, but no worse for the wear as they pull into Sterling's driveway. It's evident something is wrong as little, prickly bumps pop up on his arms as if he's been stricken with the measles and the hairs on his neck stand at attention. He sees the front door is open, and the place is as dark as the night that surrounds it. All that's heard is the rain pounding on the car's roof and the rolling rumble of thunder.

"It doesn't look good, Hamilton," Anderson utters, swallowing hard.

"No, it doesn't. Let's have a closer look. Have your gun ready."

Exiting the car, they run to the front of the house, water seeping through their shoes and mud cakes the bottom of their soles as they stop short of the door. Hamilton brings his finger up to his mouth and signals for Anderson to stay where he's at to cover him. Slow and deliberate, he moves to the open door, gun in hand stretched out before him. He reaches around the door frame, flipping the light switch on. A couple of quick glances around the corner tells him nothing is in the immediate area so, he waves the ok for Anderson to advance.

"At least he hasn't lost power," he whispers, moving into the house.

Anderson doesn't say a word; he only lets out the breath he'd been holding and nods.

Cautiously, they make their way inside. Their guns lead as they enter the living room, inspecting its dark corner. The house is in shambles and appears to be empty.

"Sterling, you here?" Hamilton hollers, knowing he will not receive an answer. "Anderson, head back to the bedroom. I'll check the kitchen."

Pistol in hand, he's not taking any chances. Anderson makes his way back to Sterling's bedroom, stepping carefully over the debris that litters the floor. In the hall, he pushes the bathroom door open—empty. Moving toward the bedroom, Anderson takes a steadying breath, hoping Sterling's not found in the same condition as they discovered the Dixons. Pushing the door, it's empty and untouched. He's shaking from the adrenaline rushing through him and leans against the wall momentarily to compose himself. When the gun in his hand stops doing the Harlem shake, he heads back to the living area.

"Anything?" Hamilton asks.

"Nothing. You?"

"No. There's no one here. Christ, look at this place, someone ransacked it."

"Yeah, but what in the hell were they looking for? What do you think happened here?"

"I don't have a clue, Anderson. Keep looking, there has to be something here—" Hamilton's face suddenly falls, blood flushing from it as if he's seen a ghost. He moves toward the turned over sofa, "Damn!"

"What?" Anderson asks but gets no response. "Hamilton, what the—" stepping near Hamilton, Anderson sees what has him so unnerved.

On the floor, spilling out from under the sofa is a pool of blood. The air quickly turns stagnate, like the oxygen is abruptly sucked from the room by a giant vacuum making it hard to suck air into their lungs. Their hearts stop. They stare vacantly at the pool, powerless to move. A single shared thought runs through their heads, *Not Sterling!*

The light glints off an object lying in the blood, jarring Anderson from his state of shock. "What's this?" Crouching down, he tugs a glove from his pocket, pulling it on his hand and picks up the object. It's round, a little larger than a half dollar and the color of bronze.

"Is that what I think it is?" Hamilton asks.

"Yeah, it's another one of those weird coins."

"Shit!" Hamilton cusses again. In a matter of seconds, he goes from a concerned friend to detective mode. "All right, you stay here. I'm calling this in and get us some help out here," Hamilton orders, hustling out the front door to the squad car.

Hamilton leans on the car with the rain battering his head like a pulsing shower and the night appears darker than it was a moment ago, if that's possible, as he grabs the mic. *Sterling where are you, man*, he thinks, pushing the talk button. "Dispatch, this is Officer Hamilton. We have a four-five-nine and a possible one-eight-seven out here at 4385 Baker Drive in Alger. I need every available officer on site and a forensics team, pronto."

An unsteady voice comes across the airways. Hamilton recognizes the voice immediately. Suzy has worked dispatch for a long time and is more of a friend than a co-worker. "4385 Baker but that's—"

"Yes, I know!" Hamilton responds, irritated. He settled his voice, knowing Suzy's as concerned as he. "We need help, Suzy," he says into the mic, his voice now pleading

"Uh, ten-four." A brief moment of silence before the radio blares to life again. "Ten-double-zero, all available officers in the vicinity of M-33 and La Porte Road, a four-five-nine and possible one-eight-seven at 4385 Baker Drive."

"Nice," Hamilton whispers when he hears the call. Ten-double zero means officer down, and any cop who catches the call will be out here in a heartbeat. He overhears responses come across the radio, not hearing whose responding as he digs his cell out of his pocket and pushes number four. When a person answers, he says, "I need a BOLO on Detective Levi Sterling." The person on the other line questions his command. "Yes, I'm serious. Just do it!" He orders then pushes end call and shoves his phone back in his pocket. He's soaked clean through as lighting strikes, illuminating the whole yard with thunder exploding before the light show ends. He runs to the house.

"Hey, Anderson, help is on its way. I'll be right back."

"Where are you going?" Anderson asks.

"I'm going to check Nefertiti's house."

"Ok, but why? When we went by the place, it was dark, didn't look like anyone was home."

"Call it a hunch," Hamilton tells him, rushing out the door.

Hamilton's he's down the road, standing in front of Nefertiti's door in a matter of minutes. The house is dark as lightning flashes, casting murky shadows everywhere. All he hears is rain falling in sheets and the growl of thunder. His fist starts to pound at the door but when it connects with the wood, the door cracks open. "Well, that's convenient," he emits, walking inside. His hand follows the wall to his left and finds a light switch. "Nefertiti, it's Hamilton, you home?" he calls out and not getting a response, he flips on the light. "You have got to be jokin'," he grunts in disbelief.

Nefertiti's house is not only void of her but whatever belongings that once occupied the home are also gone. A few dangling wires on otherwise bare walls and some leftover packing material is all that greets him. "No way," he mutters, storming out the door. "She has to have something to do with this. It's the only explanation for her to up and leave in such a hurry. She just moved here," he sputters, as his already wet feet become soaked and heavy with mud. He wipes the water from his face in an ineffectual attempt to clear his vision. The rain assaults him with no visible end in sight.

Sirens blare in the distance, getting progressively louder with their advance to Baker Drive. As Hamilton makes his way back to Sterling's house, he wonders whether or not his friend is dead or dying, laying in this wet, muddy shit in the middle of nowhere waiting for help to come.

Anderson's taking stills of the scene as he treads through the door, water dripping from him like he jumped out of a pool. Luckily, a towel sits on the table by the door. He's sure it's the towel Sterling wraps around his neck when he goes jogging, but at this point, beggars can't be choosers. He grabs it and dries his hair and face.

"Was she home?" Anderson asks.

"No, she wasn't and it doesn't look as if she'll be back."

"Huh? That's more than strange."

"Yeah, I know. The damn house is empty," Hamilton sputters, angrily. "There were no furnishings, no personal items—nothing. The only sign anyone was ever there are a few leftover packing materials."

"You have got to be shitting me. Didn't Nefertiti recently move to that place?"

"It would appear this woman is mixed up in all of this somehow."

"Goddamn, this is a living frigging nightmare."

"It's turning out that way, isn't it?"

The lights of a car pulling into the driveway shine through the window. The reflection dances across the walls, with another behind it. Hamilton opens the door to greet the officer's who've shown up and is surprised to see Martinez treading through the mud up to the house.

"Martinez, what in the hell are you doing here? Man, you should be home recovering."

"True as that may be, when I heard the call come over my scanner, and that it's Sterling... man I couldn't... is he..."

"I don't know. There's only blood, no body."

"Shit," Martinez hushes.

"You shouldn't be here."

"C'mon Hamilton, you need every man on this case. It's Sterling we're talking about! There has to be something I can do."

Hamilton muddles over his request for a moment. The last thing he needs is Martinez out here tromping through the woods in his condition. The car accident roughed him up good, and if he's honest, Martinez looks like hell. He's pale and his eyes are heavy with fatigue. He shouldn't be here. But he understands why he's here and knows for a fact he would do the same thing when it comes to one of their own going missing.

Finally, after a moment of contemplation, he says, "In fact, there is something I need you to do."

"Anything, what?"

"Go down to the precinct and make some calls. Dig up everything you can on Nefertiti."

"Nefertiti? What does she have to do with this?"

"I'm not sure. But that's what I want you to check out. I went to her place, and she's gone—everything has vanished. Nefertiti left town in a big goddamn hurry and I need you to figure out the reason."

"You are joking?"

"I wish I were, Martinez. God only knows, I wish I were."

"I'm on it... ah, she works with the zoo or something, right?"

"Yeah, she's a zoologist. If I'm not mistaken, she told Sterling she worked with the wildlife preserves in Grand Rapids."

"It's a place to start. I will call you if something manifests."

"Thanks, Martinez."

"No need to thank me yet. Let's hope I can come up with enough to find Levi alive."

By the time Martinez left, five squad cars are lining the road. The rain has let up to a drizzle and dawn is just breaking through the night sky. In short order, Amy and Brendan arrive after Martinez, followed by Officer Johnson and his partner Thomas Ryan. An hour later, men are searching the wood surrounding Sterling's house, looking for anything that can point them in Sterling's direction.

Hamilton, however, has a gut feeling they won't turn up a thing. This situation isn't right. The murdered girls... a missing medical examiner... giant cat attacks... Roy and Maggie's horrible deaths... and now Sterling's gone missing. Nothing's adding up, and he doesn't like it one damned bit.

He goes over everything they know so far, like the panther. His mind races with unanswered questions. What in the hell does a panther have to do with all of this and more curious, what part does Nefertiti play in this mess, if any? Is she the one who trained the devil cats to help her do her dirty work? If so, why? Where does Sam fit into the equation or has she suffered some horrible end in which her body will turn up in a day, a week or even a month down the road?

His head throbs trying to figure it all out, yet he knows answers won't come to him tonight. But they have to discover something, one little piece of evidence that will tie it all together. In his heart, he knows it will never be that simple. But, come hell or high water, he will locate Sterling, even if it kills him. The problem is, it just might.

Chapter 23

The Kidnap

A bright light forces Sterling to shield his eyes. Confusion prevails in his muddled mind. His head thunders as severe pain shoots from the top of his skull down his neck. Fighting to clear his blurred vision, he slowly lifts himself up to his elbow, stretching his neck with a light massage to ease the severe stiffness. A haze has formed over his sight. Struggling to focus, he's unable to make out fine details as his eyes betray him. The intense light coming from an unknown origin is not aiding in his desperate attempt to clear his vision. His lids fall shut, relaxing his eyes and giving them time to adjust. Gradually he forces his eyes open. Sterling keeps his breathing uniform, the haze lifts steadily, and his vision clears in short order.

Through narrowed eyes, his hand blocking the light which seems too bright, as the comprehension of where he is comes into focus. Trees, green grass, blue skies, a picnic table sits to his right—*a park, I'm in a park,* he thinks. Five hundred yards away, water flows from a piece of architecture cut from stone of smiling children and birds. However, a feeling nags at him that something isn't right. He stares at the fountain and confusion wades in his mind. The generation of this erroneous environment evades him for some time.

Then as if a strong wind blisters, whisking away all the murky haze, he grasps what's off with this place. It's too quiet. There are no birds, traffic, commotion, people clamoring along with their day. No breeze, smell, sound—*this place is dead,* he mulls. Then, as if the park is reading his thoughts, the soft singsong voices break the drowning silence. He strains to hear what they are saying. The voices are low, and he can't distinguish words, only the sound of tiny tones. Gradually the voices strengthen. The voices of young girls flourish, echoing through the otherwise still park, singing:

> *Ring around the rosy*
> *Pocket full of posies*
> *Ashes, ashes...*

Standing on shaky legs, straining to get his bearings to remove the clouds in his head further, he glances to his left to see a small group of teen girls who were not there only a moment ago. They startle him, but he doesn't react; he can't respond, as if something has taken control of his body forcing him to be an unwilling witness to these bizarre events. He unwittingly observes as the girls continue singing, laughing, and skipping around in a circle, just as natural as any other group of girls would. Although he's sure, these are no ordinary children.

Sterling watches the girls as their shadows fall and elongate. *No, it can't be dusk already, it can't*, he surmises. Turning his head over his shoulder, and skyward, the heavens darken as lightning strikes and thunder surges. Spinning back to inform the girls they need to go home, but they and the park no longer exist. A desolate wasteland of sand in every direction greets him. The earth succumbs to the deafening silence once more.

Where the girls were playing only a second ago, now lay the mutilated bodies of the victims from his cases. *No*, he mutters in painful gasps, pushing the palms of his hands to his eyes. "No! It is a dream, Levi. Wake up, ol' boy. Wake up," he hisses. Dropping his hands, he forces his eyes open. Darkness now surrounds him. The bodies before him now bleed. The blood flows through the sand, staining and creating a rich crimson stream.

With his head spinning, Sterling cries, "No more! Please, no more." Suddenly, a subtle sound penetrates his ears. He listens, straining to hear where the sound is coming from, but it's surrounding, engulfing and taunting him. Chanting, the same chanting he heard in his prior dream. He can't take it any longer. Falling to his knees, he screams, "What in the hell do you want from me?!"

"Levi," a soft feminine voice drifts on a phantom breeze. "Levi, it's all right. I'm here now."

Lifting his head, a woman stands before him. White cloth—gauze he believes—crisscrosses her chest, disappearing around her back to appear again nestling snug around her hips and then flowing freely around long legs. Her bronze skin shimmers, enhanced by the white cloth.

"Levi," echoes in a hushed whisper as his eyes travel up to see a face devoid of features.

"Arrrgh!" he howls in mortal fear, shuffling clumsily backward through hot sand. His eyes slam shut, not wanting to see anymore.

"Don't be afraid," resonates in overlapping voices. Prying his eyes open once more, he stiffly stands, taking a few steps back. There are three women now in front of him, faces without features. Hundreds, maybe thousands of young girls surround these faceless women. The children are standing upright facing him, staring at him with blackened, empty eyes of the dead.

He unwittingly shakes his head violently; eyes transfixed, he cannot pull his gaze from their barren eyes. His eyes slam shut as if being commanded by an unknown force, they close tightly and his head screams, *Let me wake up! Dammit, wake up, Levi!* It's no use; the horrifying site is still awaiting him when he forces his eyes to open. He has no control. He can't will himself out of this frenzied dream.

A soft, pale blue glow emerges from behind the featureless women. It floats up and over them with its pale glow creating shadows on their uniform visages. Instantly, the woman from his prior desert dream is standing before him. Unlike the other women, her features are distinguishable, radiant, stunning. Her dark, almond-shaped eyes are doused in mystery. Her elegance is without compare. An overwhelming sense of familiarity floods him. Though, he can't place where he'd encounter such a woman, other than his dreams.

Her eyes altered from deep, rich brown to intense yellow with thin-slitted pupils as she puts her hands on either side of his head. A manic rush of images burst through his mind; chanting people, blood, destruction, young girls ripped apart. Sterling hears himself scream, trying to break free from the strange woman's touch. As abruptly as they began, the images calm. The vision of a child swaddled in cloth, the mysterious woman—her eyes, her face, her lips.

"We have missed you. Please come back to us—remember. Remember. Re-mem-ber."

Nefertiti wipes the sweat from Sterling's brow as he tosses and turns, moaning in his sleep. Pulling the blanket up around his shoulders, she lays the back of her hand to his cheek, feeling his warm skin on hers, kisses his damp forehead and leaves the room. Glancing back, he's resting peacefully, no more dreams making him restless. She hates herself for doing this to him. But she'll hate herself more if invading his dream doesn't work, and she has to tell him everything.

Entering a large room with light gray walls, she looks across the room to the west wall full of a generous window overlooking the jungle. A Hyacinth Macaw sits in a tree just outside the window. Its rich blue plumage, bright yellow chin, and an eye patch bring a smile to her face. Samantha, or Saitre, her given name, paces the floor in a huff while Jamie, or Herneith, is sprawled out comfortably on the 16th-century chaise reading a book with *The Troy Dossier* printed on the cover in a bold tangerine colored letter. Also, adorning the cover, is an inkwell sitting on a crow's foot holder, an expensive bottle of scotch—the kind with a metal nameplate hanging for a chain around the bottle's neck. Next to the scotch is a piece of parchment with writing she can't read from this distance and a letter opener with a red substance on the blade—a representation of blood she presumes. Herneith loves crime novels from the 70s and 80s. One full wall of her room has a bookcase overflowing with books—ninety percent are crime novels.

When Nefertiti enters, Herneith briefly glances over the top of her book, a feeble attempt at acknowledging her presence. Not Saitre though. No, she's not the passive type—she has never been.

"Neffi." *Neffi* is the nickname Nefertiti's sisters gave her when they were young. She doesn't mind them calling her Neffi for it is more pleasing than some of the words that spill from their mouths at times. "Is he all right? Has he woken?" Saitre barks.

Nefertiti keeps her voice calm and composed. She has to. God knows Saitre won't. Saitre has a way of winding herself up into a frenzy upon hearing the slightest hint of distress. "He still hasn't woken. He's running a fever, but it's dropping, and he is sleeping comfortably, so I believe he will be fine."

"You know this situation is fucked three ways to Sunday, don't you?!" Saitre's pacing slows, but the strain in her face is evident.

"Christ, Saitre, can you please sit down for one minute and relax?" Nefertiti snaps. *There you go letting her get to you again*, she scolds herself silently. She's usually more refined with Saitre, but today she has just about hit her breaking point. Lowering her voice, she continues. "We are fine, no one saw Herneith and I leave. They won't find us here, and the new IDs and passports worked perfectly. It's not the first time we've done this, you know. Why are you so freaked this time? Saitre, there are times I wished you were as heartless as Herneith—"

"I am not heartless," Herneith protests calmly with a snide smirk, as her dancing emerald eyes appear from above her book. "I'm indifferent."

"I meant it in the best possible way, Herneith."

"I know," Herneith states, not looking up from her book. "Unlike our baby sister, I don't let the little things get to me, Neffi. I am far from the paranoid, needy, annoying, alcoholic our sister has become. You know that."

"Fuck you, Herneith!" Saitre barks, slamming her fist on the minibar, pouring herself another healthy glass of wine. "I'm two minutes younger than you, five younger than Neffi, so bite me."

"Yeah, and you're a thousand times more unbalanced," Herneith utters sarcastically, under her breath.

Nefertiti scowls at her, letting her know she isn't helping the situation. Herneith grunts, a grin forming on her lips, quite pleased with herself and although Nefertiti tries to stop it, the corners of her mouth turn up.

"Ah, yeah, laugh it up you two, but that fool practically exposed our kind. That damned Captain Nixon—"

"Dixon," Nefertiti corrects.

"*Dixon*," She snaps back. "Captain Dixon started digging into his history! Our history! If he would have dug any further, we'd all been in jeopardy. I don't understand how you two remain so damned calm!"

"For the love of the Goddess, Saitre, will you please be quiet! The way you're acting, you'd think we'd never dealt with something of this nature before. God! We have been protecting our kind for centuries, and doing a fantastic job of it, mind you. What is really wrong? Plus, the man is dead now! I mean, you're going a touch overboard, don't you think?"

"You're right, ok! I'm tense, exhausted, and emotional—"

"And drunk," Herneith spouts.

"Fuck you, Herneith. Why don't you stay out of this and keep your uppity nose in that damned book?! I played my part and played it well, mind you. You had the pleasure of sitting here on your ass doing God knows what while Neffi and I were doing everything we could to get him back!"

Herneith doesn't dignify her with a verbal response. She merely gives her the finger and turns a page.

Saitre's face twists ugly with unbridled fury, turning a shade of red Nefertiti hasn't seen before and for a split-second, she fears Saitre will fly into a full-on uninhibited rage at Herneith. Instead, she drains her glass and pours another. Then finishes what she was telling Nefertiti.

"It is, however, the first time we've been ten years without him. You can't honestly blame me for my emotional state." Saitre finishes, sighing resignedly.

"Who are you trying to fool, Saitre? You're always in an emotional state," Herneith adds, just to aggravate.

"Herneith!" Nefertiti glares at her. "Can you please refrain from your instigations?" Herneith rolls her eyes with a cynical smirk as Nefertiti turns her attention back to Saitre. "I understand, sister, but we have him back. The nightmare is over."

"Or just starting," Herneith caustically blurts.

"Herneith!" Nefertiti bites. "Will you please restrain from commenting?"

"Well, it's true," Herneith replies in her ridiculously nonchalant manner.

Usually, Nefertiti enjoys her dispassionate ways, but today she's getting on her nerves.

"Look at him," Herneith says, glaring at the bedroom door. "He still doesn't comprehend who he is, or where he is, for that matter. What do you imagine his reaction will be when he awakes, huh? Do you think, he's going to get up, wrap his arms around us, give us all a big sloppy kiss, and apologize for the last ten years of memory loss? Or, do you think when he awakens, he'll be just as confused and clueless about everything as he has remained for the past ten years?"

"You know, Herneith," Nefertiti emits, through clenched teeth. "I don't know what condition he'll be in when he awakes. But you're not helping this situation with your unpleasant comments, so please, just go back to your reading."

"Suits me," she replies as casually as being told dinner will be at 8.

"Perfect," Nefertiti states, turning to leave the room. She pauses at the door, "And Saitre?"

"Yes, *sister*," Saitre snips, finishing her second glass of wine.

"Do try to control your wine consumption today. We may need you later."

Pouring another, she smiles mockingly. "Well, of course," she replies, imitating a cheers with her glass in the air, then taking a sip.

Frustrated, Nefertiti sighs and walks out of the room. She's had all she can handle with her sisters, the family, and trying to nudge Sterling's memory back. *If that asshole in New York hadn't bashed his head with a metal pipe, none of this would be happening. Then again, it doesn't help that Herneith banged his noggin a few good times, either.* If this newest technique of invading his dreams doesn't work, she's sure she'll be the next candidate for a straightjacket.

Nearly running her mother over while lost in thought, she braces herself against the wall to keep from falling. "Mother! Jesus, you scared me."

"Nefertiti, is everything all right?" Her mother asks. "You usually are not this preoccupied." Nefertiti's mother is a stunning woman with pitch black hair that touches the curve in her back right before her bottom. She has deep almond shaped doe eyes—passed down to Nefertiti"•and though not overly tall, she has long legs with an hourglass figure.

"I'm fine. I've been overthinking this situation and there's much at risk."

"Too much, I'm sure. Don't worry; everything will work out, you'll see. It's not the first, nor will it be the last time we have to go through changing locations. You know this. But on the positive side of things, we are home."

"I do. However, this one has gotten the best of me. Saitre is ridiculously worked up—drinking of course. And Herneith... Herneith is her sweet, sarcastic self. Neither of them is helping the situation. I guess I'm just stressed."

"I understand your sisters can be a handful, they always have been since the day you stopped Saitre from trying to... well, you know. You have always been the levelheaded one in this family, Neffi. I am sorry this isn't easier for you."

"Thank you for saying so, but some days I would love to wring both of their necks."

"That's understandable. Try not to let your sisters get the best of you. With all of this behind us, we'll get back to life as it should be."

"I do hope so."

"Did you girls set the stage at his house?"

"Yes. We trashed the place and left a puddle of blood. The officers think him dead or seriously injured."

"Blood!"

"Oh, yes, blood. You can thank Herneith for that."

"What do you mean?"

"She struck him viciously on the head, again. It was hard enough that I had to stitch him up. He bled considerably."

"I told her not to hurt him," her mother growls. "After she injured him the first time, I thought that would be it." Her mother sighs, twirling her raven black hair between her fingers, a reflective action when she's displeased with something. "Ah, well, you know Herneith loves that man in her own way. And you must be thankful that Herneith is not obsessive over him like Saitre."

"I have no need to worry about that." She looks at her mother who is always so poised and refined and wonders how those qualities skipped them. Then she says, "It's not entirely Herneith's fault. Levi hasn't been himself. When he grabbed me, she tried to protect me."

"Still, he won't come back to us if she puts him into a coma. I knew we should have done this differently." Her mother manages a smile which always puts Nefertiti at ease. "But there's no need to cry over spilled milk. He's back, and he'll awaken soon."

"I hope so," Nefertiti tells her. "What if he doesn't recover his memory? What if he doesn't—?"

"Now, Nefertiti," her mother says, evenly. "He will remember. We'll *help* him remember. You shouldn't worry so much; it will bring lines to your lovely face. Now go. Get a glass of wine or something and relax."

"Relax," she repeats. "I'll do my best." She reassures her mother, resuming her way outside.

Their mother is right. And though she hates to admit it, so is Saitre. Saitre may have an obsessive, bordering on neurotic, love for him, one that Nefertiti fails to understand at times—however, she is right about Levi. What if he never remembers his true self? Where will that leave their family?

They should have done this differently. It's too late to change things now, but she knows in her heart they should have had a better plan. This family needs him. They need his memory back now before everything they've built comes crashing down.

Chapter 24

The Death Hole

It's 4am and the search parties found nil. Hamilton's been on the phone most of the night with everyone and their brother, but nothing gives. He can't identify a single person who might know anything about anyone who wants to hurt Sterling. Also, no one has heard of a woman named Nefertiti, which leaves him stumped to where this woman came from.

An all-points bulletin releases at 8:30am, plastering Sterling's face on every television station from the Great Lakes area to Timbuktu. *Someone has to have seen him somewhere,* Hamilton reassures himself. Although, in the hidden part of his soul, he knows Sterling will return or his dead body will turn up somewhere. The latter scenario doesn't sit well with Hamilton, but not finding him at least, will provide hope he's still alive.

"Hey, Hamilton," Anderson says, approaching him carefully. Ever since they found Sterling's home in shambles, Hamilton has been on edge. Agitating him anymore is not the best of ideas.

"Anything?"

"No, the teams are exhausted and have covered a five-mile perimeter without a trace." Treading lightly, he continues, "Do you think it's time to call it? If there were something to uncover, they would have found it by now, don't you think?"

Hamilton, frustrated, places his hands on his hips. Staring down at the ground with the whole damned world crashing down around his shoulders, he thinks for a good long time. A heavy sigh escapes his lips as he finally looks up at Anderson. "Call it. You're right, the men are tired. Maybe forensics will come up with something."

"Ok," Anderson replies with some relief. He starts towards the woods but stops and turns back towards the man who looks ragged and defeated. "Hamilton, he'll turn up," he reassures him, but his gut tells him a different story. However, he isn't going to say aloud what he's thinking—*Sterling is gone, or worse, dead.* He's sure Hamilton has the same conclusion running through his mind, and he refuses to add to the man's weariness.

"Yeah." He pats on Anderson's back, then Hamilton heads for his car.

"Where are you going?"

"I'm heading back to the station to make some calls. Can you get a ride with one of the guys?"

"Sure, it shouldn't be a problem," Anderson says. "Um, you should get some sleep, you know."

"Yeah, I'll get enough sleep when I'm dead. I'm calling Martinez to see what he found out from the wildlife preserve. Maybe they can shed light on Nefertiti."

"Good idea, I'll see you back at the precinct as soon as I wrap things up here."

Hamilton only nods as he ambles tiredly to the car, his mind consumed with the events over the last couple weeks—things aren't getting any better. However, he has a sneaky suspicion all of this—the murdered girls, the Dixons, Samantha and Nefertiti's disappearances, and now, Sterling—are connected. How they're connected is what he's curious about.

Getting into the car, he drives directly to the precinct. His mind wanders. He's distant and deep in thought and has to slam on the brakes to make the turn into the station's parking lot.

"Dammit, James! Keep your mind right!" he yells. "Shit!" he mutters, shoving the car into park.

His head falls on the steering wheel with a slight clunk and a weighted sigh. He takes a few minutes to pull himself together before going inside. *Sterling, where are you, man,* he thinks with his head pounding. *There should have been a trace; something to give us some idea who took you and where they took you,* he thinks, anger and fear commingling in every fiber. Sitting up, he punches the dashboard, *I will find you if it's the last thing I do.* Ok. Let's get this done," he says, opening the door and making his way into the station.

Entering the precinct is like going into a graveyard at midnight. It's eerie and empty. This precinct is small and with all the tragedy lately, all cops and detectives are on duty. Walking back to his desk, each footfall echoes as if he's the last man in the world. Isn't it enough he feels like the weight of the universe lies on his shoulders? Now, in the dimly light station, he feels like he's entered a poorly directed version of Phantoms. The empty office is cold and quiet as chills run through him when he picks up the phone dialing Martinez number. A moment later Martinez answers, "Hello."

"It's Hamilton. Did you find out anything from the people at the wildlife preserve?"

"No, I called but no one answered. I was going to try again later."

"Don't worry about it. I'll make the call."

"Ok. Sorry, Hamilton."

"It's fine. I'll talk to you later." Hamilton hangs up the phone and then dials four-one-one.

An automated voice comes over the line, "Welcome to directory assistance. For a government agency listing, please press one. For a residential listing, please press two." He presses one, and the system asks for the name of the organization, city, and state. He provides the information, frantically searching for a pen in the top drawer of his desk. He finally retrieves one and jots down the number given as the automated system says, "If you would like to be connected to this number now, please press one." Pressing one, he waits for the connection of his call. After a series of annoying rings, a deep-voiced man answers, "Grand Rapids Wildlife Preserve."

"Hi, my name is James Hamilton. I'm with the Ogemaw County Police Department."

"Hello, Officer Hamilton. What can I do for you today?" the pleasant voice on the other line, asks.

"I'm trying to get more information on a zoologist who has been helping you out. Her name is Nefertiti. I'm sorry I don't have the last name."

"With a name like Nefertiti, a last name isn't needed," the man laughs.

"True," Hamilton replies. "Do you know her?"

"I'm sorry, Officer Hamilton. I've never heard of a woman by that name here. I should know, I practically run this place."

"I see," Hamilton says, confused. "Is there any way you might be able to see if a Nefertiti working with any of the other wildlife preserves in the surrounding area?"

"I can make a few calls... um, has this woman done something wrong?" the man asks.

"That is what I'm trying to figure out," Hamilton states. "A detective of ours has gone missing along with this woman... and well, we're hoping if we can run her down..."

"You'll be able to locate your detective."

"Yes, that's right."

"Close, were they?"

"Closer than any of us knew."

"Ah, I see," the man says.

"Listen, I'll appreciate anything you can do to help me track this woman down. My number is 555-632-4800."

"Give me an hour. I'll call around and give you a shout back, how would that be?"

"Great, thank you."

"You bet. Oh, and by the way, my name's Hank. Hank Jenkins."

"Thank you, Mr. Jenkins. I'll be waiting for your call."

The line disconnects. Hamilton sits down hard in his chair, closes his eyes, and lays his head back.

"Hamilton," a voice startles him.

Jumping about out of his skin, he snaps his head around to see an exhausted, short, gray-haired woman standing next to him. "Suzy! You scared the bejesus out of me."

"I'm sorry, Hamilton. I thought you could use this," she says, handing him a steaming cup of coffee.

"Oh, yes, thank you. What are you still doing here?"

"April needed the day off, so we switched shifts. I'm working a double, but I'll have a three-day weekend," she explains, sipping the other cup of coffee she has in her hand. "I hate to ask, but has anything turned up?"

"No, but I just got off the phone and I'm hopeful the gentleman I spoke with will provide some useful information."

"I hope you find Detective Sterling. I always liked him."

"Me too, Suzy."

"Well," she sighs, wearily. "I will leave you to your work, so I can finish up mine. If you need anything, I'll be here until two this afternoon."

"Thank you."

He watches Suzy toddle away. When she's out of sight, he leans his elbows on the desk, with his face in his hand, "Where are you, Sterling? God, if you're listening, please let me find him alive."

Chapter 25

The Find

The ringing of the phone jolts Hamilton awake. He hadn't realized he fell to sleep. "Shit!" he grumbles in the startled state of awareness. "I must be more worn out than I thought." Wiping the drool from his mouth, he clumsily reaches for the phone and answers, "Hello."

"Officer Hamilton?"

"Yes, who is this?"

"This is Hank—Hank Jenkins, from the wildlife preserve. Sorry, it took so long to call you back."

"That's alright," he says, looking at his watch. "9:30!" he gushes.

"What was that?" Hank asks.

"Nothing, sorry. Did you find anything for me?"

"Well, Hamilton, I hate to tell you this, but everyone I called has never heard of a zoologist named Nefertiti. I even had them check with their contacts. That's what took me so long to get back with you."

"Son of a—!" Hamilton huffs. "Thank you, Hank, for your help, I appr—"

"Hamilton," Suzy's voice rang from behind him.

"Hank, hold on just a minute," Hamilton tells the man, covering the receiver. "Yeah, Suzy what's up?"

"I got a call from a lady. She's quite riled up."

"Suzy, I'm a little busy here."

"I know, but she said her son was playing in the woods by an old abandoned cabin back off of Elbow Lake Road and Mills. And, well," Suzy struggles to get the words out. "She said he found a human arm."

"What?!"

"That's what she said. She's freaking out. I sent a squad car to go check it out, but I thought you would want to go out there too."

"Thanks, Suzy." Hamilton gets back on the phone, "Hank, listen, I have to go, but thank you for taking the time to look into this for me."

"Anytime, Officer Hamilton. If there's anything else—"

Hamilton hangs up the phone before Hank finishes. Grabbing his jacket, he rushes out of the station and heads for Skidway Lake.

Driving down Elbow Lake Road, one would never know a series of murders have taken place. Colorful fall leaves provide a picturesque Peyton Place vibe. The sun is shining in a cloudless sky, everything to the naked eye is perfect. "Yeah, perfect my rump," Hamilton mutters as a couple of squad cars, about a half mile down from Mills Road, come into view. Pulling over to the side behind the last car, Johnson comes running over to him, his face flush, his eyes wide, and his pitch black hair in shambles.

"Hamilton, man, am I glad to see you. Suzy radioed in you were on your way. Man, this is some sick shit," Johnson fumbles, his face pale. Johnson's nervous tick is to add 'man' more than usual when he's excited or upset. It can get annoying, but the guys have learned to live with it.

"You all right? You look like hell. What the hell is out there?"

"Well... it's... It'll be better if I show you. Man, you will not believe this. Come on, follow me. We have a little hike ahead of us."

From the state Johnson's in, there's no doubt this is not anything he wants to see. Following Johnson down a driveway, they tread back through the thick underbrush of the woods. The leaves of various shades of red, yellow, burnt orange, magenta, and brown create a tapestry of eye candy. The birds chirp a warning of their presence as small mammals scurry around the forest floor. The tall treetops sway and groan in a slight wind barely felt at their level. Everything is so peaceful. How murder can be a part of something so tranquil, is the question of the day.

"When we got the call, I was the first on the scene," Johnson breaks through the sounds of nature. "The boy, Alex Hassle, was out here messing around and came across an old cabin. He told me he smelled something rancid and went to investigate," he says, talking too fast. "You know boys. He saw the old cabin and tripped over something. He'd thought he fell over a broken branch or rotted stump. But when he got up and checked, he saw a decomposing arm—no body, just an arm. Man, can you imagine that?"

"No, I can't. It had to freak the little man out."

"Oh, it did. When I got out here, I found the arm he told me about, but the stench was unbearable—too powerful to emanate for only an arm. So, I went to check out the cabin that I'm taking you to now."

"And?"

"We're almost there. You have to see this for yourself. Man, you won't believe this."

They walk a little over a half-mile back into the woods before a clearing comes into sight. Before they see a cabin, the foulest stench of rot and decay hit them. The odor reminds Hamilton of roadkill festering in the sun on a hot July day, times ten. He chokes when the aroma infiltrates his nose. "Christ!"

"Yeah, man, it gets worse the closer we get to the cabin. It's right over this mound."

"This doesn't look like a natural formation," Hamilton comments, hiking up the hard-earthed mound covered in leaves, twigs, and underbrush.

"Now that you mention it, you're right, it doesn't."

The cabin comes into view as they crest the top of the hill. It's an old, small hunting cabin that has seen better days, from the looks of it. The wood is gray with age, some of the base logs are partially rotted away. The window that he can see, has a broken pane and moths have had a field day with the once white butterfly print curtains that hang haphazardly.

Tramping up to the cabin, they don't go inside as Hamilton thought they would. Johnson leads him around to the back where the underbrush diminishes and crushed fertile soil makes a path that gets more traffic than the rest of the area.

When they clear the corner of the cabin, Hamilton sees officers standing around an opened, wooden door from a storm shelter. Four officers are present, three have a mask over their faces, and one is heaving in the bushes off to one side. Johnson walks up to one of the officers; a short hefty man, with a gray head of hair, a large nose, and gray eyes—Officer Mitch Fallen. Mitch greets them by handing them a jar of menthol and two masks.

"You'll want both," he says, through the mask. "If you think the smell out here is bad, wait until you get below."

"Thanks, Mitch."

"Don't mention it. However, I'll warn ya; even this stuff won't block out the stench down there."

"I'll consider myself warned."

Johnson makes a menthol cream mustache to stave off the stench and then fits the mask over his mouth and nose. Hamilton follows suit. Johnson glances over at Hamilton and asks, "You ready for this?"

"As ready as I'll ever be."

Johnson unhooks his flashlight from his belt guiding Hamilton down into the shelter. Mitch is right, the stench is insufferable. Despite the mask and menthol, a putrid scent seeps through. The odor of a human corpse is unlike any other. It's a rank and pungent smell mixed with a tinge of sickening sweetness that catches in the back of one's throat as it's now doing to Hamilton, as his stomach content threatens to vacate. He swallows hard with the back of his throat burning. It takes everything Hamilton has to keep from vomiting as the vile sweetness imposes an unholy taste on the rear of his tongue.

Making their way down a narrow stairway, the shelter's bigger than

Hamilton expects. The four unsavory wooden planks that masquerade as stairs lead to a four-foot wide tunnel. The tunnel isn't wide enough for Hamilton's 6'2" stature to advance down without being hunched over like an old man with a bad back. The slant of the tunnel is steep and along with his back arched, he grips the sides to prevent descending rapidly down and crashing to the bottom.

At about 100 feet, the tunnel opens to a large room where Amy's knelt down by a body. Brendan and a couple of other men are standing over what looks to be a large well in the middle of the room. On the other side of the pit are three men wearing white hazmat suits and face masks, painstakingly lowering a rope down into the well.

"That is where *they* are," Anderson says, moving over to the well.

Hamilton cautiously walks over to the edge of the well and looks down. He sees the top of the man's head they were lowering down. "Give me your flashlight," Hamilton tells Anderson. Taking the flashlight, he shines it down into the hole for a better look. What comes into view is an indescribable horror. The bile bites hard at the back of his throat, and this time he can't stop himself. Turning, he rushed over to the closest stone wall, rips off his face mask, and hurls.

"Son of a Bitch," he growls, wiping his mouth. "How many?" he asks, to no one in particular, after spitting a few times to remove the awful flavor from his palate.

"Not sure yet," Brendan states, his voice muffled through the mask he's wearing, sounding as if he's a mile away "It's hard to tell. It will take us some time to pull all the bodies, or should I say bones out of here for an accurate count."

"What do you mean bones?"

"There were only two bodies down there that still had any flesh left on them; the one Amy's examining and the one that's coming up now. The rest, from what we can tell, have been down there a long time. How long is not discernible yet. What I can tell you is, we'll need help if you want all the remains brought out of that death hole."

"Death hole," Hamilton repeats in a whisper. *A death hole is a fitting title for what I just saw*, he thinks.

"Hamilton? You ok?" Brendan asks.

"Yeah and don't worry about help. I'll get you whatever you require." Hamilton assures him. Composing himself a few more minutes, he walks over to Amy, tugging his mask back in place "What have you found out?"

Amy doesn't look up from the body. "This is the fresher of the two corpses, and this one's wounds eerily resemble the damage done to those girls. However, this is a male in his late teens—early twenties." Amy finally turns to look Hamilton in the eye, "Would you like to hear my theory?"

"Sure, why not."

"This guy, gal, or both, has been killing people for a lot longer than just the recent murders. How long, remains to be seen. But I can tell you one thing; this case is giving me the willies."

"You're not the only one, Amy."

"I'm going to get some more men out here. Is there anything you need?"

Amy pats her *tackle* box. "Nope, I have everything I need."

"Good," he says, turning to leave and hollers, "Hey, Johnson, can you get a couple of men and get this area marked off from the road? I don't want anyone near this place."

"You got it, man. I don't mind getting up out of this death hole and into fresh air."

"I hear ya," Hamilton murmurs, making his way up the tunnel.

Chapter 26

The Enemy

"This has to stop!" A familiar male voice bellows, angrily. "The world is changing; we have to change with it to survive. Don't you see that!"

"No, I don't!" a different male howls. "We are who we are!"

"I am the King and what I say, *will* be obeyed! I should have you brought up on charges for treason! The only reason you're not in shackles now, is you are my blood. However, heed my warning; do not test me, brother. Do not! For if you do, I will have you banished!"

"You won't have to. I'm leaving this rule! I'm leaving you and this tribe. I renounce my loyalty!"

"Ankhkhaf, if you do this, you'll never be welcomed back. You will become our enemy!"

"So be it! But remember, with me as an enemy you'll do well to watch your back, *brother!*"

His body is covered in a copious amount of accumulated sweat make his clothes uncomfortably cling to him like saran wrap, he wakes up screaming, "Ankhkhaf! Ankhkhaf!"

A household maid hastens over to his bedside. "C'est très bien, you had a mauvais rêve," she reassures in a soft French accent and concern in her voice.

Focusing his eyes, wiping away the sleep from them, he glances up into a beautiful oval-shaped face, the most amazing big, brown eyes staring back at him. In a disoriented haze, Sterling regards the young, slender, petite woman with dark hair pulled neatly into a bun at the back of her head. Although he's sure he doesn't know this young woman; there's something remarkably familiar about her.

"What?" he asks, trying to garner his wits.

"I'm sorry Sire; you had a nightmare, a mauvais rêve."

"Oh, yes, it was not pleasant," he replies, confusion like a thick fog in his mind. "Who are you? Where am I?!" Sterling yells as his state of uncertainty alters into a panic. Jolting upright, exploring his surroundings wild-eyed, he doesn't recognize this place and knows, without a doubt, he isn't in his room.

"Sire, Sire, veuillez, Calme Vous-même. I'll go fetch Madame Nefertiti."

Though he only understands half of what this woman says, he understands *sire*. *Why in the hell would she call me that?* He thinks before he poses the question.

"Sire? Um, miss, I think you're mistaken. My name is Sterling, Levi Sterling."

"Ah, Oui Sir... oui, Monsieur Sterling. I'll get Madame now, bien?" She says, hurrying out of the room.

"Um, bien," Sterling grunts, swinging his legs over the side of the bed. He stands up, which he discovers isn't the best idea, his head spins. His stomach becomes queasy. He's certain he'll pass out. Sitting back down quickly, so he doesn't end up sprawled out on the floor, he places his head between his hands rubbing his temples. "Take it easy, Levi. You'll figure this out," he whispers, breathing slow and deep a couple of times to dissipate the undesirable feeling.

A few moments later a slight knock comes from the door, "Levi?" A familiar voice asks.

"Yes."

"Good morning, Levi. How are you feeling?" Nefertiti appears, wearing a tan and faded teal maxi dress cut in the front exposing her shapely thighs. Her long hair is down, and it's much longer than he expected, hovering just above her hips. But as appealing as she is at this moment, it can't distract him from his anger.

"Nefertiti, where am I? How did I get here? I know I'm not in Alger!" Levi sternly spouts, lifting his weight off the bed. Dizziness permeates him once more as he's curtly forced back down.

"Levi, please. You need to—"

"Don't tell me what I need! I want to know where in the fuck I am and what in the hell happened!" He roars, holding his pounding head.

At that moment, the lovely little housemaid enters the room, pushing a serving cart like the ones used in a posh hotel. Now that his vision is a little clearer, he sees she is wearing an antique white gauze dress with a thick, tan leather belt tied around her waist, and flat strap sandals the color of her belt. *Not your everyday maid uniform,* he thinks. She gives Levi a timid smile and says in a tiny voice, "Your breakfast, Monsieur Sterling."

"Thank you, Markisha," Nefertiti tells her. "Please set the table and see to it Monsieur Sterling's wardrobe for today is brought up."

"Oui, Madame," she replies, placing the cart by the table while placing the dining setting with expert promptness and elegance without a word.

Levi waits for Markisha to exit the room before speaking again. He's confused. His head feels as if an elephant's dancing the fandango on his brain. When Markisha is gone, the spinning in his skull settles. Nefertiti hands him two aspirins and a glass of water.

"Here, take these; they will help."

Calmer, Sterling takes the aspirins without question, tossing them into his mouth. Accepting the glass from her, he flushes them down. Sitting there for a few moments, finishing the glass of water, Sterling hadn't realized just how parched he was.

He takes time to soak in his surroundings. Though one side of the room has a large window, the light shimmering through is faint for a reason unknown. The room itself is decorated in natural colors: browns and beiges, giving it that rugged, rustic look. The walls are made of reclaimed wood—something like barn wood but with a touch more class, and the furniture, chairs and sofa, have soft full cushions. *Very chic*, he thinks.

Turning to Nefertiti, he asks, "first who is that woman and second, where am I?"

"Markisha has been with us for a long time. She's, as you can tell, from France. As for where you are, you're in our home deep in the Amazon Rainforest of Brazil."

"*Our* home?! Brazil?! How in the hell did you get me here!" Sterling stands, screaming and furious. Panic engulfs him.

"Please, Levi, calm down. I will explain everything, but you have to compose yourself."

Overwrought and exhausted, he stands there with a look of fury and frustration on his face. *It's a fucking nightmare!* Runs through his thoughts. *Levi, chill.*

"All right!" he huffs. "So, tell me. Tell me why I'm here. Tell me why you stole me from my home and brought me to some *godforsaken* place. Tell me why I have been having these crazy dreams!" Taking a lungful of air to subside the anxiety welling within him, he quietly asks, "I'm not who I think I am, am I?"

Nefertiti ponders momentarily on how much to tell him. He looks considerably better, but his color's still blanched, and his body still weak from the whole ordeal. The last thing she wants to do is make him infuriated again. So, carefully she looks him directly in the eye and confirms, "No, you are not who you believe yourself to be."

"Well, that much I gathered. So, who am I? Am I even a detective or is this some charade I've been putting on?"

"You're a detective all right. In fact, it was your idea to have a certain number of us strategically placed in society."

"Strategic placements?! Well, that's just flippin' fantastic! For what possible reason would I have done this?"

"To protect our species." She waits for a reaction, but without a twitch from Sterling, she continues. "Listen, I give you my word I will tell you everything you want to know. But, I think it best for you to eat something and possibly shower."

Levi is defeated. Flustered and he has to admit; he has smelled better. Also, the aroma from whatever it is under the silver lid of the serving tray is making his stomach rumble. "Fine," he says, finally. "But can you tell me one thing before you go?"

"Of course."

"How long have I been here?"

"Two days."

"Two days!" Sterling responds, dubiously.

"I know this is all... bemusing. I would like to say I know how you feel, but I'm not that presumptuous. Please, Levi, eat and take a hot shower, you'll feel better. Then we can have a long conversation."

"Bathroom?" was the only word that came from him.

"Oh, yes, right there," she says, pointing across the room. "The door next to the fireplace. There are clean towels set out for you. You'll find a new toothbrush and razor in the cabinet."

Without another word, Sterling runs his hand roughly over his face. Annoyed, he rubs his hand back and forth through his hair, making his way to where Nefertiti pointed out and disappears behind it, closing the door.

She waits in the room until she hears the shower come on and then leaves to give Levi some time alone. He needs time to entertain everything. It's essential that she figures out the best way to tell him the truth. *This conversation should prove interesting*, she deems as she shuts the door behind her.

Before she can get fifty yards from the room, Saitre ambushes her. "Is he ok? Does he remember anything? What did he say?"

"Saitre, please, I'm not sure what he remembers yet, and yes, he is alright."

Saitre's face twists, turning skeptical. "Don't tell me you didn't get the slightest inclination he might remember something," she gushes, scornfully. "Dammit, Nefertiti, don't lie to me!"

"Lower your voice! I think he may know some things, but to what extent is yet to be revealed. Now, would you go do something—anything but bombard me with incessant questions. Try to stay calm until I talk to him after breakfast."

"Fine!" Saitre pouts. "Just let me know as soon as you have *your* talk."

Shaking her head and trying her best to stay civil, Nefertiti tells her, "Saitre, I love you, but I swear you test my patience at times. You're the most irritating, impatient person I know."

"Yeah, well, I think this situation has quantified my actions." Saitre clamors, defensively, storming away.

"God, help me to not to strangle the life out of her one day," Nefertiti breathes, more frustrated than she was before.

While Nefertiti does her best not to wrap her hands around Saitre's neck, Sterling stands under the shower head, letting the water—as hot as he can stand it—pour down his body. With his hands up against the wall—reminding him of all the people he frisked as a detective—he gazes down at the slick, white surface of the tub to the drain, thinking about his dreams and what they mean.

"Hell, Levi, you know damn well what they mean," he grumbles to himself, reaching up and rubbing his scar. It's the one thing he has to remind him of his displaced memories and it's in this moment, he realizes his dreams aren't just dreams. He now knows they are memories, a portion of them anyway. Memories of a past forgotten when a deranged lunatic stole them with one swipe of a metal bar.

It can't be. It's not possible, he scrutinizes, trying to bring forth some rational thoughts and put the dreams in perspective. The thing is, he knows nothing about his past will be logical; it's beyond the realm of any reality a *reasonable* person would have. Though he understands this—how he knows is another story. It's one of his gut feelings—hovering in the pit of his stomach, and he's certain Nefertiti will verify his fears. She'll tell him who he is, and what part she has in all of this. He comprehends she's integrated into his past, maybe more than he suspects.

The visions of the barren sand, the peculiar chanting people, the half-naked woman coddling a baby, comes rushing back into his mind with force. It's powerful enough he has to throw his hands back to the shower wall to keep from tumbling brutally to the floor. Slowing his breathing, he focuses his vision on the gleaming white of the wall, relieving himself of the site.

When he restores his balance, he reaches outside of the shower, grabbing a washcloth from the vanity. Taking the sandalwood-scented soap, he lathers himself up. *Wash all your sins away*, he thinks, with a sarcastic smirk. It's a phrase that he heard many times before. But for the life of him, he can't remember from whom or where.

Though clean and feeling one hundred percent better, he stands under the hot, running water until it gets cold, before he steps out and wraps a towel around his waist. Facing the steam-covered mirror, his reflection is obscured, looking more like a ghost staring back at him. When he wipes his hand across the glass to remove the haze, he jumps back harshly, whacking his body against the door. *It can't be*, he silently murmurs in disbelief.

Standing there staring at the mirror in utter skepticism of what his eyes are seeing, he walks back to the mirror. He pushes his faces inches from the glass examining the image reflecting back. Pulling his skin this way and that to make sure the reflection is real. "This is... is... ah, no way," he says in utter astonishment. "It is impossible!" he declares, slapping his cheeks.

As he looks at the reflection of a younger version of himself, his head swarms with the idea that he is losing all the pieces left of his damaged mind. His imagination drives wild, fantastical ideas of how he could reverse time, taking him twenty-some years in the past. Straightening his stance, he turns right and then left to view the rest of his body. The mirror above the vanity only allows visibility to mid-chest, which is no help. He turns to a full-length mirror on the other side of the room.

Strolling over to the mirror, planted in bewildered denial, he gawks at his reflection. Not that he was in bad shape a moment ago, but nature has a way of taking its toll on the human body. He turns to the side and runs a hand over his stomach; the forty-plus bulge is replaced with a toned washboard stomach he hasn't seen in years. His buttocks no longer have that slight sag; they're elevated and firm again. Examining his face; his skin is taut and youthful, all lines around his eyes have vanished and their emerald-green color more vibrant. Gone is the slight bag of his jowls, along with all blemishes and his scars. His muscular structure's more pronounced—back to that of his younger days. Even his teeth are a few shades whiter than before. His appearance tells him he's in his twenties, that he has lost twenty years in the time it takes for a shower.

"This is impossible," he whispers with a slight smile of equal measures of satisfaction and confusion, as he flexes one arm and then the other. "What is happening to me?" he asks the four walls surrounding him. Pawing at his body a few more minutes, he decides he will not get the answers he seeks admiring himself in the mirror. Walking into the bedroom, he scares poor Markisha half to death.

A sharp, high-pitched "Arrrgh," emanates from her as she spins around clutching at her chest as if she's having a heart attack. *A touch jumpy are we?* Levi thinks. "Monsieur Sterling, c'est vous. You frightened me," she huffs, catching her breath.

"I didn't mean to startle you, Markisha, but I wasn't expecting anyone in my room. What are you doing in here?"

"Madame Nefertiti said for me to bring your wardrobe for today," she states in her thick French accent, more composed, pointing to the bed.

Examining the bed, Sterling sees a pair of white, what looks like linen slacks, with a short-sleeved, lavender, button-up top. To say the clothes are not his style is a gross understatement.

Rubbing the back of his neck while viewing the ensemble, he notices Markisha showing signs of discomfort. Fidgeting, shifting her weight back and forth, head bowed, her eyes flicker between him and the floor. At first, he can't figure out what her problem is until he looks down and remembers. He's standing there in nothing but a short towel that barely covers the essentials.

"Ah, Markisha, that will be all," he says, a little embarrassed for her more than himself.

"Oui, Monsieur Sterling," she responds, her face a profound shade of blush, though a noticeable air of relief fills her person. When she reaches the door she announces, "Madame Nefertiti will be présents prochainement." Not waiting for Sterling to answer, she disappears, quickly shutting the door behind her.

"Well," Sterling says, grabbing the slacks. "This is a different look for me, but at least it's something to wear."

Chapter 27

The Analysis

At 5 a.m. Hamilton enters the precinct. It's silent at this hour, but a few men are quietly working at their desk, all greeting him with a slight nod. In an hour this place will hop like a prom dance. Men and woman closing cases, opening cases and taking calls; it gets chaotic—some days more than others. He waves at the guys saying nothing. He's had two hours sleep in the last 48 hours, and his body can't seem to manage a 'Good Morning' just yet. He's aware the baggage under his eyes is enough to go to Bermuda for a week. The lack of sleep has his thinking a little muddled. *It's nothing a hot cup of joe won't cure*, he thinks, stopping in the break room.

The recovery team was able to retrieve every bone from the well by midnight the day of their discovery. He's impressed with their speed and thankful for their competence. Since the bones reached the lab, the forensic team is working overtime, gathering evidence and doing what they can to identify as many victims as possible. Hamilton's determined to get some answers as to where these remains originated.

After nuking a freshly poured cup of last night's coffee, he heads directly to the lab in the morgue a few floors down. Entering the elevator, he takes a sip of the coffee that's more like mud and his face crinkles, *Oh that is bad*, he thinks, taking another sip. But it's strong, black and loaded with enough caffeine to get an elephant up and running. The elevator stops and the door opens to a buzz of activity as he walks down the hall to the lab entrance.

"Hamilton, you're here early," Amy says as he enters, though she doesn't look up from the bones in front of her.

"I couldn't sleep... um, who is this?" he asks, noting the short, somewhat stocky, older gentleman taking a sample from the bones. With long brown hair being severely taken over by gray, he reminds Hamilton of Sean Connery in Medicine Man—right down to his khaki color clothes and the brown leather belt.

"Oh, I'm sorry. James Hamilton, this is Dr. Jonathan Hawkins; he is the expert in his field."

"It's nice to meet you," the man says, finishing up what he's working on. "Forgive me if I don't shake hands, but..."

"Yes, I can see you're rather busy. If you don't mind me asking what *is* your specialty?"

"He's the foremost expert in Forensic Anthropology," Amy interrupts, still not making eye contact.

"Forensic Anthropology. Well, it is a pleasure to have you aboard, Doctor."

Hawkins doesn't respond, finishing whatever it is he's doing. As he finishes, he turns and walks to a table with shined steel instruments lined up neatly. Tools of varying sizes arranged in no particular order although Hamilton wouldn't know if there's a method to the instrument's madness or not. A couple of the devices are recognizable from being down here around Sam's crew: a bone saw, scissors, and a long-handled scalpel, but beyond those few, he doesn't have the slightest clue what the rest of them are or what their function is. One looks something like scissors, but instead of two long blades, it had a short, thick blade on one side and something like a flat hook on the other. Another one reminds him of a small pickax but with a catch at its end. *Very strange*, he thinks, turning his attention to Amy.

"Why did you elicit the good doctor's help?" He questions, nudging Amy.

"Hamilton, some of these bones are thousands of years old."

"What!" he blurts out in shock. "C'mon, Amy, stop fooling around," he says, hoping she's pulling his leg.

"I'm not kidding. Come over here; I want to show you something." Amy heads back into her closet of an office and switches on the light. Going over to her desk, she grabs a folder and hands it to Hamilton. "This is what we've dated so far," she explains, opening the folder and directing his attention to the top of the page. "While Brendan started on the two flesh bodies we found, I began with the last of bones pulled from the pit. As soon as I examined them, I called for Dr. Hawkins for help. I need his expertise in this matter. And I am glad I did. Because the first bones he tested are around 3,300 years old."

"You're shitting me, over 3000 years old! That's not possible," Hamilton breathes, entirely discombobulated.

"Possible or not, that is what the carbon dating revealed."

"Carbon dating? I've heard of it, but I'm not sure how it works."

"I can explain... um, your name was again?" Doctor Hawkins asks, from behind them.

"Hamilton. James Hamilton"

"Well, James, as Amy here has expressed, the carbon dating has shown these bones to be that of a human living approximately 3,000 years ago. Let me explain, the basis of carbon dating tests is the presence of carbon-14 in bones. Carbon-14 collects in the body throughout our lives. When we die, it gradually decays, so by measuring the amounts left in a specimen—"

"You can estimate when a person died."

"Excellent, Officer Hamilton," Hawkins commends. "Now, taking samples and carbon dating the remains, a pattern forms," he explains, directing him to the sheets of paper Amy holds. "Do you see it?"

Hamilton takes the papers from Amy, looking through the dates of each specimen analyzed. It takes him a moment, but there it is clear as day. "A couple of bodies every hundred years or so."

"Well done," the doctor says. "Are you sure you're in the proper field, son?"

"I am sure, Doc. But I don't quite understand. I mean, it can't be.

It's impossible, isn't it?"

"Impossible or not, that is what the data has shown."

Hamilton's trying desperately to wrap his head around the data and what *Doc* is telling him. As incredible and unbelievable as it may seem, the numbers are staring him in the face and how can one argue with facts? He doesn't feel well. He finishes his coffee, crumbles the paper cup in his hand and tosses it in the basket beside Amy's desk without thinking about what he's doing.

"Are you telling me we have a family or tribe of friggin' cannibals or something on our hands, which have passed down their sickness for thousands of years?! Here, in this small town?"

"Cannibals?" Hawkins questions, surprised. "Why would you say that?"

"Well, if this case relates to that of the murdered girls, it's a probable scenario. The girls all had their internal organs removed. Whether only some organs or all of them, all of the girls were left ripped open with something missing—chiefly their hearts."

"Really, Amy, you didn't tell me about this."

"No, I didn't, because we aren't certain if the cases connect."

"I can put that to rest," Brendan voices from behind them. "For the remains we found, I've noticed some eerie similarities, even in the male victims."

"What?" Hamilton asks.

"The male we pulled out of that pit, had his chest opened in the same manner as the girls, there's no doubt about that now. I took a sample from him and the ones we have from the girls, and they match. Also, as in the girls, his heart is missing but only his heart, everything else is intact. It's too coincidental for these two cases to be from completely different killers."

"Well, Officer Hamilton, I'm not so sure about your cannibal theory. However, ancient tribes that engaged in human sacrifices to appease the Gods have existed—a religious practice among ancient peoples.

Documentation of these rituals goes back centuries. For instance, the ancient Aztecs, Mayans, ancient Egyptians, tribes of ancient Africa, the Zapotec from Mesoamerica, and many other ancient people employed human sacrifice. For the Aztecs, the most common form of human sacrifice was heart-extraction. You see, the Aztec believed the heart was both the basis of the individual, and believe it or not, a piece of the Sun's heat.

> *Where is your heart?*
> *You give your heart to each thing in turn.*
> *Carrying, you do not carry it...*
> *You destroy your heart on earth.*

"Where is that from?" Amy asks.

"That is a Nahua poem. The Aztec believed humanity contained these celestial sun splinters. They also deemed that mankind imprisoned the divine pieces. Their beliefs held the body as imprisonment that attracted and bound fragments of the sun to fulfill its yearning. They considered all they were, given to them by the gods, so they owed them everything. These people would perform sacrifices for many reasons—yielding a good harvest, or good weather, along with several others. Often, the *chosen* were willing participants, on whom an Aztec priest would perform a ritual stretching on the sacrificial stone. The priest would then raise his obsidian knife, bringing it down to open the body, reaching his hand inside and ripping out the still beating heart, crushing it on the sacrificial stone," Hawkins explains with an air of excitement that Hamilton doesn't fully understand.

"Now, inhuman as that may sound," he continues. "The Egyptian process of mummification was more, let's say, intense. The Egyptians removed all internal organs except the heart. They removed the brain with a long, slightly hooked tool. This tool was shoved through the nose into the brain, then spun around to liquefy the brain. Then, they tilted the head forward to allow the content from the skull to discharge out through the nose. The heart was the only organ left on site or placed near the throat with a scarab or other amulet set over it to protect it in its journey amidst the netherworld. They believed the heart was a person's life force."

"That's pretty sick, Doc," Hamilton states.

"In today's society, yes, it is rather barbaric. But in peoples such as the ancient Egyptians and the Aztecs, faith was deep-seated; it ruled every aspect of their daily lives. The Aztecs held the belief that damaging the heart would produce a—"

"So Doc," Hamilton interrupts, grunting with spurious humor. "You're telling me some ancient people have been hiding out in the woods of this small-town and murdering people for thousands of years to appease their gods!" Chuckling, he continues. "I'm sorry, Doc, you must forgive me for calling bullshit on this one."

"I'm not saying an ancient tribe is still out there conducting these rituals, though it wouldn't be the strangest thing I've ever encountered. But scholars of the ancients' ways could exist—distant ancestors. Those who have studied one of these ancient tribes and have handed down this knowledge to the next generation. Or, you may have a highly educated psychopath on your hands."

"So a cult?"

"It wouldn't be too far fetched, would it?"

"No, I have to say it wouldn't," Hamilton admits, running the past few weeks through his thoughts. With a sigh, he glances at Hawkins. "I'm not putting much weight into your theory, but I'll admit what has taken place in this town was done by someone who knew what they were doing. They were either tutored in the ancient ways or have done these vile acts enough times to perfect their technique. Is there anything else?"

"I can tell you these practices have been going on for a long, long time—the bones show that much. And why not a small town? This place is perfect for these rituals, if that's what they are. It's a place that's not largely populated and has miles and miles of dense woods, making it easy to hide from the world. Plus, people come up missing daily, gone without a trace. It's not that difficult to imagine, is it?"

"Hell yes, it's hard to imagine, Doctor Hawkins!" Whether it be the lack of sleep or the fact that Doc's argument has a solid base he doesn't want to consider, Hamilton goes off. "I've lived in this town for a long time. I know these people. Shit, I've had dinner with over half the people who live here on one or two occasions. So, to think there's a sick fucker lurking in the woods, waiting in the shadows to grab his next victim, is very difficult to imagine!" Hamilton stops short, frustrated. He doesn't have to continue his rant. Everyone's face tells him they understand his point, though they are leaning toward the evidence, not his conviction to this town.

Chapter 28

The Truth

Sterling just finished a breakfast of Belgium waffles, eggs, and fried ham. He's pouring himself another cup of hot coffee when a soft knock comes at the door.

"Levi, are you decent?"

"Yes, Nefertiti, come on in."

Poking her head in, Nefertiti offers Sterling a smile and enters the room. "Good morning, are you feeling better?" she asks, sauntering over to Sterling. Her long, dark hair flowing over her bare shoulders, her gauze dress hugging her body in all the right places, her beauty should mesmerize him, but all he allows himself to be transfixed by now is the information she has about his past.

She joins him, seated on the opposite side of the small dining table, studying his mood before she says a word. Her smile fades as the seriousness of what she must tell him enters her thoughts. *No time like the present Neffi, reach down, grab some cojones, and tell him.*

"I know you must have a million questions and I realize this is all extreme—"

"Coffee?" he asks, interrupting her. He wants to know more than his dreams have shown, but there's a part of him that wants all of this to be some crazy delusion.

"No, thank you. Levi, listen—"

"Nefertiti," he interjects once more. "I know I'm not who I believe myself to be. I know there's something much bigger going on here than I can ever imagine. I also know that I mean something to you. But there's one thing I want to know before you tell me anything about myself—did

I kill those girls? Did I kill Captain Dixon and his wife? Am I some psychotic murderer?"

Nefertiti is silent for a time. Her silence makes Sterling's nerves twitch and tighten, sending millions of electric shocks through his body. All that passes through his mind is that he's a murderer, that he killed those sweet innocent girls, ripped apart the Dixons and has no recollection of doing so. When he can't take her silence another minute longer, he stridently demands, "Well?!"

"No, it wasn't you who killed those girls."

"What about Roy and his wife?"

"You haven't killed a human in a long time, Levi."

Fleeting relief rushes through him until her words penetrate his skull, *you haven't killed a human.*

"What?!" he shrieks, getting up from the table and pacing the floor. "So I have killed? When? Why? How long ago exactly? Why in the hell don't I remember any of this! Jesus, this is insane!"

"Levi, please calm down."

"Calm down? Calm down? How in the hell do you expect me to calm down when you have just told me I am a fuckin' killer?!"

"You have not killed anyone in a very long time."

"And that is supposed to make me all warm and fuzzy inside?!"

His movements are more like a caged panther pacing back and forth. Nefertiti stays perfectly still like a statue in a rose garden; the only thing that moves are her eyes studying him. *You need to chill, Levi;* he tells himself, desperately striving to slow his breathing. He forcibly decelerates. Each breath is a struggle to control, but he manages. When he senses a state of calm fall over him, no matter how fragile it is, he asks, "Why am I suddenly so young again?"

Nefertiti doesn't answer directly. She searches his demeanor for a moment with a raised eyebrow, determining his present state before she replies. When she senses that he has a subtle—feeble even—amount of control over his emotions, she responds. "We gave you fresh blood that brought your youth back to full bloom. Though you don't need blood to survive and without it you still age much slower than a normal human, with it you retain youth. It transforms you back to the youthful appearance you see now and makes you strong. However, we didn't need to kill someone to get it," she explains with a weary sigh. She sees him regarding her with a look composed of more emotions than she can place, but the one she identifies clearly is mistrust and it breaks her heart. "Please," she finally continues. "Let me tell you everything I know first, then you can ask all the questions you have. Please."

Sterling glances over at her, still pacing, though much more relaxed. He can't believe what he has heard so far. Does he want to know any more about his past? Sure, he digs into other people's history all the time, but she just told him he had killed people! *I'm a detective for Christ sakes*! His pacing slows to a leisurely gait. *Levi, compose yourself, maybe it's not as bad as it sounds. Not as bad as it seems, really? You have killed people! However, what else can she tell you that could be worse than that?* He questions himself. He strolls back to his seat, not as calm as he portrays, but he's gained a small amount control. He has to know everything, like it or not.

"Good enough," he expresses. "Tell me everything."

Nefertiti begins a surreal tale of the past. Confounded by what she's conveying, he sits quietly and listens to a fable that if he ever repeated, he'd most definitely be strapped within the confines of a straightjacket in a padded room of an insane asylum. She begins with, "Do you remember the legend I had told you of Mafdet?"

"The story you told me of the goddess who could change form and had a set of triplet girls, right?"

"You do remember."

"Of course," Sterling says, a questionable look crosses his face. "But what does that have to do with this?"

"It's not just a folktale, Levi. That story is a part of our history. You see, Mafdet was beautiful, more beautiful than anyone the tribes had ever seen. Legend says to look upon her for more than a few moments, could blind a man impure of heart. The tribes loved her dearly. She was the goddess of protection; she kept them safe and for that, they cherished and worshiped her. In return, she loved them as if they were her biological children. The tribes celebrated her for her constant shield of defense, regarded her as the goddess of wisdom and judgment."

"Yes, I remember. C'mon Nefertiti, what's this all about?"

"This will be extremely difficult for you to understand, but trust me when I tell you," she pauses, trying to decide what words to use. Then, she merely comes out with it, "I am one of the three daughters of Mafdet."

"Nefertiti, do you honestly expect me to believe you are hundreds of years old, the daughter of some ancient goddess?" Sterling laughs, nervously. However, her expression's enough to make him stifle the snicker. She's telling him the truth. It may be a morbid, ridiculous story, but she entirely believes what she says. When he doesn't see her waiver in the slightest, he falls excessively quiet.

"The picture you saw on my wall was of me a long time ago. I'm the one who has the magic touch with large breed cats; the one they once called Madam Dalaminia and the one who married Jonathan Chalthoum."

"But you told me that was a picture of your great-grandmother that her given name was Camila… why did you lie?"

"Would you have believed me if I told you the truth then?"

Sterling doesn't need to be hit on the head to see what she's getting at, and no, he would not have believed a word. He's struggling to understand any of this fantastic story now. *This is either the most remarkable story ever told or a gift from hell.* Rubbing his face, he replies, "You're right, I wouldn't have believed you. I'm having a hard enough time absorbing what you're telling me now."

"And that is why I had to tell you what I did. I am sorry I lied to you, truly I am." She studies him to get an idea of what he might be thinking and then asks, "Would you like to hear the rest?"

Sterling only nods, his words stolen.

"You see, Mafdet was once worshiped and adored; ancient peoples sacrificed in her honor. However, Mafdet was alone. She wanted a mate and children. She wanted a king. In 1281 BC, she left Egypt to seek a mate. She heard of the tribe of Ailuranthrope in Europe."

"I'm sorry, Ailura what?"

"Ailuranthrope—skinwalkers," she replies, like these people are normal and something he should already know of, then continues. "The legends described a people who were skinwalkers, or werecats. The feline god's mated with humans hundreds of years ago, and their offspring grew up to be these skinwalkers. This intrigued Mafdet, for these children were great warriors of divine bloodlines. Mafdet hoped to unearth such a warrior. So she left to search for the one who would be by her side."

Sterling watches her eyes, they almost dance as she tells him of these—these skinwalkers. His heart tells him she is telling the truth even if his mind screams that it cannot be.

"She found the tribe of skinwalkers who welcomed her and told her of their history. She met the two brothers who led the tribe, and before long, she fell in love with one particular skinwalker who, unlike the others, had unusual gifts beyond his ability to transform. He was strong, wise, empowered with the power of the moon, and the gift of sight into the future and the past. His name was Le-Banyo. He captivated her. The moment her eyes met his, she knew he was her king."

"Her love toward the older of the two brothers sparked the first signs of tension between the brothers. The younger of the two had also wanted her, so when she chooses his brother, it planted a seed of jealousy within him; one that would grow into hate and bitterness."

Nefertiti glances at Sterling for what seems like an eternity, "You don't believe a word do you?"

"I am trying to remain open-minded Nefertiti, I really am. Please continue."

She studies his face a moment longer and though he doesn't know what she is thinking or feeling; he swears there's a hint of sadness in her eyes. Then she finishes the tale.

"Mafdet and Le-Banyo built a glorious empire in Egypt. It prospered, without disease or famine—a place of protection and tranquility. Those under their rule loved and adored them. The people no longer worried about their welfare or starvation; they worshiped them, sacrificing to display their gratitude."

"Not long after their union, they were blessed with three daughters, born skinwalkers like their father. Unlike the legend, they did not need the blood of the innocent to transform back to their human form, though the people still freely sacrificed virgins to them out of honor and respect. This blessed gift of triplets only enraged the king's brother further. He grew distant from the king".

"However, in 1278 BC, turmoil erupted in the kingdom when the king decided the killing of the innocent would be no more. His brother and a few others of the realm didn't agree with his decision. They believe the sacrifices were a necessity to retain their strength and youth. But moreover, the king's brother had acquired a lust for blood, one that surpassed any that anyone could have imagined. The kingdom split and the king's brother left vowing to be an enemy of the king."

"I am Le-Banyo," Sterling breathes. "Oh God! I had intimate relations with my daughter!" He howls, pounding his fist on the table. His breathing becomes erratic. His head spins as he lowers it to the table, overwhelmed and disgusted by this insight.

"Please try to understand, Levi. We are the panthers—Skinwalkers. We're unlike any other species of werecat. Half-panther and half-human, we retain the ability to change between the two. And yes, I realize this disagrees with your morals now, but we *are* an incestuous breed."

Her words do *not* offer any comfort. However, instead of dwelling on this fraction of his being, which is utterly perverse, he asks, "Who is my brother? Where is he?"

"His name was Ankhkhaf."

"The man from my dreams?" All at once, a flood of memories come rushing back to him in a maddening surge of all he is and has ever been. He falls from his chair convulsing from the overwhelming amount of knowledge stored within him—millennia old.

"Levi!" Nefertiti cries, rushing to his side. His body shakes in vigorous tremors, his skin falls pale, and sweat runs in a flood down from his brow as his body fights to absorb all the information inundating his memory. She feels his pulse. It's erratic. His heart painfully thunders against his ribcage.

"God, Levi!" She bellows, embracing him firmly. "Mother!" she finally screams, horrified.

She listens as footsteps scamper down the hall. The door flies open and Mafdet burst through, wild-eyed with the sisters in tow "What happened?"

"I told him the whole story and when I mentioned—"

"Ankhkhaf," Mafdet interjects, evenly. Inspecting his state, she calmly replies. "There's nothing to worry about, Neffi. His mind is recovering memories. He'll be all right in a few minutes."

"Oh joy," Herneith sarcastically bellows. "Is he going to remember everything or is this only going to lead to more coddling until he does?"

"Will you shut up!" Saitre orders, running to Levi's side. "Why are you always so damned negative?! We have him back you insufferable wretch."

"Sticks and stones, sister," Herneith smirks, unaffected by Saitre's name calling. "In the light of things, I am stating the reality of it all, not negativity. As for your name-calling, I'm not the one who is a scrabbling, clingy, pretentious boob."

"That is enough!" Mafdet firmly snarls. "Why the two of you carry on like this boggles the mind."

"If she weren't so profoundly pathetic, I wouldn't have to—"

"Ankhkhaf!" Sterling shrieks, jumping up from the floor, knocking

Nefertiti over, and putting a halt to Herneith's snide comments. "God, Ankhkhaf! I have to get back," he boasts, panicked. Gawking around the room wildly, seeing Samantha next to him and Jamie, his ex-wife, across the room, he gasps, "Holy hell, it's all true. Jamie, you knew about this the whole time and never said a word? We married for Christ sakes!"

"Actually, we have never married, my dear, Levi. My name is Herneith. Please address me appropriately. And since we never married, there was no need to tell you anything."

"But we have a son!"

"No shit, Sherlock," Herneith snips.

"Herneith! That is enough." Mafdet states, firmly. Setting her gaze back to Sterling, she asks, "Do you remember?"

"Yes, I remember some—at least more than I did. I am still trying to wrap my head around it all, but I know who I am. I've got to get back." Levi glares at Herneith, "Where is my son?"

Herneith starts to answer, but Mafdet cuts her off. She's had enough of Herneith's rude and patronizing comments for one day. "Your son has his own pride now, Le-Banyo. He came of age years ago, you know."

"Le-Banyo? No, please call me Levi," he tells her, rubbing his temples. "I guess he did. God, he's what, twenty-three now?"

"That's correct."

"I'm sorry, all of this is a little much to swallow."

"Yes, I realize all of this must overwhelmed you."

"Now that, dear lady, is the understatement of the century." Levi humorlessly chuckles. Seeing the three girls together, their resemblance becomes clear—uncanny, actually. *How didn't I see this before*, he muses.

"You said you needed to get back," Mafdet says. "Get back to where?"

His recollection of previous thoughts flood back. He walks over and grasps her shoulders. "Mafdet, I have to get back to Alger, and I must go now. Ankhkhaf is there. He is the killer we've been looking for."

"How do you know that?" Saitre questions.

"His ability of sight is back, my dear," Mafdet replies, before Sterling can respond.

"Yes, it is. I saw what Ankhkhaf intends to do. It played out as if I were right next to him. It's the strangest thing."

"You will get used to it, Levi. This is one trait I fell in love with, do you remember?"

Touching her face, he says, "I don't know how I ever forgot." For a moment his emotions flow over him. He sees Mafdet and his daughters through new eyes and all the love he had for them before his memory lapsed, floods back.

However, as much as he would like to stay and talk with them—be with them—there are more pressing issues to deal with. "I have to go back. He'll kill again. He's gotten away with his morbid tactics long enough. I have to put a stop to this before he kills one more person." Suddenly, Levi spins around, his eyes wide with inquiry, his voice rough and harsh, he asks Saitre, "Did you know, or should I say, how did you know?"

"Know what?" she asks, her voice suddenly small.

"Saitre, you've worked with him as long as I have, how didn't you know it was Ankhkhaf?"

"Levi, I didn't know it was him. I mean, I'm a Medical Examiner, and I knew one of our species was the killer. I believed someone from another tribe was committing these murders, not someone from within our pride. I suspected a rogue from another pride was looking to take advantage of your memory loss to gain power over our pride and possibly even kill you. But never once did I think Ankhkhaf was the culprit, I barely remember him."

"Ankhkhaf has changed remarkably since the time of our empire," Mafdet confirms. "The girls were very young when he defied you."

"I'm sorry, Levi. Please believe if I had known who he was, I would have told you, somehow." Saitre says, almost in tears.

Releasing a formidable breath, realizing the girls did not know who

Ankhkhaf was, he wraps his arms around Saitre. "I know, and I apologize for my outburst."

"I understand," she tells him, wiping her eyes. "It's a lot for all of us to deal with."

"And," Nefertiti speaks up. "When the murders started, and Saitre told us of her fears, we knew we had to come up with a way to bring your memory back. We pushed harder than ever before to get you to come back to us, to put a stop to the killings. We feared discovery. We felt the pride was in danger, and we needed you to remember."

"I understand, at least I am trying to. But right now we have no time for this. I must get back to Alger."

"Then we will go with you," Saitre suggests.

"No!" his voice commanding. "No, Samantha... ah, Saitre, I will go on my own. I have to confront him alone."

"I don't like it," Nefertiti asserts. "Not one little bit."

He observes the women of his tribe, the ones who have stuck by his side all this time. Stuck by him and protected him when he had no recollection of who he was. The people who exhibited strength and courage in the face of an uncertain future, his family, his pride. Strolling to the window, staring out over the dense jungle, he remembers this as his home. The one they'd built after leaving Egypt in the shadow of his brother's betrayal. He observes the faces of his people as they go about their daily routine and their names follow. "How could I forget all of this," he whispers.

He watches children playing tag. A young boy hides his face in his arm against a giant kapok tree. He hears his little voice counting, 'One, two, three.' He feels a hand lay softly on his shoulder, "Le-Banyo, are you all right?" Mafdet asks.

"Levi. Please call me Levi. I have come quite attached to the name." He sighs, wearily, "So, these are our people?"

"Yes, and they have waited a long time for you to come back to us."

"Over ten years. Wow, when you say it like that."

"Yes, it seems like a long time, but with our breed ten years is just a ripple of water."

"I am sorry I left as I did."

"You can't blame yourself for something you had no control over."

"Maybe," he breathes. Too many thoughts clutter his mind. Who he is, why this happened, and what he must do now; it's all-engulfing. There's still much he's sure he doesn't remember.

"Can you tell me what the coin is all about?" He asks.

"The coin?"

"At two of the crime scenes I investigated, there was this coin or amulet left behind. In both instances, I had the strangest sensations overcome me—dizziness and nausea—unlike anything I've ever felt before. I've been trying to figure out what it means."

Reaching into her pocket, Mafdet pulls something out and holds it up to him. "Did they look like this?" she asks.

"Yes, exactly like that. What is it?"

"First, you have had those feelings often, Levi. They go with your gift of sight. As for the coin, I'm surprised you don't recall. It was our Medallion. Our family crest, if you will, from the old realm. They had a power you bestowed on them and you gave them to those you loved, but that power has ceased since you left. I assume the feeling you have with the gift of sight became penetrating and when you touched the Medallion, you awoke its power."

"Weird, but that explains a lot. It also tells me my brother is using this to make a statement of rebellion."

"It would seem so. You shouldn't be surprised. Ankhkhaf has always had difficulties accepting you as his king." Mafdet responds. "When you became king, when we united, you had everything he ever wanted."

"Including you?"

"Yes, including me. His anger dramatically increased when the girls came of age, though, do you remember?"

Levi searches the darkened, cobwebbed corridors of his memories, blazing through the thick haze-covered years, long forgotten. "I remember! I remember why. It was before our argument about the law I enacted forbidding the killing of the innocent. He hated me for that law. He never understood the world was changing, and we had to change with it. That law was the first step to blend in with the people. I mean, after all, we were supposed to protect them, to love them, not feed on their children!"

"I understand as I did then. You must remember, most of our kind agreed with you. We found other, more efficient ways after the law passed."

Another memory came to light in the dark hall of his mind at that moment. "He fell in love with—shit, I can't remember."

"Stop trying so hard. Give yourself time. Don't try forcing it."

"I will do my best. Things were much different in those days. It is strange to fathom just how different."

"I have witnessed numerous changes throughout the centuries. I guess I have become immune to their repercussions."

Crudely running his hands over his face, he concentrates. Images of the girls from many years before, awaken from hidden memories. Their species, his stature within the pride, the breed being *notoriously* incestuous. A swirl of memories move to recognition, his head pounds as he tries desperately to cope with whom he is.

"He wanted a mate but was denied," he finally says. "I remember that. I also remember he came begging me to betroth one of our daughters to him. I had told him I would not force a daughter of mine into a bond she did not desire. It was a short time after, I enacted the law. He became furious, denouncing his kinship with the pride."

"Yes, he was impetuously unreasonable."

"And he still is. I have to stop him."

"Yes, however, halting his ridiculous rampage will not be a simple task. What's your plan?"

"To be honest, right now all I want is to prevent anyone else from dying because of his vendetta against me. I'm the one fueling his ravenous retaliation, and I am the only one who can put an end to it."

"I know. I don't like it, but I know."

The girls join them. "You're leaving us again," Saitre states the obvious.

"I have to. I will be back as soon as I deal with this mess Ankhkhaf has become obsessed with seeing through."

"You mean, *if* you defeat him," Herneith corrects.

"Well, your name has changed but you sure as hell haven't. Still the same blunt little bitch you've always been, aren't you?" Sterling asserts.

"I am. Thanks for noticing."

"Please excuse Herneith. She never was graced with manners." Nefertiti scowls at Herneith.

"Girls," Mafdet warns, veering her attention back to Levi. "Come. Let us get you a flight out tonight." Taking him by the arm, they leave the room. She contemplates many scenarios. She knows all too well, there will only be one of two outcomes—the death of Levi or the death of his brother. "Please be careful," she pleads as they walk. "Your brother has no intention to concede. He will do whatever it takes to kill you, or die trying."

"I'm aware of his hate for me. I will be careful."

"He fights dirty, you know."

"Then so will I, if I must. I have to stop my brother's destructive undertakings."

Chapter 29

The Showdown

Hamilton had one hell of a day. After hearing about the bone analysis Doc completed and seeing the evidence, this quiet little town didn't seem so quiet any longer. It has hoarded murders for years, which is more than disturbing. Examining himself in the rearview, he looks like ten miles of bad road that hasn't been serviced in the last decade. The bags under his eyes would give an insomniac a run for their money. The necessity to relax and get sleep doesn't only creep up on him; it belts him alongside the head.

Entering his home, he takes his jacket off; the one he didn't need, for it's relatively warm out. He proceeds directly to the fridge, pops the top on a cold Miller, tilts it up, sucks it down, then grabs another along with the fifth of Bookers from the freezer. "Good Ol' firewater, you may not be what I need, but you're sure enough what I want," he says, his gaze falling upon the full bottle in his hand.

Turning, he heads toward the living room. He tips the fifth back, guzzling a quarter of it, plops down on the sofa, and groans, "What a rat-fucked week." Cracking the tab on his second beer, watching TV is a fleeting thought, but he decides the quiet of the night is much more appealing than another rerun of M*A*S*H. He wonders if Sterling's still alive, doing a shot for a drink. "Dammit! Where in the hell is he?!" Another swig of bourbon burns down his throat chased with the emptying of his beer. His head is swimming to some extent; he closes his eyes.

A racket jolts Hamilton awake. "What? Uh?" he grunts, annoyed, jumping up from the sofa. Another series of thumps and thuds comes from the outside. "What in the hell is going on?" He bitches, stumbling to the door.

Forcing his head clear from the combination of drowsiness and alcohol, he opens the door. Squinting, trying to steady his vision and peer through the darkness, the dim glow of the front porch light provides little help, "Who is out there?" he calls. He listens, straining to hear anything other than the crickets and the endless nerve-racking song of Katydids. A loud clanging crash arises from the side of the house, startling him. "Who, the fuck is out here?!"

Before moving outside to investigate, he grabs his gun from the side table. Now wide awake, he carefully descends the faintly lit porch stairs, turning right toward the edge of the house where he heard the clamor emanate. "Who's there?" he asks again, making his way down the length of the house, nearing the woods. A voice emerges from the blackness of the woods. It's only a whisper, carried gently on the wind. He swears the voice is familiar, but he can't quite place it. "I'm a cop, you son of a bitch!"

"Of course, you're a cop, Hamilton, and a damn annoying one at that!" a familiar voice replies, in no more than an exhale. "And I am the one you've been looking for."

"What?" he asks, straining to hear the voice he now knows is a male.

"There you go asking those annoying questions like all good cops do, right? Just like good ol' Dixon, who never knew when to leave well enough alone. Tell me, how did that work out for our Captain and his sweet, little wife? Oh, how I loved her voice, her screams aroused me."

"You son of—"

"Now, now. You may want to watch that temper, for I am the one who turned this town upside down, evoked chaos, and made police lives a living hell. I slaughtered your dear Dixons."

Hamilton sees red instantly, but he's a rational man—for the most part. On top of this, he has no idea what the psychopath hiding in the shadows is planning, so he holds his tongue, only asking, "Why? Why did you murder them?"

A sinister laugh derives from the darkest part of the wood. A laugh that triggers the goosebumps sweeping over his flesh, as the voice tells him, "Because Dixon was getting too close to the truth."

"The truth?" Hamilton asks, desperately trying to pinpoint where the voice is stemming.

"Ah, that is the question, isn't it? For I am certain that dear Sterling has not told you anything, but don't be too critical of the ol' boy, it's not his fault after all. His memories were damaged, locked away in the recesses of that puny mind of his. I tried to put him out of his misery, which you so rudely thwarted I might add. But alas, he pulled through our little excursion."

"And you're the one who left the body parts all over the yard at Sterling's?" Hamilton asks as chilling laughter comes out of the woods, a little darker and much more menacing.

"Guilty as charged. I scattered those body parts over his yard as a fucking warning to you guys. Think of it as my calling card, a small taste of my capabilities. And in leaving those gifts scattered across Sterling's front lawn, I'd hoped the little escapade would scare you cops enough that you would have the mind to cease and desist, but you cops aren't all that bright, are you? No matter, since none of you have two brain cells to rub together and understand when you're facing something more powerful and deadly than you can handle... well... at least I can say I tried."

Without warning, the realization of who he's talking to hits him hard. It's like a punch in the gut stealing his breath. He stutters, "It—it can't be you."

"Took you long enough, Hamilton. I was beginning to think you would not figure it out before I killed you. So, are you ready to die?"

Hamilton freezes. Penetrating fear races through his body as two large eyes shine through the ambiguous shadows with a yellowish-green glow. "Holy shit," he whispers, slowly stepping backward without turning.

A low, guttural growl emanates from the eyes, triggering him to cease his withdrawal. "Oh, God, please," he prays, when the snapping of small twigs and the crackling of dry leaves from the weight of the creature, courses through the night air. He raises his gun, shaking as he aims at the eyes without a body, continuing his retreat one foot behind the other.

The eyes of the thing lower, just as the glow of the light illuminates it enough so he can vaguely make out the outline of an enormous panther, sinking to the ground, its weight on its haunches ready to pounce. "For the love of—" Hamilton doesn't finish. In a fraction of a second, all hell breaks loose.

A man's voice screams, "Ankhkhaf, stop!" from somewhere in the night.

To Hamilton's shock and bewilderment the panther before him alters into a human and says, "Ah, brother, I see you have your memory back."

"I do," Sterling boldly responds, stepping out of the shadows. "Why? What purpose did all of this death serve, brother?"

"Why?!" Ankhkhaf screams.

The ground shakes beneath Hamilton's feet. He cannot believe what he is and has seen. He cannot bring himself to utter a word. A scream catches in his throat listening to the argument.

"You and you're moral discernment taking away what we were; what we still are! Relegating your own blood to the shadows while you hold your precious humans to your bosom—you betrayed us. And they," he says, pointing an unwavering finger at Hamilton, "They were our followers, they worshiped the very ground we walked on. Their sacrifices were their own, giving us our strength, our youth, and you took that away to serve your hypocritical, moral high ground. But, as always, you and your *pride* hold key positions throughout the community, pushing us further into the shadows like scavengers."

"You have slaughtered innocent children, Ankhkhaf!"

"NO! I have taken what is rightfully mine, no more. You have only yourself to thank for the additional lives that ended. My followers and I were just fine. Then, I discover you have been tramping over *our* hunting ground for ten years! I would have never known you were here if I had not seen you on the street a little over a year ago. You didn't even recognize your brother!"

"Oh, no you don't, brother! I won't allow you to lay this at my feet. I'd be lucky if I recognized my son a couple of days ago. Do *not* use my misfortunate accident as a scapegoat for your actions."

"Too late," he says, with a sarcastic grin. "The day you passed me downtown like I was a stranger, was the day I devised a plan. The next week I joined the police force, working under you, and still, there was no recognition. So, my followers and I made our kills public. I have to admit, working side by side with my dear, long-lost brother in solving the cases was my best performance to date."

"Ha! My ass! All of this has little to nothing to do with my lack of recollection of you. You're still holding onto the past. Still harboring a chip on your shoulder for what took place centuries ago!"

"But I let that go and built my kingdom here in Alger. A place where I make the rules. A place where I am king, then you! You come in with your high and mighty ethical standards, and yet again, you interfere, throwing your aristocratic weight around. You tried to destroy me once, brother. You took everything I held sacred. You put a halt to the old ways, took the woman I loved, taking it all without a second thought."

"I did not steal her from you; she chose me. Our union was never meant to hurt you."

"Hurt me?! Hurt me!" he fumes, his face reddening with wrath. "Brother, you reached in and shredded my heart just as I shredded those girls. They are dead because of your arrogance! Because of your betrayal."

"Those deaths are on your head, not mine," Sterling tells him, sternly. "You have done all of this out of your petty jealousy!"

"And I will not stop until I take all that you hold dear while you watch!"

Sterling can see the storm festering behind his brother's eyes and knows Mafdet was right; this will only end one of two ways. Ankhkhaf disappears in the dark once more, shifting into his rapacious, predatory form. The panther emits a deafening caterwaul that makes the blood run cold. A massive black cat with razor-sharp fangs and claws extending as long as a man's hand, springs from the shadows toward Hamilton.

"James, watch out," Sterling bellows as four hundred pounds of uncontrolled, raging wild cat explode into the air. A gunshot shatters the night, roaring through the evening with an ear-piercing clamor.

"Arrrgh!" Hamilton screams, tripping backward over a rock and falling forcefully to his back. His head strikes something violently. The panther's on him within a breath. His head's unclear from the fall.

"Ankhkhaf!" Sterling bellows and without a response, he again shrieks, "Anderson!" That gets the beast's attention. "It's me you want. Come and get me, you insufferable bastard. I'm right here!"

The massive panther digs his claws deep into Hamilton's shoulders as saliva drips from his fangs, trickling down his cheek. The sinking talons instigate an unbearable pain that rips through his body as the massive creature leaps from his chest. Crawling back toward the porch, he turns his head, straining to see clearly through blurred vision, "Sterling?" he mumbles.

"It's alright, Hamilton," Sterling ensures, not reverting his eyes from his crazed brother.

The panther transforms back to his human form. Hamilton observes it but still can't believe it.

Anderson smiles sinisterly at Hamilton; then his full attention is on his brother. "So, my brother, are you ready to meet your maker?"

"I am, but are you?"

A disturbing chortle comes from some nefarious place deep within

Anderson. "You think you can beat me?"

"It is time to put this to rest, don't you think?"

"And you believe you can impose your will on me?"

"No, brother, we are beyond that now."

"Then to the death."

"As you wish," Sterling utters. But before he can take a step, Anderson phases to the panther, turns, racing toward Hamilton once again.

Seemingly without effort, Sterling follows suit. Hamilton watches in dreaded terror as Sterling's vile transformation takes place. Though it happens instantly, the experience presents itself to him in unforgiving slow motion, and it is anything but effortless.

Earth shattering screams haunt the night. Sterling falls to his knees, blood boiling with the enzymes of the panther pulsing through his veins. The pain borders on agony, an ear-splitting inhuman wail pierces through the darkness.

Ripping at his shirt, tearing it from his body, he manages to stand for a moment, as his pants fall to the ground. Dropping back on all fours, his hands extend to unfathomable lengths, contorting and twisting. Splintering sounds encompass all others as severe, elongated claws slash through his knuckles. His body stretches, growing to a monstrous height. His legs distort, bending at brutal angles, snapping awkwardly backward. The fracturing and cracking of bones generate a sickening sound that causes Hamilton's guts to coil, tightening into a vicious knot. His eyes grow wider in disgust, fear and possibly fascination, witnessing Sterling's face deform. His jaw dislocates, the frontal jawbone jets forward, contorting hideously. His skin stretches and shreds as a beast tears through his chest. Short black hair sprouts, rapidly covering his body. When all the snapping, distortion, and warping terminates, a monstrous, blacker than oil, panther stands in place of Sterling.

"Oh—My—God!" Hamilton gushes.

The panther—Sterling—isn't as large Ankhkhaf—Anderson—whatever the hell he's calling himself. But soon, he'll prove he's much stronger and considerably faster. He knocks Anderson to the ground seconds before he makes contact with Hamilton. However, Sterling's claws catch Hamilton's shoulder, slashing four matching gaping gashes down to his chest as he rips Anderson away. Hamilton lies howling in agony.

The two skinwalkers—brothers—fight viciously. They circle one another less than a minute before Anderson's claw swipes across Sterling's face. His jaws snap loudly as salivating teeth sink into flesh. Claws, sharper than a Masamune samurai sword, penetrate, ripping through the skin of the beasts as they crash to the ground, tumbling the length of Hamilton's yard. Blood spews with each violent slash, fur flies, shrills of pain and anger fill the air. Neither brother fails to get up, blow after bloody, brutal blow. The two beasts rapidly become one mass of colossal fury. It's hard for Hamilton to distinguish who is who.

As the two panthers roll in and out of the impenetrable blackness, he pulls himself from the ground, holding his shoulder, as a trail of blood is left behind. He stumbles to the front door. Fumbling, he grabs his cell on the side-table and dials for help but stops.

"What the hell are you going to say? That you found Sterling, and he's an enormous cat! He, in panther form, is fighting Anderson, who's also a giant panther, on your front lawn! Hell no, they'll put me in a straightjacket for sure," he surmises, slamming the cell back on the table. Using the table to sustain his weight, he gets to his feet. He leans against the door frame, watching the ongoing fight between beast—men—or whatever the hell they are.

One of the panthers, he's confident is Anderson, rushes out of the sheet of black into view, shortly followed by, who he hopes, is Sterling. The panther that's doing the chasing springs forward, falling with his full weight on the back of the other. The sound is ungodly. He feels its vibration beneath his feet. Though the downed panther recovers quickly, it's obvious he's in pain. That does not, of course, prevent it from leaving a couple of hardy, blood-soaked ravines in the other one's ribs.

The two monsters wrestle back and forth, both seemingly on their last leg. The only thing keeping them going at each other like rabid dogs is pure unbridled hate. The animosity witnessed here tonight is unlike anything James Hamilton has ever, or with a wish and a prayer, will ever see again. For thirty minutes, the two give all they have trying to destroy one another. Cruelly, the venomous battle rages with love, hate, and passion, continues. In the end, make no mistake, this barbaric battle of strength and determination will yield no winner. There will only be the one that made it out of this brotherly Armageddon alive.

The panthers violently roll out of sight once again. The land trembles under their combined weight, crashing into it as the darkness swallows them up like a hungry, black hole in the earth. Hamilton can hear the yowls and wails, claws ripping at flesh, but he can no longer see them.

Without warning, the night fills with one last agonizing, dreadful shriek of anguish that sends icy chills down his backbone. Convinced the sound of death has rung through the night, for a moment he can't move. His very breath is ostensibly stolen from his lungs. *God, please let it be Sterling that appears*, he implores.

The oxygen rushes back into his lungs as he gasps, sucking in the fresh air. He attempts to run off the porch and see who is still alive, not thinking about if Anderson's the one, then he'll be dead in a heartbeat. He falls to his knees before he clears the porch. The blood loss makes him woozy and his head spins. *Deep breaths, James*, he commands, but his body betrays his will. Closing his eyes tight, he swallows with some difficulty. *Don't lose consciousness. Don't lose consciousness*, he repeats until his head stops its decisive downward spin. His awareness is gaunt, but he's able to see the shapes of women that emerge from the darkness. His vision irrevocably rebels and he loses consciousness.

"Levi!" Nefertiti shrieks, observing a panther lying motionless on the ground with the other standing over him.

"I told you we should have left sooner. No one ever listens," Herneith spouts.

"Herneith, not now." Herneith shrugs and follows her.

"I'm fine," they hear Sterling's voice. All the women, even Herneith, are relieved. Breathing heavily and mollycoddling his left side where his brother tore him open, he scolds. "I told you to stay in Brazil."

"I know what you said," Mafdet responds.

"Then what are you doing here?"

"We had to come."

"Yeah, little miss OCD was losing it," Herneith states, cynically.

Ignoring her daughter's sarcasm, Mafdet continues, "Yes, Saitre was out of her mind, and we... well, we had to make sure you were alright."

The women join him, standing over the lifeless body of Ankhkhaf, watching as it slowly distorts back to his human form. "You were right," Sterling says.

"Right? About what?" Mafdet asks.

"He wasn't going to concede or try to work things out. He wanted this fight to the death."

"Are you going to be ok with this?"

"I don't have much choice and taking the life of my brother may prove to have its repercussions."

A thump from behind startles them; Hamilton lies on the ground out of it. "Shit," Sterling says, darting to where he's sprawled out bleeding. "Help me get him into the house."

Sterling takes him by the shoulders as Saitre and Herneith grab his legs. Once inside they place him on the sofa, Nefertiti wearily glances at Mafdet who looks at her questionably. She nods toward Hamilton and Mafdet follows her eyes to Hamilton's shoulder. The looks between the two women do not escape Levi's attention. "What?" he asks, wondering why they were acting so odd.

"How did his shoulder get like this?" Nefertiti questions.

"It happened when I knocked Ankhkhaf away from him; it was an accident. But the marks on his chest are from Ankhkhaf, Why? What's going on?"

"So your claws ripped his skin?"

"Yes!" Sterling responds, his anger growing. "It was an accident for Christ sakes." Viewing the women's faces, he sees there's something they are not telling him. He's losing his patience quickly. "So, are either of you going to tell me why you appear as if someone just stole your virtue?"

Nefertiti glances at Mafdet and tells him, "He'll change."

"WHAT!"

"He'll become one of us, Levi."

"Now wait just one goddamn minute. You're telling me if we scratch someone, they become what we are! That's the most ridiculous thing I have ever heard."

"No," she calmly replies. "I'm saying, when *you* claw someone without killing them, they will change and become one of us."

"What in the *hell* is she talking about Mafdet?! From everything I have read—though fantasy and folklore—a skinwalker is born not infectious as vampires, werewolves, and such."

"True," Mafdet agrees. "But, as I told you before, you are different. You were born with powers we have never seen in skinwalkers before and well, this is one of them."

A cough comes from the sofa. In a weak voice Hamilton jokes, "So, I guess I'm going to be a part of the family. Hey, Sam, how ya doing?" he asks groggily.

"I'm good, Hamilton. Don't worry you're going to be fine."

"Skinwalker fine?"

"It would appear that way," Sterling tells him, floored by his reaction. "You certain you're good?"

"Considering I just witnessed something out of a Dean Koontz novel and found out that I'm going to become a skinwalker, I'd say I'm doing fairly well."

"You're taking all of this admirably."

"I don't have much choice now, do I?"

"True. I didn't know, Hamilton. I would never do this to you on purpose."

"We can talk about this later," he says beginning to come around. "So, is that asshole dead?" He glances at Sterling and regrets his words. "I'm sorry—"

"No, you're right, he was an asshole, and yes, he is dead."

"Then the three of you need to get out of here."

"The three of us? Hamilton, you must have hit your head harder than I thought, they're five of us here."

"That is more than likely correct, but what I mean is I will need Samantha and Nefertiti to stay if this is going to work."

"So you know, Sam's real name is Saitre, just for future reference."

"Good thing to know."

"They can stay and help," he says, watching for the women to confirm and then nodding. "But how do you plan on explaining this mess to the authorities?"

"Don't worry so much Levi... ah, is that your real name?" He asks but doesn't wait for an answer. Time's critical if his story is going to pan out. "I have an idea to justify the murders around here and you for that matter. Now, go."

"I don't like leaving you holding the bag."

"You can pay me back later. Now get out of here."

Mafdet hands him a card. "I'm Mafdet. Take this and as soon as everything is over, call. If you like, you can come and stay with us."

"Thank you for your hospitality."

"You are family now, Hamilton."

"Family," Hamilton snorts. "Ah, yes, before you go, is there anything I should know? I mean, about what I'm becoming."

"Only that you will become. If you can, being an officer it shouldn't be too difficult, get blood from the hospital's blood bank. It will help with the transformation. Saitre—ah, Samantha and Nefertiti will explain everything."

"Blood—from the blood bank, perfect."

He believes he may very well be in shock from it all, but he saw everything that happened with his own eyes. Unbelievable yes, but it

301

happened just the same. He will get the blood. He knows he can get his hands on some without too much trouble and, more importantly, without questions. Sam can give him the key to the lab. He will retrieve the supply needed there. The last thing he wants is to transform in front of people and worse yet, take someone's life.

"Don't worry about me. I'll take care of everything. You get out of here, so I can call the station. If we want them to accept the story I'm going to tell, disappear now and make sure no one sees you leave."

"We can do that," Sterling says. "Thank you, Hamilton. See you soon."

Chapter 30

The Vultures

Hamilton waits until they're gone before he walks out to the front yard with a gun in hand. Standing over Anderson's body, he puts one round into his head.

"Why did you do that?" Saitre questions.

"It's all part of my plan. Now, listen carefully and do exactly as I say." Hamilton tells the women what his plan is and what their part will be.

"I think this will work," Nefertiti agrees.

"Let's hope so. You have to go and don't forget to make it as real as possible." The two nod in understanding. Wasting no time, they head off to get themselves ready. He makes the call.

When the cops get to his house, he spins his tale of *believable* lies, placing all the murders on the dead man lying in his front yard. He tells them, Anderson, not only killed the girls but admitted to him he also murdered the Dixons and Sterling.

"Sterling, he's dead?"

"Yes. I questioned him about where he put the body, but the man merely laughed and said it would never be found. He came back to finish me. I presume I would not have been the last if I had not done what I did."

Hamilton continues to describe how the man attacked him, knocking the gun from his hand and pulling a hunting knife. He dictates the struggle between them for the knife. "As you can see, we each received our share of wounds before I was able to retrieve my weapon to shoot Anderson. God help me, I had no choice in the matter," he convincingly says, even managed watery eyes. "It was him or me. The man was a raving lunatic," Hamilton says. "I didn't want to kill him. I knew that man. But he was going to kill me."

"It will be alright, Officer Hamilton. Go with the paramedic, and I'll be down later to finish your statement," Detective Wilson, an older heavyset man tells him.

Before the man walks away, he inquires, "Did he say anything about this death hole we found?"

"No, but it wouldn't surprise me if he had something to do with the more recent kills we found."

"Martinez," the detective calls.

"Yeah."

"I need you to gather a few men and get over to this Anderson's place. I want that place turned upside down, do you understand?"

"Yes, sir."

When the officers search Anderson's house, they have a surprise waiting for them in the basement. Martinez is the first one down and at the bottom of the stairs, his gun leading the way, he discovers another young, mangled body. "Oh God," he utters, hearing muffled noises somewhere in the dark. "Who's there?" he calls out.

The sounds grow louder as he attentively makes his way to the back of the basement. The light from his flashlight catches something. "Sam!" He turns his flashlight to the right to see both Sam and Nefertiti huddled together in a dark, damp corner. They were gagged and bound.

"I have two live women down here!" He bellows, hurrying to where they sit on a cold, damp floor. "Get an ambulance here, pronto!"

Johnson comes bounding down the stairs, and quite by accident clicks on the light switch. The room illuminates and Johnson screams, "What in the name of—" he throws up before he finishes. There isn't just one body down here, which isn't what Hamilton expected but it adds validity to his case—like a stroke of luck. The bodies of three or four teenage females are sprawled out on the cement floor, torn open like the others.

"Get help, dammit!" Martinez howls.

"O-ok," Johnson manages before he vomits again and runs up the stairs.

"Christ," Martinez mutters, turning back to the women. "Don't worry. Help is here now. I'll get you out of here."

Hamilton wasn't there to see it but the *vultures,* AKA reporters, snapped pictures of the women being brought out to the ambulance. Damn, they were excellent actresses; they should have received the Golden Globe for their performance. The photos in the paper showed them, dirty, swollen-eyed, and bloody—it was fantastic.

Yes, Hamilton's plan worked perfectly. The scenario explained why Samantha and Nefertiti went missing and where they had gone. Of course, the women's wounds were superficial. However, they did one hell of a job beating the shit out of one another to make themselves look like Anderson put them through a series of torturous events. Hamilton got the feeling that the two had some pent-up anger between them and well, it worked. The hospital treated the women and released them after a couple of days. Both left town and no one could blame them.

Animal control cornered and captured an albino panther a week later. The unfortunate thing was, they put to sleep and autopsied it. And wouldn't you know it, there were signs the animal had been scavenging off human remains—along with pizza and other trash. Nefertiti was right; she had a magic touch with large cats. But it killed her to know they would destroy the animal.

Internal investigations got involved with the case, and Hamilton repeated the story over again, sticking to his guns about what had happened that night. They put him on probation until all inquiries were concluded, clearing him of any wrongdoing. The department closed the murder cases, including the bodies found in the well out in Skidway. 'Cop Gone Mad,' is how one of the papers headlined the incidences. All named the perpetrator as Kyle Redford Anderson.

One of the main reasons for Hamilton's clearance was due to a diary found a couple of days after Anderson's death, in his handwriting. It was

J.C. Brennan

Johnson who found the diary stuffed behind a loose cement block in his basement behind his *workbench*. The bench was more of a table loaded with knives, hatchets, and other items Anderson collected. The papers, of course, had a field day over the *tools of slaughter*, as they called them. It didn't matter that the items on that table were only items Anderson collected, not used, some being a hundred years old.

Yeah, the sadistic bastard had written everything down, minus names, thank God.

However, to make sure the authorities had no doubt concerning Anderson's guilt, some items were added thanks to Herneith and her incredible talent for forgery. No one could discern the difference, not even the expert. Within the pages of the diary were older pieces of writing, each from different periods and different ink describing the sacrifices of the innocent and his devotion to ancient sacrifice to appease his god. And even though it was all in the same handwriting—considering Anderson was millennia old—the experts along with everyone else, assumed it was a diary handed down from generation to generation. This hit the papers as, 'Words of the Ancients Create a Monster'—colorful.

Mafdet dug up an old document from her archives she started hundreds of years before. It wasn't difficult to discover a particular text to incriminate Kyle Anderson attaching him further to what one newspaper called 'The Butcheries of the Anderson Blood Cult.' And while the public thought all these brutal blood rituals dated back to some ancient tribe, the truth of the matter was, Anderson was just a sick, sadistic bastard. Hell, even in the days when people were willingly sacrificed to the tribe, before Sterling changed the law, only the hearts were removed. But Anderson took this to a whole new level. His bloodthirsty hunts incorporated removal of all their internal organs, not just their hearts. Why? He wrote in the diary he was convinced the heart gave him power, all the organs gave him supreme dominance—yeah the man was genuinely insane.

The innocent and Anderson became a full-blown circus. His name was on everyone's lips. In death, he finally got the popularity he had yearned for, although not in the fashion he expected. Psychiatrists, psychologists, news reporters—everyone wanted a piece of figuring out why Kyle Anderson had become so obsessed with the sacrificial ways of an ancient people.

One of the psychologists on the Today Show stated Anderson had, what he called, Dissociative Delusional Disorder. Hamilton wasn't sure if that was a real disorder until that moment, and he didn't care. The doctor explained that Anderson might have been suffering from this disorder since childhood, but something in his life triggered a psychotic break making him forget who he was and believe he was actually a part of an ancient tribe. Hamilton thought it was all bullshit, but then again, it was, wasn't it? After all, the doctors were forming their educated opinions on a pack of lies he, Mafdet, and Nefertiti created.

Hamilton kept all the articles from the newspapers. One of his favorite headlines read, 'Officer Survives Killing the Blood Cult Murderer.' They printed the words 'Blood Cult,' in bold, italic letters on the first page, with a picture of him arriving at the hospital in a bloody shirt, shoulder wrapped in padding, and white gauze with a bloodstain in its middle. Oh, yes, did the papers love the words *Blood Cult*; it was plastered everywhere.

All of it was very dramatic, and the newspaper that printed this particular story sold out within an hour after its release. When he showed up at the station to give the rest of his statement, he was ambushed by people wanting him to sign their paper—amazing. The only reason Hamilton received a copy was a nurse who took care of him while he healed, brought him one.

It just so happened, the first change he went through was at the end of August on a full Sturgeon Moon. Mafdet and Nefertiti knew the signs, so they all went deep in the woods in the middle of nowhere. The women chained him between two huge oak trees. They used heavy tow chains and an industrial padlock to make sure he didn't get loose.

To say the experience was painful was the understatement of the century—possibly the millennium. Words cannot describe the torture his distorted, twisted, deforming body went through on that night. Although there was a reprieve, for some time during the agonizing experience, his mind must have shut down because he could never remember the whole thing, and to be honest, he was grateful for that.

Six months after the discovery of the diary, Hamilton transferred to Brazil with a little help from some friends.

Chapter 31

The Wicked

It's been a year to the day since Sterling took the life of his brother. As he remembers more of his past, his heart aches over the death. But from his pride's perspective, blood or not, they are all better off. Levi, Mafdet, and their girls wait down in baggage for Hamilton.

"There he is," Nefertiti says, pointing to the escalators.

"I'm so excited to see him again!" Saitre beams. "He's cuter than I remember."

"Oh, boy," Herneith says, rolling her eyes. "Leave it to you to fall head over heels with a man you've met once."

"We stayed and help him out for a couple of weeks, and I did work with him as an M.E. on occasion, if you remember correctly."

"Whatever."

"Now, Ladies, why don't we welcome him." They all head over to Hamilton, who is smiling away.

"Levi, you ol' son of a bitch, how are you?"

"Never better," Sterling laughs. "It's good to see you again."

"You too. It's still Levi, right?"

"Yes, but it's Levi Holsten now. I became a little attached to the name. You still remember these lovely women."

"Hello ladies," Hamilton greets them with a kiss on the hand, which makes Saitre blush and Herneith roll her eyes again. "For the love of the goddess," she breathes.

Nefertiti elbows her slightly in the ribs. "Don't start," she whispers. Herneith gives her the *'whatever'* look, but does not say another word.

"Well, King *Holsten*, let's get my bags so we can go see this paradise you've been telling me about."

"Good enough. You will love it. We have a room all set up for you and the pride is anxious to meet you."

"The Pride? You keep saying that, what pride?"

"Our people, our family, they're excited to meet you."

"Oh. That one right there is my bag," Hamilton points to a big black bag lying on the luggage carrier.

"Is that it?" Levi asks.

"Yup, I tried to keep it simple."

"Perfect, follow me. We have a three-hour drive ahead of us, and a storm is coming in."

Saitre takes Hamilton's arm, grinning like a lovesick schoolgirl as they make their way through the bustle of the airport to the escalator. On the first floor the crowd is denser, but the exit is only five hundred feet. They reach the exit door with little resistance, weaving in and out of people. Hamilton sucks in the fresh tropical air, though humid and sticky, as they make their way to the parking lot where an older model extended jeep, the color of muddy water, waits for them.

They pile in as Sterling informs him, "It runs better than it looks."

"Are we headed for the depths of the jungle or something?" Hamilton asks.

"Yes, that's exactly where we're going. You're going to love the rainforest."

"Well, I said I was ready for a change."

"Then, you're in for a treat. Where we're going is a very remote area of the Amazon. But don't worry, we have everything we need, and it's peaceful."

"I'm not worried. I am anxious to see it. Some peace is precisely what I need after the extravaganza I've been through. Let's go."

"I can imagine. So, have you seen or heard of anything unusual?"

"If you're speaking of Anderson's clan, no, everything has been quiet. I haven't seen hide nor hair of them."

"I was worried they'd seek retribution. The female DNA at the crime scenes told us Anderson wasn't working alone. I was worried one of his devoted parasites might give you some trouble."

"That's all in the past, thankfully. Anderson's death pushed his disciples back into the shadows where they belong."

"Good, let's hope that's where they stay."

After leaving the city roads, if that is what you want to call them—more like a dirt two-track, winding them through the dense jungle—Hamilton takes it all in. It's been a long time since he's felt this carefree, not looking over his shoulder for what might lurk in the dark. He sees a few of the animals that live in this luscious, vegetation-rich land. He's able to see animals he would never experience. The Golden Lion Tamarin with a baby on its back, a few sloths, and a pair of Macaws. There are a variety of birds, but the Macaws he has seen in National Geographic, so he knows them on sight. Not even the muggy atmosphere that fashions his clothes clammy and damp in this tropical paradise bothers him.

He's not sure exactly when he nods off. He's more exhausted from his trip than he thought, the next thing he knows, Levi's nudging him awake. It's dark and rain beats against the windshield. "It looks as if we're going to get a little wet. Here," he says, handing him a vinyl poncho. "This will keep most of you dry."

"Dry," Hamilton laughs. "I haven't been dry since I stepped off the plane."

"You'll get used to it. You better take this as well." Levi gives him a flashlight. "The steps up to the house can become fairly slick with the rain."

Hamilton pulls the poncho over his head and flips the hood up.

"You ready," Levi asks.

"As I'm ever going to be."

"Ladies?" The women signal they're ready. "Ok, then let's get into the house."

Hamilton follows Levi and the women in front of him. They approach steps made of rock and as they climb; they seem to go on forever. Finally, they reach a covered landing. Though Hamilton can't see a damned thing, even with the flashlight, he notices the porch area is hidden behind trees or vines. He's not sure which.

Levi takes his poncho off and hangs it over the back of a chair that stands by a rather large, round table. Hamilton follows his lead, placing the dripping poncho on one of the other chairs. He's led through large, wooden doors that open into the grand foyer. It's not trimmed in gold or anything, but *incredible* is a sorely lacking description. This place is more than he ever dreamed. It's like a place only experienced in fairy tales. A place nature built or has taken over, but in the nicest possible way. Amazing vines run from floor to the top of the vaulted ceiling. It's nature at her most remarkable state, simply gorgeous.

"Ho-oo-ly! I thought you said this was a house, not a damned mansion."

"Yeah, I'm still trying to get used to it myself."

"How old is this?"

"From what Mafdet says, we built in back in the late 1200s. Of course, the vines have grown over the years, but they do give the place a special touch."

"Whoa, wait a minute. Are you telling me you're over eight hundred years old?"

"Older than that," he says, grinning. "In the late 1200s, yes, but BC not AD."

"No way! You're joshing me, right?"

"No, I'm not. It's hard to wrap your mind around isn't it?"

"To say the least."

"Come on. I'll show you your room." Levi chuckles.

Out of breath, climbing up the elaborate, spiraling stairway,

Hamilton notices that intertwined vines cover most of the stone walls used to build this fortress. Their thick tendrils twist and entwine with one another, creating an interlocking living entity of rich green along the walls and ceiling. *This is unreal*, he thinks, climbing another step. Finally reaching the top of the staircase, he follows Levi to the left.

"It's down here, James."

"Christ man, I'll get a workout every time I come up here."

"You'll get used to it."

"Yeah, you keep saying that." They walk down a long hall where impossibly thick ancient vines wind up the walls. Every four feet, very old pictures, some hand painted, adorn the corridor. Some are portraits showing a single person from the chest up, while others have a person posed with several panthers surround them. They're all amazing.

"Here we are," Levi utters, breaking Hamilton's admiration of the artwork. He opens heavy, wooden doors revealing a room larger than his house back in Michigan.

"Wow."

"Too much?"

"Well, It's... um, yeah. Wow. I'll need a map to get to it again and one to navigate my way around it."

Sterling laughs. "You'll—"

"I know. I'll get used to it."

"It'll give you some privacy when needed," Sterling smirks.

"No one needs this much privacy." *This is too much*, he thinks, setting his suitcase down.

After showing Hamilton to his room, one fit for a prince, Markisha's voice filters through the hall announcing dinner is ready.

"Are you hungry?"

"Starved."

"Then let's eat."

They trekked back downstairs through the maze that's now Hamilton's home, into the dining room. Hamilton stands in awe for a moment. The dining room is just as eccentric as the rest of this place. The table is long, wooden, with rounded corners—a rustic, but elegant look with chairs to match. A dining set, which appears to be handmade—possibly of clay—embellishes the table. However, society's elite would turn green with envy by the grandeur of it all. If for no other reason, its uniqueness would strike a covetousness cord.

Twenty-five people, including those he already knows, sit at the table in their wake.

"This is the whole of our pride, except for the children," Levi announces. "Everyone, please welcome James to our home."

"Welcome, James," they say in unison.

"Where are the children?" Hamilton inquires.

"Over here." Levi guides him to an adjacent room where approximately ten children sit eating. "Children," Levi says, getting their attention. "This is a new member of our family, James P. Hamilton."

"Hello, James P. Hamilton," the children's voices sing-song, welcoming Hamilton. Some resounding giggling follow their greeting.

"Wow," is all Hamilton can say.

With a pat on the back, Levi tells him, "It will take some..." He stops scanning over the children. "Where's Lucas?"

No sooner do the words escape his mouth when they hear Markisha scream. Running into the formal dining room, everyone's standing looking toward the kitchen area. Levi and Hamilton head for the screams. Mafdet and Nefertiti tell everyone to stay calm, as they follow the men. When they reach the kitchen, Markisha has her hands over her mouth, sobbing. She stands over a blood riddled child's frayed body. His blonde hair is soaked in blood, his small torso shredded, and his blue eyes stare blankly at the ceiling.

"Oh, God, No! No!" Levi howls, falling to his knees beside what remains of the eight-year-old little Lucas. "Those sick bastards!"

"Lucas," Nefertiti wails, tears streaming down her face.

"They will pay for this. I'll SLAUGHTER every last one of those child killing cowards!" Sterling yells, turning to Mafdet and Nefertiti, "Take Markisha out of here now! And keep the others out." Nefertiti wraps her arms around a grief-stricken, sobbing Markisha, leading her out of the room.

Hamilton makes his way over to Levi, who is visibly shaking. He's pretty damn sure it's from anger and grief in equal measure. He carefully kneels next to him, placing a comforting hand on his shoulder.

"Who did this?"

"Ankhkhaf's pride," Sterling says, his voice strangled with a multitude of emotion. "They're the only ones who would butcher a child."

"Why after all this time? Shit, a year has passed since that—" Something catches Hamilton's eye. "What's this?"

"What?" Levi asks.

Hamilton pulls a crude doll from under the devastated remains of the boy. "This."

Levi's looks curiously at the object. It's a doll made of cloth, X's for eyes, dressed in leaves with blood over its middle. He doesn't have a clue what it is or who placed it on the boy's decimated corpse.

"Samedi," Mafdet gasped from behind them. "Drop it, don't touch it!"

Immediately dropping the doll to the floor, Hamilton sees the terror in Mafdet's eyes. Shaking as she cautiously stumbles a few inches closer, pulling Levi and Hamilton back from the boy.

"Samedi? Who or what in the hell is that?"

"The symbol is of Bawon Samedi." She points to the chest of the small doll, and sure enough, there's a strange symbol sewn in the fabric.

"But that doesn't tell me why you look like death just trampled over you. Who is this Bawon Samedi and why are you so frightened?"

"Samedi is a Loa of the dead. He is the master of the dead. His power is especially great when it comes to Vodou curses and black magic—"

"Vodou! You're joking," Hamilton spouts.

"No. I wish I were."

"Shera, absolutely fantastic," Herneith snips, entering the room.

"Now, who in the hell is Shera?" Levi demands.

"Hell is right," Herneith snidely quips. "I see your memory isn't fully back yet."

"I guess not. Now stop playing and tell me what you know, Herneith."

"Shera is a Vodou queen, she is wicked to her core and is loyal to the great god of death, Samedi."

"Wow, you're going to mess with me right now, really?" Levi glares at Herneith.

"I'm telling you the truth," Herneith says so casually it makes Hamilton's skin crawl.

"After all, you know her more intimately than any of us do." her words drip with sarcasm though her cockiness isn't amusing. He continues to look at her questionably until she finally responds. "Christ, Levi you're the one who denied her," she says. "Your brother hated you for many reasons, and Shera was just another notch he thought you cut into him. You don't remember?"

"I..." he mutters. He thinks long and hard, pushing through the recesses of his memory. Envisioning the word Shera, trying to trace her down the darkened corridors of his brain. Slowly, a memory from the past enters his conscious mind. "I remember Ankhkhaf had followers who believed as he did. When I implemented the law of the flesh, he became enraged, livid, swearing he would be my most fierce enemy. He found a woman. He'd been told she held a great power, a dark and sinister one. She, Shera, became his most loyal follower." He closes his eyes, breathing slowly. "This woman was not of his pride; he met her in Africa. If I recall correctly, she became his lover."

"Correct, Shera became Ankhkhaf's lover, but only after you rejected her. Man, did she have it bad for you. She was in love with you, or should I say, obsessed with you."

"And?"

"When you refused her advances, she swore that she would get her revenge. I'm assuming the only reason she entered the relationship with your brother was to strike up jealousy within you, which, of course, worked although not as she intended. You were never jealous, but the fact she was so into you, only fueled your brother's hate further. You already had your sights on mother. She must have fallen in love with him at some point over the years and now is out for revenge."

"Obviously." Memories flood Levi's head. He remembers Shera more clearly. The intensity of her anger rushes over him. The power of the memories brings him to his knee. "The scent of musk and flower," he breathes, holding his head. The repressed memories are painful when they flood back. But he supposes that when his memory fully returns, the headaches will diminish.

"The scent you speak of is from the pouch she wears around her neck," Mafdet tells him. "It's a leather pouch filled with flowers and herbs and is said to hold a powerful spell of protection."

"So, she helped Ankhkhaf kill those girls, or was present."

"Yes," Mafdet confirms.

"I knew there would be retribution. I should have seen this coming!"

"Hey, dementia boy, you took a good whack to the head, scrambling your brain. Don't take this so hard," Herneith proclaims.

"Herneith! Really?" Mafdet scolds. "You should learn to be just a touch more sensitive. Or, better yet, learn to control your tongue!"

"Yeah, well, I haven't quite grasped that talent over the centuries. So, I wouldn't count on that happening anytime soon."

Hamilton interrupts the tiff going on between mother and daughter. "Levi, the female DNA at a couple of the crime scenes?"

"We can assume it was hers. She has been with Ankhkhaf for a long time."

"And she's a skinwalker?"

"Oh, yes," Mafdet answers. "She is a skinwalker, but more worrisome is her power. Shera was at the time she and Ankhkhaf met, an African Vodou Priestess or what we call Voodoo. It's an offshoot of the oldest known religions, as you may already know. Shera was, and still is, powerful. She possesses an evil beyond any other. "

"Perfect! Just what we need, a damned witch," Hamilton mutters. Then, switches the subject to something else he's curious about. "So, the sight thing you have, Levi. I remember Mafdet saying something about you having *sight* or something—you didn't see this?"

"It doesn't work that way, my friend. It comes in fragments and I don't get everything. Since I didn't remember Shera until now, I wouldn't have seen her coming."

"Or, she blocked your vision," Mafdet accesses.

"She can do that?" Levi asks.

"Oh, yes, she's powerful."

"Why am I not surprised?" Hamilton says. "So, besides having the ability to see what's coming, turning people into *cat* people with one scratch—what other powers do you have?"

"I honestly don't know."

"Mafdet?"

"He is stronger than any of us, as you saw with Ankhkhaf and he's the only one who can defeat Shera and her black magic."

"And why is that?" Hamilton asks.

"Yeah, why would I, over everyone else, be able to defeat this Voodoo Queen?" Sterling inquires.

"Because you are immune to her wiles; you always have been. Otherwise, you would be with her and not me. Her wiles and her spells of persuasion don't work on you."

"But she can still block my visions."

"Maybe not so much now that you remember her."

"Well, that's all good and well, but I wasn't able to stop her when it counted, and now Lucas is dead," his voice cracks. He has failed his pride with Lucas' death and nothing can change that.

"But the rest of us are still here, Levi," Hamilton tells him. "Listen, you have a pride here to protect from that witch, and together we'll get her and those sons of bitches, make them pay—make her pay. Uh, just how many are in Ankhkhaf's gang, pride, whatever."

"There is at least twenty, as far as we know," Mafdet answers.

"Ah ha, we have them outnumbered. That's a plus, right? We don't have a Voodoo priestess—Queen, whatever the hell she is. But we do have numbers." He reassures Levi, placing a hand on his shoulder.

"I'm not sure you understand the gravity of the situation, James. This means war and not only of the flesh," Mafdet explains.

"I figured that out on my own. If it's a war they want, then we'll give it to them."

"Yes, but a war between skinwalkers is unlike anything you've ever experienced. It's more brutal, bloody, and inhumane. Then consider the formidable spells that, no doubt, will be thrown into the mix by Shera—"

"There's a lot I have been experiencing lately, that I never have before. War is war. It's ugly, sadistic, and violent, spells or not. Levi, we've seen the worst of humanity in our years on the force. Wars have always been vile and crude. This one will be no different. Except..."

"Except what?" Levi asks.

"You're back from whatever mental block you once had and you have me." This brings a slight smirk to Levi's face. "So much for a peaceful environment," Hamilton adds. "Well, come on I'll help you take care of him. The poor kid, no one deserves to die like this."

"You're right about that," Levi whispers, covering the boy's body.

As they bury the young boy, Levi's mind contemplates what's coming. Images of skinwalkers tearing at each other, turning the jungle into a bloodbath enter his head. Death is imminent for many of their kind, even members from his tribe. He remembers once hearing of a legend about the distant species of humans known as skinwalkers. Though, in the folds of a long-forgotten memory, he can't remember from whom.

Yes, he remembers the skinwalkers, boogiemen, figures made up by adults to scare children. But he will tell you, skinwalkers are not just the made up mythical monsters from human imagination, they're real—he and his pride were living proof of their existence.

Much like humans, people see them daily—unaware there's anything different about them. Just as humans do, they kill. And as in human nature, the act isn't committed without provocation, at least for the majority. However, a few exist that are innately evil. These skinwalkers act out their aggression for absurd purposes. Fueled by warrant and revenge, they become savage murderers. Killing is their way of life—especially the murder of the innocent.

He remembers one such legend is of two brothers, born skinwalker to loving parents, a powerful tribe, and grateful followers. As the brother's become men, they quarrel over the sacrificial offerings of young, innocent, human children. Their dispute leads to one brother leaving his brother's rule and continuing a vicious, murdering onslaught. This brother rancorously takes the lives of the innocent well before their time, spawning a war.

He cannot remember how the story ends, but he's confident it will be disclosed soon enough.